DEFINING GRAY

DEFINING GRAY

A novel by
Denise Bjornson

Soaring Turtle Press
Tucson, Arizona

DEFINING GRAY

This book is a work of fiction. Names, characters, incidents, and dialogue are products of the author's imagination or are used in a fictitious manner. Any resemblance to actual events or persons, living or dead, is entirely coincidental.

Published by:
Soaring Turtle Press
P. O. Box 35403
Tucson, AZ 85740
Soaringturtlepress.com

First Edition

ISBN 978-0-9817832-0-8

Printed in the United States of America

Inside Page Design by Richard Diffenderfer

For Mike Evans

*For picking me up and
carrying me when I couldn't
take another step*

For my son, Patrick O'Brien

*Your simple 'Thank you'
made it all worthwhile*

Acknowledgments

I am filled with gratitude for all those who shared this long, (very long), journey with me...

My family—who exemplify unconditional love and support: Dad, for saying "Do it your way" enough times until I finally listened; Mom, your interest in my earliest characters encouraged me to keep writing; my sister, Debbi Hreblyn, you read my messy unfinished draft and told me you laughed, cried, and yes—I should finish it; my brothers: John Bjornson, who helped me rethink how much and how soon to give the reader, and Bob Bjornson, who began the first 'DG' edit with a pencil but soon traded it in for a sledge hammer; my partner, Mike Evans, for all things above and beyond; my son, Patrick O'Brien, for all the ways you bring joy to my life; Erin Nasewytewa, for keeping me focused on the road ahead; Shannon Kern, for finally reading 'DG'; Justin Kern, for his inspiring can-do spirit; Christian, Dylan, and Ethan Kern, and Eric Hreblyn, for rounding us out; And in loving memory of Man Sue Low who brightly shined her light on all of us.

To Mike's Evans' family for welcoming me into your lives and homes: Gordon and Joyce; John, Becky, Andy, Samantha, Jim, Beth, Cynthia, Isabel, and Willy; Gil and Gail and family, and Ozzie and Kristen and family.

Ludwig family: Bill, plain and simply, this book would not 'be' if not for you; Kim, your letter to me, at just the time I needed it, resurrected 'DG' from the bottom drawer; Amber and Sharon, for providing much appreciated faith and inspiration; And in memory of Ralph and Betty— may your former forty-acre Avra Valley property live forever in the hearts of 'DG's' readers.

Special thanks to: Uncle Richard who showed me the sights of Bismarck, N.D and challenged me to get the book published in time for the 'deuce'; Pastor Tim Laycock for providing insight for a family in crisis; Scott and Patti Cuffe for police questioning expertise; Ed and Rita, the prior owners of the Shady Dell in Bisbee, for help with the 'Spartan Manor' research; and the Gonzalez family: Luis, Sally, Celia, Francisca and Andrea, for insights into Yaqui culture and the invite to the 'Virgin of Guadalupe' ceremony.

A big 'Thank You' to my early readers for feedback and edits, large or small, but much appreciated: my family—Mike, Dad, Mom, Bob, John, and Debbi; Clarke Abbey, Alexandra Chewning, Nancy Howe, Lori Ference, Lisa Moore, Bob and Mary OBrien, Caryl Gordon, Jennifer Hensley, Tom and Glenda DeMoss, Lois Curti, Kevin Lynch, Gil Evans, Aunt Elaine Cuffe and Aunt Judy Krueger.

My gratitude goes to the team that pulled it all together: page designer, Richard Diffenderfer, for patiently correcting my endless changes; and to two dynamic duos: Mike and Tama White, for publishing consults and editing, and to Jim and Erica Johnsen for cover design and photo.

And to all of you pre-release readers, your enthusiasm was like a double shot of espresso after working a double shift—a much needed boost to keep me going! Each and every phone call, email, or message relayed by family or friend, has been immensely appreciated. I am gratefully touched by all your wonderful feedback.

To the rest of my friends and family, near and far, for special moments over the years and around the globe, and in memory of our loved ones that have passed on, I thank you from the bottom of my heart for all the shared memories and encouraging words along the way.

Prologue

It was barely past nine a.m. and already Gregory Joseph Rothman had changed the life of one woman. That was intentional. But before the day was out, he inadvertently would change the life of another.

With the morning paper tucked under his arm, he entered the small café, strode past the "Please Seat Yourself" sign, and sat in the first empty booth. He opened the *Arizona Daily Star* while the waitress, with a menu in one hand and a pot of coffee in the other, ambled over to his table.

"Good morning," she said. "Can I start you off with coffee?"

"Please," he replied while turning over the cup.

"There's a good article in there." She glanced at the paper as she poured coffee. "Our newspaper's very own editor, William Mathews, personally interviewed General MacArthur over in Korea."

Gregory looked up at the waitress with a half-hearted smile; he was not in the mood for conversation—even if it centered on the situation in Korea, but, more importantly, he wasn't raised in a manner that tolerated rudeness. *Ha!* He thought to himself. *As if calling off a wedding and ending a five year relationship—over the phone—isn't rude!*

"Thanks." He said politely. "I'll be sure to read it."

"I read it as soon as the paper hit my doorstep. It said something about the island of Formosa and our government's emergency plan." She handed him the menu. "I'm not exactly sure what it all means except I think we might be one step closer in going over there—you know—to war."

He thought about the meeting his father had with the general last month, and how the likelihood of war would affect his own future. Under different circumstances, Gregory might have been interested in conversing with the waitress on the subject. But now was not the time. "You may be right."

Later, when he was almost finished eating, the waitress approached with a fresh pot of coffee. "Can I freshen up your cup?"

"No—I'm good, thanks."

"All right then. Is there anything else I can get for you?"

"Actually, there is." He set his fork down. "Do you know how to get to Avra Valley?"

"Sure. It's before the town of Marana. Just get onto the highway, T-69,

1

heading toward Phoenix and watch for the exit—oh, I'd say somewhere between 15 and 20 miles north of here." She reached to clear the plates. "There's not much out there— you may need a map. We have some for sale at the counter." She pursed her lips in concern. "And take some water with you in case you break down or something. It's supposed to be a hot one out there today—possibly a record breaker."

"I'll be fine. I filled my canteen first thing this morning."

"Good." She gave him one last smile. "And good luck with your visit."

"Thank you." That familiar feeling, the one that chided him for being the consummate actor, sat like a cold stone in his gut. But, as always, making a good impression was essential—even if his world was falling apart. Every U.S. citizen was a future vote he might someday need. With a warm smile and a polite "have a nice day," he left the small café.

Part I

1

Randall Averson sat in the darkness, somewhat comforted by the indistinct sounds only the silence of the night can reveal. The air was thick and stale; the light of the moon showed neat but dusty surroundings. A note lay on the floor where he had dropped it several hours earlier while the words, *she's gone, she's been gone two or three days* had circled through his mind like a mantra.

The slightest movement sent tingles through his right leg and arm, and he realized he had been sitting slouched over, possibly pinching a nerve in his neck. He didn't want to move, but the pain nudged him back to reality.

He became aware of the barely audible sounds of the house, as if discovering them for the first time: the slight hum of the refrigerator, the ticking of the clock, an occasional creak from the walls. *This house has never been so quiet, he thought.*

With his eyes adjusted to the darkness, he glanced at the second shelf of the entertainment center. Light cast from an open window surrounded a pewter-framed photo in a halo. He liked the picture: a snapshot of his family all wearing shorts and shirts in different combinations of red, white, and blue taken just a month ago at a Fourth of July picnic.

He bent down to retrieve the note off the floor. As he reread it, he tried to visualize Madeline as she held the pencil and formed those letters, but he could not do it. He tried to look between the lines, at the unspoken words, hoping to find meaning which the actual words did not convey.

Randall,

> *I'm leaving. I don't know what I'm doing. It's not fair to you or the girls. I've got to leave. I'm not myself lately and I need to leave. Take care of the girls.*

> *Madeline*

The pain in his head had begun slowly, but now it throbbed. He rubbed his eyes and temples. *I've got to find you before the girls come home.*

After driving half the night, he had walked through the door just before three a.m. and was struck immediately by oppressive air he later associated with a feeling that the house had already begun mourning the loss of its mistress. He called out to her, cringing at the desperate sound of his voice, while heading through the living room, then upstairs to their bed—neatly made and empty. As if turning on the lights would tauntingly showcase her absence, he let the moonlight guide his step and only briefly turned on a light when he could not see into a curtained room.

He called out to her again as he urgently peeked into their daughters' separate bedrooms and the main bathroom. His pace quickened as he headed downstairs two levels to the basement utility room.

Empty. Where is she?

Although he had glanced past the dining room and into the kitchen when he had arrived home, and had not seen her, he imagined he would now find her sitting at the breakfast table. He slowed his pace as he climbed the stairs back to the main floor, walked through the empty dining room and kitchen, then circled back to the living room. That's where he found the note, next to the television remote, on the end table beside his leather recliner. And that's where he had sat in a state of dull shock for several hours.

Where are you? He asked silently. God I wish you were here. I wish I could hold you.

That thought brought him upright as he tried to remember the last time they had made love. It had been awhile. *Weeks? No, it can't be that long. Hell, when did I last give you a hug, hold you close, and tell you I love you?* He pulled himself out of the chair, walked stiffly into the kitchen and took some aspirin.

Maybe we've been in a rut. No big deal, we've been there before and gotten out of them. And when did you last reach out for me? You haven't been sleeping well and you often go downstairs to the sofa. You said you didn't want to disturb my sleep.

He leaned against the counter as his eyes landed on two dirty coffee cups in the otherwise spotless sink. *Did you just need some time away?*

Each possible explanation propelled him closer to considering possibilities he would rather avoid. *You won't be gone long, he decided. You'll want to help Allison pick out what she's going to wear for her senior pictures. And you were planning on talking to Vanessa about joining Weight Watchers with you. And you recently said maybe we should check Stacie's thyroid because she's pretty tiny for entering high school.* But as much as he tried to fight it, the possibility of her being with another man quickened his heartbeat and prompted cold sweat to dampen his brow. *Maybe you are with another man. You wouldn't just be on your own somewhere.* He shook his head in disbelief. *I should've confronted you back then.*

Turning away from the sink, he glanced at the round oak breakfast table and frowned when he remembered what Madeline had done the day he and the girls left on their trip. She had begun the day with the 'special breakfast'. French toast with fresh-sliced strawberries and homemade whipped cream meant it was a special day. The tradition began their first year of marriage when she made the breakfast for him the first time:

He had awoken that long ago morning to the sounds of her cooking, the smell of freshly brewed coffee, and her smiling face as he walked into the kitchen. "What's the occasion?" He asked as he nuzzled into her cheek and kissed her sweetly.

"Special day," she replied, grinning up at him.

"Special day? Let's see, it's not a holiday."

"No," she mumbled, almost as a question, giving him soft, feathery kisses up and down his neck.

Randall crossed his arms, holding himself. The memory of how affectionate they had been was almost unbearable.

"It's not your birthday."

"Nuh-uh," she muttered playfully.

"Are we doing something special today?"

"Getting warmer," she replied.

"I give up."

"Sit down and I'll tell you." She reluctantly pulled away from him, nudged him toward the table, and poured coffee.

He cut into the French toast and took one bite, savoring it. "This is delicious."

She reached for his hand, caressed it lightly, and looked into his questioning eyes. "I'm going to the doctor today. I'm hoping he'll confirm we're going to have a baby."

Randall's moment of shock was over as soon as it had come. He gently pulled her onto his lap, holding her close. "Are you sure, Maddie?"

"Not a doubt in my mind—or body!" she answered.

He looked at her with concern. "Are you okay?"

"I'm wonderful, absolutely wonderful."

Randall grimaced as other 'special breakfast' memories surfaced: the day Madeline announced her subsequent pregnancies, the loss of their daughters' first teeth, the day after he miraculously hit a hole-in-one on the golf course.

He glanced at the clock. *The sun will be coming up soon, another day gone by. I should have done something—gone after her. But where would I go?*

He began looking through the house again, this time searching for clues, but found nothing. Everything was in place; the house was clean. But he stopped cold when he saw their bedroom. It also looked the same. He rushed to the closet and threw open the doors. Her clothes were still there. The dresser—he lunged for it and pulled open the drawers—so neat, everything in order, everything there.

This is a joke! What kind of joke! She didn't take anything! A slight sense of relief relaxed his breath, but it didn't last long.

What would I know? I don't know how many clothes she has, or how many pairs of shoes.

He reopened the drawers one by one. Her panties and bras in the top drawer were a colorful and neatly folded display of nylon, cotton, silk, and lace, with matching sets together on one side and separates on the other. He could not find anything missing.

His thoughts were sarcastic. *Sure. I'm sure every husband knows exactly how many bras and panties his wife has.*

The next drawer held her pretty nightgowns, comfortable pajamas, and a few sexy negligees tucked in the back. Third drawer held her slips, panty hose, and neatly folded socks. He opened the bottom drawer. He called it her junk drawer, but Madeline called it her love drawer because she put her sentimental items in it—mostly cards or letters that were special to her.

It was full. He slammed it shut.

Randall again walked over to the closet, puzzled at the sight of her blouses, slacks, dresses, and jackets.

It doesn't look like she took anything!

While he searched for something obvious she had taken with her, he wanted to believe she was joking around—playing a trick on him and the girls—but he knew better. *Madeline would never joke around in this cruel way.*

He swung around and glanced at the bedside alarm clock.

Five-thirty. I've got to do something—but what? His eyes rested on the bed that Madeline should have been sleeping in. There was no denying that underneath the adrenaline rush, he felt exhaustion from anxiety and staying up all night, but he could not sleep yet.

Where do I begin looking for you Maddie? Friends? No—I'm not getting them involved. Police? No—you can't be missing. You left a note—you'll be back soon. Of course you will.

He went downstairs to the kitchen to retrieve the telephone book from the small cabinet beneath the wall phone. He then opened the top drawer, pushed the faded-red address book aside and took out a pad of paper and a pen.

You didn't take the truck. It's in the garage.

He began dialing every hotel in town and asked straight out for Madeline Averson's room. She was not at any of them. He then called the airlines, bus station, train station, and rental car agencies and was told they could not give out passenger information or they did not recall a passenger matching Madeline's description.

Where are you, Maddie? Tension was building and he rubbed his temples again. *Wait a minute—unless you're with a friend, you must've taken a cab. I should've started with them.*

He called every cab company and ended with the same results: no information. Randall dropped the pen and hung up the phone in a defeated manner.

Trying to gain a different perspective, he tried putting himself in her shoes. *Where did you go? You didn't take the car.* He ran over to the desk in the family room where they kept the checkbook. It was there, along with the credit cards they had stopped using months ago.

You couldn't have gone far.

Using the early morning hour as an excuse not to call her friends, he walked back up the stairs and into the bathroom, where he took off his clothes and stepped into the shower. He turned on the water and adjusted the temperature. The tepid water eased some of the tension. Ten minutes later, as most of the town was up and beginning their day, he fell naked into bed.

———

The phone rang. The sound woke Randall from a restless sleep. He quickly lunged toward the bedside table and picked up the receiver. A few seconds later he mumbled "I'm not interested" and slammed down the phone.

Damn solicitors.

For a few brief minutes he lay still in bed, noticing the lack of warmth of her body next to his. He did not know what his next step was, but he knew he had to do something to bring his wife home. He got up and dressed in a pair of jeans and a polo shirt. His five-foot ten-inch frame felt unusually heavy as he headed down the stairs and into the kitchen.

He needed coffee and began making a pot, acknowledging he hadn't made coffee in a long time.

You had it made when I got up every morning, Maddie.

He took off the lid and was surprised to find previously-filtered ground coffee, long since dried, in the basket, and leftover coffee in the normally clean pot.

That's not like you.

After cleaning the pot and brewing a fresh one, he turned from the counter. His attention was drawn back to the cabinet with the well-used address book in the top drawer.

I won't need to use it. Emily will know where she is. But a small seed of doubt accompanied that thought about his and Maddie's best friends and co-owners of their hardware store, Paul and Emily.

Emily would've told Paul if something serious were going on with Madeline. And Paul would've told me.

Randall walked the few steps to the phone. He dialed it with outward calm. Hearing Paul's voice, Randall struggled getting out a minimal greeting.

"Hello," Paul repeated.

"It's me."

"You calling from Mountain?"

"No. I came back from the reunion early. My brother, Barney, offered to bring the girls home tomorrow night." Randall's throat was dry and he wished he had waited for the coffee.

"What's up?"

"Madeline's not here. I," he paused, "I was wondering if Emily might know where she is."

"Not that I know of, but I'll get her for you."

Randall heard Paul yelling for Emily, mentioning Madeline's name, and hearing Emily respond, "I haven't heard from her."

Emily spoke into the phone. "Hi, Randall."

"Hi, Emily. Sorry to disturb you, but—do you know where Maddie is?"

"No. I haven't talked to her in awhile. Come to think of it, it's been a couple of weeks. Why?"

Randall's grip tightened on the receiver. "She left. I don't know where she is."

Emily barely let him finish his sentence. "What do you mean, she left?"

"I haven't talked to her since the girls and I arrived in Mountain. She didn't answer or return my calls. So I came back early. She left a note."

"What does it say?"

"Nothing, really. Just that she had to leave and for me to take care of the girls."

"When did she leave?"

"I don't know for sure. It could've been anytime after we talked on

Wednesday."

"Well, when is she coming back?"

"She didn't say."

"That doesn't make any sense. How long has she been gone? Where did she go?"

Randall paused, trying to slow down Emily's interruptions while he was trying to talk. "I don't know anything," he said a bit sharply. "I'm not sure when she left, or why, or where she is."

"Randall," Emily's voice rose to a fast-pitched squeal, "you stay right there. Paul and I will be right over. Okay?"

"You don't have to, Emily." But Emily had already hung up the phone. Randall replaced the receiver. He leaned against the wall, letting his forehead rest on his raised arm. Acid churned in his stomach at the thought of what the next step would be, and the next, and the next, until he found her. But one thing he was clear about: he did not want visitors. He picked up the phone, hit re-dial, listened to the dial tone and the ringing, then heard Emily's 'hello.'

"I'm sorry, Emily,—but I don't want company right now. I just needed to know if you knew anything about Maddie." Randall vaguely heard Emily release a slow exhale.

"Randall, I'm worried sick. This doesn't sound like her at all." Emily's voice softened. "I'm her best friend, I should know something."

"Well, I'm her husband." Randall stated the obvious. "And I don't know where she is."

There was a long pause until Emily broke the silence. "Have you called the police?"

With the phone sandwiched between his left shoulder and ear, Randall agonizingly leaned his torso against the wall. *Next step.*

"Randall." Emily repeated. When he didn't answer, she handed the phone to her husband.

Paul came on the line, his voice steady and deep. "Randall."

"I'm here." Randall pivoted until his back was against the wall. "Look— tell Emily I'll call the police. I'll be in touch." He hung up the phone and picked it up again. His hand trembled slightly as he dialed information. As the operator forwarded the call, he fought the urge to hang up as it started ringing.

Forty minutes and two cups of coffee later, Randall answered the door at the sound of the doorbell.

"Mr. Averson?" At Randall's nod, the officer introduced himself. "I'm Officer Ward."

Randall motioned the officer to come inside. "Can I get you something to drink, a cup of coffee?" Randall's voice was heavy, somewhat defeated. "I just put on a fresh pot." *First pot was too weak.*

"No, I'm fine, thanks." The officer followed Randall into the dining room, where they both sat down at the table. Randall pushed aside the pages of notes from his early morning phone calls and carefully placed Madeline's note on top of the stack.

The officer opened a notebook and pulled out forms and a pen. "When did you last see your wife?"

"Early Wednesday afternoon." Her image, standing at the front door waving as he pulled out of the driveway, burned into his memory so strongly the tiniest details had begun to haunt him. "That's when our daughters and I left for our annual family reunion in Mountain for "August the Deuce."

The officer seemed familiar with the annual celebration in honor of Icelandic Independence Day in Mountain, ND, about five hours away. He said nothing as Randall continued.

"Madeline didn't go with us this year. She said she wasn't feeling well, but she encouraged us to go without her. I called her as soon as we arrived at my parent's house—that evening at about six. We talked briefly, but over the next two days she didn't answer my calls."

"What did you talk about when you arrived?"

"Nothing special, she asked about the trip and was glad we made it safely. I told her I thought she sounded tired and I hoped she would get plenty of rest. She assured me she would be as good as new by the time we got back. I called the next evening, Thursday, and again on Friday morning. I was concerned when she didn't answer or return my calls, but I chalked it up to being overprotective—something Madeline has teased me about for years— and so I went about enjoying the reunion."

"When did you decide to come home?"

"Friday night—around ten." The fun he'd had that evening with his large family, eating Sloppy Joes, potato salad, and drinking beer, seemed a long time ago. "I tried phoning her again. When she didn't answer this time, I knew something was wrong."

"What about your daughters? Did they talk to her?"

"No."

"What are their names and ages?"

"Allison is our oldest. She's seventeen. Vanessa is almost sixteen, and Stacie is fourteen."

"Where are they now?"

"They're still in Mountain. They were at the Friday night dance when I decided to leave. I didn't want to ruin their weekend, so I asked my brother Barney, who lives in Dickinson, if he would bring them home tomorrow night."

"Are you and your wife away from each other often?"

"No—but, when we are, we always call to say goodnight." Randall handed the officer Madeline's handwritten note. "I found this on the end table next to my leather chair."

After the officer read the note, he asked Randall, "Is this your wife's handwriting?"

"Yes. But this is sloppy for her. Her handwriting is usually neat."

The officer made a note of that on his form. "I'll need to take it with me."

"My girls—" Randall was about to respond as if he were defending a prize possession. He let out a sigh. "They'll want to see this note from their mother."

The officer nodded in understanding. "I'll see to it you get a copy right away." He tucked the note into a plastic bag. "Have there been any problems in the home?"

"No."

"Had you been arguing?"

"No." Randall shook his head. "I learned long ago that arguing with Madeline didn't get me far." Randall realized that could have been taken the wrong way. "She would clam up if I so much as raised my voice."

"Did she ever threaten to leave?"

"Never."

"Has there been any suspicious behavior on her part?"

"No." But doubting his answer the moment he said it, he quickly added, "well—maybe. I don't know—maybe she hasn't been her usual self lately. She had trouble sleeping and she seemed—I don't know—easily distracted or something." Randall felt as if he were betraying his wife by that small admission. As a few more examples came to mind, he kept them to himself. "Nothing seemed suspicious at the time." He watched as the officer made notes.

"Any indication she wasn't happy?"

"No."

"Did she use drugs?"

"No. She doesn't like to take pills of any kind, but recently she's been having headaches. I've seen her take aspirin a few times."

"Did she go to the doctor?"

"No. Not that she mentioned anyway. They were just headaches."

"Were there money problems?"

"I'd say we're like most people, sometimes we over extend ourselves, but mostly our finances are manageable."

"Which category do you fall into right now?"

Randall shrugged uncomfortably at this further intrusion. "Business is slow, things are a little tight, but we're doing fine."

The officer looked at him intently. "Big box stores are putting the squeeze on a lot of our local merchants. I'd think your hardware store would be affected too." He looked at his notes, not expecting a reply.

"Did your wife have any mental problems or was she depressed?"

"No. Occasionally she would get—how would you describe it—melancholy, or down in the dumps, but then she'd be back to her old self."

"How would you describe her 'old self'?"

Randall pondered that question as if he had not thought about it for awhile. "Loyal—a great mother—a great wife, selfless. You know the type—always taking care of everyone else."

"She take care of you, too?"

As Officer Ward looked at Randall with a steady gaze, Randall refrained from gritting his teeth. Randall knew the officer was already assessing the situation, gathering initial impressions of the husband whose wife was missing. Randall assessed him as well, concluding the officer had seen his share of tragedies.

"Yes. She's a great wife."

"Did she have any enemies, anyone who may want to harm her?"

Randall suppressed a grin at the absurdity of that notion. "No. She's well liked and respected."

"Did you ever abuse your wife?"

"Never."

"Ever cheat on her?"

"No."

"Is it possible she was having an affair?"

As a twitch started in his lower left jaw, Randall steeled himself against pain that came with certain memories. He didn't want to think about that now, that time—years ago—when he discovered she had been unfaithful. "No." It came out abruptly. He calmly looked the officer in the eye. "She was not having an affair."

Although Randall's reaction was not lost to him, the officer refrained from making a note of it. "What did she take?"

"Nothing that I know of."

"She didn't take anything?"

Despite Officer Ward's professional demeanor, Randall could see this had surprised him.

"I went through her clothing. It looks like it's all here. Even the check-book is here." Randall's inflection changed with each acknowledgment. "She didn't take my truck, and I had her car." Hearing himself put the facts together, Randall could only come to one logical conclusion, and it scared the hell out of him. He clasped his hands together in front of him and looked the officer straight in the eye. "Do you think she could have been harmed or maybe even kidnapped?"

The intense emotion emanating from Randall was apparent. The officer answered carefully, "In kidnapping cases, there's usually contact within the first few hours. But we will follow every possible lead. I need a list of Madeline's friends, her work place, her hobbies, any clubs or organizations she belongs to."

Randall reached over for his notepad. "I made a list."

"Have you contacted any of them?"

"Only my business partner, Paul, and his wife, Emily. They are our closest friends. Both of them are as surprised as I am."

"I suggest you give me your list and let us handle it. It will save people the trouble of being questioned twice."

Like hell I will, Randall thought. "Officer, I need to do everything I can to bring my wife home."

The officer was about to offer a rebuttal, but the determination in Randall's eyes made him pause. "Okay—but I'll be taking the list. You let us know if you find anything."

The officer searched the house but found nothing suspicious. As he prepared to leave, he had little encouragement to offer Randall. "We'll do what we can to find her." But as the officer walked out, Randall imagined the officer thinking, *if she wants to be found.*

2

Earlier that day, Allison plopped down on the worn recliner in her grandparent's living room in Mountain. Her golden-brown hair hung in a ponytail past her shoulders. Her face, with just a hint of make-up, was naturally tanned from summer activities: softball, water skiing, and lying out at her best friend Judy's swimming pool. Throwing one leg over the armchair, she opened up her folder and withdrew the college brochures accumulated over the last few weeks. She had read through each one on her quest to decide which college she would be attending the following year.

Pepperdine University was her top choice. She fondly remembered visiting the University when they had traveled to L.A. in May. Since there was a large tool convention, Randall had reasoned they could write off a portion of the trip and check out a few universities at the same time.

Allison visualized herself walking along the beach on weekends or biking along a trail that stretched for miles. She could shop in Malibu or study at local coffee shops. A sense of excitement rippled through her; she could hardly wait to get through her senior year of high school.

But David won't be there, she thought with a pang. It had been exactly two weeks and four days since he had left on a family vacation to Yellowstone National Park. Allison could not wait to see him. She loved his dark hair and the way he would look at her, teasingly, raising one eyebrow while lowering the other.

She didn't know which to think about: David or college. She loved thinking about both, but, realistically, she knew the two did not go hand in hand. His grades were not good enough for a scholarship, and his family could not afford a pricey college like Pepperdine. Not that her parents could, but Allison knew she had earned it. With the highest GPA in her class, and the determination to maintain it throughout her senior year, she was certain she would be valedictorian and get a full scholarship to the college of her choice.

"Hey, Al." Allison's sister, Vanessa, waltzed into the room carrying a slice of vinarterta, an Icelandic cake of sweetened prune filling layered between seven cake-size sugar cookies.

Allison looked over the edge of the brochures and winced. Vanessa seemed to be gaining even more weight since the summer began and she had a knack for accentuating every extra pound with tight clothes and low necklines. Allison had tried to encourage Vanessa to lose weight, but Vanessa just shrugged off the comments and accused Allison of being jealous of her curves. *Yeah, right.* Allison said to herself.

With another glance at her sister, Allison reluctantly admitted Vanessa did have a flare for style. *And from the shoulders on up, she looks great.* Vanessa's thick, wavy brown hair was twisted and held in place with a butterfly clip. Loose tendrils swung lightly against her brown shoulders. Her suntanned complexion was brightened by an enviable makeup application that made her big hazel eyes sparkle. Her full lips, inherited from the Averson women and described as 'luscious' by a few of the guys around school, were lightly touched with shiny pink lip gloss.

As Vanessa took a big bite of the vinarterta, she reached down and purposely knocked Allison's leg off the armchair.

"Knock it off!" Allison yelled. "And why are you in here pigging out again? You should be outside playing football with everyone else, working those hips instead of adding to them."

Allison felt bad, sort of, for her thoughtless words. But it was the truth. Vanessa needed to lose weight, thirty—forty pounds—maybe more.

Ignoring Allison's jibe, Vanessa shrugged her shoulders and sat down on the floor. "I'm a little worried about Dad—and Mom too. First Mom decides not to come. She's never done that before. She always comes with us, and you know how much she looks forward to it. Then Dad starts getting antsy, pacing the floor. He's always trying to call her, but she doesn't answer."

"Mom and Dad are fine." Allison said impatiently. "Mom didn't feel good and Dad had an emergency at the store."

Vanessa looked startled. "What are you talking about? Dad left?"

"He went home late last night. Didn't you notice he wasn't at the parade this morning?"

"No. I was barely awake from staying up so late at the dance."

"Where've you been since?"

"I was with Stacie at the art show down at the Borg Home. I just got back—I left her there." Vanessa hastily set the plate down next to her, causing the half-eaten cake to tumble to the floor. She picked up the cake, put it on the plate, and scraped the crumbs onto the plate before looking at Allison questioningly. "So he just left in the middle of the night without telling us?"

"He told Amma and Afi, and he asked Uncle Barney to bring us home."

Allison batted her pencil back and forth, tapping it against a shoulder.

"Since when does Dad ever have an emergency at the store that Paul can't take care of?"

"I don't know, Vanessa," Allison flared, "maybe Paul isn't there." Her expression brightened in a flash. "Hi, Uncle Barney!"

"Hi, girls." Randall's oldest brother leaned against the doorway and took a drink of the coffee he carried like a seasoned veteran. He had overheard part of the girls' conversation and could tell they were worried.

Allison leaned forward in her chair. "Amma said you'd be driving us home on Sunday, right after church."

"That's right. But to tell you the truth, there was no emergency at the store." He furrowed his brows.

Vanessa gave her sister an 'I told you so' look.

"There wasn't?" Allison asked.

"No." Barney shook his head. "No—your dad just said he couldn't take another six hours in a car with the three of you girls. He asked me if I'd bring his little *scietas* home." His seriousness turned into a full-blown smile.

"We're not little shits." Allison mumbled defensively before turning back around in the recliner. The girls did not speak Icelandic, but a few choice words had survived several generations of living in America.

"Dad didn't say that." Vanessa watched her uncle shrug his shoulders and shake his head innocently.

"I don't have a problem with you driving us home, Uncle Barney." Allison started rocking herself back and forth in the recliner. "Not as long as we get to pick the radio station."

"Not a chance," he replied. "And while we're at it, let's set up a few ground rules—no perfume, no scented lotions or hairspray, no magazines with perfume samples, no messing up the car, and no taking off your shoes because there will be no stinkin' feet." He ran out of the room, grinning mischievously as the girls yelled and threw sofa pillows at him.

"Which explains why you've always been insensitive, Uncle Barney," Allison yelled when he stuck his head back around the corner. "All your sensitivity is in your nostrils."

Uncle Barney bent over, grabbed a pillow and threw it at Allison, hitting her squarely on the shoulder. He snorted like a pig and raised his arms triumphantly before walking out of the room.

Allison picked up the brochures again. "What college do you think I should go to?" she asked Vanessa. "Pepperdine was my favorite when Dad and I looked at colleges last year."

Vanessa took a look at the brochures. "Oh, come on, Sis, a private college? You're dreaming! Dad was just humoring you by going there. Even if you get a scholarship, I doubt Mom and Dad could cover room and board."

Allison stated the obvious with certainty. "I'm going to be a world class attorney and I need the best education."

"Oh, come on. What's the matter with U.N.D.? You too big for it?"

"You know it, girl." Allison sat up tall and stuck out her chest.

"You're posturing like a peacock. Get over yourself."

"Eat shit, Vanessa."

Vanessa laughed and got up off the floor. "No thanks, but I think I'll grab another piece of vinarterta. Can I get you a piece?"

"Nope. I've got to keep my figure." Allison said smugly. "I'll be spending next year at the beach."

With a roll of her eyes, Vanessa muttered "Dream on." She walked into the kitchen where her aunts were chatting away, perfectly synchronized in the kitchen routine, a well-orchestrated trio of women cooking and cleaning while talking about the different people who had come and gone from their lives. Vanessa watched them with a mixture of fascination and disgust. Didn't these women know it was the '80's? Every year they worked to feed and clean up after this mob of relatives while the men sat around drinking, playing football with the kids—and basically being handsome and charming. This, Vanessa conceded, was not very hard to do. The men in her family were handsome and charming. She reluctantly decided to give them some credit. *I guess they're the ones who usually mow the lawn and do house repairs and stuff.*

After tossing the dropped Vinarterta in the trash, she glanced at the platter of kleinurs, Icelandic twisted doughnuts, and eyeing the leftover ponnukokur's, thin Icelandic pancakes, before opting for another piece of vinarterta.

She had decided years ago that her mom's vinarterta was pretty good, but not as good as Amma's or her Aunt Marge's. Of course, Amma and Aunt Marge happened to be a hundred percent Icelandic. Maybe that was the difference. Like how the football teams were divided among the cousins, pure-bloods against the half bloods. Vanessa and her sisters were part of the half-bloods team since they were Icelandic on their dad's side and unknown heritage on their mother's. Vanessa always teased her full-blooded cousins. "Do you guys have any blood in your veins or is it just a mixture of ice and beer?" Vanessa wondered what the accumulated scores of the teams were over the years. If she had to guess, she'd say it was a pretty even match. She came to the conclusion that being a pure blood was beneficial only when cooking Icelandic desserts.

Vanessa darted out of the kitchen, almost knocking over one of the floor fans. She walked out the back door and yelled to the rest of the gang that had started a football game. "Anyone see Stace?" She heard a couple of no's as the ball was tossed and several bodies slammed into each other, falling in a heap in the rich green grass. Another game of touch football had just gotten physical.

"Who's winning?" She yelled.

"The pure butts." Her cousin Brian yelled, "Why don't you and your lazy sisters get out here and join us so we'll have a full team?"

"We played for three hours yesterday." Vanessa snapped back. "Why don't you think of something better to do?" She decided to take a walk to see if she could find her younger sister. *Maybe I should get a little more exercise anyway. This town isn't that big. If I walked around the entire town, it would probably only take a half hour.*

Vanessa liked the fact that only a few people had fenced yards and nobody seemed to mind when people cut through their yards. She crossed the narrow alleyway between two neighboring houses as she watched one family throwing horseshoes in their backyard, with people of all ages milling around.

During 'the deuce', the town—with a population of one hundred and twenty-five, regularly grew to as many as five thousand. This was evidenced not only by the crowded streets, but also by the many motor homes, campers, and tents, that sat in large backyards. During special anniversary years, the town would have as many as ten to fifteen thousand people.

A couple minutes later she reached the back of the church, the logical place to begin searching for Stacie. Walking adjacent to the graveyard toward the front of the church, Vanessa recalled one of her cousins saying that Mountain was in some record book for having the only graveyard in America on the main street. *Good for Mountain,* Vanessa thought. *I'm surprised it's even on a map.*

Vanessa thought about the other graveyard located at the edge of town, down a long dirt road. It was traditional for the cousins to walk there each year during 'the deuce.' When she was younger, the older cousins had frightened her by saying you had to exit a graveyard at the exact spot you entered or the ghosts of the dead would rise and follow you home. At the age of eight, she was scared for weeks. Now it was just a place to go—one more thing to do when the family gathered in Mountain.

Although it was such a small town, it did have a few local businesses and landmarks: one café, one small grocery store which doubled as the post office, one church, one playground, one park, a nursing home, and a dance hall. *But there are two bars and two graveyards. Is that a coincidence? She mused.*

She walked up the four steps and went inside the church, where a few people lingered around the pews, then she headed for the stairs leading to the basement, where the annual luncheon was held. People were lined up to fill their plates while others sat at tables along the walls. *But no Stacie.*

Vanessa walked back up the stairs, exited the church, and headed down Main Street to the intersection with West Street, then turned right. Portable basketball hoops were set up and three-man basketball teams of all ages and both sexes competed. Just beyond this activity was the town's only restaurant, the "Mountain Chalet," which was open for breakfast and lunch and frequented by local farmers. Vanessa entered the café and walked to the back room occupied by a few pinball machines and a pool table. *She's not here either.*

After leaving the restaurant, she walked past the front of Amma and Afi's house until she came to the far end of town where, about ten years earlier, carnivals had been held at the park. Now, the only thing happening on this side of town—other than the dance the night before—was the genealogist club helping people trace their ancestry. Down the street, west of the park, the evening's fireworks were being set up.

Circling back to Main Street, Vanessa headed past food booths and the stick-on tattoo display before she saw three beefed-up men unloading a large portable stage from the back of a semi. When she spotted punk rock dressed band members unloading their instruments from the back of a van, she couldn't wait for the street dance to begin later that evening.

Finally Vanessa spotted Stacie sitting at a picnic table with charcoal pencil in hand, fully absorbed in sketching. Quietly walking over to her, Vanessa whispered close to Stacie's ear. "Boo!"

Stacie jumped, "Vanessa, you scared me to death."

Vanessa peeked at her sister's drawing and was struck, as always, by Stacie's natural artistic ability, a gift no one else in the family had. "That's good." Vanessa was impressed with Stacie's capturing an image that was very real but seemed a tad strange when put to paper. The sketch showed the church and graveyard, the temporary stage with a rock-and-roll band and people dancing on the street across from Byron's bar. "I never thought about the proximity of the church, the bar, and the street dance before." Vanessa said with a shrug. "I guess it's a good thing—if any of us sin tonight—we don't have far to go to repent. And if anyone dies from alcohol poisoning—the clean-up crew won't have too far to carry them to their graves."

"That's sick, Vanessa."

"It's *your* sketch." Vanessa looked around at the preparation activities. "What do you say we head back to Amma's and get ready for tonight?"

"Sure." Stacie was just two years younger then Vanessa but, since she had always been tiny for her age, with wispy blonde hair, everyone in the family treated her as if she were much younger. Her overall demeanor appeared vulnerable, as if she had glimpsed the secrets of the universe and needed a little support carrying the burden. But her pale blue eyes told a different story, they held a feeling of peace and strength that defied her small frame.

Walking back to the house, Vanessa told Stacie about Dad's early departure and suggested they call home. By the time they reached Amma and Afi's house, the football game had transformed into a game of badminton. Allison made a spectacular dive for the birdie, and missed. "Al!" Vanessa yelled, "Stacie and I are going to call Mom and Dad."

Allison got up and picked a few pieces of grass off her legs. "Go ahead. Tell them 'hi' for me and I hope Mom's feeling better."

Vanessa and Stacie walked into the kitchen. Vanessa made a beeline for the phone and dialed long distance to Bismarck. It rang twice before she heard her dad answer. "Hey, Dad—you bailed on us!"

"Yeah, sorry about that."

"Well, is everything okay? Allison said you had an emergency at work."

"Yeah, yeah, it's fine—it's—uh—taken care of."

"Great." Vanessa nodded at Stacie. "Can I talk to Mom? Stacie's here with me—she wants to talk to her too."

"Uhm—can't right now, she's not home. You girls have a good time and we'll see you when you get home tomorrow night. Sound good?"

Vanessa gave Stacie a perplexed look. "Sure, Dad. We'll see you tomorrow."

"Okay—bye, sweetie."

"Bye." Vanessa hung up the phone and repeated the brief conversation to Stacie. "It was a little weird. I think we caught them in the middle of something."

Stacie frowned. "Or maybe they just want some alone time."

The house was again noticeably silent in a way that made Randall uncomfortable. *What do I do now?* Between coffee and nerves, he felt the need for activity. *I'll trim the hedges like Madeline suggested last week. And I'll mow the lawn and Mrs. Deiko's lawn too.*

He strode purposely through the kitchen and out to the garage. *You'll come home soon, Maddie, and this place will look nice for you when you do.* He grabbed a pair of gloves and trimming shears, and was about to push the garage door opener when the phone began ringing. As he raced to reach the phone, he tossed the gloves and shears on the lidded trash bin by the door and answered before the third ring.

"Hello." His voice came out shaky and too high.

"Randall, dear, why don't you come and pay me a visit."

His head fell forward with the weight of disappointment. "Good afternoon, Mrs. Deiko. I'm sorry, but I can't right now."

"Randall, I'm calling because I haven't seen Madeline in several days, and I'm beginning to worry about her." She hesitated when Randall didn't reply. "I saw the police car." Another pause. "Randall, I saw something."

There was no hesitation.

"I'll be right over."

He hung up abruptly and was soon knocking at her door. After hearing her yell 'come in,' he opened the door and saw his elderly neighbor sitting in her favorite straight back chair in the living room. She motioned for him to sit down across from her in the rocker.

Mrs. Deiko had just celebrated her ninetieth birthday a few months earlier and was proud to be living alone, with little assistance, but she appreciated the help the Aversons gave: yard work, sharing an occasional meal, and doing some light housekeeping. Living next door for more than eight years had created a bond between the neighbors.

He was grateful when she got right to the point. "Did something happen to Madeline?" Mrs. Deiko inquired.

"I don't know. I haven't talked to her since Wednesday. She left a note saying she was leaving, and to take care of the girls." He leaned forward in the rocker. "What did you see?"

Mrs. Deiko had never been a gossip, and Randall sensed she was struggling with telling him what she had seen. The gentle tone of his voice belied his desperation, "Mrs. Deiko, if you know anything that can help me find my wife, please tell me."

Mrs. Deiko looked down at her clasped hands as if looking him in the eye would fill her with guilt. "It was Wednesday night. I was at the kitchen window when I heard a car drive up to your house." She hesitated, and Randall wondered if she felt she was betraying Madeline. The fear in his gut intensified further as she continued. "I looked out the window. A man got out. I had never seen him before and, well, frankly I was a little curious." Randall's jaw tightened as he watched her take a shallow breath. "Madeline greeted him." Mrs. Deiko's eyes shifted toward the floor. "He went into the house. I went to bed at my usual 10:30, and his car was still there. In the morning it was gone. I didn't think anything of it, but then—when I hadn't noticed any activity all day—I decided to check for myself. There was no answer at the door."

Randall knew there was more to the story. He pulled his rocker closer to Mrs. Deiko and leaned toward her. He willed himself to stay as calm as possible. "I haven't talked to her in days—and I have the police involved. If there's something more you're not telling me—something that could help me bring Madeline home—please tell me."

Mrs. Deiko's eyes watered. "Maybe I should talk to the police instead." She saw his eyes widen in alarm.

"Did something happen to Madeline?" His words were clipped. "Did somebody hurt her? Maybe she was forced to write that note."

"I don't know Randall, but I don't think so."

"What do you mean?" he pleaded. "I need the truth, Mrs. Deiko."

"I know, Randall. But I only know what I saw. I didn't talk with Madeline. I may have misread the situation."

He spoke slowly. "I'll keep that in mind—but please tell me what you saw. I need to know."

Mrs. Deiko clasped her hands together. "As the man got out of the car, Madeline rushed to greet him. She seemed, well, happy to see him."

"Do you know what he looked like?"

"I didn't get a good look. But he seemed to have a tall, slender build, and his hair was dark. That's the best description I can give."

Randall's lower jaw began pulsating. "What happened next?"

"She hugged him, and it seemed very emotional—like she may have been crying and she didn't want to let him go. Then I saw them walk into the house arm-in-arm."

Randall kept his emotions tightly under control. "Thank you, Mrs. Deiko." He reached over, gently placing his strong hand on her soft, frail one. Every prior visit had ended with him asking if there was anything she needed. He tried to smile, but he felt like it was forced. He didn't ask about her needs this time.

Placing her other hand over his, Mrs. Deiko smiled reassuringly. "When are the girls coming home?"

"Tomorrow."

"Try to get some rest. If Madeline left, those girls are going to need you to be strong."

"I will." He arose from the chair. Unsteady on his feet, he felt as if he had just received another blow.

It didn't happen. She didn't leave me for another man.

He walked back to his house. With both fists clenched at his side, his lower jaw twitching, he could actually feel the veins in his neck and arms bulge. Back at home, the pain and anger was so intense, he paced through the kitchen, the living room, dining area, and back into the kitchen, as if he could trample away the pain. His empty coffee cup on the counter made him angrier as he looked toward the kitchen sink.

You served him coffee and left your damn dirty dishes in the sink, he wanted to shout.

With a trembling hand, Randall dialed the police again. After a brief pause, Officer Ward came on the line, and Randall relayed the information from Mrs. Deiko. After a few questions, Officer Ward hinted that with a note from Madeline, and now with an eyewitness that had seen Madeline hugging another man and inviting him inside, foul play appeared less likely. But Officer Ward told Randall they would talk to Mrs. Deiko, and would continue with routine investigation.

Randall hung up the phone. *She took off with another man. That's why she took little or no money, and none of her personal belongings.* A part of him couldn't believe it. It didn't make any sense. Not his Maddie.

He rushed back into the bedroom. In a fit of rage he opened the dresser drawers and began throwing her clothes: nightgowns, bras, panties and stockings—hurling them across the bed and onto the floor. He opened the closet and grabbed an armful of Madeline's suits, dresses, slacks, sweaters, and blouses. He suddenly stopped. *What am I doing? The girls can't come home to this mess.* But he was in no mood to clean it up. Instead, he grabbed his wallet, went downstairs, exited the house, and climbed into his truck. He drove around aimlessly for several hours before he pulled into the "Tree City Bar," and ordered the first of many gin-and-tonics.

3

The next evening before Allison, Vanessa, and Stacie were due home, Randall sat in his recliner, exhausted from thoughts that vacillated between blind-sided grief and overwhelming anger as he had painstakingly cleaned up the bedroom mess.

The all-consuming silence was broken as the VCR turned on and started recording. Randall glanced at the clock. *60 Minutes is starting. Madeline programmed the VCR like I asked her to.* The flashing red light on the VCR attracted his attention, but in his peripheral vision the family photo taken on the 4th of July caught his eye. As if he was hooked on a fishing line and were being reeled in, he got up from his chair and walked over to the entertainment center. His eyes focused in on Stacie as a realization surfaced. *You've been looking at Stacie in an odd way lately, Maddie. Or am I being paranoid?* But one memory in particular stood out. At Stacie's fourteenth birthday party two months ago, he had walked into the kitchen and found Madeline staring at the cake, seemingly in her own world. She was supposed to be lighting the candles and bringing the cake out to the birthday girl and guests that were gathered around waiting to sing 'Happy Birthday.' Randall had teased Madeline. "You're going to fall into the cake and mess up your pretty face," he had whispered in her ear.

"What?" She had turned to look at him. Then she shook her head and said, "I'm fine, I'm coming."

Randall looked at the family picture more closely. He began comparing the physical characteristics of each one of them. There was the obvious, with Vanessa's dark, wavy hair, round face and hazel eyes; she looked the most like Madeline. Vanessa's lips were a little fuller. Allison's oval face, high forehead and high cheekbones made her look more like his side of the family. *But what about Stacie? She slightly resembles Allison, and Allison resembles my side of the family. But Stacie doesn't.*

He looked closer. *Stacie's eyes aren't like anyone's on my side of the family, and they don't look like Maddie's. Stacie's face is more heart shaped, her nose turns up a little. Where did she get that?*

When all he wanted to do was collapse to the ground in despair, Randall remained standing. *It could be from her maternal grandparents—but we'll never know. Maddie doesn't know.* He thought of the decision he had made long ago.

Blood or not, Stacie's my daughter. It will never be otherwise.

Knowing he was running out of time to figure out what he was going to tell the girls, he turned away from the entertainment center and walked outside to the small backyard. He sat down in the denim lounge chair and glanced at the tire swing that hung from one of the two trees in the backyard. A bittersweet memory of Stacie surfaced. They had barely moved into the new house when he put up the swing. She was about six years old and her white-blonde pigtails flew in the breeze as he pushed her on the swing. She was giggling and yelling, "Higher, Daddy, I want to go higher."

You're my daughter, Stacie.

Once again he tried to focus on the present situation. *What am I going to tell the girls? I can't tell them their mother left with another man! Besides, Maddie will be back soon. I know she will. There's no reason to alarm the girls.* He concluded he would make up something to tell his daughters, a lie. His stomach lurched at the thought. But the truth was unthinkable. *Besides, a lie will give the police time to find her. I'll tell them she's on a trip with friends.* He shook his head. *But what if she's gone a long time? I'll tell them she's with a sick friend, yes—she went to help a sick friend.*

From the backyard, Randall heard the car pull up in the driveway, and he quickly walked into the house. A glance in the mirror revealed there was already a harder edge to his features. He walked toward the door as Vanessa swung it open.

"Hey, Dad." She gave him a quick kiss, then backed up a step. "You don't look too good." But she didn't wait for a reply as she walked past him and headed up the stairs.

Randall stepped outside and heard Allison teasing Uncle Barney about being old fashioned when it came to music. When she reached for the door, she gave Randall a quick hug. "Hi, Dad. You missed a great parade. Uncle Barney led the Kiwanis group in his miniature car and almost ran right into Doris Simundson when he was waving at the crowd."

Randall forced a smile for his eldest daughter and his brother Barney.

"Hi, Dad." Stacie said, carrying a duffle bag that looked like it weighed more than she did.

Randall took the bag from her, set it down next to him and squeezed her tight, a little too tight.

"Where's Mom?" Allison asked.

He took a look at them, savoring their innocence. "She's not here right now." He hoped he had said it like it was no big deal, giving the impression that maybe their mom was running an errand.

With her own bag over her shoulder, Allison grabbed one handle of Stacie's duffel bag while she motioned Stacie to grab the other. Randall watched them leave before he turned to his brother. "Thanks for bringing the girls home, Barney. I hope they didn't give you too much trouble."

"Heavens no, the girls were great."

"Good. Do you want to come in?"

Barney looked at his brother suspiciously. "You want to tell me what's going on?"

"Not right now." Randall paused, thoughtful for a moment. "I have a few things to sort out first."

Barney nodded. "I'll just head on home." He reached over and squeezed Randall's shoulder in a supportive gesture. "I'm just a couple of hours away. Call if you need anything."

"I will. Thanks." After Barney reached his car, Randall walked back inside and closed the door. Fear gripped his body as he thought of the lie he was going to tell the girls.

A sick friend, sure.

He walked through the living room, so cozy and neat. Looking at the pictures he and Madeline had taken over the years, he wondered what their future now held. The girls seemed to emerge from their bedrooms at the same time, excited about telling him what he missed during the last two days.

"When will Mom be home?" Stacie asked.

"Well," Randall rubbed his forehead, looking at the floor. "Well—Mom went—" he hesitated.

"Dad, what's the matter" Allison asked bluntly. "You don't look very good."

"No—I'm not feeling very well. Here, why don't you girls sit down for a moment, you're making me nervous all gathered around me."

The girls scattered: Allison sat in the nearby rocker, Vanessa skipped to the couch, and Stacie, to the love seat. They watched with curiosity as their dad took a deep breath.

He bowed his head and stared at the floor. *A sick friend,* he thought. *Right. Who? Carol. Sure. She's getting old.* He could not look up. He started to speak, but the lie would not come out. "She's gone, girls. She left us."

———

Nobody stirred. The girls just stared at their dad. His body language and appearance spoke of the seriousness of the situation: slumped shoulders, stress lines etched on his face, empty eyes and a defeated tone in his voice. But other than their dad's odd demeanor, there was no reason for the girls to think their life was about to drastically change.

"Dad," Allison searched his eyes for understanding. "What do you mean 'left us'? You mean went away?"

Randall felt the words stuck somewhere between his throat and his chest. *What happened to my little story?* "She's gone." He flinched at the inadequacy of his answer, but like a talking parrot stuck on a phrase, he repeated, "She left us."

Vanessa looked at both of her sisters and started laughing. It was a loud, nervous laugh that ended quickly when nobody joined in. "Dad?" It came out in a whine of disbelief. "Come on, Dad." She stood up and paced a few steps. "Guys—come on—Allison, Stacie," she pleaded, "this is ridiculous! Mom leaving!" She laughed again. "The only way Mom would leave us is if she had been abducted by aliens." She raised her hand, showing the imaginary headline that would soon be gracing the front page of the local paper, "Madeline Averson, kidnapped by little gray men."

Randall glanced at Allison and Stacie, then back at Vanessa. "It's true. I'm so sorry, girls, but it's true."

Searching her dad's eyes, Stacie's voice was barely audible. "What happened? Why did Mom leave us?"

Randall shook his head. "I don't know. I hadn't talked to your mother since the day we arrived in Mountain. For a few days I got caught up in the visiting. Even though I was worried, I talked myself out of it." He added a little guiltily, "I guess I was having too good a time."

"There was no reason not to." Allison interjected. "I mean, you didn't have any idea she would leave, did you?"

"No—of course not."

"You haven't talked to her since Wednesday?" Stacie asked.

"No, she didn't return my calls. On Friday night I called again. When she didn't answer, I knew something was wrong. You girls were at the dance— I didn't want to worry you. I talked to Barney, arranged for him to bring you home, then I took off."

Allison clasped her hands together tightly. "This is ridiculous. We're talking about Mom. She wouldn't leave us."

The memory of arriving home to the empty house remained vivid in Randall's mind. "From the moment I stepped into the house, it was obvious she hadn't been here for several days. Then I found the note on the end table." He pointed to the table next to his recliner.

"What note?" Allison jumped in.

Randall got up and went into the kitchen. When he came back he handed the note to Allison.

"Why is it a copy?" She asked.

Randall's lower jaw twitched. "The police have the original."

"The police are involved?" Vanessa asked in disbelief.

"Yes," he said defensively. "I don't know where she is. I filed a missing person's report. I had to."

"And they haven't found her yet?" Stacie asked.

Randall closed his eyes. "No."

Allison read the copy of her mother's note then passed it to Stacie, who was within arms reach. Vanessa walked over and read it over Stacie's shoulder. "It doesn't say anything that makes any sense! Where did she go?"

"I don't know, Vanessa."

"And you don't know when she'll be back?"

Randall shook his head solemnly.

Stacie stared at the words, trying to make sense of them. "I know Mom said she wasn't feeling well, but I think there's something really wrong with her. I mean—she must be really sick or something. This barely even looks like her handwriting. It's sloppy." She looked at Randall with a mixture of hope and fear. "Maybe she's in the hospital."

"No Stacie. I called the hospitals. I called everywhere I could think of."

Allison leaned forward, "Tell us who you called, and where you looked for her. Maybe we can think of something you've missed."

Randall let out an impatient sigh. "I called the police, the hospitals, the airlines and bus station. I checked accident reports. I called every place and everyone I could think of."

Stacie sat up hopefully. "Emily would know if something was wrong with Mom. She probably knows where she is."

"She doesn't, Stacie. I talked to her yesterday. She doesn't know anything."

"What about Mom's friends from the sewing group?" Allison asked.

Randall paced a few steps. "I didn't call them."

"Why not?" Vanessa asked in a brusque manner. "You said you called everyone you could think of."

Randall's patience was just about gone. "Listen," he said sternly, "The police are handling it now. Besides, she's bound to call or come home any minute now and then we can get things back to normal."

"Dad," Allison said with determination, "somebody's got to know something in this town. If we tell them she left, maybe they'll—,"

"No!" Randall yelled. With fists clenched, he turned his back to them and stared out the window. "We're not going to tell anybody else."

Allison, Vanessa, and Stacie looked at each other. Their fear increased along with the tension in the room.

"Dad?" It was barely a whisper from Stacie. "Is there something you're not telling us?"

Unable to face them, he dropped his head forward. When he spoke, each word fell heavily like a brick on sand. "She left—with another man."

"No way!" Vanessa cried out in shock.

"Mom wouldn't be with anyone but you, Dad." Stacie spoke confidently. "She would never do that—she loves you—and she wouldn't leave us. She loves us!"

"Yeah," Allison stated self-assuredly. "Mom taking off with another man is as ridiculous as Vanessa's alien theory."

For the sake of his daughters, Randall made an attempt to calm down. He purposely relaxed his clenched fists. After a few very long, silent moments, he finally turned around. "Mrs. Deiko saw them together." This time nobody commented. After another long silence, Randall told his daughters everything about his conversation with Mrs. Deiko. By the time he was finished, the absurd vision of their mother in the arms of an unknown man became a possibility to them. "We have to face it—because it's there in black-and-white. Your mother left us to be with another man."

Vanessa started crying. Silent tears slid down Stacie's cheeks. Allison stood up stoically and comforted her sisters, but her eyes remained stubbornly dry.

The sight was too much for Randall. He wanted to help his daughters, but he was too distraught to offer much support. His anger toward his wife was overwhelming, and yet he missed her unbearably. "I'm going out for awhile. I'll be back soon."

"Dad?" Stacie cried out when Randall was almost at the door. "Will you be okay?"

Randall turned and saw the fear in his youngest daughter's eyes. He knew he should be with his daughters, but it was all he could do to smile somewhat reassuringly and mumble, "Yeah." He stepped outside into the early evening twilight as the soft thud of the door closing behind him resounded heavily in his daughter's hearts.

———

For several minutes the girls remained huddled together. "It will be all right." Allison whispered. "We'll get through this. Mom won't be gone long.

She'll come home and explain all of this to us. You know she will."

Vanessa nodded her head in agreement, then dried her eyes with the back of her hand. "You're right." As if she were already bored with her emotions, she walked past her sisters and toward the kitchen. "I can't believe we declined Uncle Barney's offer to stop and get a cheeseburger because we *knew* Mom would have dinner waiting for us."

"You're hungry?" Allison asked sarcastically.

"It's dinner time and I'm starving." But Vanessa stopped long enough to consider the question and realized the rumblings in her stomach were not from hunger. "I was hungry on the way home. But if I eat now, I'll probably throw-up."

Stacie walked to the bathroom and brought out a box of tissues. She grabbed a couple and handed one to Vanessa. "There's no way Mom left with another man."

"Let's pick up where Dad left off." Allison said as she opened the drawer of the end table and got out paper and pencil. "Maybe we can figure out where she is and who she's with. We need to call everyone."

"Wait a minute," Vanessa piped in. "I agree with Dad. There's no reason to tell everybody yet. Mom will be home soon—so the fewer people that know, the better."

Allison tapped the pencil back and forth in her hand. "She's already been gone four or five days. How long do you want to wait?"

"How about until she decides to come home?" Vanessa practically rolled her eyes as she said it. "She left a note. She was seen practically making out with another man in our front yard. Mrs. Deiko saw them. The police are involved. Dad called all kinds of places. What more do you want?"

Stacie clasped her hands together in her lap. "I think there's something wrong with Mom. There must be. Didn't you notice her handwriting?"

"Maybe she was in a hurry." Allison speculated. "Or maybe she was feeling guilty. I mean—mothers don't leave their children. Maybe she snapped—you know—maybe she's having a mid-life crisis or something."

"Does that sound like Mom to you?" Stacie asked. "She loves us. She wouldn't do that to us."

Allison shook her head. "I know. We're her life—Dad and us, and this house. When would she have had time for an affair?"

"A brief fling is the only explanation." Vanessa interrupted. "Can you even picture Mom with anybody else? I mean—come on—eew. I can't picture it.

Stacie, looking disgusted, sunk lower in her chair.

Allison put down her pencil and looked at Stacie. "Maybe Dad and

Vanessa are right. It sounds like Dad did everything he could to try to find her. Besides, she'll call us soon."

"I'm worried about her," Stacie said in a defeated manner.

Allison sighed. "We'll talk to Mrs. Deiko tomorrow, and call the police to see if they've found out anything."

Vanessa scooted away from the table and stood up. "I'm going to see what's on TV. You guys want to join me?"

"You're gonna just act like everything's normal?" Stacie asked.

"Do you have a better suggestion, Stace?"

"No."

"Then I suggest you join me for a Sunday evening movie." With that, Vanessa went into the living room and plopped down on the sofa with remote in hand.

Allison picked up the blank paper. "Unless you want to use the phone, Stace, I'm going to call Judy."

"Are you going to tell her?"

"Not yet. It's too weird. I'm going to cancel our shopping trip tomorrow. I don't think I could see my best friend without telling her."

"Yeah, I couldn't talk to Claire without telling her either. But she's still at her dad's in Washington." Stacie stood up. "I'm going to my room."

Within a few minutes, Vanessa was on the sofa, flipping channels with the remote. Allison had called Judy and was now unpacking her suitcase, while Stacie was in her room, on her knees on the floor by her bed, hands clasped and eyes closed in prayer.

Please God, please bring Mom home. Thank you.

———

After three days of sharing a sense of hope with her sisters that Mom would come home, have a good excuse for all of them, and life would return to normal, Allison was becoming restless. While Vanessa and Stacie were upstairs sleeping, Allison lay on the sofa flipping channels between Johnny Carson and a rerun of "Knot's Landing." As soon as she heard the garage door open she jumped up, ran to the kitchen, and opened the door leading to the garage. She watched her dad get out of the car.

"Hi, Dad."

Randall closed the car door with an apology ready to be delivered. "I'm sorry I'm home so late."

She nonchalantly shrugged her shoulders.

"You waited up for me?" he asked.

Trying to determine his sobriety level, Allison watched him closely. She guessed he was sober enough. "Yes. I'd like to talk to you." She stepped back to allow him to enter, then followed him to the kitchen table. They both sat down. Randall reached into his back pocket and threw his wallet on the table.

"Dad, I can't…." apprehension slowed her down. "I can't imagine Mom doing this."

"Neither can I." Randall clasped his hands behind his neck and leaned back in the chair. "Except," he paused, "I don't know. I should've paid more attention to her. Instead I just took it for granted she would figure it out. Just like she always did."

"Figure what out?"

"Whatever it was that was bothering her. In hindsight, it's clear she hasn't been herself lately. Maybe it was the other man all along, or perhaps she was unhappy and recently sought the man's attention."

"I don't know, Dad, but we need to look for her. We need to let everyone know. Maybe one of our friends or relatives knows something."

"I still don't think we should," Vanessa interrupted.

Randall and Allison turned and saw Vanessa walking toward them from the bottom of the stairs.

"Do we really want them to know Mom ran off with another man?"

Hearing Vanessa say it in such a casual manner hit Randall like a punch in the gut and he reflexively leaned forward.

Allison gave Vanessa a dirty look. "We need to call all of Dad's family and—,"

"Wait—just one minute." Randall looked at Allison straight on. "Why do you think we need to get my family involved?" It was a question born of denial, and he was grateful Allison didn't answer it. He knew his girls needed to get involved, do something, anything. Taking action might help them cope.

"Go ahead. Do what you need to do." He got up, gave his two eldest daughters a hug, and went upstairs to an empty bed where the memory of Madeline waving good-bye tormented him again until he fell asleep.

The following morning, after Randall left for work, Allison poked her head into Vanessa's messy bedroom. "Wake up. It's time for action."

Vanessa briefly opened her eyes, but then nestled deeper into the pillow. "Don't you ever knock?"

Satisfied that Vanessa was awake, Allison went to Stacie's room and walked over to the bed. "Stacie—wake up."

Stacie rolled over, "Hmmm, what?" she mumbled.

"Wake up. We're going to find Mom."

"Really?"

"Really," Allison replied. "Come on—we'll talk in Vanessa's room."

They gathered on Vanessa's bed. Allison started filling Stacie in on last night's conversation. "We waited up for Dad last—"

"He was drunk," Vanessa interrupted.

"He wasn't drunk," Allison said irritably. "It's his way of coping."

"Whatever."

"Anyway, I told him we need to tell people about Mom leaving."

"That went over well." Vanessa scrunched up the pillow underneath her chest and rested her chin on it.

Allison ignored her. "He said go ahead. So I think we should come up with a game plan."

"What kind of game plan?" Stacie asked.

"Well, it's going to be hard to tell everybody the truth, but we need to do it. People are going to find out sooner or later anyway. Somebody might know something. Plus, I think we should retrace Dad's steps and see if we can find something he overlooked."

Stacie's eyes brightened. "That's a great idea. I still think Mom may need our help."

Vanessa looked at her sister impatiently. "Dad said it—it's as clear as black-and-white—Mom ran off with another man." She shook her head. "Where's the gray area?" When Stacie didn't answer, Vanessa added, "What in the world does she need our help with? Sex-tips from her virgin daughters?"

"That's enough!" Allison yelled in obvious disgust.

Vanessa threw the pillow in a burst of anger and jumped off the bed. "Mom left us—left Dad, to be with—well—with—whoever he is!" Seeing Stacie's shocked expression prompted Vanessa to calm down as she picked up the pillow. "You guys do whatever you want to find Mom, but leave me out of it, and—" she hesitated, "go somewhere else. This is my room."

Allison and Stacie got off the bed and walked toward Vanessa. Allison stopped. "If you change your mind, you can help anytime." She was rewarded with a mocking, condescending expression. "Never mind," she said, frustrated, then walked out the door.

Vanessa looked guilty when she saw the raw pain in Stacie's eyes. "I'm sorry, Stace. I just can't do this right now."

Stacie nodded sadly, gave her sister a quick hug, and left the room.

"I thought about this all night long." Allison said as the two girls sat at the kitchen table. "I think we should call everybody we can think of, anyone who might have some clue about Mom. And I think we should take her picture around town."

Stacie crossed her arms thoughtfully. "This is gonna be hard."

Allison nodded her head in agreement as she picked up the pencil. "Let's start with the obvious: Mom's closest friends, her sewing group, and the church group."

Over the next three days, they called neighbors, and friends, and searched the town for clues. They asked detailed questions, "Did she seem unhappy lately? Do you think she may have been sick? Did she mention anything about another man?" The questions, although painful and embarrassing to ask, were straightforward. They needed to know everything.

They took their mom's picture with them to the airport and the bus station. They called the hospitals in Bismarck and Mandan. But nobody knew a thing. "It's like Mom dropped off the face of the earth." Stacie said to Allison. The police had found nothing, and when Allison and Stacie had exhausted all possible leads, they gave up the search. They resigned themselves to the same conclusion their dad, Mrs. Deiko, and the police had: their mom had willingly gone with the man who had wrapped his arms around her the night she left.

4

Several long weeks passed. At Allison's direction, the three sisters took charge of the house and began a routine that would continue for months: shopping, cooking, baking, and cleaning, all with the intent of trying to cheer up Dad, and hoping Mom would return to a welcoming home.

Paul had tried to persuade Randall to take time off work, but Randall felt inadequate in his own home. He was unsure of how to handle the shift in parental responsibilities or how to help his three teenage daughters. For a moment brief as a camera flash, he would consider how they were going to be affected, but his overburdened mind could not concentrate for long.

Believing their mom would call at any time, the girls agreed to keep phone conversations brief.

With each passing day, emotions ran higher in the household. They guarded their privacy and pain as if the tabloids would be interested in getting hold of the story of their broken family in Bismarck, ND.

How could she have done this? She didn't even bother to say good-bye!

At the end of each day their hopes were dashed.

It was almost seven p.m. on Friday night when the phone rang. Stacie jumped off the couch in a mad dash to answer it. She knew she should not hope it was her mother every time it rang, but her heart jumped at the sound anyway. "Hello."

"Hey, Stacie, this is David. How ya' doin?"

"Uh, hi, David. I'm doing—okay? How 'bout you?"

"I'm doing great. I had a great vacation. I'll tell you all about it when I see you."

"Okay." Stacie smiled half-heartedly.

"Is your sister there?" David drawled.

"Which one?" Stacie drawled back, sharing a standard joke between them.

"You know which one," he replied in a teasing voice.

"Hold on. I'll get her." Stacie set the phone down, walked toward the stairs and yelled, "Al, David's on the phone."

"I'll be right there."

A moment later, Allison hesitated before picking up the receiver. Stacie gave her an encouraging nod.

"Hi, David."

Stacie was about to walk upstairs to her bedroom when the doorbell rang. She walked slowly to the door and smiled sadly upon opening it. It was all she could do to keep from crying. "Hi, Pastor Ron."

"Hello, Stacie." The overwhelming sadness in Stacie's pale blue eyes was not lost on him. "I'm sorry I didn't call first. When I got your message I drove straight over."

"That's okay. Sorry we haven't made it to church since we got home. The days kind of seem to go by in a blur."

"That's understandable." He nodded. "You know, I wish someone had called me at the emergency number I left."

Stacie shook her head. "We didn't want to spoil your family vacation." She stepped back. "Would you like to come in?"

"Yes—thanks."

They walked in the door as Allison hung up the phone. "Hi, Pastor Ron." Allison walked over to him and accepted his hug. "I can't stay. I just told my boyfriend I'd meet him at Pizza Hut in fifteen minutes."

"Have a nice time, Allison," the pastor said gently.

Allison grabbed her purse and headed out the door. Pastor Ron turned back to Stacie.

"Dad isn't home from work yet." Stacie looked down, seeming embarrassed. "Dad's putting in longer hours. He says there's extra work to do. And Vanessa took off awhile ago."

Pastor Ron nodded slightly, saying nothing.

"Would you like something to drink?" Stacie asked.

"No. I'm fine, thanks." Pastor Ron felt at a loss for words. The news had been a total shock to him. "I'm so sorry."

His kindness and sincerity was all it took for Stacie's eyes to tear up. Pastor Ron reached for her hand and, for a moment, held it between his.

"Why?" She asked. "How could she have just left us?"

He prayed the right words would come to him, something that would help ease her pain. "I don't know, Stacie." He wondered about something his wife, Caroline, had mentioned to him. In the weekly women's bible study meeting, the women were talking about parenting, specifically about motherhood. Madeline made a comment about the sin of being a bad mother. Caroline didn't think anything of it. Everyone knew Madeline was a terrific mother and wife. But in hindsight, Caroline remembered that Madeline acted a little peculiar after that conversation, unusually quiet.

Stacie stepped back and wiped her tears. "Did you hear? All she left was a note. She left with another man." She plunked down on the sofa, looking utterly lost.

"May I?" Pastor Ron asked before he sat down next to her. He had come here not only as their pastor, but also as a friend. He knew that in their eyes right now, God was very far away.

Stacie asked him, "Do you know anything? Anything that would explain why she left us?"

To say what he had been thinking would be a stretch, perhaps completely off base. "No, Stacie, I'm sorry. Your mother didn't confide in me what she was going through. I wish she had."

Stacie stared out the window with reddened eyes. "I don't understand why these kinds of things happen. Why would God allow it?" Stacie was about to enter high school, but when she innocently asked that question, she appeared much younger.

Pastor Ron answered with the truth he believed so dearly. "God doesn't intend for these things to happen, but good things can always come out of bad things."

Stacie pondered that for a moment. "What should we do now?" She asked wide eyed, with complete vulnerability.

"Keep crying."

He saw her surprised expression. "Keep healing. Keep seeking. Eventually God will reveal himself to you."

Tears misted the pastor's own eyes as Stacie's tears began flowing once more.

———

David was waiting near the entrance when Allison pulled into the parking lot. She turned off the ignition and was about to open the car door when her peripheral vision spotted him bolting toward her. She laughed as he threw open the door and pulled her out.

"Oh, I missed you so much," he shouted. David picked her up and twirled her around. With her feet still off the ground, he kissed her. Then noticing she did not share his enthusiasm, he set her down. "What's wrong?"

Seeing David almost made Allison lose the stoic resolve she had clung to over the past several weeks. Determined to remain strong, she kept silent until she could speak without crying.

"Allison, what is it?"

She melted slightly at the concerned look in his brown eyes. "It's my mom. She left us—while we were in Mountain."

"What?" He squinted; his thick eyebrows almost touched.

"She left with some man and we haven't seen or heard from her since."

"No way!"

It was clear that David didn't want to believe it.

She grabbed his hand and nudged him forward. As they entered the pizza parlor in silence, Allison vowed to herself not to lean on him too heavily. They avoided the subject until after they had ordered and drinks were delivered. Then Allison gave him the quick version.

David got up from his bench seat and sat down beside her. He put one arm around her and tried to comfort her. But she was stiff, unyielding.

When the large pepperoni pizza arrived, David moved back to his side of the table. He tried his best to cheer her up with some funny tales of his family's car trip to Yellowstone. Allison rewarded him with an occasional smile.

"I'm sorry, David. I guess I'm not very good company right now." She took his hand as he walked her to her car.

"Would you like to come over to my place? Watch a movie?" he asked.

Allison wanted to, she really did. But she felt completely out of sorts, as if somebody else inhabited her body. "Can I take a rain-check?"

David pulled her into a warm hug and gently rocked her from side to side. "Sure. It's good anytime—no expiration date." He opened the car door. "You know I'm here for you."

Allison stood on her tiptoes and kissed him on the cheek. "I know. Thanks."

She drove off.

Thanks for nothing, Mom. A lone tear escaped before she shut down her emotions.

I'm not gonna cry.

———

Vanessa had been walking for hours. She had gotten into a routine over the past couple of weeks. At first she had stormed out of the house in frustration, needing to get out, needing to find something that would ease her pain. It was as if she was about to explode—and the only way she could keep it from happening was to keep moving. She had walked several blocks to the nearest park and had tried to sit under a tree or lie down in the grass. But she was too tense and felt she had to be moving. She ventured away from the park and started walking downtown. She passed the shops, restaurants, government buildings and library. Soon her legs and her feet got sore and she headed home.

Now, several weeks later and ten pounds lighter, her body was getting used to it.

I guess I should thank you, Mom, for this crash diet I'm on. I don't have an appetite and I can't sit still. As if she were saying farewell to a friend who had overstayed her welcome, she said to herself—*goodbye ten pounds. I'm sorry we're parting due to traumatic circumstances.*

She was not scared as she walked; she was simply numb. Several times a carload of guys drove by and yelled comments like "Vanessa lard ass—keep on shakin' it!" She ignored them; she had grown used to comments like these over the years. *Besides—why did people have such a hang-up over a few extra pounds, anyway?*

She walked along the river, wondering if she would ever feel good inside. It was late, and judging by the darkening sky, it was almost ten p.m. She picked a different road to walk home, one she had never been down. It was a street with large, worn-out buildings, mostly abandoned. On the opposite side of the street sat a mechanics shop and an auto body paint shop. She walked halfway down the street when she heard bold, colorful music coming from one of the buildings. Intrigued, she looked over and saw a sign, "Sharlene's Dance Studio."

The mini blinds were partially up, so she tiptoed over to the window and crouched down to peak inside. The sight of a man and woman dancing caught her attention. The woman had a freckled complexion and curly red hair that hung past her shoulders. She wore a see-through flowered skirt over a one piece maroon leotard that stretched from her shoulders to ankles. The man had a bronze complexion and dark hair. His black pants and black T-shirt clung to his muscular build. Vanessa watched as they flowed effortlessly, changing their style of dancing with the change of the beat.

When the song ended, the man tenderly kissed the woman, picked her up, and carried her off into a back room. Touched by what she saw, Vanessa turned around and began the long walk home.

———

With the failed search behind them and the first day of school just two days away, normal activity could no longer be avoided. Summer was coming to an end.

As Randall read the Saturday morning paper, he glanced over at Stacie eating her cereal. He suppressed a guilty sigh as he recalled Emily chastising him for not taking the girls out shopping for new school clothes. He had argued with her. "Why do I need to take them shopping? I'll just give them some money."

Besides, I have things I need to do. I should check the brakes on the car— they're squealing, and I need to mow the lawn.

With resignation, he folded the paper and set it on the kitchen table. "Stacie, as soon as you're finished eating, go get dressed—and tell your sisters to do the same. I'm going to take you girls shopping."

Stacie raised her eyebrows in disbelief. "Sure, Dad."

A few hours and more than a few hundred dollars later, Randall was at the end of his rope—the excursion had been very challenging. Allison, he discovered, had expensive tastes and he continually was saying "no." Stacie's heart was not in it, and she could not decide what she wanted, so he kept encouraging her to keep looking. Vanessa was another matter entirely. Frankly, Randall was horrified at the clothing Vanessa picked out.

For heaven's sake, you're just a child! A child, he laughed to himself, as he could not deny that everything about her screamed 'I'm a woman!" When she came out to look in the three-way mirror, he gasped. "That skirt is too short, Vanessa," *and too tight,* he thought.

At the end of the day, Randall climbed into his bed, alone, again. He acknowledged to himself that, at least for one day, he had kept it together enough to do this one thing for his daughters.

How am I going to handle raising three teenage girls by myself? As he reached over and shut off the light, he vowed he would give it his best shot.

Whatever I do can't be worse than what their mother did. At least I won't leave.

———

"Come on, Stacie, its time to go," Allison yelled while walking towards Stacie's bedroom.

Stacie wished she could muster up some enthusiasm, but the first day of school brought so many memories of their mom helping with their clothes, their hair, and calming their insecurities of beginning a new school year. Going back to school without their mother's help made her absence more real. She was not coming back.

"Stacie." It was a soft, quiet whisper, and, for a moment, Stacie imagined it to be her mother's voice. She looked up and saw Allison, gently smiling down at her with an outreached hand. "We can do it together, Stacie. We have each other and we have Dad." As Stacie grasped Allison's hand, there was a question in both of their eyes as they thought about that. Their dad had been trying, but they both knew the casual drink at bedtime had become more than casual. Several times he had passed out before he had made it to bed. But nobody talked about it—they kept their fears hidden.

Vanessa breezed into the room with too much of everything—make-up, perfume, and clothes that were too tight and too short.

"I'm not riding to school with you." Allison's tone was half-serious—half-joking, and got a smile out of Stacie.

Vanessa shrugged her shoulders. "Let's get this bus rolling." They grabbed the last of their things and headed out the door. Allison sat in the driver's seat, where Mom should have been.

"Will she ever come back?" Stacie asked from the back seat.

Allison put the key in the ignition and turned to answer, but Vanessa spoke first. "Right now, Stacie, I don't give a damn. I wish you'd quit thinking about her. She's probably screwin' that man she's with right now."

"Shut up, Vanessa." Allison said through clenched teeth as Stacie sat stunned in the back. Allison drove them to school while the child-parent tapestry continued unraveling; thread by tattered thread, as each one's memory of her mother was slowly being replaced by a woman who deserted her children to be with another man.

5

It wasn't long before the cold air tiptoed in on the lengthening nights, and autumn began painting the green landscape with its vivid yellows, oranges, reds and browns.

Though Allison found it difficult to concentrate, she did her best to keep up with her homework. She hardly noticed she was spending less time with her friends, even David and her best friend, Judy.

Vanessa started a job downtown at the record store. That would have been great—except that she was staying out late, long after the store closed. Arguments with her dad didn't solve anything. He grounded her, but she didn't care. She stayed out late, dressed a bit too provocatively and flirted with any man she found half attractive. She was down to her ideal weight. With her slimmed-down, toned-up body, and the new way she moved it, men—young and old alike—were taking notice. Allison tried to get Vanessa to straighten up, but Vanessa thought Allison was plain boring.

Stacie went to school as if she were on automatic pilot—day after day, one assignment at a time. She lived for two things: church and drawing. Even though she did not feel at home in the church like she used to, she persevered, believing God would answer her prayers and bring her mother home.

Allison and Stacie did not give up the search for their mom completely. They periodically checked in with Officer Ward, and called hospitals in neighboring states. Sometimes they heard their dad on the phone asking questions about a missing woman. Knowing he hadn't given up looking for their mom brought them comfort. But ultimately, the image of her happily in the arms of another man remained foremost in their minds.

As Thanksgiving neared and the first snowfall passed, Randall felt they needed to get out of the house. After a phone call to his parents and siblings, everyone agreed to spend the holiday in Mountain. With twenty-three relatives there for the holiday and the three spare bedrooms taken by parents, the cousins sprawled out in sleeping bags in the living room and dining room where, during the night, they stepped over sleeping bodies to get to the bathroom.

Although the girls appreciated the love and support they got from their large family, it also made them uncomfortable. Everyone was struggling to find comforting words for them. When the weekend ended, they were exhausted from trying to put up a brave front.

They arrived home thinking about Christmas and agreed to make it as special as they could, just the four of them. Christmas was Madeline's favorite holiday; she had always made sure everything was done to perfection. For the sake of his daughters, Randall did his best to embrace the holiday spirit, bringing out the Christmas decorations and taking the girls to pick out a tree. Deep down, he believed Madeline would surface. *If she were coming home, this would be the time.* A small, persistent hope remained.

The girls baked together for hours, making plates of cookies, bars, and candy to give to friends, teachers, their church, and to be passed on to nursing homes and homeless shelters.

One-by-one presents were wrapped and placed under the tree. No one said a word about three gifts with "To Mom" written on them.

Christmas day arrived, but their mother didn't. Going through the motions of opening gifts, they politely thanked each other until the three gifts remained. Allison reached for the gift she had bought for her mom. "I got her a sweater. What did you guys get her?"

Vanessa was leaning against the sofa, legs outstretched. "Go ahead and open it," she said casually. "Mom won't be."

"I don't want to open it. I was just curious."

"Well, open it anyway." Vanessa sat up in response to Allison's blank stare and grabbed the package. She ripped open the wrapping and carefully pulled out a porcelain figurine of a ballerina.

"That's pretty," Stacie said.

Allison reached for it and held it gently in her hands. "It is pretty, Vanessa."

"It doesn't mean anything. I just liked it. I thought maybe Mom would like it too."

"I'm sure she would have." Allison rewrapped it and put it in the box.

Stacie leaned forward and reached for the present she had chosen for her mom. She held the package in her hands, rubbing the wrapping paper. "I bought her a bead kit."

"A bead kit?" Vanessa asked.

"Yeah. Several months before Mom left, we went to a craft fair. Mom stopped at this jewelry booth for a long time and spoke with the woman who had designed and made the jewelry. Mom loved it. When we were driving home, she told me that when she was young she had made some beaded necklaces and had dreamed of making her own jewelry some day."

Allison tilted her head. "I never knew that."

"I didn't either," Vanessa added.

Randall got up off the floor. He was glad the delicate gold necklace he had impulsively bought for Madeline was tucked away in a drawer. *It's Christmas, for Christ sake. My daughters are unwrapping presents for Madeline and she's not here. God, how am I going to make it through this day without getting shit-faced drunk?* "I think the Christmas decorations have been up long enough. What do you say we take them down?" It came out harshly. Three surprised faces looked back at him.

Calm down. He rubbed his hands through his brown hair. "You girls did everything you could to have a good Christmas, and I'm very proud of you. But it's over."

They each nodded in agreement and began cleaning up. Several hours later, before it was even time for Christmas dinner, the house was back to normal. With the decorations put away, so was the hope their mother would come back.

On a cold evening in early April, the night of their mom's birthday, Vanessa walked through the door just past five p.m. The house was quiet and at first she wasn't sure if anyone was home. "Hello, anybody?" She called out. Vanessa heard her sisters yell, "Up here." She walked upstairs and looked into her dad's bedroom—no sign of him. The door to Allison's room was open. "Hey Ally."

Allison was lying on her bed, pillows propped up behind her. She looked up from the book she was reading. "Hi."

Vanessa wasn't sure what she wanted or hoped to accomplish this evening. "I'm in the mood for spaghetti. Want to help make it?"

Allison looked at her quizzically. Dinners had been sparse around their house lately, each person fending for themselves most of the time. Occasionally one of them would put in an extra effort to make a meal for all to share. Each time they vowed to do this more often, eat together as a family, but it rarely happened.

Allison noticed the lonely look in Vanessa's eyes. "Sure," she replied briskly.

"I'll get Stacie and meet you in the kitchen." Vanessa found Stacie drawing in her sketchbook. "We're making spaghetti. Let's go." Vanessa walked over and grabbed Stacie's arm to help her off the floor before Stacie had even set down her pencil.

During dinner the small talk was strained. Each of them tried to think of lighthearted things to say, but avoiding the issue of their mother's birthday created tension between them. "I called Dad." Vanessa shrugged her shoulders. "I wanted to invite him for dinner, but he had left the office early. I wasn't in the mood to call every bar in town."

They cleaned up the dishes, then sat back down at the table, passing around brownies Allison had made while the other two made the spaghetti.

Vanessa picked up her brownie and held it up in the air. "I'd like to propose a brownie toast to Mom. Happy Birthday, Mom, wherever you are."

Allison and Stacie picked up their brownies and held them up. "Happy Birthday, Mom."

The room hummed amid the silence. "I'd like to talk about her," Stacie whispered. She looked around at her sisters, then spoke louder. "Do you realize how long it's been since we've even mentioned her name?"

"A little over two months," Allison replied. "We haven't talked about her since Christmas."

"What's there to talk about?" Vanessa said sarcastically. "We made it through my birthday, then the holidays, and Dad's birthday, without even a call from her."

Stacie's small frame drooped in the chair. "I miss her so much. It'd be nice, just this one time, to talk about her—since it's her birthday."

Allison set her brownie on the plate. "I don't know about you guys, but I have a hard time talking about her with anyone." She hesitated briefly. "Everybody I know has a mother who's there for them. Even my friends whose parents are divorced spend time with both their mom and dad. Nobody understands how I feel—nobody knows what I'm going through." Allison's eyes clouded. "I'm going to be eighteen soon. When I'm not studying, I should be having a good time with my friends before I go off to college. Instead, I'm trying to keep this family together, this house together."

Vanessa about choked. "Who asked you to play mom?" she sneered. "You're just playing the 'I'm the oldest and most responsible' crap you've played your whole life."

"Somebody has to!"

Vanessa looked around the kitchen, the dining room, and beyond into the living room. "I wouldn't give yourself too big of a pat on the back. This place is a dump."

"Stuff it." Allison's eyes narrowed in anger.

Stacie ignored the dirty looks her sisters gave each other and tried to change the tone of the conversation. "I still can't believe she left us. She was the best mom—and kind to everyone." She looked around the kitchen, at the counter, at the stove. Intimidated by her older sisters, she looked everywhere but at them while she spoke. "She did everything for us and for Dad. Remember the dresses she made for us at Easter and Christmas when we were little? And she volunteered in our classrooms. I always loved it when she would help out with our art projects and parties. She helped Dad with the bookkeeping until they hired Ruthann. And she was always cooking something. Is it okay that I miss her homemade fudge, and fresh bread right out of the oven?" Stacie's eyes welled up with tears. "Mostly though, she was there for us, listening to our problems and letting us know she loved us, more than anything in the world."

Vanessa let loose. Sorry, Stacie, but I can't take anymore of this gobbledygook. Because the first loser that comes along and gives our mother some extra attention, she runs off with the guy. Yeah, she sure loved us, more than anything in the world." She didn't even try to hide the sarcasm. "Look, Mom's probably screwin' him right now."

Allison shot up from the table in disgust. "I don't know why you keep saying those awful things about Mom. And who are you to talk anyway?"

"What's that supposed to mean?"

"It means there are rumors going around school. You're having sex with a lot of guys."

"Jealous?"

"What's wrong with you?"

"What do you think is wrong with me?"

"I think you're using Mom's leaving as an excuse to go wild."

"Well, I think you're exaggerating the number of guys I've slept with."

"So, how many has it been?"

"I don't kiss and tell. Besides, it's none of your business."

"It's everybody's business now. You're the talk of the whole school, and the talk of the town for that matter."

"I always wanted to be somebody."

"You're pathetic—and your feelings about Mom are disgusting."

Vanessa hesitated; being called on her feelings made her realize she wasn't sure how she felt about her mother. She took a deep breath and pivoted in her chair so she was facing away from her sisters. A long silence passed before she asked, "Well, how do you feel about Mom?"

A vulnerable tone in Vanessa's voice appeared to take Allison off guard. She sat back down and stared blankly at the table, swallowing hard. "I'm angry at her. It wasn't like she had it so rough. She was a housewife—cleaned the house and did some volunteer work." Her words and expressions were stronger than her voice that carried them. "Big deal! I don't care how great this guy is, Mom didn't have it so bad!" Allison leaned back in her chair and crossed her arms. "Truthfully—I'm still surprised she left. I thought she never had a life outside of us." She glared at her sisters. "I've known for awhile now, that as much as I love her, I would never be like her. I want more for myself."

They sat in silence for a moment.

Stacie looked at her sisters. *None of us see Mom in the same way.*

Vanessa leaned back in her chair and sighed. *This dinner was a bad idea— a sorry attempt to get a little closer.*

Allison pushed away from the table, stood up and left the dining room. *Happy Birthday, Mom.*

6

Vanessa walked the quiet streets of the neighborhood until she got to the large white building with the chipped paint. She stuck her hands in her pockets and swayed back and forth as she stood staring at the small sign that sat on the inside window ledge. "Sharlene's Dance Studio," it read.

She felt a surge of excitement and giggled at the familiar feeling. *Will I ever get used to this? I've been coming here for months and nobody knows!* That thought both thrilled and saddened her. It was fun doing something good for herself, without anyone knowing and without anyone having an opinion about it. But there was a part of her that wanted to share it with her family. Maybe, just maybe, they'd be proud of her for a change.

She entered the building and was welcomed in by the loud sound of Bob Seger singing "Hollywood Nights" while Sharlene moved to the rhythm in a fast beat. Vanessa never tired of watching her.

Maybe someday I'll be that good.

Sharlene kicked her right leg high into the air and slowly slid it down against her left leg before rolling forward, with shoulders hunched and knee brought close to her chest; she huddled momentarily with chin tucked in and arms around the knee. Then, as if exploding, she leaped forward as her arms shot out in back of her. Vanessa was anxious to try that move herself.

After the song ended, Sharlene turned and in a slight southern drawl asked, "How ya doin', Sweetie?" before giving Vanessa a quick hug.

"I'm doing great—other than the argument I had with my sisters last night. They're mad at me. And my best friend Suzie isn't speaking to me again. But other than that, I'm really doing great." Vanessa began taking off her outer clothing, her jacket, blouse, jeans and boots until she was stripped down to a black leotard.

"Why are they mad at you?" Sharlene grabbed a hand towel and began wiping her forehead.

Vanessa plopped down onto the bench and dropped her shoulders in an exaggerated gesture. "I don't know. I think they're jealous of all the attention I'm getting."

Sharlene sat down next to her. "What kind of attention?"

"The opposite sex kind."

"Can you elaborate?"

Vanessa's shoulders dropped even lower. "My reputation has taken on its own life form."

"Have you named it?"

"What?" Vanessa asked, then smiled, half-hearted. "Should I?"

"No. I'm just being silly. What kind of reputation."

Vanessa traced a line on the wooden floor with her pointed toes, back and forth, while gazing across the room. "Word has it that I'm an easy lay."

"Oh," Sharlene gasped. "Is it true?"

"No!" Vanessa sat up straight. The look on Sharlene's face showed concern, but Vanessa continued talking. "I don't really know what I'm doing. Here I was overweight but happy, my mother abandons us, and I—couldn't—hold—much food down." Vanessa's arms were flying as she spoke. "So I start to lose weight. I go back to school. I'm able to fit into some nice clothes. Perhaps I take it a bit too far, but why not? I look good, you know?" She glanced over at Sharlene, not expecting an answer.

Sharlene shook her head sadly. "I know you're going through a lot right now, but it sounds like you might be making a difficult situation worse."

Vanessa dropped her head back, and shook it back and forth, as if trying to shake off the reality of what had happened to her life in less than a year. A tear gathered at the corner of her eye and slid down her cheek. "You're right, Sharlene, this situation isn't good. But I am so damn angry." She jumped off the bench and paced a few agitated steps. "I wonder every day, probably every minute of every day that I'm not dancing, who is he? What does he look like? What does he have that is so great my mother would just up and leave us? And where is she? Is she across the river in Mandan or in the next state?" She paced a few more steps back and forth. "And then you know what? I was too sad to eat, but when I did try to eat my stomach was too sad to deal with it, so I drop about forty pounds—and what happens? I attract every horny, creepy, crawly scumbag in this town."

Sharlene couldn't suppress a giggle. Vanessa stopped her tirade and looked at Sharlene quizzically. "It's not funny."

Sharlene shook her head up and down. "Yes it is. Right then I pictured all these little bugs getting up out of their little hideouts, marching in your direction, just hoping to get a piece of you."

Vanessa wrinkled up her nose. "Yeah, thanks. That's real funny."

Sharlene got serious again, hesitating. "You know, Vanessa, from one outrageous dresser to another—it's not just the fact you lost weight."

Vanessa faked a surprised expression, but then dropped it. "Yeah, I know. I know I've gone a bit too far—" She grinned. "My necklines have lowered while my breasts, with the help of these padded bras, have gone up more, and maybe I've been wearing my new pants a little too low and too tight. And even my walk has changed. You know, I was in the mall and I was walking towards this long mirror—and I was surprised that the confident hip girl in the mirror was me! I couldn't believe it!" Vanessa paused long enough to see Sharlene's questioning eyes. "Okay—I know—but what can I say? Is it okay to blame it on the home front? My mother abandoned us, my dad's boozed-up half the time, my oldest sister is little miss prissy wonder bread, and my lil' sis' just withdraws into the world of paper and pencil."

Sharlene smiled affectionately. "Yeah, I'd say you could blame it on the home front." With that, they stood up, as if by mutual agreement they decided to dance their troubles away.

Months ago, Sharlene had been dancing with her husband when she caught a glimpse of someone peeking through the window. She went to the door and opened it to find a girl who was already apologizing for snooping. But Sharlene saw her excited eyes and knew she had a future student. Sharlene later found out Vanessa had been taking a quick peek through the window each time she passed by, which had been several times a week over the prior month.

Vanessa was certainly interested in dancing, but she was unsure of herself when it came to moving her body. But, driven by a new desire, Vanessa became determined to be the best dancer she could. She worked hard, stretching and strengthening her muscles, building a strong dancer's body. The improvements were quick, and she was surprised to discover she was a natural dancer. It took awhile for her to loosen up, but she trusted Sharlene, who worked with her individually in the evenings.

Sharlene had a way of selecting music that made Vanessa want to get moving. Sharlene would dance crazy, silly, anything for Vanessa to gain confidence in her movements. Sometimes they made up dances as they went along, dancing with props, hats, canes, or anything else they could dig up in the studio. Then came the partner dances. Sharlene's charming husband, Dan, took over, making Vanessa promise she wouldn't tell a soul that the local police officer was a very fine dancer.

Sharlene found she was learning from Vanessa as well. In stretching her teaching style in order to get Vanessa comfortable with movement, she found she was dancing in ways she never dreamed of. She soon learned that Vanessa was good at making up new moves, and it wasn't long before Vanessa was choreographing dances to entire songs.

"You're a natural, Vanessa." Sharlene had told her. That compliment had Vanessa beaming for weeks.

Sharlene and Vanessa danced for over two hours. Hot and sweaty, they stopped for the night, laughing and exhausted. Sharlene thought about her upcoming move with Dan to California and knew she needed to tell Vanessa about it. After quickly pulling on her clothes over her leotards, Vanessa reached the door in a hurry.

"Wait, Vanessa, hold on, please." Sharlene looked at her quizzically. "What's the rush?"

"No rush, just not in my usual mood that thrives on getting lectures from Dad." She lowered her voice. "You better straighten up young lady." It sounded like a decent impression of a father giving a lecture.

Sharlene looked at her questioningly. "Does your dad want you to stop coming here?"

"No, he just likes to complain about my schedule." Vanessa was proud the lie flowed effortlessly from her lips.

"Are you keeping up with your school work?"

"Passing grades, all the way."

Sharlene smiled. "You can do a little better than that can't you?"

Vanessa faked a hurt expression. "Of course I can. But why would I want to?"

"You're incorrigible. Are you at least going to straighten up your act so your reputation doesn't get any worse?"

"Naaaw," Vanessa said in a drawn out tone. "I'm really doing my family a favor. As long as everybody thinks I'm the town slut, it keeps their mind off the fact that my mom really is one."

Sharlene skeptically raised an eyebrow, but she knew it wouldn't help Vanessa to push her too far. She could at least be grateful Vanessa had become a stronger young woman in the past several months. "Okay, but is this 'favor' doing you any good?"

Vanessa thought about it for a moment. "I don't know, Sharlene. It's just something to do."

———

Allison tried to concentrate on what Mr. Taylor was saying, something about tips on polishing up term papers. She was doodling, very rare for the student with the highest GPA, she knew, but all she could think about was how David was not acting his usual self lately. She fought her disturbing thoughts and managed to pick up a few pointers from the teacher.

After the bell rang, she forced herself to walk out casually even though her nerves seemed to scrape across her skin. She felt edgy. She turned and faked a smile as Kyle, David's best friend, pinched the top of her shoulder from behind and matched her stride.

"Hey, Allison. How ya doin?"

"I'm good, and you?"

"I'm good too."

"That's good." She managed another smile.

"You playing short stop today?"

"Not likely. I'll be lucky if I play at all after the game I had last week."

"But you guys won last week."

"No thanks to me."

"Ah, you're being too hard on yourself."

Allison appreciated Kyle's encouraging response, but she couldn't ignore what was really bothering her. "Have you seen David?" She asked.

With a sideways glance at Kyle, she saw a change in his expression and was sorry she asked.

"Nope," he answered, shaking his head.

Deciding to find David herself, she gave Kyle a quick hug. "See ya' later."

She headed straight for the lockers where she and David used to meet every day after school. *But we haven't done that for awhile.* She looked at her watch. *Damn.* She fidgeted nervously while scanning the crowd of students to see if she could spot him. *I'd give anything right now to see your gorgeous smile directed right at me.*

She stood there for a few minutes and might as well have been wearing a sign, "I don't want to talk to you," since she abruptly ended several conversations others tried to start. Dejectedly, she walked toward the girl's locker room.

An hour later, just after Allison scored a run in the bottom of the third inning, Judy leaned over and whispered to Allison, "Get a look at the guy who's walking with Jim."

Allison picked up a jug of water and casually glanced over her right shoulder. "Wow—he's a cutie," she said before taking a long cool drink.

"That's Todd, the guy I told you about, Jim's cousin from Minot. I'm so in love."

Allison wiped her mouth with her forearm. "You just met him."

Judy ignored her. "I wonder if he's going to Steve's party on Friday night. Are you going?"

"No. David and I are supposed to go out." She said it hesitantly. It wasn't altogether true; she just assumed they'd be going out. *It'll be two years since our first date. He'll remember our anniversary, won't he?* "Besides, Steve's parties get too rowdy."

"Well, you never get into trouble, so what's the big deal?"

"Strrrike!" The umpire yelled.

"No big deal," she answered. "I just want to have a special evening with David that night. Besides, I thought you couldn't go to the party since your grandmother will be in town. So why do you care if Todd's going?"

Judy leaned over and whispered. "I don't want anyone else to have him." She shrugged her shoulders self assuredly. "He'll be mine someday."

"Whoa," Allison whispered back, "you heard it here first folks, Judy will have Todd someday."

Judy shoved Allison playfully. "And don't you forget it."

"Strike two." The umpire yelled.

"This pitcher is tough." Allison looked over at Judy, who was eyeing Jim's cousin again. "It's time to quit drooling. You're up to bat."

Judy grabbed the bat and mumbled to Allison, "I'd better look good out there." Allison's laugh followed Judy out of the dugout.

Allison glanced over at Todd again. He had lots of blonde, curly hair angling down on top of his broad, bronze back. When Jim and Todd walked a little closer in her direction, she saw a perfectly placed dimple punctuating his smile when he laughed at something Jim was saying to him.

"Strike!" She heard the umpire yell. Allison leaned forward and yelled, "come on Judy. Knock it a good one." Judy swung and missed the second pitch. "Show us what you've got, Judy." Allison chanted. Judy hit a hard single to left field.

On the drive home, Allison felt better. They had won the game six to four, and she'd scored a run. She pulled the car into the garage and walked into the kitchen. The house was silent. She walked over to the answering machine, no messages.

Why haven't you called?

She headed to the bathroom to take a quick shower.

An hour later she picked up the phone and dialed David's number. After four rings, she hung up just as his answering machine clicked on. Frustrated, she grabbed her purse and headed out the door.

She drove by several of their favorite hangouts: the pizza parlor, the arcade, and Kyle's house, but passed right on by since David's car wasn't at any of them. She drove through the streets, wondering where he could be. She drove over to David's house and felt her stomach drop to the floor as she saw Tammy Sheldon's shiny red Celica parked in front of his house.

Don't jump to conclusions. They could be studying. Wait! They are studying! Allison gave a sigh of relief as she remembered the marketing project Tammy and David were working on together for Free Enterprise Class.

Knocking lightly on the door, Allison smoothed her khaki pants and tugged at the collar of her copper colored blouse. She waited a few moments, then knocked louder. Out of the corner of her eye she saw the living room curtain move. She smiled in anticipation, but soon lost it. The door didn't open. She raised her hand to knock again but stopped herself. *What am I doing?* All of a sudden Allison felt out of place, as if she didn't belong at this home she had been welcomed in for the past two years.

She was almost to the car when the door opened abruptly behind her, then she heard David's voice. "Allison."

She turned and smiled, almost shyly. But one look at him was all it took for her to know that he wasn't her David any longer. They stood there for a moment, understanding the importance of the unspoken words. It was Tammy who broke the spell when she stepped out on the porch next to David. Allison turned around and walked to her car in shock.

Did Tammy purposely button her shirt up wrong?

Allison started the car and backed out. She heard David yelling, "Allison, please, it's not what you think."

She stepped on the gas. One thought repeated itself over and over.

I'm not gonna cry.

———

Stacie had been praying for months now; praying for her mom to come home for each holiday, praying for her safety, praying for strength and understanding, praying for help for her family. But where was God? Was her voice not loud enough? Was she not praying properly?

Because the truth was, her mother had not come home, and Stacie had no idea whether or not her mother was safe. Stacie didn't feel strong at all and certainly didn't understand the direction their lives had taken. Each one of her family members was falling apart. She could see it, feel it, like it was a tangible illness in the air that had descended upon their household. What they needed was a cure, and Stacie was sure the cure was found in God.

She prayed to God everyday, sometimes going to church after school or taking a walk down by the river. Every night before bed she lit a candle, knelt on her knees, and prayed for God to show her the way. Every morning she awoke hopeful; maybe this would be the day God answered her prayers.

Her faith had always been so strong. But something was starting to bother her, and she didn't dare admit it. She was losing patience with God. She had asked for help and, as far as she could tell, there was not a helping hand in sight.

The people who were supposed to be there for her and for each other all seemed to be in their own worlds. Just the thought of her father sent such a heavy weight to her stomach she didn't think she could stand it. How much was he drinking? Was he ever going to snap out of it? And Allison— she used to be the one who kept it together for all of them. But now Allison was going through her own troubles. Allison hadn't said a word, but Stacie had heard the rumors going around school that Allison and David had broken up. It scared Stacie that Allison, who was always so self-assured, was unraveling. Then there was Vanessa. In just a few short months she had gone from being fun-loving and a little heavy to being crude, sleek and promiscuous.

Isn't anybody or anything going to stay the same? What's going to happen to us? Needing to give faith one more try, she headed toward church.

The door to Pastor Ron's office was open, and Stacie saw him writing at his desk. She knocked lightly on the door and half-smiled when he looked up and waved from his chair.

"Stacie, come in." He stood up and walked around to greet her. "How are you?" he asked while pulling a chair out for her.

"I'm okay." She sat down while he pulled up another and sat down beside her.

They sat in silence for a few moments, Pastor Ron silently saying a prayer and asking God for guidance, as Stacie obviously gathered her courage to ask for help.

"Well—no—I'm probably not okay. I don't know what to do." Her eyes focused on the oriental pattern in the rug. "I'm so worried about my mother. I wonder where she is, and if she's okay."

He leaned forward, his elbows resting on his knees. "You still haven't heard from her?" He saw her answer with a slight shake of her head. "Are the police still looking?"

"They say they are—routine stuff anyway. You know—searching computers—databases—that sort of thing. But her name never comes up."

Pastor Ron's personal experience with God was very real, and often his strong faith flowed into his words, but other times—like now—he felt his counsel was inadequate. He did not know what to say to ease her suffering. He fought the desire to speak—because he knew the words would be his— practiced words—trite words—words of faith to fit any occasion. But Stacie deserved better; she deserved God's words—words meant especially for her. Letting go of his own will to help her, Pastor Ron reached for her hands and covered them with his own as he bowed his head in silent prayer.

Your words dear Heavenly Father. Your will be done.

Several minutes passed before he felt an inner peace, which usually came when he surrendered his own will to God's. When he opened his eyes, he saw Stacie bent over in prayer. He waited until her tear-filled eyes opened to meet his. When he spoke, his words were from the heart: slow and deliberate.

"I am so sorry for the pain you're going through. But even though I don't know why your mom left or where she is, I am certain she is not lost to God. God *does* know where she is. Maybe we can find some peace in knowing that God is watching over her."

Stacie looked thoughtful for a moment. The pastor knew she really did believe in God, and he hoped she found comfort in knowing her mother wasn't lost to God. Her shoulders lifted a little. "The rest of my family— it, well, it isn't the same anymore," she said softly.

Pastor Ron had heard some rumors. He had thought about it, prayed about it, and had been there for each of them as much as they had allowed. "I'm sure all of you are handling this situation as best you can." He hesitated briefly, "Does your family talk about your mother?"

"Not much. Hardly ever."

He reached over and clasped Stacie's hands in a reassuring gesture. "To heal yourself, you'll need to find a way to forgive your mom for leaving you."

Stacie's eyes widened. "But how do we forgive her when we don't even know for sure what happened to her? Maybe she *didn't* run off with another man." She sighed dejectedly. "Or maybe she did."

Not having an answer, Pastor Ron shook his head. "You don't need to figure it all out right away. It's going to take time."

Stacie felt a little better, realizing the last thing she needed right now was to give up on God. "Thank you, Pastor Ron." She reached over and gave him a quick hug, then headed for the door.

"Stacie," he said.

She stopped and turned around.

Pastor Ron looked at her with a gentle smile. "The strength and meaningfulness of relationships comes through in the bad times." He swallowed. "I believe there's perfection in every moment in God's plan. Sometimes we don't see it. But frequently we look back at our most difficult times as being our most precious gifts." He smiled again. "Can you try to think of that as a possibility?"

Stacie smiled the first genuine smile in a long time. "I'll try."

She walked out the door and headed home. *I'm going to make a difference for my family.* She didn't know how she was going to do it, but it was time to really try. She ignored the fear creeping in under her skin; she ignored the lead weight in her stomach due to her father's drinking problem. She ignored the fact that if Allison could get knocked off her feet, maybe she could too, and she ignored the rumors about Vanessa.

Stacie walked into the house, took one look at the place, and declared it "a dump no more."

She ran up the stairs, threw her backpack next to her desk, then hurried back downstairs to start cleaning the living room.

When did we become such slobs?

She picked up the trash, newspapers, a couple of soda cans, and an empty bag of Doritos partially hidden under the couch. Then she gathered up the dishes, a few glasses, one half-filled with tea, and a small plate with grape stems on it. She did a quick wipe of the furniture, ran the vacuum, and fluffed the pillows.

She felt a whole lot better already.

Next was the kitchen. It wasn't that bad, a few dishes on the table, an open package of graham crackers on the counter, and a floor needing to be swept. She opened the refrigerator door. *Ugh.*

Stacie brought over the trash bag and began dumping. She was almost finished when the phone rang.

"Hello?" Silence. "Hello?" A tingling sensation ran down her spine, goose bumps appeared on her arms. *Mom.* She clutched the phone tighter, her voice lowered.

"Mom, is that you?" The click of the phone dropped like a dead weight. Stacie put the phone down, shaking. Her hand was still on the receiver when the phone rang again. She jumped. "Hello?"

"Hi. Watcha doin?"

"Oh—hi Claire." She put a smile into her voice, but the disappointment was overwhelming.

"I'm in the mood for a movie. I was thinking about seeing "Can't Buy Me Love." Do you want to go? You can spend the night afterward."

Stacie pulled the phone cord over enough to be able to tie the trash bag filled with spoiled food. "Sure. I'll call and ask my dad, then call you back.

"Great! Talk to you soon. Bye."

"Wait! Did you call just a minute ago?"

"I tried, but the phone was busy. Why?"

"Oh, nothing. Its just whoever called wouldn't say anything."

"It wasn't me."

"Okay. I'll call you back in a minute."

Stacie clicked down the receiver, then dialed.

"R&P Hardware, Paul speaking."

"Hi, this is Stacie. Is my dad there?" Stacie noticed she had asked 'is he there' versus 'can I talk to my dad' like she used to. Her dad used to always be there, but now it was clear he had been leaving early to go to one of the bars.

"Well, yes, he is here. He's on the other line, so why don't you tell me how you're doing since I haven't seen you in so long."

"I'm doing fine—nothing new to tell—just going to school and hanging out."

"Well, good to hear it. Whoops—here's your dad already." Paul hadn't been able to hang up quickly enough when Randall picked up the line.

"Hi sweetheart, what's up?"

"Hi, Dad. Is it okay if I stay over at Claire's tonight? We want to go to a movie."

"Sure, that'd be fine. Do you have enough money?"

"Yes."

"Okay then, have fun and I'll see you tomorrow."

"Thanks, Dad. Love you."

"Love you too, kiddo."

7

Allison applied her makeup with a deft hand. She took the deep purple eyeliner and outlined her blue eyes, then brushed a lavender powder across her eyelids. *We were going to get married, right after college.* She and David had dated for two years and were perfect for each other. Everyone had envied their relationship. They were fun, hip, athletic, and to top it off—smart. But David and Tammy had gotten together in ways Allison and David had only talked about. They were waiting until it was right—until they were older.

Damn. Why Tammy? Allison felt reckless. *I'm going to get rid of this pain.*

The pain was unbearable. She didn't know anything could hurt so badly as David's betrayal on the heel of her mother's. Allison couldn't do anything to strike back at her mother, but the thought of having David suffer a little eased some of her pain. She wanted him to hurt; she wanted him to see what he had lost.

Ignoring David's calls and refusing to see Tammy had not helped to ease the pain.

But what could either of them say anyway? Allison sarcastically imagined them saying, *sorry we had sex instead of working on our project.* David had finally come over and practically forced his way in, saying something about how sorry he was, how he was stupid for not being able to wait. Allison gasped. She had only wanted to wait until after they graduated from high school. She had felt she would be responsible for her decisions and not disappoint her parents—her dad—if he found out. She and David would be in college and, if making love happened naturally, she would be ready. But she wasn't ready now. Not living under her father's roof.

Allison walked downstairs and was surprised to see the clean living room. Stacie was coming out of the kitchen. "Did you do this, Stacie?"

"Yeah. Just sort of got in the mood."

"Place looks great."

Stacie smiled. "So do you. Where are you going?"

"I'm going to a party." Allison flung her purse over her shoulder. "I'll see you later." Ten minutes later, Allison parked the car down the road from Steve's house. Cars filled his parent's driveway and lined both sides of the street. His parents were easy-going and frequently out of town, a good combination for a hot party spot.

She walked toward the door. The loud music did nothing to penetrate the numbness she was feeling. She felt an odd mixture of recklessness and emotional exhaustion. *I'm tired of being straight. I'm tired of being the good girl.*

"Allison!" The welcoming crowd was an instant tonic. She walked in, headed straight for the ice chest and grabbed a beer. When they asked where David was, she smiled wickedly and asked, "David who?" With each drink she took, she felt a little better.

I'll just keep on drinking.

———

Stacie and Claire were dropped off at the theater by Claire's parents right before the movie started. They quickly paid and entered just after the lights were lowered. The girls walked slowly down the aisle, trying to find an empty seat while their eyes adjusted to the darkness. Stacie jumped as she felt someone tug at her jeans and turned to try to make out who it was. She couldn't see a thing yet. "Who are you?" she whispered. Deep muffled laughter was her response. Trying to ignore it, she turned back down the aisle but felt the tug again. She turned back around just as another late movie patron opened the door, giving her enough light to see Jimmy Watts and Ed Reinke cracking up with laughter.

Stacie felt goose bumps at the sight of Jimmy. There was something just plain naughty about the way he always looked at her. It made her extremely uncomfortable. But worse yet, she knew she liked it.

"Stay away Ana!" she heard Jimmy whisper loudly.

Rolling her eyes in seeming disinterest, she turned back around and followed Claire several rows up ahead. Once again, she regretted using her full name, Anastacia, in kindergarten. Back then, the boys had quickly turned the name into 'Anastayaway', and occasionally still teased her with it.

After the movie ended, Stacie and Claire walked out of the theater and practically ran into Jimmy and Ed, who were waiting for them right outside the door.

"Hey, watch where you're going." Ed said to Claire when she bumped into him and almost spilled the remainder of his coke.

"Sorry. But you shouldn't be standing in the middle of the walkway." Claire looked at Stacie, then at Jimmy, then back at Stacie with a slight conspiratorial look.

Stacie was able to convey a "stop it" expression to Claire without Jimmy or Ed noticing.

"What'd you guys think of the movie?" Claire asked while Stacie, as always, wished she could think of something to say.

"It was good." Ed said. "Lots of cute girls. What's not to like?"

"I've been there." Jimmy jumped in, "To Tucson and to the Pima Air Museum. They really have that there—the graveyard where all the old planes are kept."

"Really? I thought it was probably just a Hollywood set." Stacie stuck her hands in her pockets to avoid clasping them together. "When were you there?"

All of a sudden she noticed the guys weren't paying attention and saw them both staring behind her shoulder. She turned to see a girl of about eighteen dressed in very tight black pants and a blouse that plunged way low. The girl's hair was slick, as well as her walk, and her make-up was overdone, dramatic. Stacie turned back around, suddenly uncomfortable.

"Boy, Stacie, for a minute I thought that was Vanessa." Jimmy glanced over at Ed as he said it, and they both started laughing. "What's up with your family anyway? You've got the town slut sandwiched between two sisters, the brainy one and the innocent of the century. I guess Vanessa takes after her mother. Who do you take after?"

"Shut up." Claire smacked Jimmy with her purse.

The earlier talk with Pastor Ron seemed almost meaningless now as Stacie fought back tears. Trying to maintain her earlier resolve to be strong and optimistic, she decided right then it was time to get over the crush she had on Jimmy.

"Come on, Claire. Let's go," Stacie said with a catch in her voice.

Claire turned back around, giving the guys a dirty look. Then she put her arm around Stacie after they walked out of sight. "You should've seen the look on Jimmy's face, Stace. I think he was really sorry he said that."

"Yeah, I'm real sorry he said it, too." Stacie stopped and turned toward her dear friend. "I'm sorry—but I'm just going to head home."

Claire smiled in understanding and gave her friend a hug before they went their separate ways.

Where's the bathroom?

Allison excused herself from the crowd of people she had been talking to for the past hour and made her way down a hallway. She opened the first door, a closet. She opened the second door and found a couple making out in a bedroom. "Oops. Sorry." She tried the door across the hall, locked. "Somebody's in here!" she heard them yell.

Allison made her way up the stairs. The bathroom door was open. She locked it behind her. The reflection of her face in the mirror took her by surprise.

Wow. She smiled. *A little extra make-up and a change in style really makes a difference.* It didn't hurt that her face had a nice tan from her softball games, and the alcohol seemed to have added a twinkle in her eyes. *I wish David could see me now.* She left the bathroom a few minutes later, wishing she hadn't thought of David, and determined to forget she had.

She rounded the corner to the staircase as the twinkle in her eye turned into a full-fledged starburst, at least that's what she imagined, thanks to a radiant smile that hung a few inches below a mop of curly blonde hair belonging to Todd. Her heel caught on the first step. "Whoa!" she yelled on her way down. Todd jumped up a step to grab her before she knocked them both down.

"You okay?" Todd eyed Allison as she straightened her skirt.

"Yeah. Nice catch." They both laughed.

"It was nice." He said with a husky voice and a wink.

That did it. His deep voice with a sexy undertone shot a wave of desire through her. "I saw you at the game the other day." She wondered if he always wore that sexy smile he was beaming her way.

"Yeah. I saw you too. You looked great out there."

By the way he said it she knew full well he wasn't complimenting her athletic ability. "Thanks." She watched him take a breath and swore his chest expanded by a factor of ten. "You're Jim's cousin, Todd."

He smiled that smile again. "And you're Allison." Leaning in closer, his whisper felt warm against her ear. "Now that we've cleared that up—," his lips, so warm against hers, led the way as his body moved in even closer. She unwittingly softened and puckered her own lips in response.

"You smell fantastic," he whispered.

Replaying the dilemma she had been in several hours earlier on which perfume to wear, White Linen, Shalimar, Chanel or Ysatsis, she felt a little smug she had made the right choice—Ysatsis.

Allison tried to find a logical thought in her head, but found it was useless. Her eyes offered her willingness as Todd leaned in again and kissed her playfully, teasingly. Her arms seemed to wrap around his shoulders against her will, and she leaned in closer too. The kiss deepened until Todd backed away and looked at her questioningly. Apparently he liked what he saw.

"Hey—What -," Allison squealed as he turned her around, nudged her up the top two steps, and opened the door to an empty bedroom.

A moment of indecision passed through her mind.

What am I doing?

But the booze allowed her a false confidence she had never known, and a feeling of recklessness she was bound to pay for later.

Todd resumed the kissing, nibbling at her lips up and down, and from side to side. He didn't neglect the corners of her mouth.

Wow. He's a busy guy. She liked every move he made. She dropped her head back, allowing him more play area around her neck while discovering his arms, chest, and back. She couldn't deny how good his body felt next to hers. She leaned into him, finding it was indeed possible to get closer still.

He is hard all over, no doubt about it.

Her fluffy pink top slipped easily over her head.

Who am I?

She felt like she was discovering a secret part of herself and liked the feeling, the fire all over her body, and the desire in Todd's eyes.

In no time they were on the bed, her skirt up around her waist, her panties down at her ankles. Todd was sucking her nipples while tugging at his pants. Allison reached down to help him. She slid her hands under his jeans and boxers, enjoying the feel of his tight buttocks, then tugged his pants down to his mid-thighs.

In her dazed stupor, she watched as Todd tore open a wrapper to unveil a condom that seemed to have appeared from nowhere.

Uh Oh. The tiniest hint of reality made its way into her consciousness. Like the fact that she didn't even know this guy, like the fact that Judy claimed this guy for her own, like the fact she was a virgin.

Nope. I'm not thinking about that now. I'm going for it. Now that she had started down this road, she was determined to toss out her virginity, right here, right now.

His hands were occupied, but his mouth wasn't. Figuring Todd could do two things at once—she started kissing him.

When his hands were free to roam her body, she raised her hips in anticipation.

Todd intended to enter her slowly, but it was like holding back a racehorse at the starting gate.

Allison gasped.

Todd stopped. It was the way she gasped—not pleasantly— that had gotten his attention. For a brief moment they were both still until realization hit Todd.

"What the hell!" He pulled out. "You're a virgin!" His words were accusatory—like it was a bad thing.

"Please, don't stop. This is wonderful—you're wonderful." She looked into his heavy, unsure eyes. "I didn't plan it this way but—" she caught her lower lip with her teeth, "a girl couldn't ask for a better first time." His expression turned doubtful so she added, "You're really nice to be with."

He looked into her big blue eyes and smiled. "Are you sure?"

She nodded her head.

"You're the most beautiful girl I've ever seen."

Neither of them bought the lines, but they smiled and responded as if they did. Their revved-up bodies wanted them to finish what they had started. Todd slowed the pace down as best he could, but Allison was raring to go.

———

Randall and Paul had been friends for many years. They had started working at the Main Street Hardware store within months of each other twenty years earlier. The owner of the store grew fond of the two and treated them almost as family. Eight years ago, when the owner decided to sell the business, he made Randall and Paul a fair offer to buy him out. The two friends had owned the store ever since and had renamed it R&P Hardware.

It had been a solid friendship. They worked well together and their wives were good friends, too. The foursome had enjoyed fun times together, including a monthly bridge game.

Randall and Paul sat at the dining room table, drinking yet another beer and going for a second round of leftover pizza. The basketball game was over, but the television in the living room was still turned up loud. The trash bin was filled with empty beer cans, but a few cans remained on the coffee table in the living room. They had enjoyed an evening without family. Allison was at a party, Vanessa was working, and Stacie was spending the night at Claire's. Paul's wife, Emily, and their two kids were visiting family in Wisconsin over spring break.

Paul and Emily had done their best to help Randall and the girls, but they could not give them what was needed most: an answer to Madeline's disappearance or, better yet, her return. They had felt helpless as they watched Randall's family falling apart.

Randall had downed twice the beers Paul had and the effects were showing. Feeling guilty for drinking with his friend when he should've been trying to discourage the drinking, Paul wondered if he should make a hasty exit now that the game was over. But in his own buzzed out thoughts, he got the impression that Randall really needed to talk. "It was nice talking to Stacie today, Randall. How are your girls doing?"

Randall caressed the side of his beer can. "My girls." He paused. "How are my girls doing? Not very damn well." Randall gripped his beer tighter and leaned forward. "I thought Ally was doing fine, but lately she's become a different person, rebellious in a quiet sort of way. Like there's a fire growing inside of her that's seeking to destroy something. I can't put my finger on it, Lord knows I haven't even tried. In fact, I haven't done a damn thing to keep this family together."

Randall choked up, barely able to control his emotions. "Vanessa is self-destructive in a way that the whole world gets to see. Anything I say or do is just a waste of time. I've grounded her, taken away car privileges, and she doesn't care. She just does what she wants anyway. And I yell at her, but I don't follow through. And Stacie, hell, that child isn't even mine."

Dead silence filled the room. Paul sat there, stunned, certain he couldn't have heard that right. Randall had just made a major declaration sound as if it was just another ordinary comment.

"What did you say? What do you mean Stacie isn't yours. Of course she's yours."

Randall took another swig of beer as if he weren't aware that he had spoken those words. He looked at Paul with regret, but also looked relieved at sharing his secret. Then he shook his head. "No. I'm not kidding. She's not mine." He leaned forward again. "I certainly love Stacie as my own, but she's not my daughter. Who knows, maybe Madeline's with Stacie's father right now."

Paul tilted his head questioningly.

"I've never told this to anyone—ever. Paul, you can't—,"

"You don't have to say it," Paul interrupted. "It stays right here."

"Madeline had this old friend from grade school—James—from when she lived in California. He managed to track her down shortly before she became pregnant with Stacie. Madeline was delighted. I teased her about her 'former boyfriend,' but she swore they never thought of each other that way. So when James was passing through, he—"

"Passing through?" Paul interrupted again. "Who goes from California to anywhere and passes through Bismarck?"

"Supposedly he and his wife were visiting his wife's grandparents in Minneapolis and he said he'd like to take a break from family and fly over for a day."

"Did you meet him?"

"No. You and I were in Chicago at that home show."

"Hmm," Paul muttered. "Madeline doesn't seem like the cheating type. But even so, what makes you think he's Stacie's father?"

Randall let out a sigh. "I came home from work early one day when Madeline was about seven months pregnant with Stacie. Madeline was on the phone, rubbing her stomach. I heard her say, "Do you want this child, James? Do you want to raise this child as your own?" Randall studied his beer again. "The time seemed about right—he had visited about seven months earlier."

"What did she say when you asked her about it?"

"I never asked her about it. I backed out of the kitchen before she saw me and left quietly out the front door. I drove around for hours until I decided what I was going to do. The only thing I was certain of was that I loved this woman more than life itself. I thought that to confront Madeline with what I heard would be opening a door that would end our marriage. I figured it would be her choice to leave if she wanted to leave, but I wasn't going to do anything to speed up the process."

Randall looked up from his beer and into the eyes of his friend. "I guess she finally decided."

They sat in silence, unaware that Stacie had decided to come home. She had just about walked into the kitchen when what she heard stopped her dead in her tracks. With the television still blaring, Randall and Paul didn't hear her come in the front door, didn't hear her tiptoe up the stairs, and didn't hear the toilet flush after she vomited.

The pain hurt so much, the darkness so engulfing, Stacie thought she would die. She managed to make it into her bedroom, but the moment she entered she knew there was even something wrong with being in her own room. Trying to find some comfort in the familiar surroundings, she scanned the room. But it didn't take long to figure out what was wrong. It wasn't the room, with her sage green bedspread and pale yellow throw pillows, or her own framed watercolors of lilies on the wall, or the various framed pictures of her family and friends that covered the dresser. No. It was not the room. It was just that every single item in this room belonged to somebody that no longer existed. Stacie, with one single overheard conversation, would never be the same.

When her gaze landed on her nightstand, time seemed momentarily suspended as a seed of intense anger planted itself right in her gut.

No. No more.

The small picture of Jesus sat next to her worn bible. They had been there for as long as she could remember. She stared at them for a long moment, wondering if any bit of comfort would find its way to her broken heart. But all she felt was overwhelming betrayal. She fought the anger that made her want to throw the picture and the bible across the floor. Instead, she picked them up and placed them at the back of her bottom dresser drawer.

Who am I?

In one last attempt to find something solid to hold onto, a lifeline that would keep her from slipping into an abyss, she went to her desk and grabbed her sketchpad and her charcoal pencils. She sat on the floor and leaned against the bed. Using the side of the pencil, she worked fast and furiously near the bottom of the page. Acting purely by instinct, and having no idea what she was trying to convey, she lightly shaded in a form. With an eraser, she smudged the charcoal, giving a soft, even look to the form. It was almost unrecognizable, but she knew it for what it was, a self-portrait that had come from the pit of her despair. The tears fell in lonely drops as she looked at her form fading into the white paper, with no clear lines of distinction, nothing to show her boundaries.

My father's name is James.

She fell down sideways on the floor, clutching a pillow and burying her face in it. She cried and cried, letting all of her hopes for her family and for herself fade away.

A couple of hours later, she didn't say a word as she heard Vanessa walking down the hall to her own room. She had no clue that Vanessa had been dancing all these months and that Vanessa was devastated having just learned the dance studio was closing down; the owners were moving out of town.

In the wee hours of the morning, nobody heard the car door shut as Todd dropped Allison off. She walked in the door a little clumsily, but as quietly as she could. She bumped into an end table before heading upstairs to her bedroom. One thought peeked in on her as she fell asleep with her clothes on: *I'm not gonna cry.*

8

This place is too damn quiet.

Sitting alone amid the silence reminded Randall of that night, almost a year ago, when he had come home to an empty house. He looked at his scotch glass and twirled around the golden liquid. Everything was falling apart and he had no idea how to stop it.

The booze. Shit. He took another gulp. He hated that voice in his head that told him to stop drinking so damn much. That voice used to be Madeline's, now the voice was his.

He went to pour just a bit more, but there wasn't much left in the bottle—so he finished it off, filling his glass half full. He knew it was too much booze, but the girls were spending the remainder of spring break with his parents in Mountain, the house was quiet, and the scotch was his only companion.

She's been gone for over eight months, without a trace, without taking a damn thing.

That last thought sneaked up on him, carrying more weight than it had before. He took another gulp.

Well, if she didn't want her stuff, what in the hell do I want with it?

Randall carelessly set down the glass, almost knocking over a small table lamp. He sprang up from the recliner and raced through the kitchen on a mission. For the first time in months, he had something on his mind other than barely making it through another day. He stepped into the garage, grabbed a wad of large garbage bags, and marched into the bedroom. In silent rage, he grabbed her clothes out of the closet and began throwing them into the bags, not giving a damn what kind of shape they'd be in later when they ended up wherever it was they were going to end up. He chose to ignore some of the memories the clothing evoked, like how beautiful she looked in the dress she had worn to the last annual Christmas party they had attended together.

I don't give a shit how she looked.

Remembering the last time he had thrown her clothes onto the bed, he vowed this time was different.

After quickly filling six bags from the closet, the adrenaline rush from the

70

anger was already fading.

Oh God, I do care, I still miss you, Maddie.

Overtaken by emotion, he dropped down on his knees to the floor and cried for the first time in these many months.

I hate you for doing this. Once the tears started, it would have taken too much strength to try to stop them. He cried, aching for the loss of the only woman he believed he would ever love. He cried over his trouble with booze. He cried for the girls who seemed to be in as much trouble as he was. When there was not one tear left inside of him, he finally stood up, exhausted, but determined to take a step in a direction, any direction.

He walked over to the chest of drawers and, slowly this time, packed away the nightgowns, the undergarments, pantyhose, socks, and shorts, that had all managed to fit into the dresser. Overwhelmed by all the bags, he made several trips to the basement, where he piled them up in a corner. He stacked a few of her books and trinkets on top of her large jewelry box and carried those to the basement also. Back upstairs, he threw away her cosmetics and toiletries. Emotionally spent and with almost a robotic motion, he opened the bottom drawer, her 'love drawer,' and just as quickly—closed it.

He was about to collapse onto the bed when he thought, *No—I'm not finished yet.*

He again opened Madeline's 'love drawer,' pulled out a stack of cards and letters and began reading. He felt in no hurry to end this task. Most of the cards were from the girls, beginning when they could sign their names. Until he couldn't bear the pain any longer, he read some of the cards he and Madeline had given to each other. A wave of regret passed over him as he realized there should have been more mementos from him.

At the bottom of the drawer he found a large manila envelope. He opened it. Inside were papers he had never seen before. His heart felt heavy against his chest while he studied the papers.

"I'll be damned," he said to the evening air as he slowly read each page.

———

Randall awoke with a monstrous headache and a nagging thought that something was different. He was anxious about something; he just didn't know what it was. He sat up in a hurry and immediately reached for his throbbing head. After a quick glance at the clock, 8:47 a.m., he lay back down and massaged his forehead.

What day is this? He tried to figure it out as images danced around in his

mind. *Yesterday I was at the office. That was Tuesday. Okay, today's Wednesday.*
"You should be at work, ya' dumb shit," he said aloud.

He got out of bed and headed toward the kitchen in his boxers. He opened the fridge, took a swig of orange juice, downed a couple of aspirin, then put on a pot of coffee.

Those papers. After climbing the stairs and entering his room, he found the papers on the floor beside the dresser. *I wasn't dreaming.*

He didn't know what this meant to him or the girls, but he did know that he felt a flurry of differing emotions, mainly a surge of anger mixed with a touch of hope.

He called the office to apologize to Paul and tell him he'd call back soon. After a quick shower, he pulled on jeans and a T-shirt and headed back into the kitchen, where he poured himself a cup of coffee. He sat at the dining room table and reread the pages. He looked at the documents and wondered how and why Madeline had managed to keep this from him for so long.

With an urgency that surprised him, he knew what he had to do. He grabbed the phone book and immediately dialed the airport. Three hours later, after making several long distance calls, packing, making arrangements with Paul, and calling his parents to let the girls know he was going out of town on business, he headed to the airport.

———

"Dad's coming home tonight from his mystery trip," Vanessa said dramatically. "I still think he was with a woman."

Allison looked up from her bowl of oatmeal and threw a look at her sister that conveyed 'you're annoying' rather clearly.

Within ear reach of Vanessa's comment, Stacie walked into the kitchen. "It's a business trip. That's what he told Amma. Maybe he went to a builder's convention or something."

Both sisters looked at Stacie in disbelief before Allison stated the obvious. "When was the last time Dad took a business trip?"

"Last year. He went to the tool convention—you went with him to look for colleges." Stacie shrugged her shoulders while stating the facts.

"I meant a *spontaneous* business trip. This doesn't have anything to do with work and we know it. It came about too quickly. If it would've been a convention or some business trip, he would have mentioned it sooner." Allison took another spoonful. "Besides—I called Paul. He did a lousy job trying to cover for Dad."

Vanessa sat down at the table with a slice of unbuttered toast and some orange juice. She leaned in close to her sisters and lowered her voice. "I'm telling you, he's with another woman." Her eyes got big and she nodded her head as if it were fact.

"No way," said Allison. "That's just your preoccupation with sex talking."

"Jealous, Miss Virgin Queen?" Vanessa sneered.

"Yeah, that's it." Allison's tone dripped with condescension.

Stacie grabbed a bowl and poured herself some cereal. "What did Paul say?"

Allison completed her dirty look at Vanessa and turned to Stacie. "He just kind of hemmed and hawed and said that something came up, and he's sure Dad will tell us all about it when he gets back."

Trying to keep the fear out of her voice, Stacie whispered. "What if he doesn't come back?"

Allison and Vanessa looked at Stacie in shock. "Dad's coming back, Stacie." Allison said. "He'll be here tonight." She gave Vanessa a warning look not to contradict her, but Allison saw Vanessa's expression soften.

"Maybe the other woman is Mom." Vanessa said it so innocently; she couldn't keep the hope out of her tone.

The statement was left hanging in the air. No one had the courage to grab it.

—

Randall came home that night to three anxious daughters. "Whoa—all three of you under the same roof on a Saturday night." He set his overnight bag in the entry and walked over to give each of them a hug.

He could see the questions in their eyes, but he wasn't up for conversation tonight. It had been an exhausting four days, and he needed some sleep before he broke the news. "It's late and your old man is tired. I'm going to bed." He grabbed his suitcase and headed for the bedroom. "We'll talk in the morning." Suddenly aware of what they might be thinking, he stopped and turned around. "It's not about Mom. I mean—I still don't know anymore about her whereabouts than you do. I'm sorry if you got your hopes up."

Three sets of confused eyes watched him as he walked away. Sure, there was disappointment that the trip wasn't about Mom, but they were just about immune to dashed hopes concerning her. It was their dad's good mood and the bright, although tired, look in his eyes that had surprised his daughters.

The following morning, Randall brought the documents downstairs and set them on top of the fridge. He opened the fridge and looked at the scant offerings. In the breakfast category, they had a few eggs but no sausage or bacon. The strawberry jam looked as if it had been there forever. He looked in the cupboard. They were almost out of bread.

He glanced out the window and saw it was a beautiful spring morning. Since the grocery store was just a few blocks away, he figured a walk and fresh air would do him good. He wrote a quick note and left it on the table.

For the first time in months, maybe even years, he felt alive with possibilities. As the brisk morning air met his face, his enthusiasm mounted. He looked at the neighbors houses in a new light, while thinking about what his life had become: going to work, mowing the lawn, drinking beer with friends while watching a ball game, or playing card games 'til three in the morning. He chuckled to himself. *The card groups hadn't issued as many invites. I'm a third wheel—no partner.*

What about the business? He liked being half-owner of the hardware store. Ever since he and Paul bought it, Randall had never thought about doing anything else to earn a living. *But I need to do something different. I need a change. I need to get away from all these memories of Madeline.* He thought about the competitive market since the other stores moved in and knew that, even if Paul could afford to buy him out, the business was no longer worth much.

He added another day to the count, two hundred and thirty nine. He had managed to survive 239 days without Madeline. Although, he had to admit, he hadn't survived very well.

Who could've done better under the circumstances? My wife of eighteen years—almost nineteen years now—was so desperate to leave she didn't even bother to write a decent goodbye note.

He tried to push negative thoughts from his mind. He was not going to let thoughts of Madeline ruin his new-found hope.

By the time Randall left the grocery store, he was a driven man. He had left his hopes of Madeline's return by the roadside.

And by God, I'm not going to pick them up again.

When he neared the house, he stopped as memories of Madeline and the girls washed over him; they were sweet as well as painful but the shock had worn off. He laughed at himself that for a moment he had thought he could forget Madeline. Still he realized this was a turning point for him. Madeline wasn't coming back. He had to face that now, they all did. He felt torn between the past and the future.

Stay here. Hold out hope. Have the stability of jobs, family, and friends. But we're all falling apart!

He knew he had to take charge of his life and be a better father for the girls. He thought about the last year.

Why didn't I see how destructive my behavior was? But the anger was still there. *At least I didn't leave.*

He thought about what their life could be a year from now if they moved. It would be a big change, but at least they'd be doing something—together.

Randall was greeted at the front door in a flurry of pajamas in cottons and flannels, pinks, greens, and purples, as Allison, Vanessa, and Stacie rushed to greet him at the door. "Whoa—you *guys* must be hungry!"

"Girls," they corrected him in unison, and laughed. They hadn't shared that exchange with their dad in a very long time.

Randall walked into the kitchen and began unpacking the groceries. "I can do all of this myself, but I'd like to eat breakfast before lunch time."

"Help's on the way." Vanessa was the first to follow him. Whatever was going on with their dad, the girls seemed to silently agree that they didn't want to break this spell with too many questions. When Randall began whistling "King of the Road," their perplexed expressions deepened.

They went all out for breakfast: eggs cooked to their liking, bacon and sausage, pre-made frozen hash browns, toast, several flavors of jam, and orange juice.

They passed around the food and filled their plates. Randall kept the conversation light, making jokes about grocery shopping and how Mrs. 'La la land' kept remarking on how it was so nice to see him in the grocery store. Her name was Lola Lender but Randall preferred his nickname for her. He felt it suited her busybody personality.

Randall put his hand on his chest, and in a high pitched voice he mimicked, "Oh, Mr. Averson, how nice it is to see you here." He rotated his shoulders in a feminine gesture. "You must be feeling so much better now after all this time has gone by."

The girls giggled cautiously.

"What did you tell her?" Stacie asked.

"Well, I told her 'I am feeling *much* better, Mrs. Lender. The women in the church have been *so* kind.' Then I winked at her and said, 'if you know what I mean.'"

"Dad, you didn't!" Allison squealed.

Stacie's eyes brightened in shock and Vanessa said, "No way!"

Randall laughed at the sight of his astonished daughters. "Just teasing. Gee whiz, can't a guy kid around in his own home?"

None of them came up with a reply. They were too bewildered at the change in him.

Allison broke the silence. "What's up, Dad?" she asked seriously.

Randall stared at his almost empty plate and set his fork down. A moment later he looked up with determination. When he spoke, his voice was calm and deep. "The night before I left on the trip, I was going through your mother's things." He paused, trying to keep the emotions out of his voice. "I had decided that it was time to get rid of her belongings." Seeing the hurt in his daughter's eyes, he quickly added "at least get them out of the bedroom—right now they're in the basement."

He stood up, walked over to the refrigerator and reached for the large manila envelope. "In the bottom drawer, in her 'love drawer,' I found this." He took the papers out of the envelope.

Allison leaned forward, reaching for them. "What is it?"

He handed her the papers. "It's property in Avra Valley, Arizona—near Tucson."

"What does that have to do with anything?" Vanessa asked, looking back and forth between her father and over Allison's shoulder at the papers.

Allison quickly read the cover page. "It's land that Mom and Dad own. Both their names are on it." She skimmed through the pages and looked up at Randall in surprise. "Mom's owned this property since she was a little girl!"

Randall nodded his head curtly. "It looks that way."

"Didn't you know about it, Dad?" Stacie asked quietly.

Randall looked at his youngest daughter sadly. "No, Stacie, I didn't." He shrugged his shoulders. "She never mentioned Arizona."

"Forty acres and a trailer," Allison said as she read over the document. "That's a lot of land." She set the papers down. "Why would Mom keep this a secret?"

He let out a deep breath. "I've been asking myself that same question for four days now. All I come up with is a big fat nothing. It goes right in the box with the other unanswered questions regarding your mother. Married to her for all these years and I don't know who she is."

Randall hadn't intended to speak openly about his feelings but, now that he had, and with tears filming his eyes, the next statement followed, "I still can't believe she left me for another man."

The girls sat there, stunned. Now that their dad had put his own voice to those words, they realized just how much he still loved their mother, and that he missed her and needed her as much as they did. They finally felt the depth of pain that had escalated his drinking.

Stacie felt a little of her heart soften at the sight of her sisters getting up from their chairs and hugging their dad. She knew she should join them. She felt the magnitude of the situation; something had changed in her dad and she was grateful. He seemed more together than he had in a long time. That he had finally voiced his own feelings of betrayal felt like a breakthrough for all of them. She did feel better, honestly, but something had changed in her also; she felt separated and didn't know how to act around her own family. She remained in her seat.

"So that's where you went? To Arizona?" Vanessa asked.

"I had to see the place." He leaned forward, pausing to rub his eyes. "It was nice. The weather was great. I should've taken some shorts—it was too warm for pants."

"Thanks for the weather report, but can you get to the good stuff?" Allison raised her eyebrows with a look of impatience. "What did you think of the place?"

Randall grinned at his oldest. He wasn't used to Allison being flippant. "It's a nice piece of property, in a valley surrounded by distant mountains and wildflowers everywhere. The trailer is small and has a rundown add-on, and remnants of what used to be a shed. But that's it."

"What was in the trailer?" Stacie asked.

"I didn't go inside. It had obviously been boarded up for a long time and without the keys I would've had to tear through the boards of the add-on. I didn't have the tools or the time to board it up again."

"So what did you do while you were there?" Vanessa asked.

"I met with attorneys from the law firm that have been the guardians of a trust set up years ago. This trust has taken care of the property taxes and fees. The attorneys said that over a year ago they had to do a full search for Madeline because the government needed to buy three acres of the property for the 'C.A.P.'—Central Arizona Project."

"What's that?" Vanessa asked.

"It's a canal that will be built to bring water from the Colorado River to Arizona to meet the state's water needs."

"It hasn't been built yet?" Allison asked.

"No, it's still in the planning stages. But when Madeline signed the papers to sell the three acres, she had the attorneys draw up the necessary papers that added my name as co-owner of the property."

"When did that happen?" Allison asked.

"A month before she left."

"Why would she keep that a secret?" Allison looked puzzled.

"I don't know. You girls know as much about her past as I do—which isn't much."

"How could we know so little about her past?" Stacie asked in frustration.

Allison nodded her head in agreement. "We all know how Mom got when we asked her about it. She didn't like to talk about it."

"Yeah," Vanessa spoke up. "What was her little bio bit that she'd give us? Something like, 'there's not much to talk about. My mom died of a brain aneurysm when I was six, I lived with my grandma in L.A. until she died when I was sixteen, then I was sent to live with my great-aunt in Fargo. Then I met your dad.'"

During the imitation of her mom, Vanessa had no idea how taken aback Randall, Allison, and Stacie were at the resemblance between Vanessa and Madeline. "What? Vanessa asked, startled by their expressions.

"You do a pretty good Mom." Allison said. Randall and Stacie agreed.

"We all have a lot of questions," Randall said as he got up and refilled his coffee, "and not too many answers, but let's move on—we have much more to talk about." He sat back at the table. "The attorneys said the trust was originally set up in 1948 by Earl Kiser for his daughter, Helen. In 1952 your mother was added to the trust. Then, in 1955, after Helen's death, correspondence from the attorney's office was sent to Helen's mother, June Kiser, in L.A. About ten years later, the mail was returned and the attorney's office had no forwarding address for your mom. Since the trust was still active and the bills were paid, the account took care of itself. When the C.A.P. needed some of the land, the attorneys were forced to find your mom. When they tracked her down, they said she had no desire to see the property and wanted the trust account to continue as it was."

"How much is in the account Dad? Is your name on it?"

"Yes—your mom added my name to that too—and there's enough money in it to pay the taxes for a few more years." Randall underplayed the amount of money in the account. As far as he was concerned, that money belonged to Madeline and he wanted nothing to do with it.

"How could she not care about the trust or the land?" Allison asked.

"For the same reason she didn't take any of her belongings, or any money. She didn't need it or want it. That man must mean everything to her." Randall regretted the statement the moment he said it.

There was silence in the room—they were long since weary of making excuses for Madeline.

"I miss her." Vanessa whispered.

"I do too." Allison said.

Stacie felt so lost. She felt that her dad and her sisters took her silence to mean that she was handling all of this better than they were. They counted on her to work it out with God, to find peace through Him.

They can't even see that my whole life has changed. It's different from theirs.

Randall's voice was low when he spoke. "I need to apologize for not handling all of this better. I've been a lousy father this past year." He dropped his head and focused on his folded hands. "I've spent way too much time drinking."

"There's a news flash for ya.... Vanessa covered her mouth as soon as she said it. She looked at her sisters, then back at her father. "Sorry, Dad."

Randall grinned, half smile, half look of regret. "That's okay. I had it coming." His smile deepened as he leaned over the table and rested his chin on his fisted hands. He remained thoughtful for a moment, not knowing how to break the news to them. He opted to get it over with quickly. "I think we should move there."

Three jaws dropped an inch.

"Move there?" Allison asked at last.

"Yes." His voice sounded steadier this time. "We need a change."

"As in sell this house—change schools—and everything?" Vanessa asked.

"Everything."

While Vanessa contemplated the reality of a move, she thought about her self-inflicted reputation. Although it had its good points, she knew there was more to her than that.

The dance studio's closing up. Mom's not coming back. All of our lives have changed.

"Dad, this is pretty cool, isn't it?" Before he had a chance to reply, she added, "I think it's a good idea." She saw her sisters look at her in surprise.

"That was easy." Randall said. "One down, one to go." He looked over at Allison and grinned. "Sorry Al, but you don't count—you'll be off to college. Have you decided on one yet?" he asked almost as an afterthought.

"Not yet. I've been accepted at four of the five colleges I applied to. Mr. Harbison, our college counselor, is helping me. Now we're just waiting for the scholarship and financial aid awards to come in. Then I'll decide." Allison thought she was going to be sick due to all of that breakfast and talk about moving, college, and Mom leaving.

Stacie was full of uncertainty.

Moving, with dad—who isn't really my dad—and Vanessa—who I don't even know anymore, and Allison—who will be off to college.

She tried to reason with herself. *He's still my dad. He loves me. He raised me.* In all fairness to him, she couldn't think of a time when he didn't treat her as his very own daughter. In one respect it made her love him even more. But, on the other hand, she felt painfully out of place. She saw that everyone was looking at her. "I, uh, I don't know. I guess it'd be okay," she said softly.

Randall smiled awkwardly. "Then it's settled. We're moving to Arizona."

9

The enthusiastic applause from Brett Smith's Salutatorian speech continued as he introduced the next speaker, Allison Averson, Valedictorian of the class of 1988.

Well you did it. Allison thought, as a wave of nausea rolled around in her stomach. *You pulled it off, Valedictorian of your senior class.* Feeling a little faint, she reached the podium and steadied herself against it. *For all the good it will do you now.*

The blaring stadium lights lit up the whole football field and cast second hand light onto the crowded bleachers. In front of her, seated on the 50-foot yard line, was a sea of maroon and gray—her classmates wearing their caps and gowns. The familiar faces were waiting for her to begin her speech.

With a quivering voice, she began. "Welcome." Her voice didn't carry through to the loudspeaker.

Come on. Get it together. With shaking hands, she adjusted the mike and tentatively tried it again. "Welcome to the graduation ceremony for the class of 1988."

That wasn't my opening line! She glanced at her notes. But between the bright lights and feeling like she was going to throw up, her notes appeared way too small. She started talking, hesitantly, highlighting the past twelve years of school, then onto dreams of the future. She tried to concentrate on the task at hand, but her thoughts kept interrupting.

I have full scholarships to every college I applied to. What a joke.

She knew that most everyone out there thought that she would be the bright star of them all, yet all she wanted to do was go home and climb into bed. She tried to put enthusiasm in her voice. Her speech was supposed to be inspiring. Some of the words were, but her voice wasn't. "Tonight we end one journey. The next door we choose to open is our choice to make."

That didn't come out right. That's not what I wrote!

She looked around at the faces of her friends, her classmates, and her family sitting in the special parents' section. What she saw didn't make her feel any better. They appeared to be bored, perplexed, or sympathetic.

"Thank you." Allison grabbed her notes and left the podium. Avoiding eye contact with her teachers and principal as she walked by, she hoped they didn't see how ashamed she felt.

I'm not gonna cry.

⸻

It was past eleven when David entered the Averson's house after Randall reluctantly opened the door. A minute later David knocked lightly on Allison's bedroom door and stuck his head in. The sight of her sitting motionless on the bed in her cap and gown brought a lump to his throat. "Allison?" He spoke in a whisper. "Why aren't you at the party?" When she didn't answer, he walked over and sat beside her. "Allison, please don't do this. You know I love you. You know how sorry I am."

A little teardrop formed, then another. She tried to steady herself against the pain and to find that familiar numb state where she wouldn't feel anything. But when David wrapped his arms around her and drew her into him, she knew she was about to lose control in a way she never had before. Breathing in his familiar warm scent melted her last resolve as ten months of unshed tears came pouring out in uncontrollable, aching sobs.

David pulled her closer still. "Please Allison, please baby, we belong together. I was stupid. I know I was stupid. Please say we can be together. I need you."

He started to cry. He knew it was over, she wouldn't forgive him—or trust him—again. Her pain was overwhelming to him, yet all she had to do was forgive him.

"I was confused, Allison. You pushed me away for months. You needed to handle everything on your own." When she didn't respond to his pleas, he gave up talking to her and just held her as the tears kept coming. He was overcome by the intensity of her tears until finally she felt limp in his arms, almost lifeless as her crying slowed.

He gently leaned back and looked into her red, puffy eyes. "Allison, look at me," he whispered.

Not knowing what to say or do to get things back the way they were, he struggled for the right words. But the sadness he saw in her eyes sparked the stark truth in his heart. "I love you."

It was barely a whisper in reply.

"I'm pregnant."

When she said it, he felt himself spiraling down into a sea of darkness. A world where he couldn't breathe; a world that was dark and empty; a place that he had entered the very day he was rollicking in bed with someone other than the girl he loved. He searched her face again; silently begging her to tell him it wasn't so.

Well, I sure did it, Allison thought. If the pain weren't so overwhelming, she might have laughed at her predicament. She had hurt him as much as he hurt her. Revenge should've been sweet, but the pain in his eyes didn't make her feel any better. All it did was reflect the horror she was feeling inside. As his expression showed a desire for confirmation, she repeated herself.

"Yes, David. I'm pregnant."

———

Vanessa couldn't believe her dad was letting her use the car. But what she really couldn't believe was that Allison wasn't using it on her own graduation night. Vanessa shook her head in befuddlement.

You blew it, Al. That speech was a disaster and you're missing out on your own grad parties. But hey—the night's slippin' by me, and I've got a stop to make before I hit the parties. And I've got the car!

Vanessa set a small package on the seat next to her. As she started the car, she smiled thoughtfully; it was the last time she would be going to her favorite place in the world. She put the car in reverse and backed into the street.

When Vanessa arrived, the door to the dance studio was propped open by a folding chair, and she could see Sharlene, in a back room, wrapping up cords of the stereo and binding them. Vanessa walked to the middle of the dance floor, her eyes roaming the empty walls as she remembered coming here the first time, less than a year ago. She was soon interrupted by a big hug from Sharlene.

"I want you to have this." Vanessa handed Sharlene the package, but placed her hand on top of it to stop her from opening it just yet. "I need to tell you something first. I bought this for my mom for Christmas. She—well—you know." Vanessa hesitated as tears filled her eyes. "I don't know what I would've done this past year if it hadn't been for you."

"Oh, Sweetie, you've been an angel in my life—don't you ever forget it."

Vanessa smiled shyly and giggled. "Wow, nobody's ever said that to me before."

Sharlene opened the package; her face brightened at the sight of the glass figurine of a ballerina. "Thank you, Vanessa. I love it." She took Vanessa in her arms and rocked her back and forth. "Your mother would be so proud of you," she said softly. "I'm very proud of you." They pulled apart, both of them wiping tears from their eyes with the back of their hands, then giggling.

"I've been doing some thinking," Sharlene said. "I think you should come to California and continue your dancing as soon as you graduate from high school."

Vanessa's eyes widened momentarily. "What? I mean—do you think I could?"

"Absolutely," Sharlene answered with conviction. "You can apply to college in L.A. and live with us."

Overwhelmed with emotion, Vanessa jumped up and down. "Are you sure? You really mean I could stay with you?"

"Absolutely again, honey. Dan and I already talked about it."

"Wow. You know what's weird?" Vanessa didn't wait for Sharlene to respond. "My dad and sisters and I were just talking about Mom. She lived in L.A. when she was young."

Sharlene smiled warmly while gauging Vanessa's mood. "Speaking sort of motherly, there'd be house rules for you to follow. You know—good grades in school, your share of housework, we'd like to know where you are in the evenings—and no drinking or drugs." Sharlene watched as Vanessa nodded in agreement. "Oh, and one more thing. It's not mandatory, but we would prefer you'd drop this promiscuous woman act."

A puzzled look crossed over Vanessa's face. "Uh, I don't understand?"

Sharlene didn't want Vanessa to continue this charade a moment longer. "Vanessa, since we last talked a few months ago about your 'new image,' I've heard a few stories. And honey, I know it's phony. It's got to be. I didn't say anything to the gossipmongers, because I know that you want your dancing kept just between your family and us. But with work, school, and dancing, there's no way you'd have time for the social life people think you have."

Vanessa looked dumbfounded. She gulped once for being called on her reputation, and gulped again for allowing Sharlene to think that her family knew about her dancing. "I'm pretty sure I'll be tired of this reputation by the time I get to California."

"You think so?"

"Yeah, it's getting old."

Sharlene shook her head with a smile. "Thank God for small blessings."

They loaded up the car with the few remaining items: the stereo, a bag of cassette tapes, a teapot, a portable stove, a few cups, teabags, cleaning supplies, a bag of leotards and socks, and some towels.

Sharlene closed the trunk of her Monte Carlo. "Time to say goodbye to the place." Arm-in-arm, they walked back inside the studio and stood staring at the empty room. Their reflections stared back from two mirrored walls.

10

"You guys ready for the party?" Allison yelled from the stairway.

"Yes," yelled Stacie in a flat voice.

"Almost," yelled Vanessa. "I'll be down in a minute."

Barely looking like sisters, they met up in the entry and headed for the door. Allison was stylish in jeans and a pink-collared shirt. Her recently layered sandy blond hair had soft curls that fell down past her shoulders. Her make-up concealed dark circles under her eyes and a pale complexion.

Vanessa had recently colored her thick brown hair a rich auburn. She had applied her make-up with her usual heavy hand, but this time it was tastefully done. Instead of going for her usual 'shock value' clothing style, she had opted instead for a sophisticated chic. Her tight low-necked shirt showed her toned form and the shape of her firm breasts, but she wore a short, tailored black jacket over it. This later presented a challenge to the guys who normally enjoyed ogling her curves. She looked incredible. Allison and Stacie just stared at her, jaws hanging. "What's the matter?" Vanessa asked as they headed to the car.

Allison and Stacie looked at one another. "You look good, Vanessa, really good." Allison said.

Vanessa's eyebrows perked up in a question mark as she looked at Stacie for confirmation.

Stacie nodded her head, yes, feeling this was one more confirmation that they couldn't be full sisters. She could never look like that. Wearing khaki pants, a button-down shirt, a little mascara and a dab of clear lip-gloss, she felt like a little girl next to her older sisters.

"Can you believe we're doing this?" Allison asked as she parked the car in the long driveway at Judy's house. "Going to our own 'going away' party?"

"It doesn't seem real," Stacie said as she got out of the back seat.

"I think it's great," said Vanessa. "Time for new surroundings, a new school, and some new men."

"Yeah," Allison said, "you've exhausted the supply of men in this town."

Vanessa was in too good a mood to let the comment get to her. She walked around the car and caught up to her sisters, then threw her arms around both of their shoulders and pushed them along a little faster.

"Let's party!"

"Not so fast, Ness." Allison scolded. "This is a surprise—remember?"

"Oh yeah." Vanessa dropped her arms as Allison rang the doorbell.

Judy winked at them the moment she opened the door. "Come on in, I'll be ready to go in just a minute." She swung the door open for them to enter. The threesome stepped into the house and moved past Judy as a roaring crowd yelled, "Surprise!"

Allison, Vanessa and Stacie scanned the faces of the crowd obviously impressed by the many friends who were there. They looked at each other and then at Judy. Then Allison reached over and gave Judy a hug. "We are surprised. You told us this was just the usual gang. It looks like half the town is here!"

"It is!" Judy beamed.

"Thank you so much," Allison whispered.

All of a sudden they were surrounded by people they had known all of their lives, young and old alike. There were people from the church including Pastor Ron and his wife Caroline; some of their former teachers; their neighbors; Paul, Emily, and the employees from the hardware store; their friends from school and various jobs, and even Sharlene and Dan, who were invited by Vanessa.

Stacie was the first to spot Randall at the back of the room. He was standing there watching his daughters with a half-smile on his face. Stacie reached over and touched both her sisters. "Look," she said as she turned her head back to their father.

"Dad's here!" Vanessa said in surprise. Randall walked over and gave them each a hug. He looked at them with such evident love and pride that for the first time in a very long time, they felt like a family again.

Stacie and her best friend Claire gravitated toward each other early on and remained inseparable most of the evening. Claire, who was leaving in the morning to visit her dad in Washington for the summer, had already postponed the trip by a week so she could attend the party.

Stacie spotted Jimmy Watts several times throughout the evening, and each time she felt a lump in her throat. Sometimes she wished she were a different person, a person who could walk up to him, yell at him for being so stupid, and then tell him how she felt about him. The little creep had meant a lot to her over the years. She felt a connection to him in some unexplainable way, but her feelings confused her and she didn't know what she'd say even if she had the nerve to say it. A couple of times throughout the evening their eyes met and Jimmy would smile his goofy smile that always seemed to be mocking her. She would return a look that she hoped looked clever, but felt it probably made her look stupid.

Throughout the evening, all three sisters kept an eye on their dad. They were glad to see he was staying away from the alcohol and seemed to be enjoying himself. He was a hit with all the older ladies who couldn't get their husbands to dance with them. Randall had always loved to dance, and he enjoyed swirling them around on the makeshift dance floor.

Vanessa took time out from her socializing and stood staring at her father in wonderment as he danced with Mrs. Deiko to a slow song. He was gentle with her, moving slowly, but Vanessa could tell what a natural he was.

So that's where I get it.

Sharlene had noticed Vanessa eyeing the dance floor during the last hour. "Honey?" Sharlene poked Dan on his side with her elbow. "Could you dance with Vanessa?"

Dan turned to his wife. "I wouldn't mind a simple dance."

Sharlene gave him a look that said, 'you know what I mean'.

"No—can't do that." The words were playful as he shook his head to his beautiful wife, hoping that charm would withdraw her request.

"Honey, look at her." Sharlene looked tenderly at Vanessa. "I'll bet not many people in this room know what that girl can do."

Dan let out a big sigh. "I'm a cop honey. Not Fred Astaire."

Sharlene leaned into him seductively and let her words drop softly close to his ear. "You're multi-talented honey, and better yet—you're leaving this town. Who cares about your tough-guy image?"

Dan gave her a sly look that let her know he would expect compensation later at home. He swallowed the last of his drink and set the glass down. "Just one thing," he whispered in her ear, "get her properly dressed. I don't want to be distracted by seventeen year old knockers staring out at me on the dance floor."

Sharlene gasped as he caught her elbow before it hit him in the side. "You're not supposed to notice." She said with a laugh.

Dan laughed in return. "Just stating the obvious."

"True," she agreed. "I'll take care of it."

Dan walked up to the disc jockey to make a request while Sharlene went and talked to Vanessa. From across the room, Dan saw Vanessa's face alight with fear as she looked over at him. Holding back a mischievous grin, he smiled reassuringly at her.

A few minutes later Vanessa returned, wearing a blouse of Judy's. "Is this okay with you, Mr. Fuddy Duddy?" she asked Dan.

Dan nodded approvingly. "Much better, *young* lady."

The current song ended and the dance floor cleared as the disc jockey announced, "We have a special treat tonight, a dance featuring one of the guests of honor, Vanessa Averson. She'll be accompanied by Dan Eppley."

Fear showed in Vanessa's face. She looked at Sharlene for help.

Sharlene smiled with encouragement, but was amazed at Vanessa's reaction. Other than running into Vanessa at the record store once, Sharlene had never seen Vanessa out in public and was surprised at her fear of dancing in front of a crowd.

Could this be the same girl who dressed in a way that attracted everyone's attention, the outgoing, smart-mouthed girl who didn't seem to be afraid of anything?

Allison had been in the bathroom upstairs when she heard the announcement. She quickly ran down the stairs and joined her bewildered Dad and Stacie.

"What's going on?" She asked.

It was obvious that the three of them were a little worried about what kind of attention Vanessa was soliciting for herself this time.

The crowd gathered around to watch. Some of the younger crowd snickered, but practically everyone was surprised that one of their local police officers was about to dance in front of a crowd.

Dan took hold of Vanessa's hand, and wrapped his free arm around her shoulders in a comforting gesture, as he led her out on the dance floor.

Her knees shook. She was gripped with fear. And it suddenly dawned on her she didn't know what they were dancing to. "What song?" she whispered.

But Dan gave her a look that told her she had nothing to worry about. The music started and she recognized the song instantly, Neil Diamond's "*Brooklyn Roads.*"

She grinned timidly at Dan as they faced one another. "Of course!" She mouthed, since it was one of Dan's favorite songs and the reason she had started calling him "Mr. Fuddy Duddy" in the first place. She and Dan must've danced to this song a dozen times while Sharlene coached them both. Since Vanessa loved to imprint her own style, she had made changes in the steps with Sharlene and Dan's approval.

Vanessa was hesitant, but she took the first step and the next one followed. Dan guided her smoothly across the floor while his eyes held hers in a sexy veil that suited the song. Vanessa gained confidence as Dan lifted her off the ground and twirled her high in the air. He brought her down into his strong arms where they spun in perfect time. Then they turned away from each other and danced on their own. Dan's moves were subtle, while Vanessa's were an electrifying choreograph of swaying hips and high kicks.

She came alive in the movement.

Everyone watching appeared stunned. Dan and Vanessa weren't just good; they were mesmerizing to watch.

For Randall, Allison and Stacie, words could not express the wonder of seeing Vanessa out there revealing a talent they had never known she possessed. Their feelings were a mixture of complete surprise, shock, amazement, and awe.

The song was nearing the end as Vanessa returned to Dan. With one hand clasped in hers and another on the small of her back, he leaned over her with her back arched toward the floor.

The applause was enthusiastic, with whistles and shouts. Vanessa and Dan took a bow. Then Dan took her into his arms in a big supportive hug and twirled her around. Vanessa smiled shyly as she saw the faces look at her with a new respect. Then her eyes found her dad's. The tears in his eyes and his wide smile said it all.

Vanessa looked back at Dan and giggled. "I've got a whole lot of explaining to do when I get home. They had no idea I dance."

The sound of Dan's laughter followed her as she walked over and was welcomed into the arms of her dad and her two sisters.

The party was well under way when Judy pulled Allison aside. "Let's go to my room. I've got something for you." They hurried up the stairs and down the hallway to Judy's bedroom. Allison had always loved this room. Ever since she was in second grade, when she and Judy became best friends, Allison would fall back on Judy's bed that seemed fit for a queen. Back then, Judy's bedroom was decorated in soft pinks and purples, and there were dolls everywhere. Judy had changed the décor twice since then, and now it was white with soft beige accents. There were framed, majestic, landscape photos on the walls. Some of places that Judy had been—and others of places she dreamed of going. The overall effect was sophisticated.

Allison walked over to the bed, ran her hand over the comforter and sat down.

Judy walked over to the dresser and picked up the small gift-wrapped box, then sat next to Allison on the bed. "It's time to replace our friendship necklace, since I lost my half." Judy handed Allison the box.

Allison smiled as she met her friend's eyes, but she couldn't maintain the smile when she felt like crying. "I have to talk to you, Judy."

"What's the matter?" Judy's tone was soft.

"I'm—." She tried to tell her the truth, "I'm—," but she couldn't. She wasn't ready to. "I'm not going to college."

Well that's part of the truth.

"No way," Judy said matter-of-fact. "You're kidding."

Allison looked away. "I'm not kidding."

Judy didn't bother to hide the shock in her expression or voice. "You didn't work that hard on those grades to quit now, before you even start."

Allison sighed. "I'm not ready to go to college. I'm going to Arizona with my family." She looked up quickly. "I don't know what I'm doing, Judy. I haven't even told my family yet."

Haven't told them I'm pregnant either.

Judy was about to state a long list of protests, but a defeated look in Allison's eyes and a houseful of guests made her think otherwise. "I know how hard this year has been for you." Judy half-smiled. "You know I'm here for you, right?"

Allison nodded her head. "Thanks, Judy, you're the best friend in the world."

Suddenly Judy felt embarrassed about telling Allison her own good news, the man of her dreams was going to the same college as she, UND, starting in the fall. It seemed trivial now.

Judy wiped her eyes, careful not to smudge her makeup. "Open your present!"

Allison tore through the wrapping and opened a small box. Allison smiled when she saw a small silver pinkie ring with a mounted teardrop emerald, all looped in a delicate silver necklace. "It's perfect." She reached over and gave Judy a hug. "Thank you."

Judy leaned back and revealed she was wearing hers. Then she picked up Allison's necklace, unhooked the latch, and reached over to put it on Allison. "When I saw it," Judy said, "it reminded me of all the times we would pinkie swear to always tell each other the truth."

Allison looked down at her pinkie ring necklace as an enormous sadness enveloped her.

Yeah—the truth. I can't this time, Jude.

———

The party was a complete success, but it had clearly been Vanessa's night. After her dancing debut, she was the star of the evening. Yet surprisingly, she was shy about her talent. Before the dance, she had captivated the elders with her charm and her peers with her spunk. She gave them the impression that Vanessa Averson was ready for whatever challenge came her way. But after the dance, she felt an exhilaration she had never known, mixed with a shyness she couldn't seem to pull herself out of. Out there on the dance floor, she had exposed herself in a way she never had before. It left her feeling vulnerable.

Randall got behind the wheel as Vanessa and Allison got into the car. Stacie came running to catch up to them. When she said goodbye to Claire, Stacie felt like she had severed her last lifeline. It was hard to let go. She opened the car door and sat in the back seat next to Allison. "You didn't drive here, Dad?"

The doors closed and Randall started the engine. "No. Paul gave me a ride from the office. Judy made it very clear that the fewer cars at the party, the bigger the surprise for you girls."

"It was a great party," Allison said. "I can't believe all the people that were there."

"That was really nice of Judy," Vanessa added. "She's such a good friend to you."

My best friend didn't even show up.

"Yeah, that was nice of Judy." Allison sunk low in the seat.

And look how I repay her.

"Vanessa, that was quite a show." Randall said sincerely.

"Thanks, Dad."

"I couldn't believe that was you out there," Stacie said. "You were so good."

"Now tell us the rest of the story," Allison urged. "You don't get to be that good by just taking *some* dance lessons."

Vanessa looked at her family appreciatively. "Thanks guys—really. But it was no big deal."

"No big deal?" Allison spoke louder. "When did you find time to learn how to dance like that when you've been screwing your way around town?"

"Allison!" Randall yelled. "That wasn't called for."

Vanessa shifted in her seat uncomfortably. "I told you a long time ago that my social life has been exaggerated."

Allison's eyes narrowed. "Exaggerated a little or a lot? Your reputation has become a legend!"

For reasons Vanessa never stopped to think about, she welcomed her reputation. "A little—I've been busy."

"I can confirm that." Randall glanced at Vanessa. "I had a nice long talk with Sharlene, your dance instructor."

"Oh?" Vanessa asked innocently.

"Oh, is right." He saw Allison's questioning eyes reflected in his rearview mirror. He spoke to Allison and Stacie. "It seems Vanessa has been dancing after hours at the dance studio for months. Sharlene was under the impression that I knew about it—since I had signed a note giving my approval."

Vanessa edged closer to the door. There was nowhere she could hide. "Sorry, Dad."

"Sorry doesn't cut it." He spoke sternly but quietly. "You and I have been going round and round for months. I've tried everything to keep you in line: restricting you, taking away car privileges, not giving you money, anything short of locking you up." Randall shook his head in frustration. "All that wasted effort of mine when all you were doing was working very, very hard at something you love, something you are very good at." He managed a half smile. "I don't know whether to hug you or throttle you."

"I'd go for throttling her." Allison yelled from the back seat.

"Shut up, Al." Vanessa yelled back.

"We don't say "shut up" in our household," Randall yelled.

Vanessa and Allison looked at each other innocently.

We do, they both mouthed simultaneously when Randall wasn't looking.

"Why didn't anybody know that you were taking dance lessons?" Stacie asked. "Several of the girls in my class take lessons from Sharlene. Somebody would've mentioned that you were in their class."

"I didn't take any of the classes."

Stacie leaned forward. "Then how late did Sharlene stay open for private dance lessons? You were always out so late."

Vanessa sighed. It had been important for her to have this experience just for herself, but that time had come to an end. "When I met Sharlene, I wanted to dance more than anything and she knew it. But even though I had already lost some weight, I was really out of shape. There was no way I was going to join a regular class. Since Dan, Sharlene's husband, had just started working the swing shift, she told me if I got Dad's permission then I could come in the evenings. Well, I got hooked and couldn't get enough of it. It had started out as one night a week, then two, then I ended up going there three to four nights a week. It was so much fun—a lot of work—but such a blast."

And she was like a mother to me.

Vanessa was unaware of the mixed feelings her family had over her successful debut. They were all proud, stunned actually, of her accomplishment, but Randall was obviously angry she had lied about it, Allison couldn't quite reconcile the Vanessa of the last year with the strength and talent Vanessa showed that night, and for Stacie, it was just one more change in her life she did not understand.

11

The boxes arrived one week before the declared moving day. With heavy hearts, the girls started packing the kitchen, wrapping dishes in newspapers they had saved for weeks. They each took a different cupboard. They tried for awhile to find conversation but they couldn't seem to get a flow that suited any of them so they gave up trying. Randall was in the garage, packing tools and camping equipment. They sorted their belongings into four separate piles: things they needed to set up house in Arizona, storage items, donations for charity, and a pile to take to the dump. They had talked about having a yard sale, but nobody was up for it.

Allison began packing her room. She started with her bookshelf. As she put some of her favorite books in a box, she couldn't think of when she last dusted. The dust, the stress. She couldn't take it. She put her hand to her belly as the nausea began.

Oh, God, am I going to love this baby or resent it? Do I know anything? Anything at all? The pressure in her chest tightened as she felt the unrecognized beginning of self-loathing. *What have I done with my life?* Her thoughts were interrupted by a hasty dash to the bathroom brought on by another bout of morning sickness.

Vanessa sat in her room, bored with the theatrics of the move and bored with talking about it. She didn't understand her sisters' emotions. In fact, she didn't understand anything about her sisters anymore. What in the world was Allison thinking of, moving with them when she should've been off to college? And Stacie, her devoted little sister who always believed things happened for the best was now as cynical as the rest of them. Already bored with the thoughts of her sisters, she turned on the radio and danced as she began packing her stuff.

Stacie knew she had to get to work; her dad and sisters were getting annoyed that she hadn't done her share of the packing, but she couldn't move. She was immobilized by fear. Her small ninety-pound frame seemed as if it was carrying a ton of extra weight.

Start packing. You're going to be all right. The voice in her head was soothing, but Stacie rebelled against it.

"No. I'm not listening."

Everything happens for a reason.

"No." She shook her head and squeezed her eyes shut.

You're not alone.

"I am alone," she said aloud in frustration. She grabbed a box and frantically began throwing things into it. She filled another box, and then another, and in her state of anger managed to pack up her room in less time than the others. It didn't matter to her that some of her things, objects that at one time had been precious to her, wouldn't make the move intact.

While Randall was outside securing a tarp over their belongings in the truck, Allison and Vanessa called for Stacie that it was time to go. When she didn't reply, they walked up to her room and found her sitting in the center of her empty bedroom looking at a rolled out drawing in her hands.

"What's that?" Vanessa asked. "A ghost?"

Stacie hadn't known what to do with the self-portrait she had attempted the night she walked in and overheard her dad saying she was not his daughter. At the time she was packing, she had no interest in the drawing and had intended to throw it away. Without knowing why, she had retrieved it from the garbage seconds after she had tossed it. And now, in these last moments in the comfort of her old bedroom, she knew why she felt the need to keep it.

Maybe someday I'll figure out who I am.

With the drawing in hand, she stood up. "No. It's not a ghost. It's just something I wasn't sure I wanted to bring." She walked toward her sisters and the three of them walked down the stairs of their empty house in silence.

The car was fully packed and hitched to the back of the large U-Haul truck that Randall would be driving. Allison and Vanessa would alternate driving Randall's truck. They had previously debated making a little vacation out of the trip, but nobody really felt like it. "Are you sure?" Randall asked. "You don't want to stop at Mount Rushmore or Crazy Horse?"

"No," they had replied, almost in unison.

Allison was loading groceries for the trip in the car when she heard another car pull up. She turned around and saw David as he shut the car door. No words were spoken as he walked up and embraced her. Allison fought back tears as she whispered to him, "I'm so sorry."

"Shhh. Shhh. It's my fault." David didn't know what to do; he just knew he didn't want to let her go. "Have you told anyone yet?" he whispered.

"No, but I'll do it soon." She grinned. "I'll have to."

David broke the hug and took one long look at her. "Allison—I, uh—"

A honking car interrupted them as Judy pulled up in her new Volkswagen convertible. She turned off the ignition and jumped out of the car. David awkwardly stepped back, but he and Allison exchanged a look that spoke volumes. She knew he was going to offer to help her with the baby; and he knew she wouldn't allow him to.

Suzie drove up in her old mustang. With a half smile, Vanessa ambled over to the car.

"Hi," Suzie said as she got out of the car. The girls stared at one another for a moment, not knowing what to say.

Vanessa's eyes teared up as she put her arms around her best friend. "Thank you for coming, Suz," she whispered as they held onto each other. "I am so sorry. I didn't have much time for you this year."

"Well, now I know why. Some lousy slut you turned out to be." Suzie managed to give Vanessa a disappointed look. "You do realize you're still the talk of the town, don't you!" They both giggled while swaying back and forth.

"How stupid we were for not talking it out. I probably should've tried harder." Suzie said.

"Yeah, we both were pretty stupid," Vanessa agreed, "but you were worse." She smiled.

"No—you were completely lame," Suzie said with a giggle. They hugged, then vowed to keep in better touch than they had during the past school year.

Stacie felt all alone as she loaded up the last of her bags in the car. She watched as her sisters said goodbye to their friends. She remembered what her mom had told her once: "If we have one really close friend, then we're truly blessed." Stacie looked at the crowd and wished her best friend were with her now.

She opened the back car door and put her stuff on the floor behind the driver's seat. Just as she was shutting the door, she was poked with pointed fingers on both sides of her waist.

"Aahhh," she yelled and jumped at the same time. She turned around to find Jimmy Watts smiling, all teeth and ears. She smiled shyly at him, reminded once again of how Jimmy looked like Mickey Mouse when he smiled really widely. She felt giddy all over, but then remembered how mad she was at him. But that little twinge of remaining anger didn't make her legs any steadier.

Jimmy's smile faded as he tried to talk. "I, uh," with his hands in his pockets he looked at the ground and, with his foot, pushed bits of gravel around in an arch across the paved driveway. He looked up to see Stacie looking hopefully at him. "I wanted to see you before you left."

Stacie turned away as she tried to keep tears at bay. She took a deep breath and turned back around to face him. "Thanks." She paused, about to say more, but he spoke first.

"Stacie, I'm really sorry about the things I said about your family. It was really rotten of me. You have a great family." Jimmy glanced around at the scattered kids hanging around saying good-bye and saw Stacie's dad locking up the house. Jimmy looked back at Stacie with an apologetic smile and, when she didn't say anything, he looked back down at the dirt and said, "I'd better let you go."

As Stacie watched him turn to leave, a few tears slid down her cheeks. She couldn't speak, so she took a step forward and reached for his arm to stop him. Their eyes met, and Stacie was surprised to see his eyes were watering, too. They reached for each other at the same time, and Jimmy held her in a big warm bear hug as she quietly cried. They were momentarily lost to the scattered people and the chatter around them.

For the first time in months, Stacie felt cared for, perhaps even loved. His bony frame that had not yet developed seemed like a tower of strength to her. She took in his musky scent and felt his warm breath against her forehead. Her nose began running, so she pulled away from his embrace and wiped her nose with the back of her hand. She smiled shyly at Jimmy, feeling the awkwardness of the moment, and almost cried again when she saw the tenderness in his eyes.

Jimmy started to reach over and wipe the tears from under her eyes, but then he caught himself. They looked at each other shyly yet intently, silently acknowledging their strong feelings for one another for the first time. They had known each other since kindergarten. Jimmy had teased her mercilessly many of those years. He knew he would miss her, but he could not say it, so instead, he smiled and said, "Who am I gonna tease now?"

The spell was broken. Stacie smiled and for a moment had a vision of him going through the rest of his high school days with no one to tease. "You'll have to find someone. Otherwise, you'll be spending the rest of your days sulking at Bismarck High." She looked into his face, trying to memorize each one of his features and trying to gather up courage to speak from her heart. It took a moment, but his warm smile helped. "I'll miss you, Jimmy."

He was more comfortable now and pulled her into another hug. He whispered into her ear, "I'll miss you, too, Miss Ana. But *don't* stay away."

Stacie smiled in the warmth of his hug. Somehow the irritation she had felt over the years about the nickname seemed to melt away as the boy who had teased her held her tight.

It was time to go. Randall had waited as long as he could, but prolonging their good-byes wasn't making it any easier for them to leave. They climbed into the two vehicles, Randall and Stacie in the U-Haul and Allison and Vanessa in the truck. With tears in their eyes, they started the vehicles and drove slowly down the road as they waved goodbye to their friends. They drove down the streets of Bismarck, through the downtown area and onto the freeway. Along the way they took in the sights, seeing them in a new light, wondering when they'd see these same buildings and landmarks again. As they drove across the Memorial Bridge over the Missouri River, they drank in the green hills and the deep blue water with boats, water skiers, and swimmers against a backdrop of bright blue sky and scattered clouds. They drove away from their hometown, their entire life—so scared to leave, but even more scared to stay.

Part II

12

Outside the diner, Gregory sat behind the wheel of his new blue Ford truck given to him by his parents two months earlier as a graduation from Stanford present. Despite a slight breeze coming in from the open windows, it wasn't long before the back of his shirt was damp with sweat and clinging to the vinyl seat.

He reached into his shirt pocket for Earl Kiser's address. His mother had jotted it down and said, "We heard Mr. Kiser bought forty-acres outside of Tucson. I hope it's not too far of a drive." With the map stretched beside him, Gregory located the street and estimated it would take a good thirty minutes to get there. He envisioned a large estate house with, perhaps, well-kept barns and horses, and realized that if he were in a better frame of mind, he would be looking forward to this visit, but he wasn't. He had no interest in driving more than thirty miles in this heat to visit an old friend of his father's.

He shook his head in frustration, well aware that his parents would soon find out he was disrupting their plans for his future. Disappointing his father right now was not a wise move. Perhaps visiting Earl Kiser would be one small point in Gregory's favor.

Gregory started the truck and followed the signs to State Route T-69 heading towards Phoenix. Since his challenging summer classes had ended, he knew it was time to face the issues that were bothering him.

Bothering me? What an understatement, I'm about to cause a bloody battle.

He felt a mix of emotions: a sense of dread, fear of repercussions, and guilt over the people who might be hurt by his decisions. Yet he couldn't ignore the tinge of excitement he felt. He was finally taking charge of his life.

Fifteen minutes later and deep in thought, he almost missed the turnoff. With a quick jerk of the wheel, he exited. A quarter-mile later he turned left onto Avra Valley Road. After a few minutes of driving on a dirt road through a mountain pass, he wondered if he might have made a wrong turn. When another ten minutes passed since he had seen any signs of civilization, he looked at the map again to verify his course.

This has to be the road.

His irritation increased as the dirt road seemed to have no end in sight.

A glance in the rearview mirror showed a long dust trail rise behind him and a layer of dust on his freshly-washed truck.

"Great," he muttered sarcastically.

Helen set the tattered book down on the bedside table. She had read it twice from cover to cover. The pages of the old pottery book were smudged with clay from her first spin at the wheel a week earlier. While the wet clay was spinning, she had thumbed through the pages of the book, looking at the pictures and reading the captions during each step of the process. But that first chunk of clay collapsed before it even began resembling the small, symmetrical bowl she had intended. Since then she had made many more attempts at the wheel, each time resulting in failure. The bowls ended up being lopsided, or having too thick a base or wall, or the clay wasn't moist enough and would feel rough to the touch.

But this time would be different. As Helen read the instructions again and studied the pictures, she felt the proper technique right down to the tips of her fingers. Excitement billowed up inside her as she hopped off the bed and quickly changed into a pair of old shorts and one of her father's stained T-shirts. She stopped just long enough to rub her cheek against the worn out cotton and whisper softly, "I miss you, Dad." Not allowing her emotions to take hold, she headed out the door to the old shed behind the trailer.

The one hundred and eight-degree temperature didn't faze her as she smiled and said hello to the struggling row of petunias she had planted early in the spring. She had purposely planted them close to the trailer, under the awning, to avoid the afternoon sun, and she watered them daily in an effort to prolong their blooms. She knelt down to lightly touch them, but quickly sprang back on her feet. Since the door to the shed always got stuck, she hit it with her fist and moved slightly to the left as the door popped open. She could hardly wait to start.

Leaning inside, she grabbed a small red bucket, walked around to the side of the shed to the water spigot and filled the bucket about half full. She carried the bucket inside the shed and unwrapped a small lump of clay, took it over to the clean workbench and started working it, kneading it as if she were preparing bread dough. Her hands began to get used to the rhythm, pulling the clay up toward her with one hand, then pushing it down with the other, slightly turning the clay on each up swing. She knew the clay was ready for the wheel when it had a smooth consistency throughout.

I've got it, just keep the feeling going.

She ignored all thoughts of her previous disasters and instead reminded herself what her father had told her many times before, "If you stick to a worthy goal, you'll succeed."

I wish you were here, Dad.

Gregory was about to turn around and forget the search when he spotted a trailer in the distance. *This must be the wrong road if this is the only sign of life around here.* After driving another half mile, he slowed down where the dirt road junctioned with another and came to a stop next to a small post. A dangling piece of wood read 'Kiser's Ranchita' painted in blue letters. Little pink and white flowers decorated the sign's corners. He stared in disbelief. "Not exactly a sprawling ranch," he said to himself. The dirt road needed grading, and Gregory had to maneuver the truck around muddy pot holes where recent rains had pooled.

He pulled up next to a dusty green Studebaker and shut off the engine. When he got out of the truck, he was struck by both the suffocating heat and the silence of the desert. Closing the truck door gently in deference to the stark quiet surrounding him, he walked down the rock-lined path to the shiny aluminum trailer.

The trailer displayed a red insignia with a profile of a gladiator and the name "Spartan Manor" in big, bold letters next to the door. Gregory stopped next to the steps and knocked lightly. He glanced at the colorful petunias thickly planted on both sides of the steps which, he thought, seemed to soften the lines of the trailer. When there was no answer and he heard no noise coming from within, he knocked again, louder, swearing under his breath. Earl Kiser, war hero, was not at home.

Is this really Earl Kiser's home?

It didn't seem right, no matter what the address and signpost confirmed. Gregory turned from the door, taking in the view of the surrounding mountains, which were far enough away to lend a feeling of spaciousness, yet close enough he could see the scattering of mesquite trees, saguaros, and cholla cactus.

A strange sound broke through the silence. He followed the sound around the back of the trailer and spotted an old wooden shed. The door was partially open.

Caught up in her excitement, and figuring it was her friend Carlotta, Helen ignored the sound of the car. She knew Carlotta would come around to the shed when there was no answer at the door.

Helen pushed the clay down hard, making it adhere to the turning wheel. Then she cupped the clay with both hands and gently coaxed the clay upwards. Keeping her energy focused and her body relaxed, she surrendered herself to the rhythm of the turning wheel.

Pushing the clay back down, she brought it back up again.

This is what it feels like when the clay is centered.

Taking a deep breath and exhaling slowly, she released the clay and picked up a thin sponge, dipping it in water. Squeezing a little water onto the spinning clay, she placed her thumb at the top center, pressed lightly and watched the clay respond to every subtle movement she made. For a moment she had a feeling of being outside of herself, of stepping back and letting the moment unfold. It was an odd sensation; she felt totally immersed in what she was doing. It seemed no time at all before the clay formed into a small, perfect bowl. She beamed in satisfaction and turned off the wheel.

She reached for the pottery knife and gently separated the bowl from the wheel. Holding it up and turning it carefully from side to side, she admired the clean, smooth lines of the bowl. She caught a subtle movement out of the corner of her eye.

"I did it!" Helen said excitedly. But a turn toward the door elicited a surprised gasp as she saw a tall, striking man with dark hair peeking in the doorway. The man's bright smile renewed her sense of joy and she grinned. With the clay pot close to her chest, she repeated herself, as if it was the most natural thing in the world to share this moment with a strange man. But this time her voice was softer and a little less exuberant. "I did it."

The irritation Gregory had felt during his long drive and the built-up tension due to his family problems lessened the minute he saw this young woman's vibrant green eyes and her smudged, yet radiant face. A few bits of clay clung to her long blonde hair that was tied in a loose ponytail. He watched as she blew a few wisps of hair out of her eyes. He couldn't resist smiling—here this girl was, out in the middle of nowhere, sitting in a dusty old shed, appearing like she had just reached her life's goal. "That's a great bowl," he offered. He was rewarded with a bright smile.

"Thanks." Holding the clay pot in both hands, she stood up and, with one foot, scooted the workbench out of the way. "Can I help you?"

He pushed the shed door fully open and stepped in. The increase in temperature just about knocked him over. "How can you stand the heat in this place?"

As a drop of sweat slid toward the corner of her mouth, Helen rubbed her face against her shoulder. "I can't for long, but I couldn't wait for it to cool down to try another spin at the wheel."

"Looks like it was a success."

She tried to tone down her excitement—but her smile practically exploded. "It was," a quiet giggle followed, "my first success."

He stepped closer and looked at the bowl, admiring the symmetry, the smooth surface, and the clean, gentle lip of the bowl's edge. "Congratulations." He turned his attention to her face, tanned and free of make-up, and smiled because a sprinkle of clay had landed at the side of her slightly turned-up nose.

Sensing his eyes were on her, she looked up. As their eyes met, time seemed momentarily suspended.

He's like the man in my dream. The quickening of her heart and the brief, sharp intake of breath happened involuntarily as she recalled her dream from several nights' earlier. Turning slightly away from him, Helen quickly regained her composure and managed to appear preoccupied with her bowl. She reached over to the worktable, picked up a pencil, and carefully, but with a slightly shaking hand, carved her initials on the bottom of the new bowl.

Gregory had always considered himself good at summing up people, and he had learned to count on his first impressions of those he met, but right now he felt as if he had marshmallows for brains.

Burned marshmallows. It's damn hot in here!

Noticing the slight tilt of her chin and the question in her eyes, he realized he hadn't even introduced himself. "I'm Gregory Rothman." His voice came from deep in his throat and had a scratchy sound to it. He was definitely experiencing something he wasn't used to—a bout of social clumsiness. "I'm here to see Earl Kiser." Gregory thought her skin paled slightly. "I've got the right place, I think." Only a brief second passed, but a bit of awkwardness lingered.

"Well, yes, you've got the right place Mr. Rothman. But he's not here."

"Will he be back soon?"

Her mind raced. *No, he won't be back soon. Not in the way you mean—in the flesh—with arms that give the best hugs, a heart as big as the night sky and eyes that always glittered mischievously. No, he won't be back soon. He's dead.* She swallowed an upsurge of emotions, as the unspoken words remained stuck in her throat. Wiping her free hand against her shorts, she closed the remaining distance between them and offered her hand. Ignoring his question, she said, "I'm Helen Kiser, Earl's daughter." They shook hands, feeling small bits of clay against their sweaty palms. As she looked into his eyes, she felt a shiver.

His eyes—yes, he is the man I dreamed about.

"Is there something I can help you with?"

Perplexed at the intensity of her gaze, he answered awkwardly, "Uhm, yes. My father asked me to see Mr. Kiser while I was in town. They're old friends from the war."

"Really? Which one?"

"World War II."

"I'm sorry." She smiled. "I meant which friend. What's your dad's name?"

Gregory grinned. "Gerald." Not sensing any recognition on her part he added, "Gerald Rothman."

She shook her head. "I don't know the name, but that's not surprising. My dad always used nicknames." The heat was getting to her, this man with dark brown eyes sprinkled with gold dust was getting to her, and the mention of her dad was getting to her. Needing to gather her thoughts, she set the small bowl on a clean area and said, "I'm going to clean this up before it dries. You're welcome to wait inside the trailer where it's cooler."

"I'll just wait outside, unless you need any help?" He watched her grab a cloth and wipe down the pottery wheel.

"Thanks—but this will just take a minute."

He backed out of the shed and walked to a nearby mesquite tree which offered a large umbrella of shade. He wiped the sweat off his brow and fanned his shirt a couple of times, wondering what kind of man Earl Kiser was, an admired war hero, who ended up in a place like this—out in the middle of nowhere in a trailer.

Helen had never minded cleaning up after all her unsuccessful attempts at the wheel, but this time was more enjoyable. She had a contented feeling of personal accomplishment that came from doing something she had questioned whether or not she could do. After wiping down the pottery wheel, she turned on the outside faucet, rinsed the cloths and water bucket, set them inside the shed, and pulled the warped door shut.

Walking toward the trailer, she felt a tingle at the sight of the young man's sweat-soaked shirt clinging to nicely formed muscles. "Would you like a glass of iced tea?" she asked.

"That would be nice, thank you." He followed her up the wooden steps while enjoying the view of her small, swaying hips. Greeted by a blast of cool air, he heard the welcome drone of the cooling system as he ducked his head and walked through the door.

"Wow," he said at his first glance inside the trailer. It was a smorgasbord of color and texture. "Nice place." The living and dining area shared the same small room. A yellow sofa ran the width of the trailer with two built-in cabinets on each end. Just to the right of the door was a Newcomb phonograph player sitting on top of a cabinet with a collection of 45's stacked below. Behind the front door was a small space heater. A television sat on a half-wall divider separating the living and dining/kitchen area. The kitchen had a small Dixie oven-stove and a red icebox with "GM Frigidaire" in silver lettering emblazoned beside the silver handle. Green and white floor tiles lay in a checkerboard fashion under a pair of green coiled rugs.

He looked over at her and watched as she also looked around the trailer. He wondered what she was thinking. Was she trying to see the place from his perspective? Hints of sadness in her eyes made him think otherwise.

"This place looks brand new," he said. Gregory saw her eyes turn peaceful.

"It is. Dad bought it just a few months ago."

"Do you," he paused slightly, "live here with your dad?"

"Yes—I mean no," she said hesitantly.

Again Gregory felt as if he had said the wrong thing. Turning toward the sofa, he noticed two framed pictures on the wall. "May I?" After Helen nodded, he took a few steps and looked at both pictures. "Is this you and your dad?"

She smiled, but it didn't quite reach her eyes. "Yes."

The first picture showed a younger version of Helen, standing next to a Cessna, smiling from ear to ear. In the other, her dad stood next to the airplane, leaning against the cockpit door. He looked as if he had been laughing. Gregory smiled, imagining her doing something silly before she snapped the shot.

She tilted her head. "I've been trying to think of some of the men's names Dad mentioned when talking about the war. He mainly talked about Sludge and Cooter." She paused, trying to remember some of the others.

"I don't know." Gregory leaned into the table. "My father never mentioned nicknames."

"Dad had pictures from the war. I'll get them out so we can see if your dad is in one. Please, have a seat," she added as she walked down the hallway.

Gregory pulled out a chair and sat down at the dining room table. He absently pushed a crystal vase of purple and pink petunias away from him and rested his forearms on the table. "Your flowers are nice," he said when she walked back in the room with a large envelope. He thought she looked cute in her stained man's T-shirt and dirty tan shorts.

"Thanks—I picked them this morning." Standing next to him, she opened the envelope, pulled out a handful of pictures, then separated the war pictures from some old family pictures. "There are only a few."

Gregory looked at them. "Here he is."

"Let me guess, Cooter, right?" She leaned over and pointed to the man her father had called Cooter. After Gregory shook his head 'yes,' she added, "I should've known, you look a lot like him."

Gregory looked up at her questioningly.

"Well, your jaw line," she mumbled in response.

"I guess there's some resemblance," he conceded, "although I'm having a hard time envisioning my father with a nickname like Cooter."

"I think it stood for 'you old coot.'" She shrugged her shoulders mischievously. "I don't know why."

Gregory grinned. "I do—he *is* an old coot." He watched her walk to the kitchen, take out two glasses, fill them with ice, and pour the tea. "I'm from Los Angeles—Glendale, actually," he called after her. "I hear our parents lived just a few miles from each other, but they didn't know that until our fathers were stationed together."

"Oh, I didn't know that."

"Will your father be here soon?"

"No. He's gone. He, a—" their eyes met briefly and she quickly glanced away. Her tone shifted as she said, "well, he—" Her voice broke into a whisper. "He died." She shook her head yes, as if having to convince herself it was the truth.

Gregory stood up, took a few steps toward her but stopped at the divider. "I don't know what to say. I'm stunned—I'm sorry—truly sorry."

She avoided his gaze while handing him a glass. They both awkwardly said thanks at the same time, he for the tea, she for his condolences.

"He died last month of kidney failure."

Shaking his head in disbelief, he said, "I've been in Tucson since mid-May. I was so wrapped up in my studies that I waited until now to visit." He couldn't believe his selfishness. His father had asked him each time he called, and Gregory said he was too busy. He looked up, and she saw his regret.

"There was no way for you to know. Dad didn't want anyone to know." She took a sip of tea. "I'm sorry you made the long trip out here for nothing."

Compassion warmed his face. "Don't be sorry." He stepped closer to her, hesitated briefly, and then reached for her hand. He squeezed it gently. "I'm glad I did." Something special was already happening between them; it was reflected in each other's eyes as they searched for clues as to how they could be so comfortable with one another. It was Gregory who broke the spell. "So, when you said you don't live here with your father—" Noticing the sudden tenseness in her fingers, Gregory regretted the question before he even finished asking it. He started to apologize but she held up her hand to stop him from speaking.

She stood up and took a couple of breaths, exhaling slowly, then turned around and smiled. "Sorry." She was curious at his sudden change of expression. "What?" she asked, wondering what caused it.

He leaned into the table. "You haven't grieved," he said simply.

She folded her arms against her stomach. "Dad and I said our good-byes before he died."

Gregory leaned back, about to question her, but quickly thought better of it. When he spoke, his words were sincere. "I can't imagine what that must have been like." He leaned forward and looked around the trailer while rubbing the bottom of his glass. "So he bought this trailer for you?"

She smiled warmly. "Yes. It was my dad's last gift to me. He knew I loved it here, and he always wanted me to have a place to come home to. So he sold his airplane to pay for the trailer and utility lines."

"That's quite a gift."

"Yes. When he found out he wouldn't be living much longer, he put all of his energy into getting this place ready for me."

Gregory smiled. "He must've loved you very much." But Gregory was confused. He leaned forward in a subconscious move to be closer to her. "Haven't you been living here with your dad since your parents divorced?" He had heard that Helen's mother still lived in the house that was not too far from where his parents lived, a house Helen most likely grew up in, in an established area east of L.A. Gregory knew he was getting personal, but for some reason, good manners seemed to be lost on him for the moment. "My mother mentioned running into your mother quite a few years back, at some charity event, I believe."

"My parents never actually got a divorce. My mother would never have allowed that."

Gregory watched as she seemed to go off into another world. She picked up a napkin and wiped the 'sweat' forming on the side of her glass in smooth, slow strokes. They sat silent for a moment, her focus on her glass and his focus on her.

Aware of his gaze, Helen looked up, appearing comfortable with him. "Dad was great; there was never a question about which parent I would live with." She half smiled. "But Mom wouldn't allow that, so they compromised and sent me off to boarding school in New York. Besides, Dad was away much of the time."

"He didn't live here?"

"No, he lived in Tulsa. He was a pilot instructor for Spartan Aviation. At Christmas and summer vacations, Dad would pick me up and fly us to

Tulsa. And every chance we got, we came here." She thumbed through the remaining photographs, pulled out a picture and handed it to Gregory. "That little thing is what we used to stay in before Dad bought me this trailer.

Gregory grinned when he saw the picture of a really small trailer. "I hate to say this, but this looks like it would be the last place I'd want to spend the summers."

Helen laughed. "Sometimes it was really miserable and we would wonder what we were doing here, but the summer rains would come and, like Dad would say, we had front row seats to one of Mother Nature's breathtaking shows. The lightning storms were spectacular, the sunsets so beautiful. It was magical."

Greg's expression turned thoughtful. "It's obvious you two were very close."

Her expression softened. "He was everything to me." She smiled contentedly. "I enjoyed school, but I always looked forward to being with Dad. When I was with him, everything was an adventure. When it wasn't raining, he'd take me flying at sunset. Afterwards, we would eat dinner at the café near the airport. That was our home away from home: Prop's Café. I've worked as a waitress there every summer since I was fourteen."

"I thought you had a special way with the tea."

She grinned. "That's right. Years of experience—and I appreciate good tips."

Acting like he was going for his wallet, he winked. "I'm sure I don't have enough on me. I guess I'll have to work it off."

"That would be easy around here."

"You think so? This place looks pretty great."

"Thanks. But I was thinking of planting flowers, forty acres of them. That's a lot of caliche to break, and that's real backbreaking work." Her tone was playful, but her expression serious. "I could use a little help."

"I don't think you have enough tea for that."

"I have a box of Lipton. You need more?"

"Maybe another box or two."

"Can't you just picture it? Heat-stroked, wilted flowers everywhere you look?"

They both laughed. The sound of her own laughter took her back to the last time she remembered laughing: the day before her father slipped into a coma. Her dad had made the scattering of his ashes a funny deathbed wish. *"Split up my ashes,"* he had told her. *"Bury some with a newly planted iron-wood tree. I like the knotted wood and you like the pink flowers. Plant it in a pot,"* he said like an afterthought. *"That way you can take it with you back to college. Yeah—I like that idea. You can replant it here later. Then have my old friend Ralph take you up in his Cessna and drop some more of my ashes on this land. And finally, I'd like you to bake some cookies or something for your mother with a little 'Ashes de Earl' in them. Maybe she'll choke on them. Then at least I'll die knowing she can't hurt you anymore."*

Between most fathers and daughters, those comments would be morbid. But Earl and Helen had let love and laughter heal the emotional wounds inflicted by June Kiser.

I miss your sense of humor, Dad. I miss you.

Helen's eyes drifted toward the open window. A few long seconds passed until she looked back at Greg. He pointed at the picture of the previous trailer. "What was it like staying in this little thing?"

"Oh—we loved it. We named it the "desert rat," because it took such a beating from the harsh sun. And boy, sometimes when the rains came we thought the trailer would be knocked over or swept away. But it always survived intact, just like the rats." She grinned in response to Gregory's interested smile that urged her to continue. "We slept outside most of the time, on cots, under a sea of stars. If we had to sleep indoors, Dad would insist that we flip for the bed. Somehow I always won, and he'd end up sleeping curled up on the floor with his legs scrunched up under the table." She smiled at the memory. "I'd try to get Dad to switch with me and have him take the bed, but he always insisted a deal was a deal."

Tears seemed to surface out of nowhere. Her throat caught while trying to speak. "The day before he died I asked him—I said, 'Dad—do you remember the toss for the bed?' He nodded his head 'yes,' so I asked him if he was on the level—about the coin toss."

The intensity of the pain, the loss of her beloved dad, could not be contained any longer. Gregory saw what was coming and quickly reached for her as she tried to finish. But she didn't finish. He could see her trying to fight it but her face was flushing, her eyes welling with tears. When the tears began flowing silently down her cheeks, Gregory gently pulled her close and adjusted his position slightly so that her head rested comfortably against his chest.

He held her tight as she cried. "It's okay," he whispered.

Her tears came from deep inside as she soon realized it hadn't been strength that kept her from grieving, but rather that she had been in a state of shock and numbness since finding out about her father's illness. The comfort she felt by being in Gregory's arms acted like a safety net that allowed her to feel the loss of her dad's passing. Year after year of precious memories surfaced: her dad making pancakes shaped like teddy bears for her when she was little. The numerous times he got out the needle-nose pliers when she got splinters from the prickly pear or cholla cactus. The twice-weekly phone calls he never missed when she was away at school. The books they read out loud together. And most memorable—countless hours in his plane, chasing clouds.

All Gregory's senses were engaged as their heat-soaked bodies clung to one another in her sorrow. He took in different little things about her: the dainty beaded bracelet on her left wrist; the hollow between the base of her neck and her collar bone; the mixed scent of lavender in her hair and his sweaty body odor which still held a hint of his musk aftershave. They were so close that he wouldn't have known whether the salty taste in his mouth came from his own sweat or from her tears.

Helen began to calm as she heard Gregory's soothing voice saying, "It's going to be all right." Finally her sobs subsided.

Gregory leaned back and wiped her tears with the back of his fingers. Her face was puffy and red from tears, yet to him she was radiant.

She moved away from him to get a tissue and discreetly blew her nose. He sat down on the sofa. Turning back toward him, she said, "Sorry."

As she was about to explain, he held up his finger. "Don't apologize. You needed that."

"Yes. I guess I did." She reached for their teas, handed him his glass, and sat down at the other end of the couch, facing him slightly.

"Are you up to telling me your dad's answer?" In response to her quizzical expression, he continued. "Was your dad on the level about the flip for the bed?"

Her expression turned thoughtful, and then she grinned. "Dad winked at me, and said 'of course I was.' But he knew I was onto him." Helen's smile turned bittersweet as she looked out the window. "I really, really miss him."

Gregory saw her eyes mist over again.

"Anyway," she said, "enough about me. Tell me about you."

Taking a lighter tone, Gregory replied, "That's funny, I hardly know anything about you other than you went to boarding school, spent summers with your dad, and just had your first success at pottery making."

A gust of wind rushed through an open window, sending the curtains up in the air and bringing Helen back into the moment. "A storm is on its way." She got up to partially close the window, leaving it just slightly open for the fresh air, and sat back down on the sofa. "You said something about your studies. Are you going to school here?"

"Yes. I'm enrolled in the University of Arizona Law Program. I just finished taking a couple of summer courses. Are you in college?"

She sat there for a moment, brow creased in thought, then she leaned forward and crossed her arms against her knees. "Is there some reason why you are reluctant to talk about yourself?"

In a move to avoid the intensity of her gaze, he had taken a drink of tea and now just about spit it out. He swallowed. "Guilty," he admitted. He set his glass down on the end table. "I just received my bachelor's degree in Political Science from Stanford. I wanted to live someplace different to get my law degree. A friend of mine goes to school here, and he really likes it, so I thought I'd join him." Gregory looked over to see that her expression hadn't really changed. "That's about it."

The sound of thunder ripped through the trailer as the wind sent the curtains flying. Helen looked out the window, saw the dark, thick clouds, then turned her attention to Gregory. She studied him for a moment as contradictory images played in her mind—the man in her dreams had brought her a gift. *Compassion—that's it.* She made her decision and stood up. "Thank you for stopping by. I uh—" she saw a look of disappointment on his face. "Well—the roads can get flooded quickly during a monsoon storm. I wouldn't want you to get trapped."

With a polite nod, Gregory stood up, stepped around Helen, and took a few steps into the kitchen where he placed his glass into the shiny stainless steel sink. "It was nice meeting you, Helen," he said formally, a hint of sadness in his gaze.

"It was nice to meet you, Gregory. Thanks for driving all this way and—" she hesitated, looked into his eyes. "Thank you for listening, and letting me cry on your shoulder." She grinned appreciatively while opening the door for him.

"Thanks for the tea." He moved closer to her and the door. They said goodbye at the same time, and both smiled awkwardly as he turned and left.

Helen stepped off onto the top step and watched him leave. "Please thank your dad for me. It's really nice that he remembered my dad."

She thought he was gone, but then he poked his head back into view. "I will." He winked, masking his disappointment behind a smile.

Helen walked back into the trailer and stood there for a moment, listening intently as he opened, then closed his truck door. She headed for the bathroom and for the first time was aware of the messy clothes she was wearing. She took one look in the mirror and gasped. Tiny chunks of clay dotted her face and ponytail. Her tears had blended with some of the clay—leaving her face smudged and streaked. And somehow she had been oblivious to it throughout their visit.

"Leave it to you to meet a remarkable man with dirt on your face," she said with a laugh.

13

Mile after mile of farmland rolled into view: fields of barley, beets, corn, and alfalfa. Randall, Allison, Vanessa, and Stacie headed south on highway eighty-three, past large rolls of hay scattered over recently harvested fields. Sunflowers, with their large blossoms of bright yellow petals and rich brown centers facing the eastern sky, presented a colorful distraction after the miles of green crops.

Allison had been driving for twenty minutes. Not a word had been spoken; she and Vanessa were both lost in their own thoughts.

Vanessa slouched low in the seat, her head resting comfortably on a pillow propped between the seat and the window. Memories of her childhood in Bismarck were playing through her mind. Nothing stood out that made her life special until this year. There was a feeling down deep inside of her that she was having trouble identifying. When it finally surfaced, she sat up uncomfortably.

"Al?" She said it hesitantly.

"Yeah?" Allison answered roughly. She had been dwelling on her unrealized dream of being on a beach in a bikini when her classes were over for the day.

Allison's tone was enough to keep Vanessa quiet. "Never mind." She was unsure of herself, of the guilt she was feeling over how this had been a good year for her. She was almost grateful that her mother had left.

"Can you believe this?" Allison bellowed, "We have to take a detour down farm roads."

Vanessa glanced up ahead. "These aren't farm roads." She was rewarded with a scowling look. "They aren't," she argued.

"Look around, Vanessa. What do you see?"

"Farms, but these are main roads that lead to town."

"Yeah—main dirt roads with mostly tractors going by." A few minutes later they encountered another detour sign that ended up taking them through more miles of fields. "At this rate we should arrive in Arizona in about three months," Allison shouted.

Vanessa looked at her sister impatiently, "Just drive," she said before leaning forward, ejecting the Rita Coolidge tape, and loading another.

"What are you doing?" Allison yelled. "Put that back in there."

"We need some more upbeat music. This stuff is putting me to sleep."

"Well, go to sleep then. When I drive, we listen to what I want. You can listen to whatever you want when you drive." It came out in a whine and Allison was embarrassed at the tone of her voice. "Does that sound fair to you?" she asked huffily.

"Sure. Whatever." Vanessa put the tape back in, then fluffed up her pillow, closed her eyes, and turned away from Allison. A few minutes later she repositioned herself, trying to get comfortable. She turned toward Allison and folded her legs up onto the seat. She rested there for a few minutes, then opened one eye. "I think we should change drivers every hundred or so miles."

"Why?" Allison asked with her eyes still on the road.

"Because I prefer driving and I prefer listening to my own music. At least that way we'll have equal time."

"Sure. Whatever." Allison mimicked Vanessa, then asked in a normal tone, "Can you hand me the peanuts?"

Vanessa reached into the small backseat of the truck, fumbled through the bag of snacks and handed the peanuts to her sister.

"And some apple juice?"

Vanessa threw her an irritated look, then unhooked her seatbelt in order to reach the ice chest. "Will that about do it for you?" she asked as she handed Allison the juice.

Allison smiled. "Thanks, Sis." She turned up the stereo and began singing, "We're all alone" along with Rita as Vanessa covered her ears with the pillow, silently muttered *Oh brother*, and fell asleep.

"Vanessa, wake up!" Allison gave Vanessa a whack on the arm before pulling off to the side of the road.

"What!" Vanessa yelled. "Why did you wake me up?"

Allison turned down the radio and put the truck into park. She couldn't resist singing her own rendition of an old tune her grandfather used to sing. "Lord, I'm one hundred miles away from home. Away from home, away from home, away—"

"Aahhh," Vanessa screamed, "You pulled over at exactly one hundred miles?"

"It was your idea," Allison said innocently, and in case Vanessa didn't believe her, Allison showed her the odometer mileage she had written down when they left the house. "Besides, it will probably be the longest hundred miles of the trip."

"Unbelievable." Vanessa threw down her pillow. "I didn't mean exactly one hundred miles." But Allison was already out of the truck and walking over to the passenger side.

"Hundred miles down, a whole bunch more to go." Allison said when they were both in the truck. Vanessa immediately took the tape out and put in "Shake it Up" by The Cars. She cranked up the volume and began tapping the wheel as she stepped on the accelerator and pulled out onto the highway. It wasn't long before they caught up to the U-Haul.

They were just outside of Pierre, South Dakota, when Vanessa slowed the vehicle down and pulled over onto the side of the road.

"What's up?" Allison asked.

"Your turn to drive." Vanessa put the truck into park and got out. Allison laughed, taken by surprise. She hopped behind the driver's seat and checked the odometer reading. "You drove 128 miles, Vanessa. The deal was 100."

"So I forgot to look. Sue me."

Further down the road, they hit the junction with I-90 and headed west.

Randall pulled over at a drugstore in Wall, SD. Both Randall and Stacie got out of the U-Haul and waited for the truck to pull in beside them.

Allison rolled down the window. "Why are we stopping here?"

Randall put his hand on the door and leaned in just enough to talk to both of them. "Did you see the sign? This is the famous Wall Drug Store."

"Famous for what?" Allison asked.

Randall frowned. "Famous for advertising cold water during World War II. They advertised it all over the world; everyone wanted to come to Wall Drug to get some cold water, and that's exactly what I'm going to do!"

He turned and walked toward the drug store while his three daughters stared at him in disbelief. "We know he hasn't been drinking," Vanessa said. "So he must be smoking something."

Allison huffed and Stacie rolled her eyes as they climbed back into the vehicles and waited for their dad.

They stayed the first night in Rapid City. Early the next morning they headed toward the quaint towns that surround Mount Rushmore. When they neared the monument, nobody wanted to bother going into the park. Instead, they drove along the road, spotted the enormous heads of the former presidents, then pulled off to get pictures. Fluffy white goats perched stoically on the nearby cliffs provided another photo opportunity.

They headed west on Highway 16 and stopped for a quick walk at Jewel Cave National Monument. They were treated to beautiful fields of mustard as they left the Black Hills behind.

Entering Wyoming, they were greeted by a large, rusty metal Bison that stood on top of a hill as they watched the surroundings change from forest into endless rolling hills of pale green grass. They turned south on Highway 85 and every hundred miles, give or take a few, Allison and Vanessa stopped to change drivers.

In the U-Haul, Stacie was about halfway through reading Danielle Steele's "The Ring" when her dad yelled "Ha! Look at that." He pulled into a gas station as she looked around.

"What is it, Dad?"

Randall got out of the U-Haul and reached behind the seat for the camera. "It's time for another picture. Hey!" he yelled, seeing that Vanessa hadn't slowed the truck down. "Hey," he yelled again, waving and running as fast as he could as she sped by him.

Vanessa glanced in her rearview mirror and saw someone running down the side of the highway, waving his arms. She put on the brakes and slowed down. "Is that Dad?"

Allison turned around and saw her dad waving his arms. "Yes—I wonder why he wants to stop here."

Vanessa headed back toward her dad. When they pulled up beside him, she rolled down her window and lowered her sunglasses. "Is this a scheduled stop?"

Randall shook his head and smiled in exasperation. "No. Your old sentimental father just wanted to take a picture of his girls."

Allison and Vanessa looked up ahead and saw a big sign that announced, "Three Sisters Gas Station."

"Cool." Vanessa put the car into drive and drove toward the parked U-Haul.

"Um," Allison muttered. "Don't you think it would've been nice to give Dad a ride back?"

Vanessa put her hand to her mouth in a quick reflex. "Oops," she giggled. They got out of the car and Vanessa walked over to her dad as he was jogging toward them. "Sorry, Dad," she said to his perturbed glare. "I just thought you wanted to stretch your legs more."

Randall snapped the shot of his three daughters, once again hoping and praying they were traveling down a road that would bring better times for all of them.

They stopped for dinner in Colorado Springs, but decided to keep driving. Although they were beginning to get cabin fever from being cooped up in the vehicles, they were getting excited about reaching their final destination. It was nearing midnight when they reached Trinidad, Colorado. Most of the hotels were booked and the only vacancy they could find was at the "Budget Inn," where the only thing cheap was the hard bed and the small, thin towels.

Nobody had a good night's sleep, but Allison had the toughest night of all.

Randall woke to the sound of Allison vomiting in the bathroom. Jumping out of bed, he hurried over to the bathroom door and knocked lightly while asking, "Are you all right?"

Allison didn't want this, not now, not today when they already had so many other things to think about. She mumbled, "I'll be out in a minute," then quickly rinsed her mouth and brushed her teeth.

When she opened the door, Randall's concern escalated. "Is it a flu bug?"

She couldn't tell him yet. "I don't know, Dad. I'm just not feeling well."

"Let's get you out of here."

They took quick showers and packed up in record time. Stacie helped Allison gather her things.

"Dad," Stacie said, "I think I should drive today." She hadn't felt confident enough to drive on the trip since she'd just gotten her driver's permit a month earlier, but she could see that Allison needed to rest.

"Are you sure, Stacie?"

"Yep."

"Okay, great." Randall gave her a confident smile. "You'll do fine."

Allison rushed to the bathroom one more time. When she came out looking pale, Vanessa took one look at her and said, "You look awful. Whatever you've got, I hope it isn't contagious."

Allison made no remark as she headed out the door and climbed into the U-Haul with her dad.

It was going to be a long day, but they were determined to get to Tucson that night. They drove with as few stops as possible.

With encouragement from Vanessa, Stacie soon gained confidence in her driving, and it wasn't long before she relaxed her tight grip of the wheel. When she pulled over to the side of the road at exactly one hundred miles, Vanessa gave her a high-five as they switched drivers.

Vanessa glanced over at Stacie, as a strange thought seemed to drop out of nowhere.

Stacie has been acting differently lately. Vanessa thought about the past few months, and it didn't take much to recognize some changes in Stacie's behavior. *You haven't been going to church, your drawings are different and you haven't tried to get us to do things as a family in a long time.* "How are you doing, Stacie?"

Stacie looked at Vanessa in surprise. "I'm fine. Why?"

"I don't know. You just seem different lately."

Stacie's eyes clouded with a hint of sadness. *I am different.* She slouched down against the pillow and made up an explanation. "Just a lot of changes—too many."

Vanessa took that as a reasonable answer. "Yeah, I know what you mean. Since it was after 11:00 p.m. when they arrived in Tucson, too late they agreed to set up beds and, knowing they needed groceries, they opted to check into a hotel for the night. With sore necks and stiff muscles, they practically stumbled out of the vehicles.

By the time they had breakfast and checked out of the hotel, it was after nine a.m. After buying groceries, they walked out of the store and gasped at the intense heat. "I thought this was supposed to be a dry heat, Dad." Vanessa said sarcastically. She didn't get a reply.

They took the Avra Valley road exit and headed west through a mountain pass lined with cacti, bushes and scattered trees. After two thousand miles, they were finally on the last leg of their journey.

About twenty minutes further west, they turned onto a dirt road that obviously had seen very little traffic over the years. With each pothole Vanessa hit, Allison thought she was going to lose it again. Vanessa seemed to be oblivious to Allison's troubles.

"Can you slow down?" Allison barely whispered.

"Huh?" Vanessa drove over another rough spot.

"Will you please slow down and try to miss some of these potholes." What little strength Allison had vanished. Her anger and self-disgust increased until she no longer felt in control of her emotions. She fought back tears.

Vanessa swerved to miss a hole, which lurched them both sideways. "Jesus, Al, what's the matter with you?" They hit another deep pocket, which sent them airborne in the seat. "I'm not going that fast. I'm just trying to keep up with Dad, who doesn't seem to be having trouble with the road in that big thing." She glanced over at her sister. "Are you about to cry?"

That made it worse for Allison, and she did begin to cry.

Vanessa shook her head in disgust. "I don't get you, Allison. For the life of me, I can't figure you out. What are you doing here, in this truck with me in this God forsaken desert, sobbing like a baby, when you should be heading off to college?"

Vanessa's tone had somehow gone from disgust to tortured sweetness, and it totally did Allison in. "Oh, God, Nessa, I'm pregnant."

Vanessa slammed on the brakes and jammed the truck into park.

I didn't hear that. She momentarily leaned her head on the steering wheel as Allison's sobs turned into silent tears.

There's no way you're pregnant, Sis.

Allison took off her sunglasses and, with the back of her hand, wiped the tears off her face. "This is one for the books," she said. "Vanessa Averson—speechless."

Vanessa managed a sad smile as she turned to face her older sister. Compassion was a feeling she hadn't felt in a very long time. "This is the type of thing that's supposed to happen to me. I'm the reckless one in the family." She saw that her dad had stopped up ahead, so she put the truck back into gear and slowly picked up speed.

"Sorry," Allison said sarcastically. "I didn't mean to infringe on your 'family troublemaker' territory."

"Infringe? You just knocked me right off my throne. What in the world can I do to top this one? Look at you—at the top of your class, giving a speech about—," Vanessa stopped and turned to Allison as the realization of her sister's situation dawned on her. Their eyes met, a connection made as Vanessa felt her sister's pain. No sarcastic words tumbled out of Vanessa's mouth this time. They drove the rest of the way in silence.

Stacie had been sitting low in the seat, her eyes barely above the door. As they were about to reach their destination, she scooted up to get a better look.

In the air-conditioned vehicle, the desert didn't seem so hot, but it did look lifeless. The whole area seemed to lack color and vibrancy. She looked around at the scattered mountains that appeared to be as brown as the ground—*brown. No grass at all?* Most of the shrubbery appeared to be dead. The trees appeared to be leafless. She did a double take at the trees with their pale green stems. The sky even lacked color; it appeared pale blue, almost white. She could have cried—normally would have, but she just felt numb to it all. She thought of their beautiful hometown with its deep, rich greens and beautiful river dividing the towns of Bismarck and Mandan. The dark hole inside of her got a little bigger.

I don't belong here. I don't belong anywhere.

Stacie was the first one to see the trailer off in the distance. "Is that it?" There was no enthusiasm in her voice.

Randall looked over at her, feeling the weight of her reaction on his shoulders. "Yep, that's it." He didn't come up with any encouraging words to say.

They turned on a dirt road marked at both sides by old metal posts. The used trailer Randall had purchased had been delivered and set up.

Randall and Stacie got out of the U-Haul and looked at the land in every direction. Stacie tried to smile when he looked her way, but the tears were about to fall. He walked over to her side of the vehicle and pulled her into a tight hug. "I'm sorry, Sweetie. We'll make this work somehow." He lifted her chin up and planted a kiss on her forehead. They turned around just as Vanessa and Allison were getting out of the truck.

Vanessa slammed the door, stared at the surroundings in disgust, and declared "We've gone to hell."

14

It had not rained in four months; the plants had dropped their leaves and looked lifeless. The prickly pear cactus were so dried up one could vaguely make out their lacy skeleton underneath. Their normal healthy gray-green color now looked almost yellow. The giant saguaros looked like emaciated old men, barely able to withstand another day.

As the family stood, speechless, surveying the surroundings, the heat soaked through their bones and stripped away what little strength they had after the long trip.

"Dad," Allison whispered. "I've got to get out of this heat."

Randall turned and looked at her. "You look white as a ghost."

"I think I'm just car sick." She gave Vanessa a warning look.

Randall got the keys out of the glove box and walked toward the trailer. "So what do you gals think?"

There seemed to be a collective sigh among them. "This isn't at all like you described, Dad." Vanessa said. "Where are the flowers, the vibrant colors, the contrasts between the purple mountains, deep blue sky, green trees and plants, and the colorful poppies?"

Randall looked around. The desert was nothing like he had seen it several months earlier. "I'm not sure. Maybe the vegetation couldn't survive the heat."

"I hope we can," Vanessa quipped as they followed him to the trailer.

As Randall fumbled with the keys, Stacie spotted the small boarded-up trailer and add-on that her dad had told them about. A tingling sensation rippled through her. She couldn't wait to see what was in there.

Everyone had mixed feelings about living in a trailer. When they stepped inside, they were struck by the small size of the rooms but also sensed a cozy feeling. "It kind of feels like we're camping," Stacie said, not unkindly.

A bit defensively Randall replied, "It will do for now."

The front door opened into the living room with a combined kitchen and dining area right next to it. The brown carpet, along with orange and brown wallpaper in the kitchen, reminded Allison of her old Brownie Troop days. A decorative half-wall separated the two rooms. The master bedroom and half-bath were at the front of the trailer on the other side of the living room. Off the kitchen was a short hallway, which contained the washer and dryer. Down the hall were two small bedrooms separated by the main bathroom which, Vanessa mentioned, "mercifully has double sinks."

"You girls decide on the bedrooms; draw straws or whatever. I don't care." Randall said. "Allison, you can share a room or sleep on the couch until you start school."

Allison's stomach did a somersault. Vanessa turned away and headed down the hall so nobody could read her expression.

They started the swamp cooler right away, as Randall had prearranged for the cooler to be overhauled at the suggestion of the seller. But for more than twenty minutes it did little more than push the hot air around until it finally gave some relief. In the meantime, they agreed that although the trailer appeared clean, they would disinfect it top to bottom before doing any unpacking.

Several hours later, when every room was cleaned and either mopped or vacuumed, and the ice chests and groceries were unpacked, they made a light lunch of turkey sandwiches and cold drinks.

"I'm not ready to get back to work," Allison said. "Can we make a bed on top of sleeping bags? I'd like to lie down."

"Good idea." Vanessa said. "I vote for waiting until it cools down a little before we do any more work."

Randall smiled. "I hate to tell you this, but that probably won't happen until about October."

Vanessa grinned. "I'm not asking for that much time. I'm just hot and sweaty. I stink and I have a headache—probably from not drinking enough water." She looked at both her sisters and frowned. "But gee, I think I look better than you guys. You still look pale, Allison, and Stacie—you're all pink."

Randall looked at his daughters and agreed with Vanessa. He grabbed four paper cups and filled them with water from a large jug and handed them out. "Okay," he said, "take a longer break if you need one. I'm going to unload boxes onto the porch but I'll need help with the furniture later on."

"Dad, are there keys to the small trailer?" Stacie asked. "I'd really like to take a look in there."

"We don't have keys, but it will be easy to break into the add-on. The wood is shot. Just knock some of the boards down."

"Anyone care to join me?" she asked.

Allison was already lying comfortably on a sleeping bag and Vanessa had just grabbed a magazine from a tote bag. They both mumbled, "no."

Stacie stepped outside and briefly enjoyed the intense heat against her skin. But that moment was soon over as the heat seeped into her bones. She looked toward the road they came in on, but there was no road in sight that led to the old, small trailer. While wondering where the boundaries of the forty acres ended, she studied the land in a panoramic view, feeling comfortably surrounded by nearby hills and distant mountains. She looked at the vegetation, the trees, and the nearby bushes. Everything looked dried up, dead.

She eyed the old trailer. It looked as if it had been planted there, taken root, and belonged as much as the desert plants. It was sitting at an awkward angle, leaning a bit too heavily on the fragile built-on addition. She counted her long strides until she reached the door of the add-on. Sixty-two yards from their trailer, she guessed. That was much farther away than the next-door neighbors in Bismarck.

She tried the door handle, but it didn't budge. As she tried a little harder, the structure shook and debris fell to the ground. She wondered how hard she'd have to push for the whole thing to collapse. Deciding to find the easiest spot to break in, she walked around to the back, careful to step over bushes and small cacti.

The windows were partially boarded; the remaining plywood was worn and splintered. She stood on her tiptoes to peek through an opening in the back door, but she wasn't tall enough. Giving a good yank on one of the boards, she almost fell backwards as it came off too easily. Her curiosity was stronger than the slight discomfort from the splinters, so she removed two more boards. Her shirt and shorts, moist with perspiration, caught a slight breeze and cooled her momentarily.

Sweat dripped into the corners of her eyes as she rubbed the remaining dirt and debris from the window with her hand. Standing up on the tips of her toes, she looked through the window and was surprised to see furniture.

Knowing there was a possibility of finding some clue from her mother's past, adrenaline kicked in. She walked back around to the add-on and found a few rickety two-by-fours. Believing she'd found the weakest spot, she kicked. A slow trickle of blood appeared where she scratched her leg, but it didn't stop her. She kicked again, this time more carefully. A few more kicks and she was able to crawl through the boards.

Slivers of light peeking through worn-out lumber guided her entry into the dusty add-on. The odor was only slightly stale, as what little remained of old carpets and furniture was dry. Remnants of shredded, warped wallpaper lined the walls, along with what appeared to be narrow, sandy tubular columns, which, she later learned, were termite tunnels formed from the eaten wood. An old sofa and chair frame remained, while some of the stuffing was scattered nearby. Droppings of small rodents were scattered around the floor.

She pressed on anyway, carefully stepping over debris as she neared the door of the trailer. Beside the door was a faded red, partially chipped figure of a man's profile and the words "Spartan Manor." The steps appeared to be broken, so Stacie stood next to them and gave the door a slight tug. It opened after a harder tug, and she carefully pulled herself up into the trailer, feeling a little like a trespasser encroaching upon someone else's territory. Everything inside the trailer was surprisingly intact. She could almost imagine her mother living there. *But did she?* With a quick glance at the living room, Stacie saw a faded yellow sofa and chair, a coffee table and an end table. A broken lamp was lying on its side on the end table.

She turned her attention to the kitchen, where dead bug carcasses sprinkled the old stove, refrigerator, and sink. A small kitchen table and two vinyl chairs sat against the opposite wall. She quickly opened the cupboards and found them empty.

Down the short hallway was a very small bathroom, then a bedroom which had a full-size bed and a small dresser. She opened the dresser drawers, checked under the bed and in the closet. She found nothing. Except for the furnishings, the place was empty.

Disappointment swept over her. Nothing—no clues anywhere that Mom had ever lived there. Stacie walked back toward the living room and was about to step out of the trailer when several photos hanging next to the front door caught her attention. The photos were faded, distinctive features mostly gone, but the first photo was a man standing next to an airplane in the desert. Stacie wondered how they were related, or if they even were. She looked at the next one and saw a young girl standing next to the same plane. Goose bumps broke out as Stacie took a closer look at the faded picture. Then Stacie looked at the last picture and gasped as a shiver swept through her. This picture was a close-up shot, and Stacie felt as if she was looking at herself reflected in the picture. It was a young woman holding a little girl. Stacie looked back and forth between the two pictures and saw that the young girl next to the plane was the same woman holding the girl.

Stacie ran from the old trailer and toward the newer one. She walked inside as quietly as she could, but she was taking quick gasps of air.

Randall saw her and went to the kitchen. "Sit down, Stacie, your face is beet red. You're not used to this heat." He poured Stacie another cup of water, found a wash cloth, dampened it with cold water, and handed it to her.

"I got in there." She took a drink. "It was really hot!" She drank the rest of the water while wiping her face and neck with the cool washcloth.

"Did you find anything?" Vanessa asked from her temporary bed while Allison sat up, grabbed Randall's pillow, and then covered her head with it.

Stacie got up and refilled her cup. "Yeah, there were three pictures on the wall." She took another drink. "There was a picture of a lady." She looked at her sister, then her dad. "It was like looking at a picture of me."

There was silence for a moment until Vanessa sat up. "Cool." She reached for her sandals. "I want to take a look."

Randall, Stacie and Vanessa braved the heat, and a few minutes later stood looking at the pictures. "Stacie, you look just like this woman." Vanessa had glanced at the woman, but her attention went to the little girl. "And this is Mom," she said in a quiet whisper. "I know it is."

Randall and Stacie took a closer look. "I agree. It's Mom," Stacie said.

Randall wiped the sweat from his brow. "Man it's frustrating not knowing more about your mother." He turned and looked around the trailer, imagining her living here. "Maybe she didn't remember this place."

The heat was getting to them, so Randall and Vanessa quickly looked through the rest of the small trailer, already referred to as 'Spartan Manor' by Stacie.

Allison awoke from her nap as if coming out of a coma. She opened her eyes slowly, rolled onto her side, and looked at the kitchen. All the walls were covered with a light oak paneling. The kitchen had almond-colored appliances, and the wallpaper was light beige with differently shaped teapots painted orange and brown. She decided it did not look as bad as she had thought it would. A tear escaped and slid down her cheek. "This is home," she whispered to herself.

She was torn between finding her family and lying there. She rested for a few more minutes.

I can't put off telling Dad. I can't sleep on the couch forever. I need to see a doctor. She sat up and wiped her eyes. *I need help.* She stood, grabbed her travel bag, and went to take a cool shower.

The rest of the afternoon was filled with unloading the truck, the car, and the U-Haul, then piling everything on the porch. The sun was still high in the sky when they took a break for dinner just after six. Nobody felt like finding the pots and pans, so they agreed to have sandwiches again for dinner. They moved the sleeping bags and blankets out of the way and formed a circle on the floor.

"Listen to that," Randall said.

The girls perked up their ears. "What?" Allison said, "I don't hear anything."

"Exactly—not one noise."

Vanessa took a bite of her sandwich. "That's a little weird," she mumbled. "Maybe the world has come to an end and we're the only survivors."

"Why don't we get our stereo, or the T.V.?" Allison asked.

"Yeah," Stacie agreed, "Knots Landing is on tonight."

Randall finished his sandwich and got up to get a bag of chocolate chip cookies. "Why don't we just enjoy the quiet for one evening?" He sat back down and took a couple of cookies. "Who knows, maybe it'll be a night we'll always remember."

"Hey, Al," Vanessa caught her attention, then pointed to Stacie. "Stacie got into the old trailer and found some photos on the wall." Vanessa scooted to reach the cookie bag. She grabbed two, changed her mind, and put one back. She looked at her sister while holding the cookie right in front of her mouth. "You need to see them."

Allison looked at them expectantly. "Is Mom in any of them?"

Vanessa munched on her cookie. "Yeah, we're pretty sure. There's one of a woman who, by the way, looks a lot like Stacie—and I mean *a lot*. She's holding a little girl who we're pretty sure is Mom."

Allison raised her eyebrows. "Really? The woman must be our Grandma Helen." She got up, put her plate in the sink and wiped her hands on her pants. "I'm going to go take a look." She walked out the door and into the heat that had barely subsided, although it was almost 7:00. The sun was still fairly high, but a few scattered clouds captured the light and cast varied shades of orange across the countryside.

She walked carefully, stepping over and around a few low bushes. When she reached the building, she crawled through the hole Stacie had made and stepped up into the trailer. Her eyes rested immediately on the photo of the woman holding the little girl. She quickly glanced at the other two photos, then again at the first one, acknowledging the strong resemblance to Stacie. The woman holding the little girl didn't appear to be much older than Allison was now. "Maybe it's genetic," she said to herself, "having babies in our family before we have a chance to grow up ourselves."

The stale odor was making her queasy, so she darted out of the trailer, then the add-on, and into the fresh warm air. The colors in the sky had deepened. She admired the glorious sunset that finally gave color to the pale, dry desert.

She wanted to go for a walk, but the desert was foreign to her. She had no idea what was out there, or if it was safe. She walked back to their trailer, opened the door, and yelled inside. "Hey guys—come outside and see the best thing about this place so far."

Vanessa was in the shower, but Randall and Stacie walked outside and gasped. "I guess it's true, there's nothing like an Arizona sunset," Randall said. The sun was just about to hide behind the distant mountains and the sky displayed a showcase of dazzling peaches and bright yellows.

Stacie turned around to see what was behind her. "Look over here," she said.

They turned to see that behind them, the scattered clouds were a deep magenta against a rich blue sky. The mountains were a colorful combination of pink, purple and rust.

Stacie darted for the truck, feeling inspired for the first time in months. "I'm getting my sketchbook." The colors wouldn't show in her sketch, since most of her art supplies were packed, but she hoped she could capture the feeling the sunset evoked using just a charcoal pencil.

Randall and Allison stood side by side. "I can't believe we're here," he said. "I hope I did the right thing."

Allison looked at him questioningly.

He let out a sigh and crossed his arms in front of him. "This move won't affect you much, but what about Vanessa and Stacie?" He looked all around him. "This place is night and day compared to where we just came from."

The tension in Allison grew as she tried to comfort her dad. "I think it'll be a good change for all of us."

Randall turned to her in surprise. "Think so?"

A little ground squirrel caught her attention as it scurried from a bush and then down into a hole. She turned to her father. Instead of giving an answer she said, "Dad, I need to talk to you."

The tone of her voice prompted him to look into her eyes. Something was wrong. Randall called out to Stacie who was shutting the truck door and walking back towards them. "Allison and I are going for a walk."

Stacie sat down on the trailer steps. "Okay," she answered, already moving the dark pencil across the crisp, white page.

Randall and Allison headed off in the direction of the setting sun. The small scattering of plants left plenty of room to maneuver. They walked in silence for about five minutes until they came to a sandy wash with a bank a foot high. They moved a few small rocks and sat down.

Allison had lived this moment repeatedly in her mind. She had rehearsed a hundred ways to tell her dad about the pregnancy and had imagined as many responses. She bit her quivering lower lip and tried to calm herself.

Randall sat patiently, imagining different scenarios: something about Vanessa or Stacie, but not for a moment did he suspect anything was wrong with Allison. *Except,* he thought, *she hasn't talked about college lately.*

He cleared his throat before asking, "Is this about college?"

Allison bit her lower lip again. She tried to talk but the words did not come out.

"Is this about college?" he repeated.

She nodded her head and wiped her eyes. "Sort of." She stood up, hoping to find strength by standing. "I'm sorry, Dad. I'm scared, really scared."

Randall thought his heart was going to break from whatever was causing his daughter this much pain. "Whatever it is, Al, just say it."

She looked at the spot the sun had been minutes before. A halo of light was still suspended in the sky. "I did something stupid, Dad, really, really stupid." She took a deep breath and heard herself say the words as if someone else were speaking them. "I got pregnant."

Randall *couldn't* have heard right. That was all there was to it.

"Dad?" Her lower lip began quivering again.

She said she was pregnant.

Randall was shocked, dumbfounded, and couldn't think of what to say. He looked at Allison. He saw her, all of her, when he looked in her eyes: shame, regret, remorse, but mostly a sadness so deep he wondered if she would ever be the same. He stood slowly, took her in his arms, and held her tight as the last of daylight faded away.

—

Vanessa was halfway through blow drying her hair when she thought, "What am I doing this for?" She turned off the dryer and put it in a drawer under the counter. She grabbed a big hair clip out of her purse, flipped her hair into a twist and pinned it tight. Ignoring her make-up bag, she moisturized her face and left the bathroom.

She opened the front door, hitting Stacie in the back. "Ow," Stacie squealed. "Watch where you're going."

Vanessa shrugged her shoulders. "Watch where you're sitting."

Stacie rubbed her back as Vanessa sat down on the step below Stacie. "Where are Dad and Al?" Vanessa asked.

"They went for a walk."

"Hmmm," Vanessa stretched her legs down the remaining steps, her feet almost touching the concrete slab below. "That's good."

Stacie looked at her quizzically. "Why is that good?"

"Because they need to talk."

"About what?" Stacie's comment was half statement, half question.

Without hesitation, Vanessa leaned over and whispered, "Sis is pregnant."

Stacie's eyes widened. "No way!"

But Vanessa confirmed it by nodding her head.

Stacie looked out at the horizon. "It's getting dark out there. Let's get the flashlights out of the truck and go find them."

The half-moon slowly appeared and lit up scattered clouds. Allison was sitting on the side of the wash, staring at the sand while her father paced back and forth.

Randall's shock had worn off, and replaced with a myriad of questions. He stopped pacing and turned to her. "Just tell me all about it. Who's the father? What do you want to do? What about college?" He rubbed his forehead. "Are you going to get married?"

Allison looked up at him with a confused smile. "I don't know. I don't know, I don't know, and no." She changed her expression with each answer as she thought about the question.

Randall shook his head. "What?" They both smiled, the tension temporarily broken.

"This is hard, Dad. Can I just start at the beginning?"

He sat down beside her. "Good idea."

Allison grabbed a stick and began making circles in the sand. "Well, I went to a party, dead set on getting drunk and getting over David. Instead I got drunk—," she turned her head away from him and looked up at the sky, "and got pregnant by a guy who I don't even know."

Randall took a deep breath. "He was just a guy at the party?"

"Yes. A college kid just passing through town."

"Did you try to find out who he was?"

"No. Why would that matter?"

"It matters." Randall said sternly. "The guy needs to know what he did to my daughter. He needs to take responsibility. The baby needs a father." Each statement got more punctuated until Randall dropped the last sentence with a thud. He looked at her doubtingly. "Unless you're planning on getting rid of the baby?"

"No." She said it quickly, urgently. She leaned down, resting her upper body against her legs and drew another circle in the sand. "I did think about it, but I couldn't do it."

Randall let out a sigh of relief. He couldn't picture his daughter going through that ordeal. But he couldn't picture her having a baby either. Either way, it was a nightmare. "So, you're going to have this baby without the father."

"Yes." She tossed the stick, then wiped out the circles with her hand. The sand felt surprisingly cool.

"You're not going to college." He let out a big sigh. He hadn't realized until now how much he was looking forward to his daughter's future success. Neither he nor Madeline had gone to college. They were so proud of their eldest daughter who had set her goals high, and now he felt overwhelmed at the loss of those dreams.

"I'm sorry, Dad. I'm so sorry." Her lips started quivering again as she said it.

Randall reached over and grasped her hand. "I'm sorry, too."

Allison needed to talk about her first time having sex; how it should have been with someone she loved instead of someone she didn't even know.

How did I let this happen? She had asked that a thousand times, and still she couldn't accept what she had done.

"Dad?" she barely whispered.

"Yeah, Sweetie?" He answered tenderly while images of all the drunken nights, while his girl's lives were falling apart, played through his mind. His heart was heavy with guilt as he blamed himself, and Madeline.

"It was my first time." She said it so sadly it broke his heart.

He looked down and saw her wet eyelashes sparkle as they captured the moonlight. He held her again while she cried. It was all more than he could bear, and yet he had to bear it; his grandchild was on the way.

Randall and Allison heard Vanessa's chatter as she talked about bugs and snakes and strange noises in the night. They turned and saw two flashlights headed their way.

"We thought you guys might have gotten lost," Vanessa said much too cheerfully.

Stacie gave her a dirty look that was lost to the darkness. "We thought a flashlight would be useful."

"Thanks, but I think we're through talking now." Randall looked over at Allison for confirmation. She nodded. They both got up and joined the other two and made their way back to the trailer.

Vanessa bumped into Allison and whispered in her ear, "You did tell him, didn't you?"

"Yes, I told him."

Vanessa shrugged, satisfied. "Well, good, and I told Stacie, so it's all out in the open now."

Allison's mouth dropped open. "Thanks a lot." She said it bitterly, but at the moment she was too emotionally spent to care.

"You know," Vanessa said, "I thought your boobs were bigger. It didn't even occur to me that you were pregnant, so I just thought maybe we Averson girls are lucky and get a second growth spurt."

Allison whacked her arm.

When they got back to the trailer, Randall brought out an extension cord and hung a spotlight outside. It was still hot out, yet tolerable compared to the mid-day heat. While Vanessa and Randall began unloading furniture directly into the trailer, Stacie brought boxes in from the patio, and Allison began unpacking.

Because of the measurements that Randall took when he bought the trailer, the furniture fit perfectly. As each piece was put in place, it felt more like home.

Since Allison's situation changed the bedroom dynamics, which had not yet been resolved, the girl's agreed to leave the beds in the U-Haul for the night. It was past ten when Allison and Stacie moved sleeping bags and blankets into two back bedrooms before getting ready for bed. Ten minutes later they were both lying in the dark, with just a hint of light coming through the window.

"It must've been a bit of a shock to hear my news." Allison said with little emotion.

"Yeah, it was." Stacie rolled onto her side and faced her sister. "Are you okay?"

Allison remained on her back but turned her head toward Stacie. "No, but I will be." She gave a little laugh. "Like Dad says—,"

"It's an imperfect world." Allison and Stacie said it together, mimicking their father's tone of voice.

"How much did Vanessa tell you?" Allison was tired, but she felt she might as well get everything out in the open in one day.

"Just that you're pregnant." As Stacie's eyes adjusted to the darkness, she could see Allison's face illuminated by the moonlight. She couldn't believe this was happening to her sister, but at least it explained Allison's behavior over the past several months.

Allison rolled over onto her side, facing Stacie. She told her everything that she had told Vanessa and her dad, and she stuck with the lie of not knowing who the father was. "I can't believe I was so stupid."

"You weren't stupid, Al," Stacie said it gently, lovingly. "You were just in a lot of pain."

Allison laughed sarcastically. "Yeah—but we all were. Mom left all of us." She paused. "You're the only one out of all of us that has kept it together."

Stacie took a deep breath; she wasn't going to argue with her, she didn't want to talk about herself. "What are you gonna do?"

"I don't know. I was hoping I could figure it out once we got here."

Stacie rolled onto her back and stared at the ceiling, "You will."

15

Between keeping everyone fed and having cold drinks on hand, Allison washed bedding and cleaned countertops and cupboards. Vanessa and Stacie spent the day unpacking boxes and putting everything away. Randall, who had driven into Tucson that morning and bought a wheelbarrow, shovel, cement and a shed kit, was busy prepping the ground to pour a concrete slab.

Nobody wanted to turn the oven on in this heat, so they prepared bean burritos on the stove and gathered around the solid maple table that was much smaller, with the leaves removed, than it had been in their large dining room in Bismarck.

Allison knew she couldn't put it off any longer. She needed help, yet she was embarrassed to ask for it. Faced with decisions she wasn't prepared for, her stomach did a somersault as she blurted out— "Dad, I need to see a doctor." She looked down at her plate. "And I don't have much money."

Randall placed his burrito on the plate as if he'd been slapped right back into reality. "Of course." They didn't have much in savings and, since Allison would not be a college student, he wondered if she could be covered by his insurance. "Did you see a doctor in Bismarck?"

"No. I knew we were moving—and, well, I didn't want to see Doctor Mathis."

He nodded understandingly; Dr. Mathis had been their family doctor for many years.

"I don't know how I'm going to do it," Allison said with determination, "but I plan on supporting myself and the baby."

Randall managed a small smile. She'd be working instead of studying for tests, changing diapers instead of changing her wardrobe, staying up late with feedings instead of staying out late on a date. "Let's get you checked out by a doctor first, and then you can worry about a job," he said.

Then he realized what was likely worrying her most. "Allison, you and the baby have a home with us for as long as you need. We'll make room."

She looked down as her eyes welled up with tears. "I'm sorry. I'm really sorry."

Vanessa reached over and grasped Allison's hand as Stacie stood up to give her a hug, but no words of encouragement were offered. Nobody could predict how they would manage having a baby in the household.

The next few days were filled with a never-ending list of things to do. Everything was a challenge: finding the things they needed and putting them away; discovering there were no major grocery stores in Avra Valley or nearby Marana so they would need to drive to Tucson to do the shopping. All the things they had taken for granted: laundry, cooking—everything seemed harder and took longer.

It didn't take long each day for the triple digit temperatures to sap their strength. They got into the routine of utilizing the early morning and later evening hours to run errands or work around the house. Randall left most of the trailer for the girls to organize, but his bedroom and small bathroom were off limits. "Hey, a guy's got to have some privacy in this place."

As the humidity increased, the evaporative cooler was practically useless. They listened to the weatherman on the evening news and learned that, although the monsoon season was running late this year, the seasonal winds would soon be bringing heavy storms.

Having anticipated the day the phone would be installed, they cheered when the technician turned on the service. Randall declared the off-peak hours of the first weekend as long distance frenzy time. "We'll burn up the phone lines!" he told the girls. The first call was to Amma and Afi, followed by Randall's siblings as the phone was passed around so everyone had a chance to talk. Per Allison's wishes, they agreed not to mention the pregnancy to the family yet. She said she'd tell everyone soon.

After the relatives were called, they drew to see who got to call their friends first. Vanessa won and quickly dialed Sharlene's number in California. The phone rang five times before the answering machine picked it up. "Darn." Vanessa said, disappointed that she couldn't talk to Sharlene in person. The phone beeped. "Hi, Sharlene. Hi, Dan. This is Vanessa calling from Hell. Oops, sorry, shouldn't have said that. But anyway, it's that hot here, or hotter than, if you know what I mean. Um—I was just calling to say hi, and that I miss you—and that Stacie and I drove through the town where we'll be going to school and it's tiny, I mean real tiny. There's not even a dance studio. Can you believe it? I'm going to have to drive about thirty miles into the big city of Tucson to take a dance class." She threw her hand into the air in frustration as if they could see her. "And there are no places to walk to from high school. We have no choice but to pack a lunch or eat in the cafeteria." She paced a few steps. "Oh, well, I'm prattling on here." She gave them the phone number and asked them to call her when they got in. "I miss you guys—a lot. Hope to talk to you soon. Bye." Feeling deflated, she clicked the receiver but held onto the phone. "Stacie, it's your turn," she yelled.

Regretting her hasty packing, Stacie couldn't find Claire's number at her dad's house in Washington and there was nobody else she wanted to talk to.

Allison didn't feel like talking to any of her friends either. At least, if she didn't talk to them, she didn't have to continue lying to them.

They had been there a week, with three more before Marana High School started. Vanessa was not enthusiastic about beginning her senior year in a new school and Stacie was nervous. Randall took them both to the high school to register and sign up for classes.

They were greeted warmly by Mr. Brown, the school's principal, who happened to come out of his office as they were talking about having just moved. "You came from Bismarck? It's cold there." He rubbed his hands together as if to keep them warm. "You'll like it here much better."

They grinned at the absurdity of that statement. "At least you can dress for the cold weather, but there's only so much clothing you can take off in the heat," Vanessa said jokingly. "Unless you have a liberal dress code."

"Not that liberal." Mr. Brown grinned. "You'll just have to try the latest methods for surviving in the desert: go to matinees or the mall, eat lots of popsicles, go swimming, or run through the sprinkler. If those aren't available to you, then I suggest you wear a wet bandana on your head."

They all laughed. He asked questions about their personal interests, told Vanessa about the school's dance program and told Stacie about the art classes. The girls left the school feeling confident they could talk to the principal if they ever needed help.

The following day everyone got up early to go with Allison to her doctor's appointment. Allison had chosen Dr. Rachel Martinez because she was one of the few female OB-GYN's on the Northwest side of Tucson. Randall, Vanessa and Stacie waited for more than an hour in the waiting room while Dr. Martinez took extra time with her new patient. She discussed the pregnancy and what Allison could expect in as much detail as time permitted. She also recommended several books she wanted Allison to read, suggested some dietary changes, and jotted down the number of a support group for unwed pregnant women.

Allison walked back into the waiting room with a satisfied smile on her face and a prescription for pre-natal vitamins. "I like the doctor. She's really nice."

Randall put his arm around Allison's shoulder and gave her a squeeze. "I'm glad."

"Did she tell you when your due date is?" Stacie asked.

Allison tried not to smile, as she had been able to tell the doctor the exact date of conception. "Yes, the baby is due January 17th."

They drove around Tucson, admiring the mountain views, the quaint downtown area, and the grassy lawns of the University of Arizona. They stopped at The Blue Willow Restaurant, where they enjoyed lunch on the patio and were cooled by water misters. On the way home, they stopped at Tucson Mall to get school clothes for Vanessa and Stacie, and maternity clothes for Allison.

"Do you remember buying school clothes last year?" Vanessa asked as they entered the mall.

Allison and Stacie nodded their heads, remembering the overwhelming grief they were feeling just a year ago. "A lot has happened since then," Stacie said.

Allison smiled sadly, thinking of the past year. "Yeah, too much."

Deciding to meet in two hours at the center fountain, Randall took off to Sears to buy a new vacuum cleaner. And he said he'd look for a few new shirts and slacks to wear for job interviews.

By the time they returned to the car, they had missed most of the summer's first monsoon storm. They were surprised by the amount of water that had gathered in puddles along the sides of the road. "Wow, and we didn't even know it was raining." Allison said. Although it was now barely drizzling, they ran to the car.

"Whewweee," Randall yelled. "Feel that drop in temperature. Now that's more like it." After tossing shopping backs into the trunk, they piled into the car. Randall had put the new vacuum cleaner in earlier, and there was barely room for the remaining bags.

"Do we have to go home already? Can't we go to a movie or something?" Vanessa was practically whining.

Randall looked at his watch, and then started up the car. "It'll take us almost an hour to get home—just in time for dinner." He backed out of the parking space and started forward.

"But, Dad—can't we just skip dinner or grab something quick? There are some good movies out right now."

Randall looked in the rearview mirror. He saw Stacie staring out the window and Vanessa's lips in a pout as she sat staring out the opposite window. "Vanessa, is there something wrong?"

Vanessa snapped her head to her dad in surprise.

Is there something wrong? She thought sarcastically. *Is there anything right?*
"I don't know. There's just not much to do out there. It's boring."

Randall glanced over at Allison before he pulled onto Oracle Road. "What do you think, Al—Stacie? Are you up for a movie?"

"Yeah, that'd be fine." Stacie muttered. Allison nodded her head.

"Okay then, it's been a fun day, we might as well turn it into a fun evening as well." As he parked the car at the theatre, he felt overcome with a long forgotten feeling of gratitude.

We're going to be okay, all of us. His eyes welled with tears as he turned towards his daughters. "I love you girls, and I'm proud of each of you." Embarrassed at his emotions, he quickly added, "Come on. Let's go see a movie."

Allison, Vanessa and Stacie piled out of the car, looked curiously at one another, then gathered around their dad and gave him a hug. "We love you, too, Dad," they told him.

16

Monsoon season arrived. The seasonal high pressure winds from the Gulf of Mexico brought torrential downpours of rain to the parched desert floor. The clouds burst, sending sheets of rain onto the cracked, dry, soil. It wasn't long before washes and riverbeds herded the rushing water through the desert and temporary waterholes filled. During the night, toads would gather at these waterholes, having just climbed out of the underground burrows that had been their home for almost a year. They would mate, fertilize eggs, and as tadpoles grew in precious puddles of water, the toads would eat as many insects as possible before the soil dried up again. The surge of activity was like an entire sleeping town that awakened for a few nights a year to celebrate life and store up enough food in their bellies to survive another year.

Vanessa sat on the porch step, appreciating the cool breeze the monsoon wind brought before the storm. Over the past week, she had come to love these afternoon storms. The sheer force of the winds, the rain, deafening thunder and crackling lightning was a bit frightening, yet intensely exciting. In truth, she felt the storms were the only exciting things that had happened since they had arrived.

She knew something was bothering her, but could not pinpoint it. She thought about her family. Her dad and Allison left every morning to look for work, and Stacie kept occupied by cleaning and fixing up "Spartan Manor"—which is where she had taken off for a few minutes before, with cleaning supplies in hand.

They had been here less than two weeks and had finished settling in. Now it was just ten days before school started, and Vanessa couldn't come up with one good reason why she should be going there. Frustrated, she spoke out loud. "I should be home in Bismarck, working, and going to Sharlene's dance studio."

But the studio's gone, and there's really not that much to go back to. The thought saddened her. She felt so misplaced. "But I don't belong here either."

The breeze stopped blowing, and for a moment there was no sound whatsoever. The absolute stillness got her attention. Then a slight breeze gently moved the topsoil. She smiled thoughtfully; it seemed as if the soil were hesitantly trying a new dance step. The wind picked up, gathering loose dirt and sweeping it up, creating a swirling vortex of dust, debris and pollen.

Something stirred within her. She felt a sudden urge to do the impossible. She got up from the step and rushed out to greet the oncoming storm. The breeze intensified, brushing across her face as she stood against the wind. She felt the moisture in the air and breathed in a refreshingly clean scent. Remembering the soil that had swayed back and forth, she began moving in a similar fashion, with the wind, wanting to move just as it moved, sometimes gracefully, sometimes harshly. As much as she could, she became the wind and the swirling dust, as varying degrees of hot and cold swept against her skin.

As a few warning drops of rain hit her face, Vanessa lifted her arms just in time to greet the downpour, which was colder and harsher than she had expected. She stood there for a moment getting completely drenched, then for several minutes danced her finale as if the whole world were watching. Just as she bowed her head in closing, lightning and thunder exploded in the sky and she bolted to the safety of the trailer.

She fell against the steps panting. After her breathing returned to normal, her face drew into a broad smile. She knew exactly what she needed to do.

———

Waiting impatiently for her father's return, Vanessa had been pacing in front of the trailer for over an hour. The storm had passed. She had changed into dry clothes and had made several phone calls. She supposed she could help her sisters make dinner, but she was so wound up that the small kitchen seemed like a cage.

When she saw the truck, it was all she could do to stop herself from running out to greet it. As Randall pulled up along side the trailer, her excitement turned to fear. *What's he going to say?*

She smiled as he got out. "Hey, Dad, how did it go?"

Randall walked toward her, pulled the already loosened tie from around his neck and put his arm around her as they walked together toward the trailer. "It went pretty well, actually. I think I got a job at the cement plant."

"That's great, and it's so close to here."

"It will beat driving into Tucson everyday."

Vanessa wanted to talk to her dad in private, and with any luck, before dinner. "I really need to talk to you about something."

The atmosphere thickened as Randall looked at her questioningly. Too late, Vanessa realized that the last time he had heard those words his college bound daughter had announced her pregnancy.

"I'm listening," he said cautiously.

She hadn't intended to get off to a heavy start. "It's okay, Dad. It's nothing bad."

He let out a sigh of relief. "Okay—do you want to go for a walk?"

With a shrug of her shoulders, she smiled. "Yeah—I mean, it's not necessary, but it would be nice."

"Okay. Give me a minute to change clothes."

A few minutes later they were walking toward the wash where Allison and Randall had talked in the moonlight two weeks before. Vanessa had grabbed a couple of garbage bags to sit on, since the ground was wet. The wash was muddy, so they sat under an ironwood tree, avoiding branches heavy with mistletoe that almost touched the ground.

"So, what's up, Ness?" Randall prodded.

Vanessa straightened out her garbage bag. "Hmm, I—" she let out a breath in exasperation. "I'm not really sure how to start."

Randall looked out across the horizon. "I liked the part when you said it wasn't that bad."

"Well, it isn't."

How can I do this? But she knew she had to. She sat up straight and took a breath, regaining her composure. "Dad, I don't want to go to school here."

There, she had said it.

Randall did a good job of stifling his grin, but he couldn't control the sarcasm. "So, are you dropping out? Going to school by correspondence? I know!" His face took on an enlightened expression. "You want me to home school you!"

With an answering smirk on her face, she punched him lightly on the shoulder. "None of the above." Her tone took on a more serious note, "I know what I want to do with my life. I want to be a dancer, or choreographer, or teach dance. I don't know for sure which it will be, but I want to be involved somehow in the dancer's world. I'm already behind as far as my age is concerned. This year could make or break my future career."

He raised his eyebrows at the exaggeration, but he let her continue.

"There is no dance studio nearby. I'd have to go into Tucson for lessons."

"What's your plan, Vanessa?"

"I called Sharlene in L.A. If it's okay with you, I'd like to live with them my senior year. I can work with Sharlene almost every night. She said that if I keep my grades up, behave myself, and work hard at my dancing, they'd love to have me."

Her words made sense, but that didn't matter a bit to Randall's heart. "No."

Vanessa looked crushed. "Dad, I'm gonna rot out here." She said it quietly to his retreating back as he got up and headed back to the trailer. She looked around at the expansive desert. "I just don't belong here," she said to no one.

It was half an hour later and dinner was ready when Randall walked out of his bedroom and sat down at the kitchen table. Allison and Stacie looked at each other questioningly. He hadn't spoken a word since he got back from talking with Vanessa.

He felt their stare. With a heavy heart, he asked, "Can one of you go tell Vanessa it's time for dinner?"

Allison stopped setting the table and walked out of the trailer. She found Vanessa in the same spot her dad had said he left her. She was sitting curled up with her head and shoulders draped over her lifted knees.

"Dinner's ready."

Vanessa lifted her head, unashamed to show her tear-streaked face. She looked at Allison, almost defiantly. "I want to go to Los Angeles. I want to live with Sharlene and Dan for my senior year in high school and work my butt off dancing. I want to work harder in school than I ever have and maybe even try to get a dance scholarship at UCLA."

"Wow." Allison stood there, stunned. "Dad doesn't seem too happy about it."

Vanessa's eyes sprouted fresh tears. "I know." She took a few shallow breaths as she tried to control her crying. "I feel so awful for wanting to leave, but I feel so excited about making these things happen."

Allison sat down and put her arm around Vanessa. Vanessa leaned her head against Allison's shoulder. "What am I gonna do, Al? Dad has such hopes of getting us all on track here, you know—bringing us closer together—like we used to be."

Allison couldn't bear the thought of her family getting any smaller either. "I don't know, Sis. I'd hate for you to leave, too."

Vanessa's sobs pierced the silence. She knew she was going to leave, knew it was the right thing for her to do, but it broke her heart. She swung her arm around and clung to Allison.

When Vanessa regained her composure, they walked back to the trailer arm-in-arm. Before going inside, Vanessa stood up tall and took a few deep breaths.

She was going to fight for her dreams.

———

Hardly a word was spoken at dinner. They passed the casserole around, the salad and the green beans, and tried to lighten the mood with small talk. But the tension remained, and it was not long before attempts at conversation dissipated.

They all seemed to be relieved when the meal was over, and even though it wasn't their turn, Allison and Stacie offered to do the dishes. Vanessa nodded an appreciative thanks as she hurried out the door to catch up with her dad.

"Dad!" she yelled after seeing him bolt off in the distance. "Dad!" she yelled again when he didn't turn. A surge of anger squeezed out some of the sadness. She took off in a sprint after him.

Randall wanted to run. He wanted to hide. This move was supposed to be the impetus to get them moving in a better direction. He had tried so hard.

God knows I'm trying. He hadn't been drinking. It had taken everything he had in him to stay away from the bottle. Everyday, every evening, he wanted a drink. He'd give anything right now for a drink.

He thought about Madeline's desertion, leaving his business, quitting drinking, the move, Allison's pregnancy, looking for work, and now this. Now his middle child wanted to leave before her time. It was too much—it was just too much for one man to take—too many changes. He was so full of emotion: anger, sadness, and guilt. When he heard Vanessa approach, he turned to face her.

The moment their eyes met, Randall felt his emotions suck the life right out of him. He collapsed to the ground in tears. The look of compassion in his daughter's eyes was the same as her mother's. He had buried his pain in a bottle, and buried it by moving to Arizona. But a certain look in Vanessa's eyes told him the truth: he was a broken man who couldn't run any longer. There was no place to go. He had to face it.

Vanessa rushed over to him. She cried with him, holding him as best she could in an awkward position. The crying quieted after several minutes. "Dad," she said it hesitantly, "are you okay?"

Randall rolled over and sat down, feeling a hard squish beneath him. He leaned over and looked around to find flattened coyote scat, which thankfully was dry, on his shorts. Noticing Vanessa try to suppress a giggle, he grinned and said "I am now."

Vanessa helped him up, then grabbed a stick and offered it to Randall.

"Thanks," He said as he took the stick, then flicked the remaining scat off his shorts. He flung the stick as if he was skipping a stone. He looked at Vanessa and sighed, a little embarrassed at his breakdown. "Ness, that wasn't all about you."

Vanessa shrugged her shoulders. "I know, Dad. We all figured that was bound to happen sooner or later."

Randall grinned half-heartedly. "You did, huh?"

"Yeah."

"Sweetie—I've cried before."

"You have?"

"Like a baby. Just not in front of you girls." He turned serious. "About California?"

Vanessa's eyebrows perked up cautiously. "Yes?"

"Do you promise to do all those things you said? Get good grades, work your tail off, and most importantly, behave yourself?"

Vanessa thought for a moment. "Can we define good grades and behave myself?"

Randall shook his head in exasperation, wondering if he had spared the rod too many times with her. His mind jumped back to her dance at the going-away party. He was so proud of her and amazed at her ability. She had worked hard, had focused her energy in a positive direction during a very difficult time. It was much more than he had done.

"I'm going to miss you."

Vanessa's jaw dropped. "Do you mean it?" she asked it hesitantly, as if afraid he would change his mind.

Randall had had enough emotions to last him a long time. He walked over to her, turned her around and propelled her toward home. "Yeah, I mean it. We could use your bedroom." This time he caught her fist before Vanessa landed her second punch of the day.

17

A spray of flour burst in the air as Allison rolled dough across the countertop. She sang along with the radio as a tap-tap-tap partially blended with the song. The tapping sound got louder and she finally realized somebody was at the door. "Just a minute," she yelled. She set the rolling pin on the counter, wiped her floured hands against her shirt, and walked to the door.

A quick peek through the peephole sent her heart racing. *Judy!* With one hand over her heart in a reflex move to calm her nerves, she opened the door hesitantly, hiding her stomach behind it. "Judy, uh—hi." Her tone held no enthusiasm.

Judy cocked her head and spoke sarcastically. "Oh Judy, it's so good to see you. I've been so lonely out here without my best friend. Thank you for coming all this way to see me."

Allison dropped her head to her chest, sighed resignedly, and stepped around the door. Judy's expression turned to shock.

They stood in awkward silence as Judy's piercing gaze shifted between Allison's eyes and her protruding stomach. "Why didn't you tell me?"

Shifting uncomfortably from one foot to the other, Allison whispered, "I don't know." She opened the door wider. "Come in."

Judy climbed the steps and entered the trailer. They hugged, awkwardly. Judy looked around at the familiar furniture and knick-knacks from the house in Bismarck. "The place is nice, it's homey."

"Thanks." Allison shut the door. "Have a seat." Admiring Judy's cute haircut, perfect nails and make-up, her fashionable clothes, Allison felt like a beached whale next to a beautiful swan. "What brings you to Arizona?"

"My Uncle George invited us for Thanksgiving. Since Mesa's only a little over an hour from here, I thought I'd surprise you." Judy smiled uncomfortably. "I've been so worried about you. For the life of me, I couldn't understand why you were hanging out here and not going to college." She crossed her legs nervously as Allison stood silently looking around the room.

"How did this happen?" Judy gasped, then smiled. "I didn't mean that."

Allison sighed. "I should've told you, but it's been hard, really hard. So much has happened. And I guess—I guess I was embarrassed."

"I'm your best friend. You shouldn't have been embarrassed with me."

Judy tilted her head sideways. "Did you and David get back together?"

Allison shook her head uncomfortably. "No." In an attempt to ward off further questions she added, "I had a one night stand with a college student who was just passing through town. I don't even know his name."

"Oh," Judy said with obvious shock.

"Can I get you something to drink?"

"Water would be fine." Judy struggled to keep her eyes off Allison's stomach.

Allison put ice in a couple of glasses, filled them with water, and handed one to Judy before sitting across from her. They sat silent for a few moments, Judy shell-shocked, Allison resigned.

"Allison, this wasn't in your plans at all."

"Neither was being abandoned by my mother."

Judy ignored that statement. "You want to be a lawyer. Are you giving that up?"

"Do I have a choice?"

Judy leaned back in her chair. "Have you considered giving your baby up for adoption and going to school?"

"No."

"My God, Allison, you're too young to be a mother."

"I know I am, Judy. And I don't know what I'm going to do. But I'm not going to wonder every single day of my life where my baby is or if my baby's okay. Is my baby healthy? Loved? Happy? Alive even?"

"Adoptive parents really want children. They're probably great parents."

"I know, but will my baby know that I, his real mother, gave him away? Will he or she wonder why I didn't want him? Feel abandoned?" With great effort, Allison held back tears. "Jude—every single day I ask those same questions about my mom. She abandoned us. I'm not going to follow in her footsteps."

Judy sat up straight, scooted her chair over closer to Allison, then leaned over to give her best friend a hug. "I don't know what to say. I'm flabbergasted. I never would have guessed this in a hundred years. But you know what?" She took Allison's hands and held them firmly in her own, then looked directly in her eyes. "I'm proud of you."

"Proud of me?"

"Yeah. You're making the best of a difficult situation. Having a baby without the father takes a lot of guts." Judy shook her head and sighed. "What's it been like—the pregnancy—living here?"

"It's been fine, I guess. I'm past the morning sickness stage and I'm not huge yet, so I guess I'm doing pretty well. And I've been working at a convenience store down the road. 'Joe's Stop for Food and Gas.'"

"Catchy name." She took a drink.

Allison grinned. "Other than that, I just take care of myself, go to the doctor, and help out here as much as I can."

"How are your dad and sisters?"

"Dad got a job at the cement plant near here. He's doing well. He's starting to get things together." Allison glanced sideways. "He hasn't been drinking."

Judy smiled. "That's great."

"Vanessa is in L.A. She's going to high school there."

"Wow! How come?"

"She's living with Sharlene and her husband. You know—the prior owners of the dance studio. Sharlene invited Vanessa there for college. Vanessa didn't like it here, so she asked if she could go early and finish school there."

"And it's working out?"

"So far it is. She calls us once a week, plus Sharlene talks to Dad and confirms that Vanessa is following house rules. My outrageous sister seems to be toeing the line and then some."

"That's good to hear. And Stacie?"

"Stacie's fine, I guess. She doesn't really say." Allison rested her hands on her belly. "Enough about me and my family—tell me about college."

Judy talked about college life, but briefly. She didn't mention the guy who had asked her out on a third date. She felt uncomfortable at the differences in their lives and would have felt silly talking about a guy when Allison was about to have a baby.

They finally gave up on the small talk and just looked at each other for a moment. Allison smiled with teary eyes. She reached over and grasped Judy's hand. "It's good to see you, Judy. I didn't realize until now just how much I've missed you."

Judy smiled sadly. "I've missed you too, Al." After ten minutes of awkward conversation, silences, and finally promises to keep in touch, Judy pushed back her chair and stood up. "I've got to get back to Mesa. I promised Mom and Dad this would be a quick trip."

Allison walked Judy out to her car and waved goodbye as Judy drove away.

———

A week before Christmas, after putting a load of clothes on the line and cleaning the trailer, Allison lay back in a lounge chair. She could not believe how mild the winters in Arizona were. Other than some steady rains and a few chilly days, the temperatures had been moderate. Today was warm enough that she felt comfortable in a pair of cotton stretch shorts and a long-sleeved shirt. It felt good to soak up some warm afternoon sun. She smiled as the baby moved its foot across her enlarged belly. "Once again, baby, you're waking up when I'm ready to take a nap." With her hand resting softly above the noticeable protrusion, she closed her eyes and fell into a light sleep. A short time later the sound of a car awoke her.

Opening her eyes in the direction of the sun, she could not make out the vehicle. It drove up slowly, as if the driver was unsure. The door opened and someone got out. Allison cursed the sun that showed the silhouette of a tall man, his movements barely familiar.

"Allison?"

Allison sat up. Her eyes instantly registered shock when she saw curly blonde hair and blue eyes. "Uh, Todd—is that you?" She struggled out of the lounge chair. "What are you doing here?"

He looked down at her stomach. "Why didn't you tell me?" The question hung between them as he watched Allison's eyes widen.

"Why is it any of your business?" Allison tried to act defiant. "How did you find out?"

Todd ran his fingers through his hair. "Judy."

Allison frowned. "Judy told you? I didn't know you guys were in touch."

He ignored the question.

Allison lifted her chin. "So you just show up? You couldn't have called first?"

"I didn't know if you would see me, and I wasn't going to take the chance that you would take off before I got here." A guilty expression on her face confirmed he had made the right decision by surprising her. "Did you and David get back together?"

Allison remembered how kind Todd had been that one night when, afterwards, she had told him about David.

"So—I was the revenge, huh?" Todd had asked. "Yeah." She paused, "Not very smart, was it?"

Now she could see the question in Todd's eyes—the hope that the baby wasn't his, and she understood. She had spent countless hours wishing the baby were David's, and crying that it wasn't. "I—," she crossed her arms in front of her, resting them on her belly as she gazed out at the desert. "David and I didn't get back together."

"Is the baby mine?" He saw her eyes widen with that 'deer in the headlights' look and was pretty sure he knew the answer, but he needed to hear her say it. "I'm flying back home the day after tomorrow. My parents are expecting me home for Christmas, they don't even know I'm here." His words were clipped and tense. When she didn't respond he added, "I'm enrolled at UND next semester, yet I may have a baby on the way. Do we have a lot to talk about or not?"

Allison shifted awkwardly and said "yes" without looking at him. She didn't see the effect her answer had on him, how he had to force his shoulders back and brace himself so the weight of his newfound responsibility didn't force him to the ground.

It wasn't as if it was a surprise to Todd. Every minute since Judy had casually mentioned Allison's pregnancy, Todd had felt certain the baby was his. "Why did you leave without telling me you were pregnant? Didn't you think I had a right to know?"

Allison's hesitation lingered, one second spilling into the next, until she finally opened up. "I was in denial the first several months. I couldn't believe I actually got pregnant my very first time. It didn't seem real. I didn't know what to do. When my father said we were moving, I was glad to get away from there. Nobody had to know. Not right away, anyway. And you barely knew me. I couldn't tell you, and frankly, I can't believe Judy did."

"I had a right to know." he said accusingly.

"Did you? We hardly know each other."

"That doesn't change the facts."

"The fact is—this is my baby, Todd—my responsibility. I'm not going to trap you with a child!

"You couldn't have trapped me any more than I trapped you. Neither one of us planned for that night to happen—but it happened to *both* of us."

Allison was embarrassed to ask the question, but it had been on her mind frequently throughout the pregnancy. "What about the condom? I saw you unwrapping it—you put it on. Didn't you?"

Todd had also thought about that. "I was drunk, and sloppy." He shrugged. "You were moving so fast. I wasn't thinking." He took a slow step toward her. "Look, I plan on doing the right thing now."

She swallowed, eyes narrowing a fraction. "What does that mean?"

With a hand squeezing the back of his neck, he turned away from her. When he finally pivoted back, his words were slow and deliberate. "I'm going to be there for the baby."

The strength of his words stopped her breath. Intensity gathered around them as she tried to think of something to say to discourage his strong conviction.

"When is the baby due?" he asked, beating her to the punch.

"January 17th."

"We don't have much time."

"For what?"

"I don't know!" Todd said sharply. "I'm angry with you for not telling me—I would've had time to think things through." He ran his fingers through his hair, looked at the ground, then back into her eyes. "I wasn't raised to bring a fatherless child into this world. I will be in this baby's life one way or another."

I'm gonna kill Judy, Allison thought, *my best friend? Yeah right.* But Allison took one look at this young man's tall stature and strong arms and felt some weight fall off her shoulders. The past year had been incredibly draining. Now, all of a sudden, the situation had completely changed. She wasn't alone. Her baby had a father. They barely knew each other, but right then, she didn't care—he wanted to be a father to their baby. "Can I get you a glass of iced tea?" The comment broke the tension, so her next words were lighter. "It's sun tea. I'll bet you haven't had that in awhile."

"I'm not sure I've ever had it. But I'd like some." He followed her into the trailer and, after she poured two glasses of iced tea, they sat down at the kitchen table. "How has the pregnancy been so far?"

"It's been fine. I had morning sickness for the first three months and during the move, but since then it's been good." She happened to glance at the clock then sat up in surprise. "I slept longer than I thought."

"Well, that explains it." Todd said nonchalantly.

"Explains what?"

Todd smiled. "That indented mark across your face from the lounge chair."

Allison's face registered shock at his blunt remark. "That's not very nice."

"I didn't say anything about the dried slobber at the corner of your mouth." Todd mumbled with a grin.

Allison reluctantly smiled while wiping her mouth with her sleeve. "I don't believe you said that. But it doesn't matter right now—you have to leave. My dad's going to be home soon—and you can't be here when he gets here."

"Can I drink my tea first?" Todd didn't wait for an answer as he downed the whole glass in several large gulps. "Okay, Allison," Todd's voice turned more serious, "I'll check into a hotel in Tucson and call you from there. Will you come see me tonight?"

"Yes." Allison quickly grabbed a piece of paper and pencil, jotted down her phone number and handed it to him. She looked at him awkwardly as she walked him to the door. "I'm, uh, a little overwhelmed right now and don't really know what to say—other than thanks for coming."

Todd wanted to give her some words of encouragement, but he too was overwhelmed. He left the trailer carrying a heavy burden of responsibility on his broad shoulders. His father's words echoed in his mind. *Honor, integrity, decency—without those, a man is nothing.*

"Well, Dad," Todd said to himself, "I wonder if this is what you had in mind."

———

Randall walked in the door. His work clothes were heavily dusted with lime and clay. "Hey, Sweetie." he said to Allison who was resting in the recliner, appearing to be nonchalantly reading a magazine. "How was your day off?"

"Hi, Dad." She put down the magazine. "It was fine. How was your day?"

"Challenging." Randall headed for his bedroom. "Where's Stacie?"

"She's at Spartan Manor—studying."

While Randall showered, Allison's nerves rapidly frayed. Fifteen minutes later he came out wearing a clean pair of jeans and a T-shirt.

She knew this conversation wasn't going to get any easier by delaying it. "Dad," she jumped in, "we need to talk."

Randall threw his head back and laughed. "Don't tell me—you're pregnant." He got serious when he saw the anxiety in Allison's demeanor. "I'm sorry. I've grown to have a strong dislike for conversations that start out like that."

Capitalizing on his jovial mood, she jumped in. "The baby's father came and visited me today."

Randall's brow creased as his eyes narrowed.

Allison took a deep breath. "He said he wants to be a part of the baby's life."

"I don't understand," Randall said suspiciously.

Allison shifted in her seat uncomfortably, remembering all too well the lies she had told. "Judy ran into him at college and mentioned I was pregnant. He asked a couple of questions and guessed that he might be the father."

"Wait a minute—you didn't even know his name, and yet he knew enough about you to put the pieces together?"

Allison bit her lower lip. "I sort of knew who he was."

Randall paced a few steps.

"Dad?" Allison felt tension build between them. "Dad?"

Randall stopped pacing and looked at Allison with steely blue eyes. "I don't believe this."

"I'm sorry, Dad."

"You're sorry?"

Allison felt she'd fall with the weight of the dejected look in her father's eyes. "I didn't know what to do."

Randall spoke deliberately. "You begin with the truth. I've always been able to count on you to tell the truth." He sighed before his next words came out in a tumble. "You told me you didn't know who the father was. Yet you knew who he was all along, and you weren't going to say anything?" He was yelling now. "I can't believe you would bring a child into the world without telling the father!"

"I'm sorry." It came out in a whine as her eyes filled with tears.

"So what are you going to do now?" he asked abruptly.

Allison wanted to run from this conversation. Her dad had never spoken to her in that tone before. She spoke in a jerky voice. "I don't know what I'm going to do. He's only here for a couple of days, so we'll try to figure it out."

"Great. Just great." Randall dropped his head and rubbed his forehead. "And who's 'he,' by the way? Does the father of my grandchild have a name?" Randall asked sarcastically.

"Todd." Allison took a breath. "Todd Waverly."

"Well, good. My grandchild has a dad after all." Randall headed out the door. "I need some fresh air," he called over his shoulder.

18

Several hours later, Allison stood in front of the bright red door with the gold plated number 217. She hesitated for a moment before knocking. She could hear Todd rushing to the door. He greeted her with a reassuring smile. She felt herself relax. "I brought you some dinner," she told him.

"Thanks." Todd took the containers out of her hands. "It smells great. I was getting hungry."

"I hope you like lasagna. And there's some garlic bread and a salad."

"I love lasagna." He closed the door after Allison stepped into the room. "Here—take off your jacket and have a seat."

She glanced around the room and spotted a single duffle bag in the only chair. "You travel light."

"I was in a hurry." He reached over and set the bag on the floor. "Would you like the bed or the chair?"

"I'll sit on the bed so you can eat at the table." Allison took off her jacket and sat on the edge of the bed while Todd took the foil off the plate of lasagna and bread, then took lids off Tupperware containers of salad and cake.

"Wow—chocolate cake, too!" He glanced over at Allison. "This is really nice. I haven't had a homemade meal like this since school started."

"How is school?" Her question was polite—her own regrets well hidden.

"I took the last of my finals yesterday." His tone was light as he cut into the lasagna with his fork. "I have one semester under my belt and I'm enrolled for next semester." His tone shifted slightly as he hesitated, staring at his plate. He felt intensity build within him as he thought about his first semester: his ice hockey team where he was currently second string, the general education classes he took while still not knowing what his major would be, his friends—and Judy. Aware of Allison's full attention on him, he turned toward her but didn't meet her eyes. "My situation has changed since I started college—and I don't know what to do about it."

Allison sat up straighter and crossed one leg under the other. "You can't give up college."

Todd was just about to take a bite when he hesitated, then glanced at Allison. Judy had mentioned her friend's educational goals. His voice was deep, but caring. "You did."

They both fell into their own thoughts and remained silent while Todd finished eating everything but the cake. After his last bite, he wiped his mouth and took a swig of soda before asking, "How did it go with your dad?"

"It was okay." Allison swallowed, and her eyes started watering. "My dad is really mad at me."

Todd didn't know what to say. "Do you want to talk about it?"

Allison swallowed again as her eyes filled with tears. "I'm sorry. It's just that...." She closed her eyes for a long moment. "I used to always tell the truth—no matter what the consequences. And, since this happened, I haven't been honest with anyone."

Imagining the burden Allison had been carrying these past months, Todd swallowed his own anger toward her for not telling him the truth. "What happened?"

"I lied to him." She bowed her head. "When I told him I was pregnant, I said I had no idea who the father was. I destroyed his trust in me."

Todd stood up, then sat next to Allison on the bed. "I should've been there when you told your dad."

Allison heard the compassion in his tone and looked up into his big blue eyes. "Have you ever hurt so much that you just want to run from the pain, but every direction you turn just brings a different pain?" She blushed. "My broken heart led me to that party, and the pain led me into your arms. I'm sorry."

Todd nodded. "I'm sorry, too."

They sat in silence till Allison asked, "Do your parents know?" It was a combination of a whimper and a whisper.

Todd shook his head. "No."

"How do you think they'll react when you tell them?"

He took a deep breath before answering. "They'll be disappointed."

But they'll expect us to get married before the baby is born.

"Listen Allison, we need to figure out a way to do this—together."

"We don't even know each other."

His voice was deep, unapologetic. "We'll have to learn."

Her voice trembled as she asked, "What does that mean?"

Todd wasn't prepared to carry this conversation further. In reality, he knew he wouldn't be prepared for about five more years—after he finished college—after he found a good job—after he'd had time to figure out some things about himself—but mostly—after he found the woman he wanted to spend the rest of his life with. With a slight shake of his head, he knew none of that was going to happen. Instead, what he was about to do made his head throb and his stomach weak. "I won't be an absentee father."

"Okay." With her brows furrowed, her reply was more of a question than an admission.

Todd felt momentarily paralyzed, stalling for time and yet equally determined to get this conversation over with. "I don't think you understand what I'm trying to say." He took a slow deep breath and turned toward her. "We should get married. I can't have you raising my child on your own."

Allison gulped.

Get a grip, girl, and do what's best for the baby.

In an attempt to do something other than dwell on what he had just said, Todd reached over for the cake. "The dinner was really good, by the way. Did you make it?"

Allison smiled. "I made the lasagna, my dad made the salad, and Stacie made the cake."

"Who's Stacie?"

Allison grinned at the absurdity of the situation. "This is so unreal. You mention us getting married, but we know practically nothing about each other. Are you sure we should do this?"

"No," he said sincerely, "but can you think of a better solution?"

With the argument she'd just had with her dad still painfully in her mind, Allison felt even more vulnerable than she had before. Options seemed few.

Todd is my baby's father. Maybe we can make it work.

Even though she didn't respond directly to his marriage statement, there was an immediate understanding between them that her next statement meant a 'yes.' "Stacie is my youngest sister. She's a sophomore. My other sister is Vanessa. She's living in Los Angeles with a friend for her senior year."

"See that?" Todd grinned. "We're already getting to know each other. I have an older sister, Cathy. She's ten years older and was supposed to be an only child. I'm a mistake."

That brought a smile to Allison's face. The way he said it showed no signs of neglect from his parents. "Where does she live?"

"In Seattle. She's married, with four children. Her husband's an engineer. She's a homemaker, and I hardly ever see her."

"And your parents?"

"They live in Minot. My dad will be retiring in a few years from the Air Force. My Mom is a nurse who works part-time. They're both in their early 60's." The mention of his parents brought Todd to a standstill once again. He put his fork down, forcing out his words. "If we're going to do this—get married I mean—we might as well do it before the baby is born."

Allison gulped down her fears and held back tears.

This isn't the way it's supposed to be.

But with the baby's arrival only a few weeks away, she knew there was a lot to work out. "Where would we live?"

"I don't know. Maybe if I can get a job here—I mean in Tucson, it'd be okay. We could give it a try."

"Really? You think you could live in Tucson?"

Todd looked stunned, but spoke lightly. "I lived in Tucson for three years when I was in elementary school, and my dad was stationed at Davis Monthan Air Force Base. I have fond memories of Tucson. Besides, I've moved around so much, this feels like home about as much as any other place."

Allison felt relieved. "Are you sure about this—about us?"

Todd forced a smile. "Yeah. Besides, you're everything I'd want for the mother of my baby."

Allison cocked her head quizzically.

Todd's eyes softened. "You're beautiful, smart—and you have a great swing."

"What?"

His smile widened. "Softball. I was at your game. I saw how you hit that ball."

Allison smiled in return. "Is that an important trait?"

"Yes. I happen to know from experience that you're clumsy around stairs. But it's reassuring to know you're good at a sport. You know—traits to pass on to the little one."

Allison flushed at the reminder of their night together. "Todd, I know nothing about you.

He leaned forward in his chair. "I'm here."

Allison smiled. "Yes—you're here. So what would you think about coming over for dinner tomorrow night? I'm sure my dad will want to meet you."

Todd nodded resignedly. "Sure."

"Six-thirty?"

"I'll be there."

"I get off work at four. You can come early if you want."

"I might. But I think I should spend some time in Tucson—take a look at the job market." He scooped up a bite of cake and held a forkful in front of Allison. "Would you like some cake?"

With a grin, Allison nodded. As Todd fed it to her, he captured and held Allison's blue eyes with his own, which were just inches away. As she bit into the rich chocolate cake, Todd asked her, "Will you marry me?"

With her mouth closed tightly, Allison laughed in response to Todd's teasing gaze, and then nodded her head yes.

"Good," he whispered. "Because under the circumstances, that's the best proposal I could come up with."

Allison's eyes instantly filled with tears. "I woke up this morning just like I have every morning since I found out I was pregnant: worried about *my* baby's future. But tonight I'm going to go to bed knowing that *our* baby is going to have a good life." A tear slid down her cheek. "Thank you."

Todd kissed her gently, but quickly—a kiss to seal their agreement. With that one kiss, they knew they had a long road ahead of them. Between low-income jobs, setting up a home, medical bills, and future child-care expenses, they were starting their young adult lives with a deficit coming their way at full speed.

———

Grateful for the slow day at 'Joe's Stop for Food and Gas', Allison sat at the register with her feet propped up on an upside-down trashcan beneath the counter. As long as nobody asked for cigarettes, she found she was able to handle most of the customers while remaining seated on the barstool. She closed a magazine after reading the story on J.R. and the rest of the Ewing clan, rested her hands on her belly, gazed through the glass door, and let her mind wander.

How can I marry him? I don't even know him! Is he a nice guy? He could be a chauvinist, a slob, a drug abuser.

Probably not. He was so sweet to me, so understanding when I told him about David. And his truck was clean—spotless, actually. That's got to mean something. He's Jim's cousin. I've known Jim practically all of my life. Jim's a nice guy. They've inherited some of the same genes. That's good. Is he responsible? A hard worker? He's so cute, and that dimple!

The bells sounded, signaling another customer. Out of the corner of her eye, she saw a flash of pink sweater and a blue baseball cap dash behind the cereal aisle. Bolting upright, she stretched her neck in order to get a better view. A flash of pink and the tip of a black boot rounded the opposite end of the shelves before Allison had a chance to follow the movement. Chills coursed down her back and her heartbeat picked up. "Hello? Can I help you?"

Nothing, no sound. Getting up off the stool, Allison nervously looked at the alarm button near the register. A swirl of pink flew into the air, arms raised. A booming voice yelled, "Surprise!"

"Aaahhhh." Allison jumped, frightened by the intruder. But beneath the moment of terror was the obvious recognition of the loud, obnoxious voice. "You scared the hell out of me, Vanessa."

Vanessa peeked out from behind the counter and hurried toward her sister. "Lordy girl, you've gotten big as a cow."

Allison had just about been ready to give Vanessa a hug. Instead, her arms dropped down to her stomach, her lower lip seemed to double in size as it jutted outward, and her nostrils flared. She took a few quick breaths that preceded an onslaught of tears.

"Oh, Allison, I'm sorry." Vanessa's voice sounded sincere, although a little impatient.

Allison found herself crying while enveloped in fuzzy pink chenille. A flowery perfume hit her sinuses, ending her sobs with a couple of sneezes.

"Yuck." Vanessa stepped back. The expression on Vanessa's face as she looked down at the snot on her sweater made Allison giggle so hard her belly bounced up and down. She found herself supporting the weight with her hands below her stomach.

Vanessa raised her eyebrows. "A bit moody, are we?"

Allison laughed even harder. "Very. I seem to be either laughing or crying lately. I don't know what's wrong with me."

"Maybe you should see a doctor."

That comment obviously struck another funny bone, as Allison continued laughing. But as Allison's replacement, Jill, walked in the door, Allison's giggles quietly subsided. A few minutes later, Allison and Vanessa walked to the car. Vanessa had already explained that Dad had dropped her off at the store.

"Can you drive?" Allison took the keys out of her purse and tossed them to Vanessa. "My back hurts and my feet are killing me," she explained.

Snatching the keys in mid-air, Vanessa asked, "So what's up with Dad? Man, he was grouchy when he picked me up at the airport."

"Grrr."

"What kind of answer is that?"

"The kind that says the last two days have been more than I can handle."

"How's that?"

"I'm getting married."

"You're *what?*"

"Yes—married. My knight in shining armor appeared at my doorstep yesterday. He's going to do the right thing by 'our' baby."

"Our? You mean he's the baby's father?"

"The one and only."

Vanessa laughed. "Whoa. This is too much. But why is Dad upset? You'd think he'd be happy about it."

"He probably would've been if I had told him I knew who the father was from the beginning."

"Wow, Allison, you told a major fibber."

"Yeah, major."

"When do I get to meet my future brother-in-law?"

"Tonight—the same time Dad and Stacie meet him. Todd's coming for dinner."

"Cool."

"Yeah, cool." Allison repeated without enthusiasm as she sunk down in the seat.

Allison took one last look in the mirror. There was no way around it—she felt she was past the 'glowing stage' of her pregnancy and, in these final weeks, was looking like an overripe melon. She was at least thankful the black tunic she had chosen for the occasion offered a little sophistication. When she heard the knock at the front door, she looked at her stomach. "Well baby, your daddy is right on time, and he's about to meet your grandpa. Wish me luck."

Vanessa stormed in. "He's here—and you are one lucky momma, Al—he's a hunk."

Before Allison had a chance to respond, Stacie walked in behind Vanessa and smiled at Allison's trepidation. "You look beautiful, Allison." Stacie said.

Allison half-smiled in appreciation. "Thanks. And thank you—both of you, for making dinner."

"Well, with those bags you had under your eyes," Vanessa said, "it was obvious you needed a nap." She took a step closer to Allison and smiled sincerely before Allison delivered a snide comment in return. "Stacie's right. You really do look beautiful."

"Okay—whatever—let's go already." Allison straightened her back as much as possible and followed her sisters out the door.

An hour later, as they were passing around the strawberry cheesecake, Allison sat in silence as everyone else laughed at Todd's jokes. Somehow, he had won over the entire family. He was down-to-earth, completely relaxed, and he exuded a mix of quick wit, intelligence and undeniable charm. Allison was also won over by him, but she knew her dad's approval of Todd didn't alter any of the tension between her and her dad.

"It's great timing that my little niece is going to be here before I have to leave." Vanessa said cheerily.

"Niece?" Todd asked. "Is it a girl?"

Allison shook her head. "I don't know. Vanessa just wants it to be a girl."

"Oh, it's a girl. Allison is carrying low. If the baby is low, it's a girl." Vanessa took a bite of cheesecake and mumbled, "Or maybe it's the other way around." She shrugged her shoulders. "When are you guys getting married anyway? There's not a lot of time left."

All eyes were drawn to Todd. He answered while looking at Allison. "We hadn't talked about the date yet. But maybe we could get married right away."

Allison knew he wanted the wedding to take place before the baby came. But she felt it was too soon. Without even looking at her dad, she could feel his disappointment. "Fine. That'd be fine with me."

"Yippee." Vanessa flew around the table hugging everyone, seeming completely oblivious to the tension in the room.

Two weeks later, after a 'hit and miss' holiday season of a little laughter and lots of tension and frayed nerves, Allison and Todd stood before the justice of the peace in downtown Tucson. Todd's parents didn't make it, but they promised they would visit soon after the baby was born. Todd understood that what they really needed was a little extra time to get used to the changes.

Allison had found an ivory satin two-piece dress at a second hand maternity store. The dress's crowning achievements were a high, flowing neckline, tapered sleeves that ended in diagonal points over her hands, and a long draping skirt. Fresh gardenias clipped to one side of her upswept hair added an exotic flare.

Clad in black pants and a charcoal-colored jacket borrowed from Randall, Todd smiled at Allison and leaned over to whisper, "You look beautiful."

So far so good.

Allison thought. She managed a slight smile in appreciation, but her nerves were shot. She looked at her sisters and thought Vanessa was downright sexy in a shimmering gold dress which, thankfully, Todd seemed immune to, and Stacie looked precious in a lavender dress. When she looked over at her dad, she saw tears in his eyes. When their eyes met, the look that passed between them said it all: hurt and disappointment, but ultimately love.

The ceremony lasted eight minutes. A few pictures were taken in the judge's chambers before the wedding party left the room and went outside. Standing in the courtyard, beneath the exotic tiled dome of the courthouse, Vanessa snapped several pictures of Allison and Todd before a passerby offered to take a few pictures of all of them together. The last picture was taken by Todd, one of the three sisters and Randall standing side-by side under an archway, when suddenly Allison's first contraction came on strong enough to leave no doubt.

"The baby's coming," she announced simply.

Born a little after 4 a.m. the following morning, Jason Robert Waverly missed his parent's wedding by less than twelve hours.

19

Towards the end of July, a year and a half later, Randall rushed through the front door of the trailer and yelled toward the back, "Are you ready, Stacie?"

"Almost," she answered from her bedroom. She put her sketchpad and charcoal pencils inside her oversized leather briefcase—last year's Christmas gift from Randall, then dangled her purse over her shoulder and grabbed her suitcase. She was about to walk out the door before she turned back, hesitating.

I can't go a week without them.

Swinging the briefcase under her right arm, she hurried over to the desk and pulled a pack of Marlboro's out from under a magazine in the bottom drawer. She put the cigarettes in a zippered pocket in the briefcase and left the room.

While throwing clothes into a suitcase, Randall shouted to Stacie in the other room. "Can you call Allison? Tell her she has to be ready to go as soon as we get there."

"Okay."

Allison hung up the phone as Todd walked into the bedroom and asked, "Who was that?"

Lately, Allison thought, *the tone of his voice always seemed to be mocking her or edged with anger.*

She wondered how long it had been that way and wondered if her voice seemed that way to him also. "It was Stacie. Dad had to go to work for a meeting this morning, and it ran late. He wanted to make sure we'll be ready to go as soon as they get here."

"I'm not surprised he had Stacie call," Todd said. "I think he's caught on by now that your clock runs a good fifteen minutes slower than everyone else's."

Ignoring the barb, Allison folded the few remaining tops she had just pulled from the dryer and stacked everything into the open suitcase in an orderly manner. Out of the corner of her eye, she could see a mocking grin on Todd's face. She turned and faced him. "What?"

"Nothing," he said innocently. "It's just that I've never seen you be so neat with anything."

Allison studied Todd for a moment, unable to pinpoint what she was feeling. The only thing she knew for sure was that his eyes were not as blue as they used to be, his curly blonde hair was not as soft, and that dimple on his left cheek did not seem as cute as it once did. She ignored this remark, just as she had the last one. She did not have the time or energy to participate in her share of the endless bickering. She zipped up the suitcase, grabbed the handle and carried it past Todd and into the living room of their small apartment. Setting it down by the front door, Allison mentally went over the packing list she should have made.

Todd followed behind her. "I'm going to wake up Jason. I'd like to spend a little time with my son before you guys leave me."

It was the way he enunciated "leave me" that prompted Allison to count to three before she commented. With barely controlled anger, she blurted out—"is that what all this is about? You've been pouting for a week, and it's making me crazy. You could've come with us!"

"I don't want to go with you." Todd had perfected the art of yelling quietly so as not to wake their son. But his distorted facial expressions picked up the slack. "I've been working my butt off for two years—"

"A year and a half," Allison interrupted.

Exasperated, Todd shook his head, "—for a year and a half without a break. I don't want to go with your family for my one vacation."

"What about last year in L.A.? We had a nice time. We had fun at Disneyland."

"I don't consider a trip with your family—to see Vanessa graduate from high school, a vacation. And spending money on Disneyland when Jason was only six months old wasn't the best use of our money. Now you'll be spending the money we don't have on another vacation that I don't want!"

"But I do!" She struggled to keep from yelling. "You're not the only one who works around here. Besides Jason, I watch two other kids in this small apartment. I'm chasing them all day long and I'm tired." She fought back the tears that always seemed right under the surface. "Besides—this isn't a typical vacation. It's my grandparents' fiftieth wedding anniversary. And Dad is paying our airfare—offered to pay for yours too. So what are you complaining about?"

Todd ran his fingers through his sunny blonde hair. "Just forget it." He walked past Allison toward Jason's room, but stopped and turned around. "Since your dad's running late, call him back and tell him he doesn't have to pick you up. I'll take you to the airport."

Vanessa looked at her watch for the twelfth time in the last hour. Patience, as far as she was concerned, was not a virtue—it was a pain in the ass waste of her precious time. In fact, she'd been down right crabby ever since her dad had told her she'd have to wait at Tucson International Airport, after flying in from Los Angeles, until they could all fly together to North Dakota. She heard her dad's voice in her head; *it's only a two-hour layover. I would barely get you home, then we'd have to turn right back around.* "Thanks a lot, Dad," she muttered sarcastically as she shoved the issue of 'Cosmo' she had just read cover-to-cover into her large black leather handbag. She figured she'd pass it on to Allison to give her something 'hip' to read.

Leaning back in the stiff chair, she stretched her legs out in front of her. After two minutes she checked her watch again, sprang out of the chair, and decided to wait for her family at the entrance.

She walked past the security booth and down a corridor decorated with artwork done by first graders from a local elementary school. She chose to ignore the display—just as she had the other four times she had passed this way while stretching her legs. A moment later she stood near the main entrance, looking out a window next to the large sliding glass doors. It wasn't long before a smile brightened her face when she saw her family. Suddenly giddy with excitement, she nibbled lightly at her melon painted fingernails and giggled at the sight of her adorable little nephew dressed in khaki shorts and a U of A tee-shirt. Quick visual impressions of the rest of the family registered: *Dad looks pretty good, fit and tanned, Todd and Allison look like the typical all American—but very young—family except Allison looks a little pale, and Stacie—oh my God!* Wondering what had happened to her angelic little sister, Vanessa did a double take. *What's with the whacked out hair and the heavy make-up?*

Stepping back a bit, Vanessa watched them enter the airport and head toward the escalators. "Yoohoo," she called. They all turned around while Vanessa caught up with them and greeted them with hugs, high-fives, and saying *Islanskur Matur.*

She smiled brightly at Jason, who recoiled shyly into his Grandpa's shoulder. "Do you know what *Islanskur Matur* means, cutie pie?" Vanessa asked her nephew.

Jason shook his head no.

"It means Icelandic Power. You've only got 25% of that running through your veins, little one. But don't worry, that's plenty."

"How was the wait, sis?" Allison asked in a bratty manner.

In her sweetest voice possible, since she was still trying to get Jason's attention, Vanessa responded, "Up yours, Al."

"Off to a good start already." Randall grumbled as he gestured for the group to get moving toward the ticket counter.

Todd leaned in close to Allison. "I'm gonna get going."

Allison turned around, eyes wide. "You're not going to wait until we board?"

"No. I want to get the car into the shop. If I get there early enough, I might be able to get it back before the day is out."

Allison reached for Jason. "Say bye-bye to Daddy."

Todd leaned over and gave Allison a quick kiss, then smiled brightly at his son. "You be a good boy for Mom." He kissed his son on the forehead. "Daddy loves you." Todd said goodbye to the rest of the family and headed toward the exit.

Allison watched him walk away. His strong build and good looks made women's heads turn wherever he went. She remembered the different emotions that knowledge had invoked in her over the past eighteen months—insecurity, pride, and now the worst of all, indifference.

What's happening to us? How do we fix it?

As they got off the plane in Minneapolis, where they had a two hour layover, Randall carried Jason, who had been tugging at his ears and crying off and on for the past hour.

"I'm hungry," Vanessa said. "Can we have lunch?"

"That's fine with me," Randall said after Stacie and Allison nodded in agreement. "But I promised Jason I'd take him for a walk as soon as we got off the plane. Decide on a restaurant, and Jason and I will meet you there in a little bit."

At the restaurant, Stacie pointed to a large, empty, corner table. Allison hung her purse over a chair and sat down. "My poor little sweetie. I did everything I could think of to help him pop his ears. I hope Dad's doing okay with him."

"I'm sure he's fine." Vanessa slithered into the chair next to Allison. "That kid of yours is so cute. It's good to see something good came out of your messy predicament. I'll never forget the day you and Todd got married. Geez, I'm still surprised Dad showed up."

"That was a long time ago." Allison barked irritably.

"Hey, look at it this way," Vanessa continued, "that baby of yours has worked wonders for your relationship with Dad."

"Mind your own business, Vanessa."

"Well it has, hasn't it? Dad forgave you for all those lies you told him."

Allison spoke in a controlled whisper. "Yes, Vanessa, Dad and I are fine."

Finally.

Vanessa looked at Stacie critically. "Stacie, I've been biting my tongue ever since I first saw you, and I can't take it any longer. When did you start wearing all that makeup? I think your foundation and lipstick weigh more than you do."

"Spoken from the drama queen herself," Allison piped in.

Vanessa gave Allison a dirty look. "Well, excuse me, Allison, but you're obviously slipping in your self-designated mother role." Vanessa took a sip of her iced tea, then offered up an excuse for her rudeness. "We only have each other for the advice we should be getting from Mom." She turned back to Stacie. "I'm sorry, Stacie. I just think you're cuter without it."

Stacie got up. "I'll be right back." She headed to the restroom.

Vanessa glanced over at Allison, whose eyes were focused on the salt and pepper shaker. "Hey, Al" Vanessa waited for a response. "Allison, listen to me. Stacie's smoking."

Allison looked up. "What?"

"I saw the pack of cigarettes in Stacie's bag a minute ago. Can you imagine how silly she must look smoking those things? She's so tiny. What do we do?"

Out of the corner of her eye, Allison saw Randall and Jason enter the restaurant. "Nothing right now. We'll have to talk about it later."

After flying in a small shuttle plane to Grand Forks, they rented a van and drove to Mountain, where they began the 'August the Deuce' celebration and enjoyed Amma and Afi's anniversary party.

Before the weekend ended, the three sisters went for a private walk in Mountain, where Allison and Vanessa confronted Stacie about the cigarettes. Stacie assured them it was no big deal to quit smoking and threw her cigarettes in the trash in front of her sisters.

On the same walk, Allison and Stacie learned all about Mitch, a junior in college Vanessa had met months earlier at a frat party. Despite her insistence that the two were just friends, it was obvious to Allison and Stacie that Vanessa would prefer it if Mitch would drop his current girlfriend.

And on the same walk, Stacie and Vanessa learned from Allison that getting married at the age of eighteen, because you're pregnant, to a guy you don't really even know—or love—isn't the easiest way to begin a marriage.

No kidding, they both thought.

They spent two days in Bismarck, visiting friends and their favorite places, they drove by their old house, stopped in at the hardware store, the church, and the nursing home Mrs. Deiko now lived in. It was an emotional visit for all of them.

They boarded the plane coming back feeling much closer to their relatives. But more importantly, they had managed to chip away a little distance between themselves.

Part III

20

Strong winds blew in dark thick clouds, casting shadows across the desert as Gregory headed back toward Tucson. When he reached the dangling 'Kiser's Ranchita' sign he smiled, visualizing Helen painting the flowers. As he turned out of the drive, the first fat raindrops came smashing down on his truck in a violent greeting.

He didn't want to leave. At this moment there was no other place in the world he'd rather be. He forced himself to keep his hands on the wheel, his foot on the gas, and to keep measuring the distance between himself and that spirited young woman.

Driving eight miles through a pouring rain had seemed like a hundred, the pull was so strong to go back to her. He rationalized reasons why he shouldn't go back: he had just met her, he did not want to mislead her, it was a vulnerable time for her.

And she told me to leave! Maybe she wouldn't want me to come back!

But he could not help himself. Surprised at the runoff of water already building on the hard soil, he carefully turned the car around. He shook his head, knowing he was a damn fool, but nothing could wipe the smile off his face.

Helen had turned off the shower, opened the bathroom door, and reached for a towel when she heard a car drive up. At lightning speed, she dried her feet, wrapped the towel around her, ran to the other end of the trailer, and peeked through the window. The sight of Gregory's truck put an instant smile on her face. Running back to the bedroom, she jerked the towel off her body, wrapped her wet hair in it, then reached for her yellow chenille robe.

The storm was delivering a steady downpour as Gregory pulled up to Spartan Manor. He parked as close as possible and jumped carefully from paver to paver while running to the door. He hesitated when he reached the door. Before he had a chance to knock, the door swung open. Her face, framed by a fluffy blue towel, looked at him questioningly. Their eyes met and held each other's, searching.

Smoothing his hair back did little to ease his tension. In order to be heard above the splattering of raindrops against the aluminum trailer, he spoke loudly. "The roads were pretty bad." Grimacing, he looked down at the concrete slab, embarrassed by his lack of courage. He exhaled a slow breath and looked back up to meet her eyes. "The roads aren't that bad. Do you want me to go?"

"No." She spoke the word in a soft whisper while she shook her head at the same time. They exchanged a silent, knowing look, but her next words de-emphasized the intensity of their emotions. "It's nice to have company." She spoke loudly. "This storm is pretty bad. It's good you're not driving in it." She moved aside. "Come on in."

He pointed at his shoes, then quickly took them off and set them by the steps. He followed her inside and closed the door behind them.

She walked to the back and brought out a clean towel. As he said 'thanks' and patted his face and arms dry, she pulled the towel off of her head. Her long wet hair fell in a wave against her back. "I'm going to get dressed. I'll be just a minute. Please, have a seat."

A few minutes later she walked out of her bedroom and saw him sitting at the table, thumbing through a September 1948 issue of *Flying* magazine.

Without moving his head, he looked up as she walked through the kitchen. His heart jumped at the sight of her. She was wearing tan pedal pushers and a navy blue top tied at the waist. Although the clothing was flattering, revealing slender curves, Gregory had enjoyed seeing her in stained work clothes and a bathrobe, so he thought he would likely find her attractive in anything.

To avoid yelling, she walked up beside him to speak close to his ear. She leaned in, close enough to feel heat emanating off the curve of his neck. A mixture of cologne, freshly fallen rain, and sweat combined in an erotic scent; she breathed again, deeply. Her voice came out in a deeper, raspier tone as she pointed at the magazine and said, "Dad had his last airplane listed for sale in the classified section."

Her damp hair brushed the nape of his neck, sending a shiver throughout his torso. With her warm breath still lingering, he had to force himself to pay attention to what she was telling him. He flipped the pages to the back of the magazine as she reached over his shoulder, turned a couple of pages in the classified section, and pointed. He silently read, *CUB J3, Lycoming 65, dual ignition, new exhaust stacks, fuselage and engine, cowling complete; new engine mount, tank and tachometer.* He skipped to the end of the ad. *$1700.00. Earl Kiser.*

Crooking his finger, he motioned her to bend down so he could speak into her ear. "That must have been hard for him, knowing that was the last plane he would ever own." They both felt it, the warm words brushing against skin, the closeness of their bodies. But they steeled themselves, not letting it show.

"It was. He loved that plane, but he was getting weaker all the time. When he said good-bye to the Piper Cub, he said good-bye to flying."

Gregory closed the magazine, then got up to set it back in the rack next to the phonograph stand. He turned around and faced Helen, then leaned toward her again to speak. "I didn't mean to drop the ball on the conversation earlier, but the truth is—" He stopped. "That was rude of me. I'm sorry. The thing is—" He shook his head and let out a slow breath. "I've been making decisions lately that are going to hurt others. I haven't figured it all out yet."

She spoke loudly enough for him to hear. "It's okay. You don't have to say anything. You came out here to meet my dad and—I'm glad."

He leaned back in an attempt to read her expression, then relaxed on seeing the warmth of her eyes.

Leaning forward, she stood on tiptoe. "It looks like this storm could last awhile. Would you like to change into some dry clothes? I kept a few things of my dad's. They might fit you."

Gregory smiled in appreciation. "My luggage is in the truck. Would it be all right if I got cleaned up?" She mouthed a 'yes,' so he signaled he was going outside. He stepped onto the porch, slipped off his socks, rolled up his pants, and dashed for the truck as the rain continued pouring down.

Stepping outside, Helen took a deep breath of fresh air and marveled at the heightened colors the rainstorm brought out in the typically dry desert. An impulsive urge to bolt off into the storm made her eyes twinkle with realization. She felt a joyful sense of being alive, a feeling she hadn't felt in many months.

Maybe it's okay to smile for awhile, to feel things other than pain and loss. That would be nice.

As Gregory bounded back onto the porch, Helen once again marveled at his tall, lean, muscular build. The shed had seemed so much smaller with him in it, and now—thoughts of him being in the small shower made her grin.

He followed her to the back of the trailer and watched her open a built in drawer across from the bathroom. She pulled out a clean towel and washcloth. On the outside of the door, she took her wet towel off the hook and hung up the dry one, then handed him the washcloth. She stepped into the bathroom, grabbed her hairbrush and lotion, stepped back into her bedroom and—with a mischievous smile—she motioned him inside and yelled "good luck!"

Perplexed by her choice of words, he tilted his head and eyed her questioningly. But one look into the bathroom gave him his answer, and he started laughing. He turned around and saw her laughing too. "How am I supposed to fit in there?" he yelled. "I'm as big as the whole bathroom!"

She turned and walked back into the living area, leaving him to figure it out.

He stepped into the bathroom in front of the small sink and stood next to the toilet. Above the sink was a small, mirrored cabinet. On his left were the shower knobs, the showerhead stuck out above the cabinet in the corner. There was very little standing room.

During his shower, the downpour changed to light drizzle. Less than fifteen minutes later he stood near the kitchen, watching Helen as she chopped celery. The front door was latched open and a cool breeze circled throughout the trailer.

"Do you like tuna sandwiches?" Helen asked as she continued chopping.

"Yes." He took a step closer to her, standing right in front of the stove. "Can I help?"

Eyeing him suspiciously, she asked, "Have you ever helped in the kitchen before?"

With a quick laugh, he replied, "I don't know. Not that I can remember, but I'm sure I could do something."

She smiled. "There are apples in the fridge, and a bag of chips in that cupboard." She pointed over her shoulder. As he moved past her, she scooped up the celery and put it in with the tuna. "How was the shower?" She grinned with amusement.

"I managed." Gregory gave her a look that dared her to think otherwise. "At least I did until I dropped the soap on the floor." Enjoying Helen's surprised laughter, Gregory continued. "It was a challenge getting the soap off of the floor when I couldn't bend over to get it."

"How did you?"

"I had to sit on the toilet seat with my head scrunched up under the sink while fishing around for it on the floor." He chuckled when Helen broke out in laughter again. He opened the small fridge and reached for a couple of red apples. "Your old trailer was a lot smaller than this one. Did it have a shower in it?"

Helen stirred the tuna with salad dressing and put it on bread with lettuce and tomato. "No, Dad rigged up a shower outside. He attached a curtain to the shed that circled around a big metal bucket. We would stand in it and wash up using a garden hose."

They sat down at the table and began eating. "Were you here in the winter?"

"Sometimes we'd fly in and stay for about a week over the holiday break. During those times we would heat up water on the gas stove and sponge bath."

While eating, they talked about college and their studies until a sudden hailstorm ended all conversation. Helen ran to the door, unlatched the hook and, with a yank, pulled the screen door closed.

They watched the brief hailstorm while a backdrop of sunlight illuminated the surrounding mountains. It only lasted a matter of minutes and was followed by a heavy rain that lasted for almost an hour. Few words were spoken during the storm; neither Helen nor Gregory felt the desire to compete with the thunderous sound of raindrops against the aluminum siding. When the rain subsided, they stepped outside. The colors stood out vividly: brilliant blue sky, the green cacti and shrubs, the soil that now appeared a rich chestnut color, and a full rainbow arched against the northwest sky.

For Helen, everything in life felt perfect in this moment. The dream surfaced once again, but she saw it more clearly this time: a beautiful rainbow, this man's eyes looking at her with such compassion, and a gift that he gave to her.

But what was the gift? Was it really a gift of compassion—or something else? That part of her dream was still out of reach.

Gregory gazed across the colorful rain-soaked desert and felt this was the best day of his life. He took in a noticeably deep breath; the sound of it filled the silence.

"That's the creosote bush." Helen told him. "When it rains, the wet leaves give off that wonderful, fresh scent." There was a subtle change in the air as she felt, rather than saw, him looking at her. When she turned and met his gaze, her heart filled with the warmth of his eyes.

He reached for her hand. Neither was surprised at the heat their contact delivered. "I have never felt this comfortable with anyone in my life. And— considering we've just barely met, well—it's strange."

She was touched by his words. "It's this place. I think there's something magical about it that helps us get to the heart of matters. Every time I come here, I feel as if life takes on a different perspective. I come here with all these layers and masks. But I get rid of them one by one, like a snake shedding its skin. I get to what's real, and I find that love and truth are all that matters."

Gregory tilted his head thoughtfully. "Maybe it is this place." He reached out and gently caressed her cheek, "Or maybe it's you that's magical."

She closed her eyes and leaned her head in closer to feel his caress. She hoped he would open up to what was bothering him, but he remained silent. When she opened her eyes, she knew it was time to confront the pain that she saw in his.

"Are you all right?" she barely whispered. Feeling a certain peace over his change of mood, she did not regret the question. Honesty and forthrightness had always been mainstays of her personality.

Resting his hand in the nook of her neck, his expression turned serious. "This place is so beautiful right now, so peaceful. It's the exact opposite of the situation I'm headed for."

She could see he was hurting. "Would you like to go for a walk?"

"Yes," he said without hesitation. As she went inside the trailer to get her shoes, he went to the truck to get a dry pair.

They walked down the dirt road and maneuvered around an occasional puddle. "It's so quiet here—not a soul in sight." He looked around. "I've been—I *was*—engaged for more than two years." He looked over and saw Helen's surprised expression. "Just this morning, I called off the wedding." He clasped his hands together tightly. "Over the phone."

He saw her eyebrows rise in surprise, but she remained silent. "Never in a million years did I think I could be so cruel," he admitted in a weary voice.

"What happened?"

"Sandra, my fiancee, visited me over the 4th of July. The visit left us both feeling strained."

Strained? He thought. *She complained about everything: the heat, the dirt, the lack of greenery, the shops and the restaurants she felt weren't adequate.*

"After she left, I threw myself back into studying, yet I couldn't deny what was bothering me. I didn't want to marry her. I was going to break off the engagement when I got home, but when she called this morning, going on and on about wedding plans I—I had to stop her."

Helen looked down at his hand, started to reach for it, then pulled back. "I'm sorry for both of you, but are you sure this isn't a case of cold feet?"

Gregory nodded sadly. "Not a chance."

"Then it will probably be better for both of you in the long run."

"But I'm not just letting her down—" He stopped and turned to face her. "I'm letting down my whole family, my parents, grandparents, and her family too."

"You don't think they'll understand? These things happen." She watched him as he paced a few steps, his anxiety apparent. "Gregory, is there more to this?" His brilliant dark eyes connected with hers. This time she did reach for his right hand while his left clenched the back of his neck.

Her touch brought such comfort it surprised him; it soothed the tension. "Yes, there's more to it." With her hand still in his, he started walking again. "I can't seem to remember making a conscious decision to go into politics. It was simply what was always expected of me. My mother comes from a long line of politicians. You may be familiar with the name Halborough."

"Oh." Helen said in recognition of the respected political family.

"I've already let my parents down by not continuing my education at a prestigious college." Gregory shrugged, "They relented—allowing me this one small rebellion. But until I had time away on my own, I hadn't realized that Sandra was my parent's choice—not mine. This is going to be another blow to them."

They walked in silence until Helen spoke. "How did Sandra take it?"

He considered it for a moment, as if he hadn't thought about Sandra's reaction. "She took it well, actually. She was silent for a while, then suggested we talk about it when I get back."

"Don't you find that a little odd?"

"No, surprisingly I don't. I think she was probably relieved. I think she probably felt the same way, but hadn't known how to stop the plans that were already in motion."

"So you're more concerned at this point about your parents' reaction."

"My parents won't be as understanding, or as reasonable. They have my life and my political career planned for me: I get married, finish law school, then join my uncle's firm. Around the age of thirty, I run for a seat in the House or, if the competition is weak, aim right away for a higher office. I'll have two adorable children along the way, as long as we have at least one by the time I run for office. Oh—and, of course, if the country goes to war in the near future, I will enlist and serve my country." By the time he was finished, his monologue had taken on a lighter note.

She shook her head in amusement, then in a serious tone asked, "What is it that *you* want?"

He turned to her thoughtfully, about to say something, but when their eyes met his expression changed. "What I want?" His voice was light but turned heavy as he spoke confidently. "I want to kiss you."

Helen smiled, unintentionally giving her consent as she glanced at his lips. He took a step closer, slowly leaned into her, and lightly touched her lips with his own. It was meant to be soft and gentle, but the heat sparked a longing that intensified the kiss.

He felt unfamiliarly vulnerable, like his actions were completely, yet wonderfully, given over to the moment. There was no fighting it, and no making sense of it. He stopped the kiss, but his lips remained sweetly against hers. About to say something, he hesitated, and instead he reached out and rested his hands on her shoulders. He wove her blonde hair into his fingers and drew her closer. This next kiss lingered, explored, deepened.

"I really should go," he whispered. "I have so much to deal with at home, but I'll be back in a month. Can I see you then?"

"I uh—" she was surprised at the confusion she felt. "I'll already be back to college."

Although disappointed, he nodded in understanding. They turned and headed back the way they had come.

When they reached the porch, he stopped, not intending to go inside.

"Are you driving all the way to L.A. tonight?" she asked.

"No, I'm going to spend a few days in Flagstaff and see the Grand Canyon before I head home. It's out of the way, but nobody's expecting me for a few days. I need some time to think before I face everybody."

Heaviness formed in the pit of her stomach. "Can I pack you some food for the trip? I have leftover chicken in the fridge." She had tried to take on a casual tone, but the words were clipped.

He smiled warmly. "That'd be great."

Once inside, he spotted paper and pencil in a small box by the phone and began writing. Helen fixed him a plate of food, wrapped it in foil, then put it in a bag. When she was finished, he quickly folded the paper and set it under the vase of flowers.

"This is my address at the apartment I rent in Tucson. I hope you'll write when you get settled in college."

She forced a smile, unsure of what was bothering her. "I'll write, as long as you write back."

Sensing her change of mood, he tried to lighten it. "Plan on writing a lot of letters." He winked.

They walked out to his truck in an awkward silence. The connection they felt just a little earlier seemed to be replaced with the hard truth of reality: they both had commitments to tend to. He opened the truck door and set the plate on the seat.

Helen spoke casually. "Good luck, Gregory. I hope everything works out for the best."

He nodded. "Thanks, I hope so too." He wanted to reach out to her, to hold her close to him, but something stopped him. He didn't know whether the uneasiness came from what he was soon to face at home, or if it was something between Helen and him. He opened the door and got in. As he started up the truck and backed out, they waved goodbye.

She felt an overwhelming sadness as she watched the back of his truck bob up and down, crossing the dips in the road.

Oh God. This is silly. What's the matter with me?

Turning away, she walked back toward the trailer. Once inside, she rested against the table. She crossed her arms and held them close to her stomach for comfort. Wondering if she'd ever really see him again, she caught sight of the paper securely held by the vase.

It's just an address.

But something compelled her to reach out and unfold the note. Her heart quickened as she read his words. In addition to leaving his address, he wrote:

> *A lot can happen when you follow a long dirt road into the middle of the desert. I miss you already and look forward to the next time I see you.*
>
> Gregory

The sadness dissipated and a smile lit up her face. She grabbed her car keys before running out the door. Her Studebaker screamed down the dirt road, and it wasn't long before she caught up to Gregory. Honking the horn, she slowed down as he pulled over, then she stopped behind him. Her adrenaline rush kept her going as she bolted out of the car. As soon as he stepped out of his truck and their eyes met, she stopped dead in her tracks. She felt a slight flush of embarrassment as she saw the question in his eyes. But then the next thing she knew, she was in his arms, kissing him as tears slid down her cheeks.

"I don't want you to go," she whispered. "We could have these few days together."

He searched her eyes. "Are you sure?"

"Yes," she said urgently, then quietly, "yes. I don't understand it, but I don't want you to go."

Gregory walked over to her car, turned off the ignition and took the key. He scooped her up into his arms and placed her carefully in his truck. "We'll come back for your car a little later. Right now, I don't want you out of my sight for a minute."

But they didn't make it back to the trailer right away. All reasoning left him the moment he saw the first hint of passion in Helen's satiny green eyes. When she nestled into him and traced a row of soft kisses from the base of his neck to behind his ear, he gave up thinking about starting the truck.

There was a familiarity that existed between them. But more than that, a longing, stemming from deep within, a sense of knowing that their lives had been meandering until they found themselves alone together in the middle of nowhere. Helen burned with his touch, ignited by a heat of passion that she would not allow herself to deny. They wanted each other, perhaps for no other reason than that they could. Who was going to deny their passion? Who was there to tell them not to?

Helen was young, and inexperienced with the desires of the flesh, but mature beyond her years when it came to knowing her heart. She had always trusted life, let it happen, and let it take her where it would go. She lived one day at a time, appreciating her life for what it was: a gift. Not something to master, no desire to tame the world or bend life to suit some hidden agenda. She lived, accepting the present moment at face value. And at this moment, she accepted the incredibly wonderful man who had entered her tiny desert oasis, had replaced some of the pain in her heart with a spark of joy and was now giving her body a heat unlike anything she had ever felt before. She gloried in the moment, enjoying the look in his eyes that held secrets promising what lay ahead for both of them. She allowed her heart to do what it wanted: dwell in the unexpected joy of being with him.

This was a different time for Gregory, where different rules applied. For the first time in his life, he stepped off the golden path that he had been on his entire life, one with dreams incredibly large, with measured goals along the way, goals that up until now he had slowly reached one by one. Whether they were his or his parent's dreams didn't matter; they had made up his entire life. And right now he wouldn't have known where his parents' dreams ended and where his own began. He didn't care. At this place, Helen made time stand still for him. Obligations, which had been a part of him for so long, were lost in these ethereal moments, where the depths of Helen's eyes mirrored everything he felt for her.

What they started in the seat of Gregory's truck ended hours later on the red and white quilt covering the full-size bed in Helen's room. After their lovemaking, they held each other tight, never wanting this moment to end.

21

Randall jerked awake at the sound of the phone ringing.

What time is it? He got up out of the recliner and glanced at the clock on his way to the phone.

2:50 a.m. Oh, God, I hope she's safe.

He grabbed the phone. "Stacie?" He barely heard the frightened cry.

"Daaaad."

"Are you all right?" He spoke urgently.

"Dad—there's been a—an—an accident."

Oh, God, No. "Are you okay?"

"Yes."

Randall barely heard her. "You're not hurt?"

"Just a little."

"Where are you?"

"I'm—I'm at the—the hospital. Can you come and get me?"

"Which hospital?"

"Northwest."

"I'm on my way." Randall ran to the truck.

Please let her be okay.

He drove down Sandario and took a right onto Twin Peaks road, heading into Tucson. His mind jumped around with thoughts of the past year. *How did Stacie end up in worse shape than Allison or Vanessa? She's my little angel. What happened to her?*

He got on the freeway, angry with himself for falling asleep.

But what could I have done? Looked for her?

He grabbed the steering wheel tighter. *Yeah—I should've gone out and looked for her.* He glanced at the speedometer, trying not to go too much over the speed limit.

She's just in with the wrong crowd. That's it—that explains the smoking, the drinking. Oh God. Maybe I've been too lenient. Hell, maybe I've been too strict.

Randall left the dark night and entered the fluorescent, fast-paced world of the hospital emergency room. Spotting her immediately, as well as two police officers, Stacie's friends, plus some of their parents, he had three simultaneous thoughts: *Oh God—she's hurt, Thank God she's alive,* and, *she didn't leave home dressed like that!*

"Stacie!"

"Daaad." At the sight of him, Stacie started crying.

When he got closer, Randall's heart fell. Underneath streaks of heavy makeup, he could see that Stacie's right eye was swollen shut. Bruises and scrapes marked the entire right side of her face, her lip was swollen, and her hair was matted. Her black leotards were ripped, revealing a nasty cut on her thigh, and her short black skirt and blue skimpy top were splattered with blood.

One of the officers acknowledged Randall, telling him they'll be with him as soon as they finish the paperwork on the other girls.

Randall reached for Stacie, gently, thankful her injuries weren't worse.

"Dad, Lena's hurt."

"Who's Lena?" Randall asked softly.

"She's a girl from my school." Stacie pointed in the direction of an elderly, dark-skinned woman. "I think that's her grandmother."

Randall looked in the direction Stacie pointed, but before he had a chance to ask any questions, a nurse walked up to them.

"Mr. Averson?" The nurse didn't wait for a reply. "The paramedics reported nothing life threatening, your daughter's vitals are good. But we'd like to take a head and foot x-ray. Since she wasn't wearing a seatbelt, she hit the windshield hard and was lucky she didn't go through it." The nurse handed Randall the clipboard and told him where to sign. A nurse's aide walked up with a wheelchair. "We'll have her back before long." The nurse helped Stacie out of her seat and into the wheelchair. Randall grimaced as he saw Stacie limp on her left foot. He watched them go down the corridor until they turned a corner.

What happened?

Randall glanced over his shoulder at the dark-skinned woman. She had been pacing back and forth, and her back was now turned to him. He walked toward her; she turned around upon hearing his footsteps. Randall took a sharp gulp of air when they made eye contact. The intensity and strength of her gaze caused him to hesitate. He forced himself to take a step forward.

"I'm Randall Averson, Stacie's dad."

The woman studied him for a moment, not saying a word.

"I guess our girls were in a car accident together."

With a quick huff, her eyes closed momentarily. She looked back at Randall in a scrutinizing manner. "If that's what you want to call it."

Randall felt uneasy. Her words were as powerful as her gaze. "I don't know Lena. Are you her grandmother?"

"Yes."

"Is she all right?"

"That remains to be seen." She turned away.

Randall took a step closer to her. "Look," he said while facing her back, "I don't know what happened."

With barely controlled anger, she turned back around. "Lena and *your* daughter were not in an accident *together*, Mr. Averson. Your daughter and her friends swerved off the road and ran right into my granddaughter's car." Her next words were slow and harsh. "Your daughter and her friends were out drinking. They were driving a Blazer. My granddaughter was coming home late from an out of town volleyball game. Her team had just been dropped off at school and she was driving home in her Corolla."

Randall grimaced. Since Stacie's friends showed no signs of obvious injuries, Randall asked, "Are Lena and Stacie the only ones hurt?"

She let out a sharp breath. "Yes, Mr. Averson. Your daughter will be fine and, as you can see, her friends made it through with barely a scratch." She turned away angrily, obviously expecting the conversation to be over.

"What happened to Lena?"

"Two broken ribs, a punctured lung, some internal bleeding. The doctors are trying to find the source of the bleeding and get it stopped. That's it for starters."

Randall sat down on a bench near where the woman was standing. "I'm sorry."

She turned to him, as if sensing the depth of his sincerity. She relaxed, looked at the bench and sat down a few feet from him. "I'm Carlotta."

Randall offered his hand. When she accepted it, he placed his other hand on top of hers and, for just a moment, their eyes connected, conveying the hope for Lena's safety that needn't be spoken. They turned away from each other in silence.

A few minutes later, Stacie's friends and their families walked over to Randall and Carlotta. Some introductions were made, apologies given, and hopes and prayers offered for Stacie's and Lena's recoveries. When the officers approached, Randall said quick good-byes to the families who were preparing to leave.

He walked to a more private area with the officers—who wasted no time in getting to the point. "Your daughter was engaged in underage drinking with a blood alcohol level of .12, and we suspect drugs were also involved. We need you to read and sign the arrest document, then both of you will need to appear in court on the date listed below." With a heavy heart, filled with guilt, Randall read over the document. As he signed it, the officer added, "Your daughter was lucky, Mr. Averson. Her injuries are fairly minor, and this is her first offense. She'll likely only be sentenced to a reasonable amount of community service and counseling." Randall thanked the officers, then went and sat down near Carlotta.

It was over an hour later when they turned at the sound of the clicking wheels as the nurse wheeled Stacie back into the waiting area. The nurse explained to Randall that Stacie had suffered only superficial injuries: a few cuts and bruises, and some damaged soft tissue in her ankle that should heal in a few weeks.

After the nurse left, Stacie got out of the wheelchair and hobbled towards Carlotta. "I'm so sorry. I feel so bad for what we did to Lena."

Carlotta looked up, about to respond, but Stacie's one-eyed gaze from a face washed clean of make-up sent a chill down Carlotta's spine. Something was familiar about this young girl. Then, when Stacie's expression turned quizzical, Carlotta did a double take and froze.

Dear God in Heaven. In addition to worrying about Lena, Carlotta had fought to restrain her anger all evening. And now, looking into the eyes of one of the culprits, it was like looking at her old, dear friend Helen, as if Helen had come back from the dead. Overcome with emotion, Carlotta managed a mumbled 'thank you,' while silently promising herself to sort it out later.

Lena first.

Stacie sat down next to her dad. No words were needed between the two. They would stay here with Carlotta until they learned of Lena's prognosis. Within minutes, Stacie fell asleep on the bench.

Knowing it was going to be a long night, Randall stood up. "Can I get you some coffee?" he asked Carlotta.

She said yes with an almost imperceptible nod. A few minutes later he returned with two steaming cups. He handed a cup to Carlotta, then sat a couple of seats away from her as he gently lifted Stacie and rested her head on his lap. He gently finger-combed Stacie's matted hair away from the cut on her forehead.

Carlotta saw the unspoken emotions in Randall, mainly love, fear, and vulnerability, and she felt comfortable with him. "My daughter and son-in-law, Lena's parents, are vacationing in Spain. I've—I've left a message at their hotel, but I just pray to God I have good news for them when they return the call."

The happy-go-lucky man Randall had been before Madeline left would've assured Carlotta that she would have good news for Lena's parents. But he had been knocked down too much the past few years to be able to offer up hopes—when heartache may as easily follow. "Let's pray for good news," he replied.

They sat, mostly silent, for more than three hours, until the doctor finally came out. Randall nudged Stacie awake, but they remained seated as Carlotta spoke privately with the doctor. Randall said a quick prayer of thanks when he saw by Carlotta's body language that the news was good.

A moment later, Carlotta came over and told Randall and Stacie what the doctor had said. "They stopped the bleeding. Lena should recover completely. She'll be in the hospital for a week or two and will need to take it easy for a couple of months."

After offering Carlotta any help she needed, which she declined, Randall and Stacie left, promising they would help in anyway they could.

Three weeks later Stacie was rocking back and forth in her dad's old brown recliner as she waited for him to return from running errands. She looked at the framed photographs on the end table: Allison's wedding day, the day Jason was born, Vanessa's High School graduation, and Jason's first and second birthday pictures. Stacie had added the latest photograph, a snapshot of all of them in Mountain.

Where are you, Mom? You're not in any of these.

When Stacie heard her father's truck pull in the driveway, she got out of the recliner and opened the door. "Hey, Dad."

"Hey, Sweetie." Just as he had each day since the accident, he took in little things about her: the swelling was gone, the cuts and bruises were still noticeable, but had faded significantly, and her walk seemed almost back to normal. "You ready for the session?"

"Nervous, but ready."

"You'll be fine. Remember, I'm the parent. The counselor will probably be tougher on me than on you. I'm the one that didn't see you were in trouble. And for that, I am very sorry."

"It's not your fault, Dad. I was pretty sneaky when it came to keeping my drug use from you."

Randall squeezed her shoulder as they walked to the truck. "Well, we're just lucky your juvenile officer feels that, since your drug use was a new development, as long as you pass the periodic drug tests, you won't need a treatment center."

Stacie snapped her seatbelt as her dad started the truck. "Oh—is that what he told you when he asked me to leave the room?"

"Yes." *Among other things,* Randall thought. *Including how one of the other girls already had a DUI, and how as a parent I need to do all I can from letting this happen again.*

"Well, that is good because, on top of everything else, I don't think I could handle being taken to a treatment center."

"Then it's a deal?"

"What's that?"

"No more drugs or alcohol?"

Stacie's eyes filled with tears. "It's a deal. Every time I think of Lena lying in that hospital room, I know I don't want to ever again be a part of something that can cause somebody harm."

Randall felt the sincerity in Stacie's words and quietly sighed with relief as Stacie continued. "Did you know that Lena might have made Student Athlete of the Year? And that her volleyball team is still hoping to go to State?" Stacie snapped her fingers. "So just like that, something she's been working towards for years has been taken from her. She didn't get a choice." Stacie fought back tears. "I still can't believe Lena forgave me."

"I'm sorry, Stace. I really am. I mean—you watched as my drinking got out of control. And you saw how sometimes I drove when I shouldn't have. Some of us just get lucky and arrive home without any accidents. But that doesn't make it right."

Stacie's smile was bittersweet. "Thanks, Dad." When her dad reached over and squeezed her hand, Stacie squeezed back. "You know what's really weird? Since Lena's parents agreed I could talk to her, the place I've wanted to be most is sitting in that chair next to her at the hospital. I'm really glad I get to spend time with her."

Randall glanced at his daughter. "Which reminds me, when I was out running errands, I stopped in at the hospital with a bag of bagels for Lena's family. Carlotta let me know that they all appreciated us being there, and she told me that you have had a special way of cheering Lena up."

"Really? I can't imagine that. I just try to help her with stuff—you know, hand her juice or water, bring her a lip gloss—stuff like that."

"Oh yeah? Is that it?" Randall said with amusement. "I was told Lena has some new artwork in her room."

"Oh that! Yeah—" Stacie grinned. "I guess I got a little carried away. But that was almost two weeks ago. It's old news!"

"Not for me. I hadn't been back since I took you there a few days after the accident. And I've gotta tell you, that drawing is quite impressive. I can't believe how huge it is—taking up almost half the wall."

"Thanks. I keep adding to it. When Lena wakes up, she tells me more and more things she likes. It's been a challenge adding otters, dolphins, rocky road ice cream, the Beatles, antique hair barrettes, and gourmet cooking to her volleyball and team mascot mural!"

"From the way Carlotta says it, it has given Lena a lot of joy. And they all like how you framed the mural with Lena's get well cards."

"Well—it's the least I could do. Especially since Lena's closest friends can't visit very often, since they are practicing everyday."

Stacie had been more withdrawn than usual after the accident, so Randall felt grateful for the easy flow and candor of their conversation. As they turned onto Avra Valley road he said, "I forgot to ask you about your first volunteer session. How was it?"

"It was fun, actually. The kids seemed to have a good time. A lot of them set the ball down on the lane and pushed it—so most of them were gutter balls. But the kids laughed a lot and had fun."

"I thought you were picking up trash on the highways today."

"No—that's next week. Today was helping physically challenged children learn to bowl."

"Hmm—that does sound like fun."

"Most of the volunteer options seem like they'll be fun. I think I'll learn a lot and it should be challenging and rewarding. But the one thing I'm dreading is the all day juvenile delinquency class I'll have to attend in a few weeks."

"It seems the system is set up to do all they can to try to discourage a young offender from breaking the law again."

"Yeah. I think it'll work for me."

"Good—that's music to a parent's ears." Randall parked the truck at the counselor's office. "Now let's go see what this 'Mr. Day' has to say!"

More than an hour later they left the counselor's office. "Can we have lunch at Props?" Stacie asked. "I've wanted to go back there ever since we learned Carlotta is the manager."

"That's right—she is. Plus the food's great and I'm hungry. So that's a great idea."

As they neared the airfield, Randall said, "I could use some fresh air after that counseling session. What do you say we look at the planes first?"

Stacie nodded her head. "Fine by me."

Randall parked next to the airfield office. Most of the hangars were closed and locked up, but several were open: one containing a red-and-white Cessna, the other revealing a bright yellow Piper Cub.

"This reminds me of the picture in Spartan Manor. That plane in the picture, Great-Grandpa Kiser's, was probably flown out of here."

"Yeah—it probably was," her father agreed. "Wonder what this airport was like forty years ago?"

Stacie saw one man wiping down a Decathlon. "Maybe you should learn how to fly, Dad." She looked up and saw his surprised expression.

"Nah, I'm too old for that." He affectionately tapped her nose. As they walked around the airport, they nodded 'hello' to a few pilots and mechanics before arriving at a row of blue-and-yellow planes used by the trainers. Stacie watched as Randall ran his hand over the shiny finish of the paint.

"I mean it, Dad. I think you should take lessons."

Randall turned when he heard a plane coming in. The plane tapped the runway lightly, bounced back up, and then came back down for a smooth landing. "Expensive hobby." He put his arm around her shoulders. "Let's go eat."

Props Café lot was lined with cars. When they opened the door they saw the restaurant was full, every booth filled, but there was room at the counter. They sat down on two adjacent bar stools. Randall ordered the southwestern chicken sandwich with green chiles' and Monterey Jack cheese, and Stacie ordered the avocado mushroom burger.

Stacie turned to see a young waiter rush through the double doors that led into the kitchen. She looked around the restaurant. "This place is packed and hardly anybody has their food." She looked at the people, some waiting impatiently, but most of them chatting happily, sipping their drinks.

Randall looked around as the front door opened and Carlotta rushed through it. He saw her eyes brighten in surprise at the chaos around her, then she yelled, "Sorry for the delay everybody. We had a few emergencies this morning."

Randall stood up to catch Carlotta before she rushed past them on her way to the kitchen. "Hello, Carlotta."

Carlotta stopped and turned around. She smiled when she saw Randall and Stacie. "We just got Lena home from the hospital. It was a complete surprise! We were expecting her to be let out on Monday, but the doctor came in, checked her vitals, and said there's no reason she needed to stay there the rest of the weekend."

"That's great." Stacie said shyly. "Is there anything I can do for her? Does she need anything?"

Carlotta shook her head 'no' as she opened her purse and dropped her car keys inside. "I'm in a hurry. We're short handed around here." She took a few steps forward, and then stopped, turned back around and looked at Stacie. "Have you ever been a waitress before?"

"No."

"Lena worked every Saturday." A knowing look passed between them. "I could use some help."

Without uttering a word, Stacie jumped off the barstool and followed Carlotta into the kitchen. A few minutes later, she was busy filling drink orders while Jimmy, Lena's little brother, ran the cash register and took patron's orders. When Stacie delivered her dad's lunch to him, she handed him her wrapped burger. "I'll eat at home later—pick me up at four." Then she was off cleaning tables, mopping up a few spills, and delivering food orders while Randall ate lunch alone and tried to subdue his ear-to-ear grin.

Later, with the restaurant closed and Jimmy and Stacie already gone, Carlotta sat alone on a barstool next to the cash register. The restaurant was sparkling clean, thanks to Stacie's fastidiousness. Carlotta reached under the counter and pulled out an old brown photo album. The photo album contained pictures of every person that had ever worked at the restaurant. Carlotta opened it up to the first page and looked at the familiar photo of herself and her dear friend Helen. A smile warmed her face, but tears glistened in her eyes.

I can't wait to see your little girl all grown up now. I wonder if Bailey will remember me. Carlotta thought of her granddaughter and the long recovery that still lay ahead of her. *Lena first.*

A few weeks later Carlotta finished up in the kitchen and walked to the large double doors that led to the restaurant. She stopped and looked through the door's plastic window. Stacie was refilling the napkin dispensers after another hectic Saturday lunch crowd.

I hardly know a thing about you, Stacie. You're so quiet. And where is Bailey? You never mention your mother, but she must be Bailey.

Carlotta pushed through the swinging doors and walked toward Stacie. "Do you need any help?"

Stacie opened a napkin dispenser and reached for a thick wad of napkins. "I'm almost finished. I already refilled the salt and pepper shakers, and the ketchup."

Carlotta looked at Stacie discerningly. "Stacie, I'm glad you are helping out. You've been a real blessing."

Stacie closed up the dispenser. As she had been doing for the past two weeks, she again managed to hide her exhaustion behind a smile. "Thanks." Due to the many and varied volunteer opportunities, she had managed to schedule her community service hours around school and waitressing. Unbeknownst to Carlotta, Stacie had every spare minute booked until Christmas so she was able to keep her Saturday's open to help out at the diner. Her dad had been concerned, but Stacie assured him that keeping busy was just what she needed—and the excuse she needed to turn her life around and find new friends.

"I stopped by and saw Lena before work today. She tells me she'll be coming back to school next week."

"Yes, she healed nicely. She's a tough girl." Carlotta smiled warmly. "She told me you two have become friends and that she invited you to the 'Virgin of Guadalupe' ceremony.

Stacie smiled shyly. "Yes, Lena's a special person. She told me about the parade for everyone who has been through something tragic or needs a special blessing—or something like that."

Carlotta smiled at Stacie's description. "Yes, there is a parade. And Lena will be walking in it this year." There was a brief lull as Carlotta debated whether this was the time to ask about Bailey. The thought of her healthy granddaughter made the decision easier. "Would you like to join me for a piece of pie? There's something I'd like to talk to you about." Carlotta didn't intend to make it sound so serious, but truthfully, it was, and she didn't want to mislead Stacie.

"Sure." Stacie followed Carlotta into the kitchen where they dished up two pieces of cherry pie. A few minutes later they sat down at one of the booths, facing one another.

"Stacie," Carlotta hesitated, "I've been meaning to talk to you, but I was waiting for something."

Stacie looked at her quizzically. "Waiting?"

"I was waiting for two things, actually. I was waiting for Lena to get better, and I was waiting for your mother. I haven't seen her and you never mention her."

Stacie swallowed a bite of cherry pie and tried to quiet the unexpected flutter that rose within her. "I, uh...." She glanced around the room. "I—" she looked at Carlotta and was somewhat calmed by the warmth in Carlotta's eyes. Stacie seemed about to speak, but she couldn't get the words out.

Carlotta reached for Stacie's hands across the table and held them in a firm grasp. "You're the spittin' image of my dear friend, Helen. You must be Bailey's daughter."

Stacie, who had been momentarily comforted by Carlotta's gesture, jerked her hands away. She shook her head back and forth. "No," she almost shouted.

She looked around the room as her stomach tied up in knots. She didn't understand the surge of energy that was pouring through her. She and her sisters agreed that Helen Kiser must be their grandmother. They had accepted it. But hearing it from Carlotta was a shock. "Who's Bailey? My mother's name was Madeline."

The room began spinning. Stacie felt herself move, but she didn't know what she was doing. She felt disoriented, lost, spinning on a fast merry-go-round. Suddenly she became aware of two strong hands holding her shoulders. She heard her name being called and glimpsed Carlotta's face before she was wrapped in an encompassing hug.

Carlotta held Stacie close, whispering comforting words over and over again until Stacie's breathing returned to normal. When she felt Stacie relax, she stepped away just enough to look into Stacie's eyes. "Can you talk about it, Stacie?"

Stacie's lower lip quivered. "What—what happened to me?"

"I think you just had an anxiety attack."

Stacie shifted uncomfortably. "Who's Bailey?"

Carlotta looked concerned. "Maybe we should postpone this talk until another time."

"No—please—I'll be okay." When she saw Carlotta's doubtful expression, Stacie added, "I've just been very busy since the accident and—well, I forget to eat sometimes." To make her point, Stacie sat down and took a bite of pie.

The truth, it's the best way. And Helen would want that now.

"Okay, Stacie, but first I'm going to get you something more to eat." Before Stacie could finish a rebuttal, Carlotta had walked straight back to the kitchen and returned a few minutes later with a turkey sandwich and a glass of milk. She silently waited until Stacie had finished eating.

"Helen's daughter's name was Madeline Cari Kiser," she said quietly.

Stacie's eyes widened. "That's Mom's name."

"Yes—Bailey was her nickname." Carlotta held back saying that the nickname was very special; it had to do with a story Bailey's father had told Helen. "Why haven't I seen your mother? Are your parents divorced?"

"No—", Stacie looked defeated. "Mom abandoned us three and a half years ago."

Carlotta drew in her breath. "No. I can't believe that."

"It's true. She didn't go with us to our family reunion. We came home and she was gone. We haven't seen her, or heard from her since then."

Carlotta tried to picture Bailey, the happy little girl with brown curls falling down her back, as a woman who would leave her own children.

What happened to you, Bailey? What did your grandmother do to you?

"There are several pictures of a woman who looks like me hanging on a wall in the trailer. We figured that had to be our grandma."

Carlotta remembered one of the pictures that hung by the door. She had taken it on Bailey's third birthday. Helen had swept Bailey up in her arms and Carlotta had taken the shot. It was Helen's favorite picture. "Yes, that's your Grandma Helen."

Stacie managed a faint smile. "Can you tell me about her? The only thing my mom ever said was that her Grandmother June raised her, and that her mother died when she was young. She always changed the subject when it came to her family, said she didn't want to talk about it. We learned not to ask."

Carlotta sighed knowingly. She felt that all of her years of worrying about Bailey were now being justified. "Stacie, I think I better talk to your dad first. Have him call me and we'll see when we can get together and talk."

Stacie jumped up. "I'll call him right now. He should be home. Maybe he can come right over."

Carlotta needed time to think. "I can't see him today. I'll meet with him tomorrow or some evening next week."

Stacie looked at Carlotta shyly. "I'm sorry I flipped out."

Carlotta pulled Stacie into her arms once more. "It's okay. It's a lot to take in."

—

Stacie couldn't wait to get home.

Darn—Dad's not here. When she pulled up to the driveway, she threw the car into park, turned off the ignition and jumped out. She ran into the trailer and headed straight for the phone. She dialed Allison's number as fast as her fingers would move. It rang eight times before Stacie heard an emotional hello.

"Allison, what's wrong?"

Allison started crying at the sound of Stacie's voice. "Oh, Stacie, Todd and I—well—we're getting a divorce."

"Allison!" Stacie heard Allison's uncontrollable sobs. "It can't be true. You guys are great together."

"Yeah, sure we are." Allison mumbled. "That's why he left me."

Stacie thought she heard a giggle amongst the sobs. "What happened, Al?"

"I don't know. We've been fighting a lot lately. Look Stace, I don't want to talk right now."

"Okay. But is Jason all right?"

"He's fine. He's at playtime. Just please don't say anything to Dad. I'll tell him when I'm up to it."

"Okay. I'm here if you need me."

"Thanks."

Stacie hung up the phone, her previous enthusiasm all but gone. She glanced over at a picture of Todd, Allison and Jason as her heart filled with sadness for the three of them. She picked up the phone and dialed Vanessa's number in L.A. A breathless hello answered the phone.

"Hi, Vanessa, it's Stacie."

"Oh, hi, Stacie, I'm just heading out the door. My friend—you know, Mitch, sprained his ankle. I made him some chocolate chip cookies, and I want to get them over to him while they're still warm. Can I call you back?"

"Sure. Tell him I hope he heals quickly."

"I will. Talk to you later."

Stacie hung up the phone, went into her bedroom and plopped down on the bed. She thought of Carlotta's strong embrace that brought her back from the anxiety attack. A tear slid down her cheek. The tremendous pain that had long since dominated her emotions, had dimmed: she did not feel so alone.

22

"But, Dad. You can't leave. Carlotta's going to be here soon."

Randall looked at his youngest daughter with regret. "I'm sorry, Stace. I couldn't sleep last night thinking about it. The more I thought about it, the more angry I got. It's as if your mother walked right back into our lives. But is she here?" He asked sarcastically. "I'm trying to get on with my life. She's been gone over three years and—"

"I know." Stacie interrupted in a soothing manner, *And you have enough reminders of her because of us. But mostly because of me.*

Randall grabbed his keys. "I'm sorry." He left the trailer and headed for his truck.

When Stacie heard a car drive up, she went out to greet Carlotta just getting out of her car. "I passed your dad." The unspoken question was in her voice.

Stacie nodded. "I'm sorry, Carlotta. He doesn't want any reminders of Mom." Stacie was relieved when Carlotta nodded in understanding.

Carlotta looked around, taking everything in: the spaciousness of the desert landscape, the mountains in the distance, the scattering of wildflowers, and the small trailer. "After Helen and Bailey were gone, I took care of this place. I had a key—and for years I'd come out here, sweep away cobwebs, set traps for mice, but one day I just stopped. I don't even know why. Busy I guess."

Memories swept over her and she felt transported in time. She turned to Stacie and smiled. "You would've loved your grandmother." Carlotta saw Stacie's face brighten with a smile that seemed sent straight from Helen.

"Really? What was she like?"

"Well, for starters, she was a beautiful woman, but never acted like it. Her truest beauty came from within. She had a big heart, good instincts, and she saw the best in everyone."

Stacie tilted her head in confusion. "Mom said there wasn't much worth remembering about her childhood."

"I'm sorry to hear that. But I can honestly tell you Bailey was a very happy little girl. She and her mother were very close." The memory of Helen's death flashed in Carlotta's mind, bringing back the pain of that time.

"Helen died when Bailey was in kindergarten."

"We never heard how she died. What happened to her?"

"It was a brain aneurysm. Helen had been having severe headaches, so she went to see her doctor. When she was diagnosed, the only surgeon who could perform the surgery was out of town. They tried to find another surgeon who could be flown in but it was too late. The aneurysm burst just three days after diagnosis."

Stacie's eyes clouded. "That's horrible."

Carlotta held Stacie's hand in a comforting gesture. Carlotta didn't feel that it was her place to add that Bailey had been alone with Helen when it happened. Although Carlotta had tried to be with Helen and Bailey around the clock as soon as they'd gotten the news, she left for just a short time to get groceries. When she returned, she found Bailey crying over Helen's lifeless body. The paramedics literally pulled Bailey away from her mother. Only then did Bailey realize Carlotta had been trying to comfort her. Bailey collapsed, completely exhausted, into Carlotta's arms.

"What happened then? What happened to Mom?"

"After the funeral, your mother went to live with her grandmother, June, in California. And I never heard from Bailey again."

They were silent until Stacie again saw Carlotta looking at the small trailer. "Would you like to see Spartan Manor—the small trailer? After I got it cleaned up, Dad and I restored it. Last year he got utilities hooked up so we can use it as a guest house."

Carlotta knew seeing the old trailer would be bittersweet. "I'd like that."

"We tore down the add-on. It was in pretty bad shape."

"I can imagine. I'm surprised it was still there." As they neared Spartan Manor, Carlotta added, "There used to be a short wooden fence here. I remember one day coming over to visit, Bailey was standing on one of the wide fence posts with her arms outstretched. She had such a determined look on her face that I didn't want to disturb her. Helen came out and told me that Bailey was concentrating on which way the slight breeze was blowing. It was part of her daily weather report. She said she was going to be a weatherman when she grew up."

"That's funny. I can't picture Mom doing that."

"Your mom had spunk. I believe she could've done anything she set her mind to." Carlotta walked inside Spartan Manor and felt instantly transported back in time. "Oh my, this is amazing. You've changed a few things, but so much is the same. I can't believe it—look at the floor—the tile! It looks just like it did when the trailer was brand new!"

"Dad and I thought it would be fun to duplicate the original look."

Carlotta pointed at the futon to the right of the door. "There used to be a yellow sofa over there."

"Yes," Stacie replied. "We took out some of the furniture, but the table, bench seat, and the bed frame are here. We added the futon in here and a new mattress in the bedroom. Other than that, we tried to keep everything the same. We repainted the kitchen appliances, refurbished the maple walls, and got everything working."

Carlotta looked at the kitchen with the bright red icebox, the stainless steel sink, and the white Dixie oven-stove. She loved the hodgepodge colors—just as they had been forty years earlier. One memory surfaced, Helen cooking dinner while Bailey was coloring at the table, and another one followed. "Every Christmas, Helen and Bailey would make care packages for the birds—edible balls of nuts and fruits hung on the trees."

Stacie smiled. "That sounds really neat—and fun." She quietly followed Carlotta through the small trailer. They peeked into the small, sparkling clean bathroom, then stepped into the bedroom. The bed, with the original headboard, was covered with a beautiful red-and-white quilt.

"My mom made that quilt." Stacie said.

"It's beautiful. And it looks perfect here." Carlotta recognized the significance of the quilt, handmade by a woman that apparently had no recollection of her happy memories here.

"You did a wonderful job restoring this place. Your grandmother would be thrilled."

"It was fun." Stacie said appreciatively. "Spartan Manor is my special place. Nobody took to it like I did."

Carlotta smiled.

Helen—I swear I feel your presence, and I believe you're smiling now.

"It's a beautiful day, Stacie. Why don't you take an old woman for a walk around the property? Is it still forty acres?"

"Thirty-seven now. The Central Arizona Project took three acres." They walked out of the trailer and into the sunshine. "Supposedly within a year or so the C.A.P. will be bringing in their bulldozers to make the canal."

"It's coming right through your property?"

"Yep." Stacie pointed east but ran her hand back and forth in a north-south direction. "Right over there."

Carlotta grinned. "Speaking of water, during the summer months, Bailey made sure—with her mother's help—that the animals had a water source. Birds, squirrels, rabbits, javelina, and coyotes could be spotted at her waterhole. There was one coyote that used to visit frequently—he had a slight limp. Your mother named him Gimpy."

Stacie grinned. "Tell me more about them."

"Well, your mother loved being outdoors. She loved everything about the desert. Always running around, digging in the dirt, building castles out of the sand in the washes. She'd bring a bucket of water and mix mud. Bailey had a knack for making beautiful things out of the dirt, just like her mother."

"What did grandma do?"

"She was a potter. She made dishes, bowls, platters, and cups. In just a few years, she made a name for herself locally. Her business was beginning to expand so quickly she was becoming unable to keep up with the demand. But she wanted to build a house and be able to pay for it as she went, so she worked as hard as she could to earn the money. She had the house plans drawn and was ready to break ground when the headaches started."

"That's so sad."

"Here—I'll show you where she was going to build it." They walked until they came to a large Palo Verde tree. "This is the spot she had chosen."

Stacie looked around. "My dad sometimes talks about building a house. Maybe he could build it in this spot."

Carlotta thought for a moment.

How much and how soon?

But *'be patient'* kept coming to mind. They walked in silence as a soft early spring breeze caressed their skin.

Stacie looked at Carlotta. "Do you know who my grandfather is?"

Carlotta's eyes softened as a tender memory surfaced. "No. Helen never said who he was, but what she did say was that he was the love of her life, but she would never be able to be with him. I suspect he was somebody important, because she said his destiny was more important than his love for her."

"That's so sad."

"It wasn't meant that way. Helen didn't have regrets."

"No regrets? None?"

Carlotta grinned. "I think you could say if she stubbed her toe she would've wished she hadn't. But when it came to the important things in life—relationships and life events—Helen felt strongly that things happen for a reason."

Stacie thought about that for a moment. "This is so strange, meeting you, and learning about my grandmother and my mom as a little girl."

"Your grandmother would've considered this part of life's perfection."

"What do you mean?"

"Helen's saying was 'Life is perfect, despite it's seemingly imperfections.'"

"Really? That's kind of funny. When anything goes wrong, my dad always says, "It's an imperfect world.""

Carlotta smiled at the contrast. "Your grandma never worried about the past or the future. She had a way of accepting every moment of her life for what it was, good or bad." Carlotta stopped walking and turned to Stacie. "What do you believe in, Stacie?"

Stacie looked toward the distant mountains. "I don't really believe in anything."

"Nothing?"

Stacie shook her head. "I used to believe in God. I spent most of my time at church. I loved it there. But I don't believe in God anymore."

"Why is that?"

She turned toward Carlotta. "God never answered any of my prayers, and he didn't bring Mom home."

"Do you know what your grandma Helen would've said to that?"

"What?

"Trust God."

Stacie took a deep breath. "How could she be so sure of her faith when God didn't even give her the man that she loved?"

"She accepted that he was not meant to be hers forever. But he gave her a very special gift—your mother." Carlotta opened her heart to Helen's memory in order to give Stacie a more accurate description. When she spoke next, the words came from deep within. "Helen loved your grandfather with every part of her being. And she carried that love, even in his absence, into her relationship with Bailey. That kind of love, whether it lasts a day or a lifetime, is precious and rare. It's beautiful to witness the outcome of that kind of love."

A tear slid gently down Stacie's cheek, but Carlotta's words acted as a soothing salve seeping into her wounded heart.

Arm in arm, the two women walked back to the main trailer in silence.

———

Carlotta awoke with a start. The image of Helen was so strong in Carlotta's mind that she looked around the room as if she'd find her there.

It was just a dream. She glanced at the clock and saw that it was just after 4 a.m.

But it was no ordinary dream.

Carlotta pulled down the flowered duvet and got out of bed. She grabbed her cotton robe while slipping her feet into a pair of sandals.

As she stepped outside, the dark April morning was crisp and clear. The stars shone like fine points of light against the expanse of dark sky. Carlotta fumbled with the lock on her storage room door as quietly as possible, not wanting to wake her neighbors. The lock turned on the third attempt, and, as always, she told herself she'd get a new lock soon. She stepped inside and reached overhead for the twine and gave a quick yank. Light exposed the room. She placed a stepladder in front of a tall shelf. After climbing two steps, she reached up high and pulled down a large brown box, maneuvered it partially onto her shoulder, then carefully went back down.

I'm getting too old for this.

The dream of Helen played over in her mind as Carlotta, sitting at the kitchen table, opened the box. Carlotta had long ago learned to trust her dreams, especially the ones that came through with such clarity and with a message she knew to be real. Most of the items in the box were to be saved for Bailey. But in the dream, it was clear that a few things were to be given to Stacie and Randall.

Carlotta went through each item in the box, savoring the memories with an open heart. She opened a gift box and moved aside the tissue paper to see Bailey's christening gown. A smile crossed Carlotta's face as she remembered that perfect spring morning over forty years earlier. Next she pulled out a bag of Bailey's baby teeth, her baby book with various pictures, measurements and shot records, her kindergarten class picture, and a large assortment of artworks dating from the time she was old enough to hold onto crayons or paintbrush.

Carlotta took out the things that were meant for Stacie and Randall and closed the box. Memories washed over her yet again, Helen's tragic death, followed by Bailey staying with Carlotta for the next three months while she fought for custody. Carlotta had never forgotten the day Bailey was dragged from her arms and handed over to June Kiser. The painful memory still left a bitter taste in her mouth.

Helen's legal document to give custody to Carlotta should anything happen to Helen didn't carry much weight, since Bailey was born out of wedlock. The courts had ruled in favor of the wealthy, white grandmother over Carlotta, the Yaqui Indian woman who was a cook at a café and living on a reservation.

Carlotta put the box back in the storage room and locked the door. Knowing she wouldn't be able to get back to sleep, she spent the next couple of hours making a few extra dishes to take to the Virgin of Guadalupe ceremony. Then she bathed herself, put on some clean clothes, and called Randall.

———

Stacie was already showered and dressed when she walked down the hall and saw her dad at the kitchen table and drinking coffee. "Good morning, Dad."

Randall looked up from reading the paper. "Morning. Are you about ready to go?"

"Yep. I'm just going to get a bowl of cereal." Stacie headed for the cupboards.

"If we leave now, we can stop and eat breakfast along the way."

With one hand on the cupboard door, Stacie turned around and looked at Randall. "What do you mean, 'we'?"

Randall got up from the table and put his coffee cup in the sink. "Carlotta called early this morning. She urged me, in a very polite manner, to attend the ceremony. I agreed. So let's go."

Stacie giggled. "Are you sure?"

"No, I'm not sure. I'd rather rearrange rocks in the desert, but that woman is hard to say no to."

Stacie shut the cabinet door and headed back toward her bedroom. "Let me grab my purse!"

Two hours later Randall and Stacie exited the freeway as they neared Phoenix. The town of Guadalupe, located South of Phoenix, is a Yaqui reservation named after the "Virgin of Guadalupe." Randall followed the directions given him by Carlotta. He turned down several streets until he reached the street of Lena's other grandmother's house.

"There's Lena." Stacie pointed a couple of houses over, then waved as Lena walked toward them. Stacie rolled down the window and stuck her head out. "Hi—you look great." Lena's long black hair was pulled back in a ponytail and tied with a bright red ribbon. She had looped a similar ribbon through the belt loops on her Calvin Klein jeans. She wore a white cotton blouse with elastic sleeves which puckered just above the elbow.

"Thanks." Lena grinned while spinning around. Her shoulders swayed and her large, dangle hoop earrings bounced.

Stacie laughed while opening the door.

"Hello, Mr. Averson." Lena said as Randall got out of the car. "Grandma Carlotta is waiting for you inside. You'll have just enough time to meet my other grandparents and the rest of my family before the parade starts."

They walked into the small house. Lena's family and friends stood in the kitchen while others sat around the dining room table eating homemade soup and fresh tortillas before leaving for the parade.

Later that evening, Stacie remarked to her dad. "It's kind of strange, huh?"

"What's that?"

"It's just like being in Mountain for the Icelandic festivities. Parade, church, lots of food and family, then party!"

"Yeah—I see what you mean."

"Dad—you know how I told you about Lena going to New York?"

"To cooking school?"

"Well, she suggested that since I don't have a clue what I'm going to do with my life, I might as well go to New York with her. Not to school—I'd stay in New York while she's a half hour away at the Culinary school in Hyde Park."

"No way. That is no place for you," Randall insisted.

"Well, Carlotta told me that Grandma Helen believed that you have to go where your heart takes you."

Randall nodded his head thoughtfully. "That's good advice. But you have to check in with your brain, and with your father. Both of them say 'No.'"

"How do you know what my brain says?"

"You have a pea-brain, Honey. It's easy to read! Ouch!" he exclaimed as Stacie's elbow landed in his side.

They spent the drive home talking about the future: about Stacie's upcoming graduation from Marana High School and the possibility of her going to New York City.

23

On the eve of Stacie's high school graduation, the three sisters headed toward Spartan Manor with flashlights beaming ahead to watch for snakes. Once inside, Vanessa sprawled out on the futon. "I can't believe you're not going to go out partying with your friends all night long on your graduation night, Stacie. Boy, when I graduated, I stayed out the entire night and most of the next day."

"We remember, Vanessa," Allison said as she sat down at the table. "We were there—in a hotel—hoping you'd come by and see us before we left."

"Oh, geez, bring that up again, Al, just because you stayed home on your grad night. I can't help it if I'm the only one who knows how to have fun around here."

"I want to be with you guys." Stacie said. "I'm not going to see you for awhile. New York's a long ways away."

"I still can't believe Dad's letting you go," Vanessa said.

"I'm eighteen, Vanessa—besides, Dad let you leave home when you were seventeen."

"Yeah—but that was with strict supervision. Believe me, it doesn't get any stricter than living with Sharlene and Dan. Break any of *his* rules and you're likely to end up in jail."

Allison grinned. "I still can't get over the time he went over to your friend's house and acted like you were under arrest for breaking curfew."

"Yeah—it was only twenty after twelve, but he said, 'By golly, when I say be home by twelve, I mean twelve—not twelve o' one, not twelve o' five. I mean twelve.'" Vanessa lowered her voice as she said it. "What can I say— he took his surrogate father role very seriously." Vanessa glanced at Stacie's navy blue cap with a gold tassel and her blue gown. "Isn't it a little weird that none of us graduated from the same high school?"

"It is weird," Allison agreed. "We lived in the same place for so long, and it ended up none of us graduated in the same state! It's hard to believe so much has changed."

"Like who would've believed you'd be married and divorced by now." Vanessa quipped.

Allison ignored the jibe as Stacie grabbed a sports bag she had brought in with her.

"I have a surprise for you guys." Stacie opened the bag and pulled out a worn leather journal.

"What is it?" Vanessa asked.

"It's Grandma Helen's journal. Carlotta gave it to me when Dad and I went to Guadalupe."

"That was over a month ago. How come we're just hearing about this now?" Allison asked.

"I tried to talk to both of you, but neither of you returned my calls. So I just decided to wait until we were all together—which is now." She sat down purposely between the two of them and opened the journal to a page that was marked with an old strip of ivory ribbon. "Here—listen to this—"

"I never expected to fall in love that day, but it happened the moment our eyes met. Within a few hours, we were in each other's arms. In our hearts we knew we belonged together, in the dark we whispered promises we would never be able to keep. We should have spent a lifetime together; instead we shared three days."

They sat speechless for a moment until Allison spoke in a mere whisper. "Who was he?"

Stating the most obvious answer, Stacie whispered. "Our grandpa, whoever he is."

"The journal doesn't say?"

"No." Anticipating their next question Stacie continued, "And we already know that Carlotta doesn't know who he is either. She said Grandma Helen was determined to keep his identity a secret."

"Why?"

"Grandma Helen believed he was an important man whose destiny was more important than their love." Stacie turned to another page. "Here's something else—and I'll warn you—it's a long one—*"We were lying on a blanket under a sky alive with stars. I was completely relaxed with his arm wrapped securely around me; my skin tingled where he lightly caressed my arm.*

"Tell me a story." I whispered, longing to hear his warm voice.

He asked, "What kind of story?"

"Something special," I told him. "Something you haven't shared with anyone else."

I watched him gaze at the fingernail sliver of the moon. It was only moments before he told me the night sky reminded him of a special night long ago. A satisfied smile turned up the edges of his mouth and he rolled over on his side, facing me. "I know just the one." He kissed me and rested his hand on my belly. Then he told me—

"When I was nine years old, I spent the whole month of June with my grand-

parents on their farm in Minnesota. It was a kid's dream. They were such happy people, full of life and of love for one another. My grandmother was always in the kitchen cooking, and I remember the wonderful smells of her homemade pies and dumplings. My grandfather took me fishing and taught me about farm equipment. One night grandpa and I stayed overnight at the lake. It was a beautiful night—the sky lit brightly with stars. I asked him then to tell me about his life. We talked for hours, but there was one story that especially stayed with me. Grandpa told me 'all it takes is one person to touch your life in such a way that you'll be changed forever. You'll feel like you were blessed with the presence of an angel.' That's how he felt, he said, when he was my age, nine years old, and a stranger came to his parents' farm—the same farm he and I were camping on that night. His parents were hard-working people with four kids and another on the way. My grandpa was the oldest. His father, my great-grandfather, was very strict, and his mother was frequently tired. They had the same schedule every day: hard work from sunup until sundown. They didn't seem happy or try to make life fun. Winter was settling in and they were busy chopping wood, hunting for food, canning, and making quilts. One day, just before supper, there was a knock at the door. My great-grandfather answered it to find a young man asking for work. Great-grandpa said no and told him to go away. A couple hours later, when he was closing up the barn for the night, he saw a form lying on the road coming into the property. He ran over and found the young man, collapsed. Great-grandpa got him back to the house and my great-grandparents saved his life by feeding him and keeping him warm. Within a few days a big snowstorm hit, one of the biggest in recent history, and they were all snowed in. The young man, named Tom Bailey, slowly regained his strength, but by then Granddad's parents had begun to like him, and they asked him to stay the rest of the winter. Bailey, as he was called, brought joy into the household. He had a way of bringing out the best in everyone. My grandfather told me, "He was a hero. He brought love and laughter into a hardened household. He was like an angel, and it was a happy time for all of us." Grandpa told me that his parents were able to hold onto some of that joy for the rest of their lives."

His eyes softened at the memory. I reached over and cupped the top of his hand with mine and said, "That was a beautiful story."

"Do you know why I chose that particular story for you?" He playfully touched my nose with the tip of his finger and followed with a warm kiss at the nape of my neck.

I closed my eyes. "Because this is a perfect night, just like the night you stayed by the lake with your grandfather."

He interwove his fingers with mine and brought my hand up to his cheek. Before he replied, he looked deeply in my eyes. "It's because for the first time in my *life I know what he means. You're my angel, you've changed me forever."*

Overcome with love and gratitude, I turned my cheek into his hand and kissed the tips of his fingers. "Thank you."

He brushed his lips at the corner of my eye where a teardrop hovered, then pulled me on top of him where he held me close.

And that, my dear sweet angel, is why I call you Bailey.

Stacie closed the journal as she watched her sisters wipe their eyes. The story, especially learning about the origin of their mother's nickname, had the same effect on Stacie each time she had read it.

Questions followed, but because Stacie had already told her sisters everything she had learned from Carlotta, there were no new answers. "I have a big day tomorrow." Stacie said. "You guys can stay up all night reading this if you want." Stacie looked at Vanessa. "But before I head off to bed, I just want to know if you checked into those things I asked about."

Vanessa's eyes widened. "Yes, I did, and Mitch helped. We sifted through old newspapers on microfiche at the library and we—"

"Wait a minute." Allison interrupted. "Back up. What are you talking about now?"

Vanessa swirled her legs around, going in one swift movement from lying on her stomach to sitting on the floor with her legs stretched out in front of her. "Well, we knew that Mom had once lived in L.A., but after meeting Carlotta, we knew when. So Stacie asked me to find out anything I could."

Stacie, looking a little guilty for excluding Allison, spoke up. "I'm sorry I didn't tell you, Allison. I just thought you were dealing with a lot already."

Memories of the past several months played over in Allison's mind—the arguments between her and Todd, the continual seesaw between bouts of crying and trying to put up a good front around Jason. That perpetual feeling of shame that had invaded her life several years earlier now added another layer—she hadn't been available to her sisters, and now she felt unreliable and not needed. "It's not your fault, Stace. You did try to talk to me."

"Listen up, guys." Vanessa jumped in. "I found the obituary for June Kiser, our great-grandmother. She died in 1965. That's probably when Mom moved to North Dakota."

"Why are we just hearing about this now?" Allison asked a little irritably. "When did you do all this?"

Vanessa rolled her eyes impatiently. "You're hearing about it now because I just got into town today. And—I was busy at school and didn't start looking into this until the day before yesterday, after I finished finals."

"Is that all you were able to find?" Stacie asked, getting back to the subject.

"No—there's more." Vanessa wobbled her head back and forth as she smiled teasingly at Stacie. "There's a lot more—so don't rush me." Vanessa glanced at Allison, then back to Stacie. "Along with the obituary, we found this—" Vanessa reached into her handbag, pulled out a folded copy of a newspaper article, and handed it to Stacie.

WOMAN FOUND DEAD

June Kiser, age 59, died Saturday of injuries sustained in a fall down her staircase. Authorities have not ruled out the possibility of foul play and an investigation is pending. Having lived in Glendale since 1932, Mrs. Kiser was an active member of the women's Junior League, and has been instrumental in many local charity events. She is survived by her granddaughter, Madeline Kiser.

"Let me see that." Allison looked over Stacie's shoulder and reread the article. "Can you imagine what that must've been like for Mom? First grandma dies when Mom was only six. Then great-grandma Kiser dies when Mom is only what—sixteen?"

"Yeah—she had just barely turned sixteen."

"Did you find a follow-up article?" Stacie asked. "Was it an accident or was there a burglar or something?"

"We looked through several more months of microfiche, but we didn't find anything." She didn't tell her sister's that she and Mitch had gotten hungry and bored after sitting at the UCLA library for more than three hours.

"What about the address I gave you? Did you check that out?" Stacie asked.

"What address?" Allison asked.

Stacie reached for the journal, opened it up to another page, and took out a torn envelope with a card inside. "It's a birthday card—from June Kiser to Grandma Helen. It was mailed to this address from Glendale, and inside it's simply signed *Mom.*"

As Allison opened the card and confirmed what Stacie said, Vanessa responded to Stacie's questions. "Well, here's an interesting part—Mitch was surprised when I showed him the address. He said it was just a couple blocks over from where he grew up. We drove right to the house without consulting a map. It's a really nice area. The houses are huge! It's hard to believe that Mom lived there at one time."

"So what happened?" Stacie asked.

"We knocked on the door. The woman who answered was really polite, and, after hearing our story, said she'd only lived in the house for eight years and didn't know anything about the previous owners. We thanked her and left, but when we were almost out to the car, she ran out and said that the neighbors across the street, the Smiths, had lived there for many years and that they might have known June Kiser."

Stacie's eyes widened in anticipation. "Did you go there?"

"Of course we went there."

"Did you meet the people?" Allison was becoming impatient with the storytelling.

"Yes. Mr. Smith answered the door. It was a little weird. He did a double take and after I explained who I was he said, 'of course you're Madeline's daughter.' Then he smiled and said, 'Either that, or she's only aged a few years in the past thirty.' He invited us in and asked how Mom was."

"What'd you tell him?" Allison asked.

"I told him the truth, that she had left home a few years ago and that we didn't know where she was. I told him she never talked much about her childhood and that we hadn't even known she lived in his neighborhood until recently."

"What did he say?" Allison asked.

"Well, it was odd. He just nodded his head as if he understood. It seemed like he was being very cautious about what he said. But he called her Madeline. He had never heard of the name Bailey. He said that if we see our mother, please let her know that he would like to hear from her."

"That's it?"

"Well, I asked what Mom and Great-Grandma June were like. He said Mom was a beautiful young girl with a big heart. And he didn't know Great-Grandma June very well. But it seemed to me that there were a lot of things that he didn't want to say."

Allison plopped her head down on a pillow. "This is so weird, meeting Carlotta, and now finding out where Mom lived in L.A. I've been having this funny feeling lately, as if there's a much bigger picture to this than we ever thought. I feel like this has become a big puzzle that we're supposed to be putting together, but we're still missing some pieces."

"What do you mean?"

Allison turned to answer Stacie's question. "Shortly after you told me about Carlotta, I remembered a time before Mom left. Mom and I had gone to the grocery store. I had been in the magazine section. When I caught up with Mom, she was standing in the produce section staring at a Native American woman. When I asked her why she was staring she just shrugged her shoulders, saying something about her was familiar." Allison looked at her sisters with a far off look in her eyes. "And do you remember Dad saying that maybe Mom had been acting strange before she left us? There are probably all kinds of clues—we just don't know what they mean."

Vanessa tilted her head thoughtfully. "We could make ourselves crazy over this. In the end, what does it matter anyway? Mom left us. We tried to find her, but we have no idea where she is." At Allison's obvious irritation, Vanessa corrected herself. "Okay, Allison, you guys tried to find her—and so did Dad. Mom doesn't want to be found. It's been four years—four long years since we've seen her. And isn't it frustrating? We may never know the answers. So why are we torturing ourselves with this stuff when nothing adds up anyway?"

"I need to know." Stacie blurted. "I need to figure out who I am."

Vanessa and Allison looked at Stacie peculiarly. Allison spoke, "You know who you are just as much as we do, Stacie."

Stacie looked down at her hands. "I just think we'll never be at peace until we know what really happened to her." Stacie picked up the journal, closed it, then handed it to Allison. "I can't believe we've stayed up this late. I'm exhausted—and going to bed. Tomorrow's my big day."

Allison and Vanessa inconspicuously winked at each other. It was an even bigger day than Stacie was aware of. The after-graduation party for Stacie and Lena was not a surprise. But Stacie had no idea that her friend Claire and many out of town relatives were going to make it to her graduation ceremony and would be surprising her at the party.

"Wait, Stace—don't go yet." Vanessa reached for her purse and took out two small packages wrapped in purple tissue paper with small, sparkling, silvery bows. "I bought us all something."

Allison and Stacie opened their gifts and each pulled out a delicate necklace with three red hearts intertwined. There was a printed saying attached. It was titled, *Loving Heart,* and said, *Have you remembered to love yourself unconditionally, to forgive yourself for not measuring up to your own expectations? Remember that each day is a new day to begin the path to your dreams. But loving yourself and others unconditionally is the foundation to make those dreams come true.*

Before her sisters had a chance to comment, Vanessa said, "I bought these for two reasons. First, I was drawn to the three hearts—which, to me, obviously symbolizes us. But when I saw the name of the company who designed the hearts, I was blown away."

"Why?" Allison asked.

"Look at the back of the printed card." Vanessa responded.

Allison and Stacie turned the cards over.

"Bailey's Hearts." Stacie whispered.

Silence expanded in the room as tears welled up in three girls eyes.

"Thank you, Vanessa." Allison said.

"Yes, thanks." Stacie reached over to give Vanessa a hug.

"There are all kinds of these, each with its own saying. Next time you guys come to L.A., I'll take you to the shop and we'll pick out another.

24

"Wake up! Wake up!" Allison and Vanessa stood over Stacie's bed, shaking her.

"Go away." Stacie mumbled, her words quickly turning into a shriek upon being tickled. She jumped up. "Okay—I'm up!"

"It's about time." Vanessa looked at her watch. "It's almost eleven. But Al and I figure we have enough time to take you shopping."

"I slept too long! I've got a lot to do. I told Dad I'd clean the house before Amma and Afi arrive."

"It's done, sister." Allison said. "Vanessa and I swept the porch and *quietly* cleaned the house, since Dad had said to let you sleep. He's going to vacuum while we're gone."

Stacie grinned. 'Thanks, guys. I'll just take a quick shower."

Allison and Vanessa looked at one another, then shook their heads. "Nope—be ready in five."

"No way!" Stacie yelled.

"Way," Vanessa snarled. She opened up several of Stacie's dresser drawers and pulled out a bra, panties, and a pair of shorts. Then she went to the closet and grabbed a shirt. "We've slaved away all morning in your honor as if we were Cinderella and you, the wicked step-sister. We've waited long enough for you, Sleeping Beauty, to get out of bed." She pushed the clothes into Stacie's arms. "Now we want to have some fun!"

Stacie giggled. "Well hi-ho out the door and let me get dressed in private."

Allison crossed her arms authoritatively. "Why do you want us out of here? Are you hiding something, lil' sis'? A tattoo maybe? A hickey? Or maybe a cigarette stash?"

Stacie laughed while shoving them out the door. "I have no body art of any kind, not yet anyway, and I quit the habit. Now get out of here." She shut the door with a smile on her face, relishing this rare fun time with her sisters. A few minutes later she walked into the kitchen. Vanessa and Allison were standing by the front door, ready to leave. "Don't I get breakfast?"

"We fixed you breakfast." Vanessa pointed toward a glass on the counter. "The instant kind."

"Thanks," Stacie uttered sarcastically. "Where's Dad?"

"He went to help a friend. Some guy named Spencer."

Stacie suppressed an involuntary grin that, ever since meeting Spencer a few weeks ago, embarrassingly appeared every time she heard his name. "So what's Dad helping him with?" She took a drink.

"Dad's helping him move into Spartan Manor," Allison answered.

Stacie just about spit out the vitamin-charged chocolate milk. "What?"

"He said that Spencer, and Spencer's little sister, needs a temporary place to stay, so he offered the little trailer for awhile. Do you know him?"

"Yeah, I met him a couple weeks ago."

He's so cute! She thought.

"He works at the plant. I think Dad's kind of adopted him, Spencer's about nineteen or twenty, has never known his father, and his mother is in rehab. Dad said that Spencer is currently taking care of his little sister, Lizzy. She's only four years old." Stacie hoped her voice sounded casual.

Vanessa grew impatient. "Let's go—we can talk in the car."

Stacie finished her drink in several gulps and was grateful for the break in conversation. "Is it okay if I brush my teeth?"

"Not the dentist recommended three minutes. If you haven't gotten the hint Stacie, we're in a hurry."

A few minutes later they piled into the car with Allison behind the wheel.

"Is this blue bomb ever going to quit?" Vanessa asked.

Stacie put on her seat belt in the back seat. "Dad says it got us all through high school. It doesn't owe us a thing."

Vanessa patted the torn dash. "You've been so good to us, baby." Then she turned to Stacie. "Al and I stayed up until three going through that journal. Grandma was incredible."

"I know." Stacie leaned forward. "What really got to me was that after talking to Carlotta and reading the journal, I realized I knew more about Grandma Helen than Mom does. Isn't it strange to think that Mom didn't remember her own mother?"

"I remembered something," Allison interrupted. "When I was in band in the sixth grade, we were putting on a special concert for grandparents. Amma and Afi drove down from Mountain to be there, and it prompted me to ask Mom again about her parents. I was adamant that I wanted to know why I didn't have any grandparents on her side. Mom got upset. I remember her saying something like, 'my mom died when I was young, but she wasn't a good woman. I don't know who my father is, and I never want to talk about this again'."

Stacie spoke quietly. "All of us knew not to talk about Mom's family. But why did Mom think grandma wasn't a good woman? It's obvious she was special."

Shifting sideways, Vanessa rested her left arm on top of the seat. "It must have something to do with her time in L.A. I mean, wasn't it a little obvious in the journal that Helen loved her dad? Her memories of him were so sweet, but she never mentioned her mother. Yet Great-Grandma June was still alive—that's who Mom went to live with."

"You're right, Vanessa," Allison said. "Maybe you should try talking to Mr. Smith again. Maybe you could ask him some more direct questions this time."

"No. The person we should be asking is Mom. What good does it do to find out about her childhood?"

They sat in silence for awhile, burdened with this new information that still didn't tell them what they wanted to know the most. *Where was Mom? Why did she leave them?* The pain was like a crusty old scab.

"Judy's coming into town next month." Allison said, deciding to change the subject.

"It's neat how you guys have stayed so close," Vanessa said. "How long is she staying?"

"Permanently. She's moving here."

"Why would she do that? What's here?" Vanessa asked.

"Me—for one. She got a job at the U of A, she likes the weather, and she's looking for a change."

"Hmm. My friendship with Suzie fizzled after a few failed attempts at letter writing and a couple of awkward phone calls." Vanessa tilted her head toward Stacie. "What about you, Stace? I'll bet you've kept in touch with Claire." Vanessa suppressed the urge to wink at Allison conspiratorially.

"Yeah, we still write each other. But I can't believe it's been almost three years since I've seen her. She was at her dad's in Michigan last year when Dad and I made it back for the family reunion."

"That's too bad." Allison made eye contact with Stacie in the rearview mirror. "I never asked you if you saw any of your old friends while you were there."

Stacie giggled. "You didn't ask a lot about anything. You were a little preoccupied at the time."

"Yeah, I guess I was."

Vanessa looked at Allison seriously. "What's going on with you—and Todd—and Jason? How are you guys doing?"

Allison glanced Vanessa's way. "Todd and I are doing better at divorce than we did at marriage. The main thing we're doing right is taking good care of Jason and making sure he feel's loved. And in an odd way, we're sort of supportive of one another. But everything else in my life is a major struggle."

"Have you thought about going to school?"

"Well, that would solve everything." Allison said sarcastically. "Do you have any idea how much money and time it takes to raise a child? I'm working at a bank for just over minimum wage. It occurred to me recently that my wardrobe costs way too much in proportion to my lousy pay. We have to look good for our customers though, you know?"

"Maybe you should quit the bank and go to work somewhere where you don't have to look so good." Vanessa's tone was half-joking, half-serious.

"That's logical," Allison again replied sarcastically, and then shrugged her shoulders. "At least the benefits are decent."

"Well then, start taking night classes."

"Vanessa, my life isn't anything like yours—okay? I'm tired all the time. I barely have enough energy to work full-time and be a decent mother. I can't keep up with the laundry. How am I going to add homework on top of it?"

"I don't know, but sooner or later you're going to have to try." Vanessa shifted her attention to the back of the car. "And what about you, Stace? I don't exactly understand why it is you aren't going to college."

Stacie felt a rare moment of insanity as she started giggling. The giggling turned into laughter when she saw Vanessa's confused expression. Making eye contact again with Allison in the rearview mirror made her laugh harder.

"What is with you?" Vanessa asked.

Stacie took a few deep breaths as her giggles subsided. "I just think it's funny that you've turned out to be so practical."

With that, Allison started laughing too. For the first time, it felt good to laugh at the turns their lives had taken. "She's right—*Mother,*" Allison said to Vanessa.

Vanessa haughtily faced forward. Try as she might, she couldn't keep a smile from creeping up.

Stacie leaned forward as Allison pulled into Gadabout Salon. "I thought we were going shopping?"

"Nope." Vanessa said innocently. "We're here to be spoiled. We should've done this before Allison got married, but none of us had any money."

"Do we have money now?" Stacie asked.

Allison got out of the car and grabbed her purse. "No, we're still financially challenged. But that's what credit cards are for."

They walked into the salon. Three hours later they walked out, refreshed and energized. They had enjoyed being pampered: haircut, facial, manicure, and pedicure.

"Queens for a day." Allison said as she started up the car. "Now on to Price Club to pick up the cake, then home in plenty of time for Stacie to get ready for her big night."

Stacie zipped up a red-and-white flowered, short skirt and pulled a white silk top over her head. She fluffed her wispy blonde hair with her fingers, grabbed her cap and gown, and left the bedroom.

"Hey Stacie, Lena called. You don't have to pick her up." Vanessa scooped up freshly cut cantaloupe and added it to the large watermelon bowl. "She said Carlotta wants to talk to Dad, so she's going to drop Lena off here."

"Okay."

"I'm finally going to meet Carlotta." Vanessa washed plump green grapes to add to the watermelon, strawberries and cantaloupe as Allison cut some limes to spritz the fresh fruit.

"She's looking forward to meeting you, too."

Just then Randall walked from his bedroom into the living room. Stacie saw a wave of emotion pass over him as he spotted her cap and gown.

Vanessa noticed it also. "Oh, Dad," she crooned, "what's wrong?"

"Nothing." He said in a muffled tone, looking at the large cake decorated with an artist's easel sitting next to the Statue of Liberty. Then he looked at each of his daughters. His eyes watered as his attempt to keep his emotions under control backfired.

As Allison and Vanessa walked toward Randall, Stacie looked on. It brought back the memory of the last time her dad had cried in front of all three of them. Stacie had stayed back then—because she wasn't his daughter. She remembered how the pain at that time felt like a knife plunging deep. The memory was intense. But new memories with her dad now played out in her mind: long walks with her dad out in the desert and building a fence together around a backyard and garden area; she and her dad watching movies and popping popcorn; then meeting Carlotta and Lena. Stacie sighed; she had an awful lot to be grateful for. Her contented expression turned into a smile as she joined her dad and sisters in a group hug.

Randall closed his eyes momentarily, obviously basking in the love he felt for his daughters.

As the hug naturally broke up, Randall broke the silence. "I'm sorry, girls. I just couldn't contain myself." He looked down to see three pairs of sympathetic eyes directed his way. "They're tears of joy really." He backed up a step as those eyes turned curious. "I'm just so glad I finally have my girls raised and out of the house." He took another step back before getting ready to bolt outside. "You girls were a handful!" He barely got out the door before Vanessa, Allison, and Stacie tore off after him.

Stacie and Vanessa had the speed of youth. Randall had determination, but not the endurance. Allison soon realized she needed more exercise, since she couldn't keep up with them at all. As a car turned into the drive, Randall, who was losing ground to Vanessa and Stacie, gave up the chase. He halted and turned around. With a pointed finger held up in a scolding manner, he looked at Stacie. "Now, now—we have company. Carlotta and Lena are here."

They both started laughing. "We'll get you for this, Dad." Stacie said.

Randall put his arm around her. "You already did," he said seriously. "You're leaving home. You're leaving me."

———

As soon as Carlotta got out of the car, she immediately walked up to Vanessa, took both of Vanessa's hands and held them firmly in her own. "You have Bailey's eyes, her mouth, and her hair." Carlotta took Vanessa in her arms and held her as the memory of Bailey being pulled out of Carlotta's arms all those years ago washed over her.

"I can't stay long," Carlotta said. "I would love to sit down with you, maybe after all the company leaves."

"I'd like that," Vanessa replied.

After making plans to meet the following week, and declining Vanessa's offer of a glass of iced tea, Carlotta signaled Randall to talk with her. There was still a lot of work to do before the party that evening.

"So let me guess," Randall said to Carlotta as they sat outside. "You had a dream last night."

"That's right Randall, I did. And you're going to love this one."

"Does it have something to do with the party tonight? Are you having second thoughts about having a bunch of Icelanders and Yaquis in the same room? Don't worry about it. It'll be fun."

Carlotta smiled, remembering the conversation she and Randall had enjoyed a few weeks earlier, when planning the party, about a few obnoxious, racist relatives on both sides who could possibly stir up some trouble. "No—it's not that." Carlotta reached into a duffel bag she had brought, took out a large manila envelope and handed it to Randall.

"What's this."

"Your next project."

"What do I need a project for?"

"You've completely restored Spartan Manor, you've built a fence, and the landscaping you've done is beautiful. What else do you have planned?"

Randall sat silent for a moment.

Nothing. I don't know what I'm going to do next.

He opened the envelope and pulled out blueprints and a pencil sketch of a house. "This must be the house Helen designed. Stacie told me about it."

"The dream was so vivid, Randall—the house was beautiful, and you were having a Fourth of July picnic with a lot of family and friends.

And Madeline was there, but it would be cruel of me to say it.

"You were happy, Randall."

"I don't know, Carlotta." Randall let out a heavy sigh. "I was desperate for a miracle when I brought the girls to this place. And really, if I had given the decision to move here more thought, I probably wouldn't have swallowed my pride long enough to come to a place that Madeline owned. The first year the girls and I were here, I asked myself over and over again, what am I doing here? But I owed it to them to stay in one place. I figured this was the only connection I could give them to their mother. But I've never had any intention of making this my permanent home. I figured I'd leave this place when the girls were gone."

"And where would you go? Where is home now? Where is the place for the girls to come home to? Is it Bismarck?"

"I can't imagine moving back there—too many memories."

With a soft voice that conveyed a heart full of compassion, Carlotta stated simply, "Build the house, Randall. Its time has come."

———

Considering there were over three hundred graduates, the ceremony passed quickly. Knowing Stacie and Lena would want to spend more time out on the football field with their friends, their families encouraged them to stay a little while longer.

Forty minutes later, Stacie and Lena stood at the door to Props Café. A quick glance at each other elicited immediate grins before Stacie pushed open the door.

"The guests of honor have arrived!" Lena yelled. She and Stacie looked at each other again and laughed.

"Aahhh!" Stacie yelled. Her hands went up to her mouth as she gasped in surprise. Amma and Afi stood in the doorway, smiling as everyone in the packed restaurant yelled, "Surprise!" Grandparents, aunts, uncles and cousins from both families greeted the guests of honor.

Jason ran up to Stacie before she barely had time to greet her grandparents. "We really surprised you huh, Aunt Stacie?"

Stacie bent down and picked Jason up, twirling him around. "You sure did." She touched her forehead against his and gently rubbed noses with him.

"Know what?" Jason asked.

"What?"

"Nessa tol' me she was my favorwit aunt. I told her nuh-uh, Aunt Stacie is."

Stacie laughed while glancing over at Vanessa, who did not seem amused.

"Someday he'll be mine, Stacie," Vanessa said. "You'll be so far away he'll forget all about you."

Todd walked up, gave Stacie a quick hug, then took Jason from her. "I'll take him, Stacie. You go say hi to the rest of your relatives. They came a long way to see you."

"Thanks, Todd." Just as she handed Jason to Todd, she caught a glimpse of an old, familiar friend. "Claire!" Two seconds later the friends were hugging arm in arm while Lena was swept away in the welcoming arms of her relatives.

The next several hours were spent in lively chatter amongst the two families. Allison felt a tinge of regret as she introduced Todd and Jason to her relatives. It was the first time most of them had met Todd, who was now her ex-husband. Occasionally Allison glanced at him throughout the evening, wondering if there might still be hope for them. But she realized the feelings were born from guilt, not love, so she tried her best to let them go.

Later in the evening, Stacie and Lena took a rare moment from visiting and sat down next to one another. They looked at everyone, visiting, drinking, nibbling on cake, cleaning up messes, some of the adults playing darts, and the younger kids playing tag outside.

"It's like having Mountain, North Dakota and Guadalupe, Arizona mixed into one." Stacie said. Neither Stacie nor Lena denied that there were a few people in the room who'd had some racially challenging moments during the evening. "Who is your uncle who is prejudiced against Native Americans?" Lena asked.

"My Uncle Gary," Stacie whispered. "He's the one talking to your dad." She unobtrusively pointed to the booth where the two men seemed to be talking amiably.

"Figures. My dad has a knack for mischief. He probably sniffed out the racism factor and is probably telling your uncle some made-up pagan stories just so he'll have a tale to tell later."

"Would your dad do that?"

"Why not? He's got a thick skin when it comes to racism. Maybe because he thinks many whites are ignorant."

"Well if it helps any, Uncle Gary doesn't limit his prejudices to Native Americans. He's prejudiced against every person who isn't white, or whose religion is anything other than Baptist, and he believes women should've remained home—definitely shouldn't be able to vote. Basically, he's prejudiced about everything."

"Well, everyone else seems to be having a good time. And you're right—our families do seem similar."

Stacie nodded her head in agreement. "Yep, they're all right. Loving."

"And nurturing," Lena interjected.

"Bickering," Stacie quipped.

"Drinking."

"Fun."

"Irritating."

"Very." They both looked at each other and laughed. "I think we should get out of here. You know, go somewhere else—move away."

"I agree. How about New York?" Lena asked teasingly.

"Good idea!"

Lena looked back at the crowd. "Hey, everybody!" she yelled.

Most everyone stopped what they were doing and looked Lena's way. "Stacie and I are going to New York City!"

They were rewarded with cheers, hollers and whistles from the large group.

—

Stacie grabbed the folding chair and sat down gently, distributing her weight so she wouldn't stress the worn chair. She had her sketching pad with her and began outlining her favorite ironwood tree with its leafed branches hanging in every direction.

By this time, she seemed to know the secrets of this tree, each branch, each nest, each knot. She looked over at the small saguaro and began sketching it also. She took her time, making sure her pencil noted the indentation where it looked as if the saguaro had been wearing a belt. She sketched the holes that had been made by woodpeckers and the base that was woody and aged. She added her ironwood and her saguaro, then quickly sketched in a few creosote bushes and bursage plants. She planned to hang this in her

New York apartment as a reminder of home.

After completing her sketch, she sat quietly until she heard footsteps approaching. Knowing it was her dad, she turned to see him standing there, thoughtful. She returned his smile and tenderly noticed the glistening of tears shining in his eyes. "Have I ever told you just how proud I am of you, Stacie?"

She grinned, set her sketch down and went to give him a hug. "Actually, you did, Dad, one time when I was in first grade and I punched out little Ricky for looking under my dress."

Randall laughed. "If that was the only time I told you what an incredible young woman you are, then I'm long overdue." He rocked her back and forth, not wanting to let her go. "Lena just called. They're on their way."

"I guess this is it then." She looked up and gave him a bittersweet smile, and knew that right now she didn't care that he wasn't her real father, because even though the last few years had been tough, she loved him more than she could love any other father. She knew he felt the same closeness with her. "What are you going to do, Dad, out here all alone?"

"Oh, I don't know, maybe I'll work on improving my golf game."

"Why not learn to fly?"

"That's not a bad idea. It's better than the one Carlotta had."

"What's that?"

"She said I should build Grandma Helen's house."

They were interrupted as Lena arrived with cheers and hollers, her parents smiling and waving in the front seat. "Let's go already, Stacie girl. We've got a plane to catch and some fiiissssshhhh toooo fryyyyy." Lena was so excited it was contagious.

Stacie felt her own enthusiasm mount. "Righto, girl. Let's go."

Randall winked at his youngest. "I still can't believe I'm allowing you to do this. You stay out of trouble. Do you have your money, traveler's checks, I.D.'s? Do you want to change your mind? You can still do that, you know."

Stacie laughed. "I'll be fine, Dad." She gave him one last long hug. "I love you, Dad, bigger than the sky."

Randall knew he had to let her go, and it almost tore his heart right out of his chest. "I know you will." He forced himself to give her a gentle nudge, but couldn't resist adding, "Expect a visit from your old man real soon."

"That'd be great." Stacie got into the car.

As Lena's dad started the engine and stepped on the gas, Lena quickly rolled down the window. "Mr. Averson—I forgot to tell you—Grandma Carlotta said that it needs to be adobe."

"What?" he yelled?

Lena called back as they were pulling away. "The house—she said to tell you to build it with adobe bricks."

Rendered speechless, Randall grinned as he watched them drive away, both Lena and Stacie waving at him from the car window and blowing him kisses. He waved back until they were out of sight.

The desert was so quiet; he knew he was completely alone now. He headed back to the trailer.

I do need something to do.

He stopped when he saw the trailer, then he turned in the direction where his mother-in-law, a woman he'd never met, had sat years before in the shade of a large palo verde tree and drawn up plans to build a house.

That would be crazy. It should've been Madeline's house—not mine.

"Ah, what the hell."

A smile crossed his face. *Adobe. Damn, that woman's pushy.*

Part IV

25

Gregory slept so deeply that the song of the spade foot toads, during their mad rush to mate during the brief monsoon season, was lost to him during the night. Nor had he felt the breeze coming through the open windows that gently caressed him as he dreamed. But when he awoke, he immediately sensed her absence in the bed. Rolling over onto his side, he ran his hand along the sheet where she had slept, curled up beside him, all night. He knew he belonged to her. He marveled at the soothing comfort inside of him, knowing he had never felt like this before, knowing without a doubt where his heart belonged.

"Helen," he called out, his hand still resting where she had lain. "Helen?" He spoke louder, into the quiet trailer. Getting up, he put on his trousers and looked down the hall. When he realized she was not inside, he grabbed a shirt, put on his shoes and walked outdoors. It was only a bit past eight, and already the heat clung to the moist air. Since her car was still there, he first checked the shed. Since she wasn't there, he went for a walk—circling the trailer in a wide arc.

When he caught sight of her, he stopped—mesmerized by how beautiful and natural she looked. She was wearing a wide, floppy hat and a summer dress hiked up to her knees while sitting cross-legged on the ground, sketchbook on her lap, under a large mesquite tree. He quietly walked toward her as she gazed, deep in thought, at the landscape. Then she began to sketch.

She seemed so absorbed in what she was doing that he wasn't surprised when she didn't hear him. He was now close enough to touch her. He did so playfully, kneeling down and smothering her with kisses to the back of her neck and shoulders.

She laughed, tossing her head back to expose more places he could reach. "This is heaven on earth," she sighed.

He sat, with legs straddled, behind her and drew her close. "Hmm, you feel good, you smell good." Gregory glanced at the drawing, and then maneuvered to see it more closely. She had sketched a rustic, southwestern style house surrounded by vegetation and distant mountains. He could see the exact spot where she had it situated. "This is fantastic."

She tilted her head and looked up at him. "Yeah?"

"Yeah. It's designed as if it belongs here. It suits the surroundings perfectly."

"I'm going to build this house someday. I've known for some time this is the spot I should build, but this morning I woke up knowing exactly what I wanted the house to look like." She stood up, excited. "Here—I'll show you." After helping to pull him up, she began outlining the area. "Here's the front door, two big double doors with long narrow windows on each side. It will have one big room for the living, dining and kitchen area. The bedrooms will be off a small hallway over there." She pointed to the right of the imaginary living area, "and it's going to have a good-sized courtyard that will connect to my pottery shop." She paced the area, and, when that wasn't good enough, grabbed a large stick and drew a big outline in the sand. "There will be plants and flowers everywhere, some in a garden and some in pots."

He smiled at her enthusiasm. "Can I help?"

"Ohhh." Her hand reached up to her heart as she swooned. "Absolutely, you can." She ran into his arms, and he picked her up and twirled her around. Between planting kisses on his cheek and neck, she whispered, "I think we'd better finish college first."

He gently set her down and looked seriously into her eyes. "Have you thought about what I asked you?"

"About going to college here? Yes, I have. It's too late to apply for next semester but I'll plan on being back here in January."

He picked her up and twirled her around again. "That's my girl."

When her two feet were back on the ground, she said, "How about your girl making you some breakfast." She picked up her hat that had fallen to the ground.

"Are there extra bedrooms in that house of yours?"

"Huh?" She asked, unsure of his meaning.

"You know—for the kids. I don't want them sleeping in our room."

Helen's smile originated from deep within her and it lit up her eyes. "If we have a baby boy, I'd like to name him Thomas. If she's a girl, I'd like to name her Bailey. That special story you told me last night really touched me. I'd like to think an angel brought us together, just like Tom Bailey brought your grandparents together."

Gregory's eyes warmed. "Thomas or Bailey—I can picture that." They walked back to the trailer arm in arm.

An hour later, it was time for Gregory to leave. Helen walked him out to the truck. They were afraid to promise too much, to ask for too much. But neither of them had felt love and life as fully as they had felt it over the last several days.

"I have so much to look forward to when I come back. I can't wait to start my life here—with you," Gregory said.

Leaning into him, she rested her forehead against his chest and nestled her head under his chin. She melted into him further as his arms came around to hold her. They stayed there for a few minutes, enveloped in tender warmth. Then she pulled away so that she could look at him. He raised his hand, looking questioningly at her as he wiped the tears from her eyes.

She spoke—scared to speak the words she was feeling, but somehow knowing she needed to say them. "If I were to never see you again, I would feel so blessed to have had this time with you." She blinked as tears again filled her eyes. "I will always, always, love you and will carry you with me forever."

Overcome with emotion, Gregory held her close, then cupped her face gently between his large, strong hands. He couldn't say goodbye. He couldn't say anything. Touching her lips with his, they felt each other's tears blend and become one.

———

Helen could not pinpoint when it was she felt herself change from drifting by in a blissful high to allowing words of doubt to echo in her mind. She knew those words; they felt familiar to her. The voice was steady and sure. It was her own voice, tantalizing her with words she could not bear to hear. *He's not coming back.*

She had already received three precious postcards from him. He had mailed the first the very day he left, then one each the following two days. *I miss you already. Be back soon. It's cooling off with every mile. How's the pottery going? I ran out of gas, daydreaming of you, had to hitch a ride twenty miles to the nearest station. I'm home! Got home late last night, parents are throwing me a 'surprise' party tonight. Wish you were here.*

But that was it, nothing else now for more than a week.

But today a letter arrived. She looked at the envelope that lay heavy in her hand. She stroked the letters that formed her name and address. She visualized his hand grasping the pen and somehow felt the pain in his heart as he wrote the letter. She did not need to read it to know she would never see him again. She felt it—sensed it—as deeply as the heat soaking into her bones. But she needed to hear his words of goodbye. She went back inside the trailer, grabbed the old red quilt, then walked outside to the mesquite tree that had provided shade for the two of them just ten days earlier. It was miserably hot outside, but she needed the soothing comfort of the desert more than she needed cool air. She shook the quilt, laid it in the shade, and sat down. She opened the letter slowly, as if delaying hearing the words would prolong their time together. But the words came too soon.

Dearest Helen,
I don't know where to begin. I don't have any idea how
I can even get the words out that I have to say to you. Sandra
is pregnant.

Helen dropped the letter and jumped up, trying to breathe as her chest squeezed into her heart. She felt her future fall in shattered bits all around her. She tried to pace—tried walking around in circles. *No, Dear God, please, please don't take Gregory away from me.* The storm inside of her built until the pressure couldn't be held in any longer and she heard herself scream in pain and agony. "No, God, No! Don't do this. Please don't, please—don't do this." The scream turned into sobs so deep, her breathing so hard, she knew right then it was possible to die from a pain this deep. She fell back onto the blanket, onto her side, curling up into herself, as sobs shook her entire being.

Memories of her three days with Gregory played over and over in her mind like a turning kaleidoscope. Doing chores that were fun because they did them together: dishes, cooking, fixing the shed door, and hanging her "Kiser's Ranchita" sign so it didn't dangle. They arose early for the sunrise and drank wine as they watched the sunset. They hibernated like many desert animals, napping and making love during the hottest part of the day. Several times their lovemaking was so raw and passionate it surprised them both and left them breathless. Or it was playful as they squeezed together in the shower, washed each other, and enjoyed lovemaking as Gregory sat on the closed toilet seat while she sat on him. The night before he left, they made love so sweetly and tenderly they both cried afterwards. And the laughter; no one had ever made her laugh so hard or so deeply before. He held her, encouraged her, while she cried more tears over the loss of her beloved father. And in between the laughter and the tears were many tender moments as they shared past memories and future dreams. They had lived an eternity in those three days.

She did not know how long she had been there, but her first conscious thought came as a white wing dove flew to a nearby branch. Her sobs slowed. Breathing was difficult—quick intakes of breath while her lungs tried valiantly to get enough oxygen.

She tried to focus on the dove, or watch the cottontail that she knew was off in the distance, or notice the ground squirrel as it playfully sped by, but the pain inside her blinded her to the life that was going on around her. She tried to listen to the soft breeze through the trees or the beautiful song of the curve-billed thrasher that was perched nearby on the arm of a saguaro, but all she could hear was the sound of Gregory's voice speaking the words he had written in the letter.

Sandra is pregnant.

She tried to find God in the beauty of her surroundings, the soft wispy clouds up above and, once again, by glancing at the dove above her, but all she could find was emptiness so big she felt she would disappear.

She looked at the letter; her eyes remained there for several minutes, as if contemplating whether the pages were her enemy or her friend. She reached over with the realization that this was as hard for Gregory as it was for her.

Oh, Dear Gregory!

She propped herself up on one elbow and once again began reading.

> *I've been wandering around the last few days completely in a daze, feeling anger, and guilt, but mostly an overpowering sense of loss over you, over us.*
>
> *I say to myself, 'if only she would've told me sooner'. She's known for over a month, but said she wanted it to be a surprise. A month! And during that month I had the best three days of my life. And, God help me, I don't know whether to be eternally grateful for that time with you, even though I will feel the pain of losing you forever, or whether it would have been better for it to never have happened.*
>
> *There are so many things I want to tell you, to share with you. I want to share my life with you, Helen. But these words are the only thing I have to offer. I love you with all my heart, and I curse the hands of fate that have played this cruel trick on us.*
>
> *I know I should be doing a better job writing this letter to you, taking more care in the words I choose. But the truth is—there's not a damn thing I can say that will make any of this go away.*
>
> *Helen, I meant it when I said the time spent with you was the best time of my life. I never knew I could feel a connection with anyone as deeply as I felt it with you. I am sorrier than you'll ever know.*
>
> *Please forgive me, my love,*
>
> *Gregory*

The tears fell quietly this time, rolling past her left cheekbone and back toward her ear as she stayed huddled on her side. The sun was no longer high in the sky, but was finding its way over the horizon in its bid to say good-night. The early signs of a beautiful sunset were making its mark across the sky and reaching toward the surrounding mountains, illuminating their life lines, crevices, and stretch marks, just like a soft light on an old woman's face.

Helen was too withdrawn to care about the car that drove up, or the knock on her door, or the voice that called out, "Helen?" She didn't respond to the soft sound of footsteps that seemed to know where to find her. But when the sound of those steps stopped in front of her, tears began to flow once again as she saw her friend's well-worn sandals and dark, dusty feet.

"Carlotta." Helen looked up into the face of her dearest friend, who immediately dropped down and cradled her in her arms. They cried together as the glorious sunset cast shades of peach, magenta and purple against the deep blue sky.

26

The patio at 'Cushing Street Bar and Grill' had a lively Friday night crowd as Allison and her co-workers enjoyed dinner, drinks, and live music during their monthly outing. She was in the middle of her 'customer of the day' story, about a woman asking for a five-thousand dollar loan to train and primp her cat for an upcoming cat show, when the waiter came up to Allison and informed her she had a phone call.

Allison excused herself, followed the young man inside, and picked up the phone. To block the noise, she covered her other ear with her hand and said 'hello' into the phone.

Jenny, her fifteen year-old babysitter, immediately cried into the phone, "Jason was out riding his bike and—and this big dog ran after him. It scared Jason. He lost control and ran his bike right into the curb. It happened so fast, and the training wheels just—I don't know. They just didn't hold him up. He landed on the asphalt—on his face."

Allison's body tensed. After some specific questions, she was able to determine there was no need for an ambulance, but he might need stitches. Allison gave Jenny instructions to slow the bleeding and, after a brief explanation to her co-workers, she dropped money on the table to cover her bill and quickly left the restaurant.

Jenny, with Jason in tow, was standing near Allison's designated parking space when Allison pulled in. After comforting him briefly, they drove straight to the emergency room. As soon as Jason was in the care of a nurse, Allison called Todd and left a message.

More than an hour later, when Jason's cuts were stitched and the wounds cleaned, Allison left Jason with Jenny in the treatment room and walked to the front desk to use the phone.

Where are you, Todd?

She didn't bother leaving another message, since Todd rarely answered his phone and kept the volume on the answering machine turned low. Since the hospital wanted to keep Jason for observation the rest of the night, and Jason had been crying for his daddy, Allison went back in the room and explained to her son that she would try to find his daddy. After Jenny made a call to her parents, it was agreed she could stay at the hospital until

Allison returned.

The day's heat was finally giving way to a cool breeze as Allison drove to Todd's apartment. As he lived less than five minutes from her; neither home was far from the hospital. She parked in the nearest available spot and ran up the stairs. She came to a sudden jolt as she saw through the window the faint outline of her former husband in the arms of a woman with short, cropped hair.

"No, please no."

An upsurge of anger swelled within her as she ran to the door and pounded on it.

"Just a minute," Todd yelled from inside.

Through the window, Allison could see their surprised expressions. She waited, fidgeting as she heard the bolt unlock and the door burst open.

"Allison, what are you doing here?"

"It's Jason. He's been in a bike accident, you son of a bitch!" She walked past Todd and over to her longtime friend. "It was *you* all along. Why couldn't I see it?" Allison dug her fingernails deep into her own flesh, fighting every impulse to slap Judy.

Todd grabbed Allison by the arm and swung her around. "We'll deal with this later. Tell me about Jason."

With angry eyes, she said, "He's at UMC. His face is badly cut and he got stitches in his forehead. They're keeping him overnight to make sure there's no concussion—and—he wants his daddy. But right now, I'm just sorry you are his father." She started to turn when Todd grabbed her.

"Now just you wait a minute."

Allison jerked out of his hand, turned on her heels and ran down the steps. She ran from the two people in the world who knew her best. In the safety of her car, fear for Jason and betrayal from Todd and Judy escaped her in huge, racking sobs.

Oh no.

Thoughts about personal things she had told Judy in confidence regarding her relationship with Todd—especially during the divorce—added a layer of shame and vulnerability. She cried while driving to the hospital, barely keeping hysterics at bay. Once she arrived, she sat in the car until she calmed down.

Pull yourself together—you have to for Jason. Once inside, she headed straight for the restroom and took a good long look at herself in the mirror.

"Maybe this is what rock bottom looks like. At least I hope this is as bad as it gets," she said to her reflection.

She blew her nose and, using hand lotion and a paper towel, removed smeared make-up and mascara, then washed her face. After applying a touch of lip gloss, she took another look in the mirror at her red, puffy face and knew it would have to do.

On her way to Jason's room, she made a stop at the nurse's station. "Hi. How's my boy doing?"

"He's doing fine. Were you able to reach his dad? Jason has still been crying for him."

Allison tried to relax her clenched fists. "Yes, he'll be here soon." As if on cue, Allison heard the familiar sound of Todd's footsteps coming up behind her. She turned around and didn't catch herself before asking, "Where's your girlfriend?"

"She's parking the car." Todd replied, not apologetically. "Where's Jason?"

Allison pointed to his room. She stood there feeling paralyzed, unsure whether to follow Todd or to create some distance between them. The knots in her stomach made the decision for her; she headed toward the outside sitting area. The small courtyard with potted flowers was softly lit. Allison walked past a grouping of tables and chairs and sat on a wooden bench facing away from the hospital doors. Anger, humiliation, and betrayal were feelings she tried to ignore as she spoke prayers of gratitude for Jason's overall well being.

It could've been worse.

When the door opened, she didn't have to turn to hear Judy's soft, hesitant steps walking toward her.

"I never stopped loving Todd." Judy's voice from behind her was heavy with guilt. "I tried to get on with my life. I dated other men and even became engaged to someone, as you well know. But I couldn't marry him."

Allison almost laughed as she turned around and faced Judy. "Well, aren't you Miss Integrity—pining away over your best friend's husband while saving your fiancé from a loveless marriage."

Judy's posture straightened as she leaned forward. "You want me to feel sorry for you? You actually think you're the poor victim here? Well, sorry, but I don't feel that way. I don't know how we got into this mess but I'll tell you one thing—you deserve how this has turned out—every last bit of it. You're just lucky that Todd and I still love you and want what's best for you. Otherwise, you'd have nothing."

"How dare you! You stole my life right out from under me."

"I didn't steal Todd away. If anybody did that, you did!"

"What are you talking about?"

"I'm talking about high school. You knew how I felt about him and you went after him anyway."

"You barely knew him," Allison replied hotly.

"The feelings were there. The hope was there. And later, Todd and I were getting close in college. Do you have any idea what that did to me? When Todd admitted he was probably the baby's father? It just about killed me. And you know what? I think you were so miserable because of your mom and because of David that you didn't care who you hurt. You set your sights on Todd and didn't care at all about me. And you got him. In the meantime, you have messed up my life, Todd's life, and your own along with it. The only good thing that's come out of this is Jason. And right now, as pitiful as you've become, you don't deserve him."

Judy stormed toward the door, but before she went inside she paused. With one hand on the doorknob, she turned back around. Her words were spoken softly. "You once said that Todd was an optimist, a dreamer. That's true, but the follow up *is* there. The problem was you, Allison. Todd has always been honest with me. We had been dating for only a month when I saw you were pregnant. When he told me the truth and what he was going to do about it, it broke my heart. But I respected his decision, and I respected him for doing what he thought was right. He told me the truth. You didn't. He did his best, and all you did was let him know it wasn't good enough." Judy opened the door and walked out.

As the door closed between them, both women recognized the end of their friendship.

27

The end of the fall semester of Vanessa's junior year at UCLA was just two weeks away, but as she hopped out of her old yellow VW Super Beetle and ran through the gate and up the stairs to Mitch's second story apartment, thoughts of upcoming finals were the last thing on her mind. She pounded at the door and breathlessly called out his name, "Mitch, it's me—Vanessa. Open up."

She was knocking again when the door swung open. Vanessa hopped up and down, her arms flying, "I've got the best—" she cut herself short as her heart did a somersault and landed right in her stomach at the sight of him. It was after two in the afternoon, yet Mitch was wearing a pair of gray sweats and an old t-shirt, his hair was uncombed and he hadn't yet shaved. But she didn't need the physical description to see the disheveled look in his eyes. Her enthusiasm left her like air rushing out of a deflating balloon. "Are you okay?"

With a tilt of his head, he invited her inside. Sarcasm tinged each word as he said, "I'm fine, just fine," while shutting the door behind her.

"Mitch," Vanessa whispered. "What is it? What's the matter?"

As if awakening from a trance he jerked his head and blinked, then quickly smiled. "I just have a lot on my mind." He walked toward the kitchen. "Can I get you something to drink?"

Yes! Champagne would be nice! I came here to celebrate! Vanessa wanted to say.

She hesitated. "I'll take a glass of water." She followed him into the kitchen and sat down at the oak table. "Do you want to talk about it?"

He plunked a few ice cubes into a glass. "Not much to tell. Jeannine and I broke up."

"Oh, I'm sorry." Vanessa about choked on her thoughts.

It's about time!

She masked her face with a look of concern when he turned from the faucet and brought her the glass of water. "Thanks."

Angling the chair off to the side so he could stretch his long legs toward her, he sat down next to her. "It was inevitable—I guess."

No kidding.

"I'm sorry." She looked up at him sadly. "You're still in love with her."

He let out a deep sigh as he stared at the floor. "I don't know." His peripheral vision caught Vanessa's painted burgundy toenails as her feet wiggled back and forth. His head tilted slightly as he took in the silver, high-heeled sandals that framed her somewhat calloused, but clean, tanned feet. The gray bell-bottoms attached to the slinky gray pants flowed back and forth with the movement of her foot. He watched for a moment, slowly following the slinky material up past her knee until he settled around her hips.

Whoa.

His heart rate picked up at the sight of her tanned belly exposed about an inch between that sleek gray material clinging low at the waist—decorated with a silver chain hanging loosely in the belt loops—and a tight, white, spandex tank top which outlined her firm, small breasts.

"Mitch?"

He raised his eyes and smiled in a flirtatious manner. "New outfit?"

A giggle escaped Vanessa. She reached for the water and took a quick sip, stealing a quick glance his way.

"Hey." Mitch's face lit up. "Didn't you come here with some news?"

"Yea, I did. Do you think you can handle it in the state you're in?"

"Why don't you try me?"

"Well, remember the choreographing contest I told you about?" At his nod, she continued with her voice low and deep. "I won." Her eyes widened at his surprised expression and she began giggling. "I did! I won—first place!"

"That's great!" Mitch stood up and pulled her out of her seat and twirled her around. "Congratulations!"

"Thanks, but there's more." Vanessa broke the embrace and backed up a step. "My dance production will be part of the UCLA Arts Performances next year! It will be a full blown production—professionally done—and, are you ready for this?" Vanessa clenched her fists and shook them back and forth in excitement. "I get to be one of the judges for the dance auditions, *and* I'll be helping produce it."

"You're kidding," He said, shocked.

"Uh, uh." Her grin was a mile wide.

"That's awesome."

"I know. Can you believe it?"

"No! Yes! It's great! Will you be dancing in it?"

"I don't know. I'd have to audition also. It's two different things though: producing what I created, and actually being in it. I'm not sure I'll want to do both. Auditions aren't until the spring. I'll decide then."

"I get a front row seat."

"Only if you come and celebrate with me tonight."

"But I'm feeling sorry for myself tonight. I'm hardly in the celebrating mood."

"I'm sorry—that was thoughtless of me." Vanessa bowed her head, making her look almost sincere. But then she raised her head with a sheepish look in her eyes. "Can you fake it?"

He smirked. "I'll give it my best shot." He stood up and headed for his bedroom. "I'll be ready to go in five."

Vanessa peered at him over her shoulder and playfully wrinkled up her nose. "Make it ten. You need it."

Mitch turned around. "You think the show will be that good? You're asking a lot—maybe too much for a front row seat."

"Oh," Vanessa responded, "it'll be worth a shave."

After having Thai food for dinner, they drove to the beach to take advantage of the clear, crisp sky lit by a three-quarter moon. Vanessa exchanged her high heels for warm socks and tennis shoes, then grabbed her red, fleece-lined windbreaker out of the trunk. As they walked toward the water, she lifted her chin slightly, as if to appreciate the cool breeze gliding over the breaking waves. Mitch caught her movement out of the corner of his eyes and felt as if he had been awakened from a trance. "I haven't been very good company."

"It's okay." Vanessa's pace slowed just a bit. "It's hard to sustain that kind of high for very long anyway. Since I found out, I feel like I've been flying all over the place, so it's good to be back on earth again."

"You're being generous."

"No, not really. Besides, it's not your pitiful mood that landed me on my feet again. I've been thinking about my mother, wondering if she ever walked along this beach when she was young."

"It must be awful, not knowing what happened to her, or where she is."

"Very. I vacillate between sadness and anger. It's like those feelings moved in a long time ago and took up permanent residence." Vanessa patted his shoulder. "Come on, let's run." She took off in a sprint.

Mitch watched her for a moment, the fluid movement of arms and legs propelling her forward, while the slinky gray pants—folded up at the cuff—hugged her firm bottom that peeked out beneath the windbreaker. He smiled in appreciation, admiring the view, and then took off after her, realizing he always had a good time when he was with her. His long strides closed the distance in no time, but he slowed down to match her speed as soon as he reached her. They ran for over twenty minutes, both of them trying to ease the pain of unavoidable hurts in their lives. Finally Vanessa slowed and softly tumbled onto the cool, welcoming sand. He fell down beside her.

They lay there panting until she rolled onto her side, facing him. "Hey." She gave him a comforting smile when their eyes met. "Did you do everything you could to talk her out of breaking up?"

"Nah, I thought about it, but her mind was set." Mitch's eyes were drawn to the curve of Vanessa's waistline, then he glanced back up into her hazel eyes. "I let her go without a fight." As if it was the most natural thing in the world to do, he scooted close to Vanessa and lay on his back, resting his head in the saddle of her waist.

She softly caressed his thick mane of dark hair. "I'm sorry. You guys were together a long time."

"Yea—probably too long." He took off his shoes and plunged his feet into the sand until they were buried. "You're kinda' sweet this way, Vanessa. You should feel sorry for me more often."

"Don't get used to it. Compassion is overrated."

Mitch grinned, but was already thinking about something else. "So how come you never seem to stay with one guy for long?"

"Love 'em and leave 'em. That's my motto." Vanessa changed the subject. "How's your sister doing?"

Mitch raised his eyebrows, noticing her ploy. "Mindy's great. She's doing well in school, working hard in her AP classes. She plans on studying biochemistry in college."

"Wow, that's impressive."

"Tell me about it."

"Did she get all the brains in the family?"

"Probably so. I was adopted."

"Yeah, right." Vanessa ignored him.

He buried his feet even further in the sand. "Did I tell you my grandfather will be here for Christmas?"

"No. Is he coming from Mexico?"

"Yes—but he has a beach house here too. It's been in the family for generations." Mitch took a deep breath as he counted the visible stars… three. "I don't see him very often."

"How come?"

"He only visits once or twice a year." Leaning his head closer to Vanessa's, Mitch said, "My dad and grandpa aren't very close. In fact, my family rarely talks about grandpa."

"Why not?"

His voice took on a heavier note. "He's 'a disgrace' to the family." Mitch wiggled his toes around. "But I've always looked up to him."

"Why would they think he's a disgrace?"

Mitch tilted his head and looked at Vanessa questioningly.

She tilted her head sideways. "What?"

"You don't know who my grandfather is." It wasn't a question.

"Should I?"

Mitch smiled.

"I'm getting irritated, Mitch. You're making me feel stupid." Vanessa scooted out from under him, stood up and took off in a fast walk, but stopped almost as quickly as she had started. She turned back around to face Mitch. "Rothman? Greg Rothman? You're related to *that* Rothman–Halborough family? The wealthy, highly political family?"

With an innocent demeanor, he answered, "Used to be—anyway—highly political, that is. I think there's still some money hangin' around, maybe enough to be considered wealthy. I guess it all depends on what your definition of wealthy is."

Ignoring his banter, Vanessa walked back toward him. "You're related to the 'Runaway Senator'?"

"Yep." After Vanessa's dramatics, Mitch's reply seemed anticlimactic. He popped all of his toes out of the sand, then his feet. Vanessa walked toward him and offered her hand. He took it, leaned forward, and stood up. After brushing the sand off his backside, he turned Vanessa around and got them walking.

Vanessa matched his stride and said, "I remember my history teacher mentioning Greg Rothman a time or two. Truthfully, I don't remember much from the class, but Mr. Taylor seemed to respect your grandfather's choice not to run for president."

Mitch smiled contentedly. "That's nice to hear. A lot of people supported his decision but a lot didn't—including my grandmother."

"What happened?"

"They're divorced"

"That's sad."

Mitch shrugged his shoulders. "They both seem content." He moved closer to her, and, arm-in-arm, they walked back in the soft glow of moonlight, comforted by the feeling that their friendship was deepening.

They slowed down when they neared the parking lot, prolonging their time together, enjoying the soothing sounds of the surf.

"I'd like you to meet him."

"Really? I'd like to, but I'll be in Avra Valley. We were supposed to have our first Christmas in the new house. My dad hoped he'd be finished by then, but it's going to take a couple more months. We're all supposed to go there anyway."

Without hesitation Mitch said, "Invite your family. Maybe your dad would like a break. He can always say no. Besides, there's plenty of room at the beach house. They could stay there, and Grandpa would love the company. He'd probably take us sailing."

The moonlight barely captured Vanessa's skeptical frown. "Just like that, huh? Your grandpa wouldn't mind a house full of strangers during the holidays."

"No, he wouldn't. My grandpa thrives on meeting new people. He says it's the reason he keeps on working."

"He still works?"

"He co-owns a dive shop in San Carlos. He still goes out on the boat almost every day. He loves it."

"Wow, sounds like an adventurous lifestyle."

"I guess it is." Mitch smiled at Vanessa's description. "So what do you say?"

She looked into his eyes, searching for clues to see if their friendship had somehow changed to something more intimate. "Are you sure?" But his expression showed the same good friend Mitch. If there was a change, he wasn't giving anything away.

"It'd be fun. The more the merrier."

"Okay. But make sure it's okay with your grandpa first. Then I'll ask my dad and sisters."

"I'll call him tomorrow."

Vanessa paced the floor, debating her plans, unsure if this family gathering was a good idea. Deep down, she wanted Mitch all to herself. She knew the minute she got together with her sisters she'd revert right back to her same old obnoxious self. Mitch would probably hate her that way.

"Quit putting it off," she murmured to herself as she picked up the phone. She heard Stacie's voice say "hello," and was already answering back when she realized it was the answering machine. After beeps sounded off in her ear, Vanessa hastily muttered words about everyone coming to L.A. for

Christmas. She hung up the phone to call Allison and breathed deeply a few times, feeling like a complete idiot for making such a big deal out of it.

Jason yelled a big, out-of-breath 'hello' as Vanessa moved the phone away from her ear. "Is this Jason Waverly, the young man who can throw a baseball all the way to Kentucky and who can whistle the Star Wars theme song without taking a breath?" She smiled as she heard a cute little giggle on the phone line.

"Who is dis?" he asked.

"Jason, this is your favorite Aunt, Aunt Vanessa."

He giggled again. "Nuh, uh. Aunt Stacie is."

Vanessa smiled at his honesty. "Well not for long, kiddo. You spend a week with me and you'll forget all about wicked Aunt Stacie! You sound so grown up! How old are you now, Jason?" There was silence on the other end. "Jason, are you holding up your fingers?"

"Uh—huh."

"Well I can't see them over the phone, Sweetie. How many are you holding up?"

"Free."

"Three? You're three years old already?"

"Uh, huh."

"Jason, Sweetie pie, I hate to tell you this, but you're still two. You'll be three next month."

"Oh."

"Are you feeling all better now after your bicycle accident?"

"Uh, huh. Daddy got me new bike. I don't wide it on the stweet."

"That's good, Honey. Hey, can you put your momma on the phone for me? I need to talk to her."

"Mo-ommmy", he yelled, half into the phone as Vanessa again held the phone away from her ear. She heard Allison in the background.

"Who is it, Honey" and Jason answer, "It's Aunt Nessa, Mommy." The phone dropped with a bang.

"Hi, Vanessa, sorry about that."

"Hey, Al—that kid of yours is sounding more grown up all the time."

"Tell me about it. It's hard to keep him in clothes, he grows out of them so fast."

"Ohhhh," Vanessa crooned, suddenly missing her little nephew. "Has he grown that much since I last saw him?"

Allison glanced over at Jason who was currently pushing around a Tonka dump truck. "You'll recognize him."

"That's good. I don't want to miss out on too much. Hey—to change the subject, we need to talk about Christmas. Mitch invited all of us to spend Christmas with his grandpa at a beach house in Malibu. I called Dad already. He said that'd be fine with him."

"Really? I'm surprised Dad would leave that place for a few days. He's working so hard on it that I have a difficult time getting him over here for dinner."

"I think he sounded relieved. He said he's itching for a road trip, so he'll just keep Stacie's flight into Tucson and then you guys can drive over. I've gotta tell you about Mitch's grandpa. He lives part of the year in San Carlos, where he owns his own dive shop. Mitch said if the weather's good, we can go sailing in a boat that a friend of his grandpa owns. Maybe see some whales or do some deep-sea fishing."

"Sounds wonderful." Allison visualized herself laying on the beach, getting a tan and drinking a fruity alcoholic drink, maybe a daiquiri. She'd heard of others, but didn't have a clue what they tasted like. "What are the odds of getting a tan?"

"If it's a sunny day, the worst thing that'll happen—besides a sunburn— is that we'll get goose bumps while tanning."

"Have you talked to Stacie yet?"

"I just left her a message."

Not wanting to say certain things in front of Jason, Allison asked Vanessa to hold on while she switched phones. A minute later she whispered, "Sorry—I don't want Jason to hear me talking about a trip, especially since I don't see how it could work. There's no way I can bring Jason, since Todd's parents are coming for Christmas, and he and 'Miss Snooty Pants' have a big bonanza blowout planned for Jason on Christmas day."

"How about having Todd keep Jason for the week?"

"No—" Allison moaned. "As much as I'd love to come, there's no way I'm going to miss out on Christmas with Jason. I have him Christmas Eve, then Todd will come over early Christmas morning for the Santa Clause presents."

Vanessa sighed. "Well, what about leaving after Jason opens his presents from Santa?"

"That might work. I'll talk to Todd. Maybe he and Judy can keep Jason for a few extra days."

"And I'll talk to Mitch." Vanessa twisted the phone cord in her hand. "So I take it you and your best friend in the world, 'Miss Snooty Pants,' haven't reconciled?"

"Reconciled? How in the world could we ever get past this one? Are you telling me you'd still be friends with her?"

"There's no way in hell that I'd still be friends with her. But we're different."

"I guess not that different."

"Have you started dating yet? You probably should, you know, tit for tat. Todd's gone on with his life. Sex would probably do you some good. Maybe you wouldn't be so grumpy. Unless you're getting some without telling me?"

"Geez, Vanessa! I don't ask you about your sex life. Although," she snickered, "I wouldn't have the time to hear about it."

"Real funny."

"Well, are you as active as always?"

"I thought you didn't ask."

Allison dropped her chin to her chest. "Just ignore me." She took a deep breath, then went over and sat on the bed. "What's the deal with you and Mitch?"

"Mitch? He's as handsome, charming, adorable, and sexy as ever. And such a dear, dear friend—but only a dear friend."

Allison laughed. "What's it going to take to get you guys over that friendship plateau?"

"I don't know. He's completely oblivious to my womanly charms."

"I thought you could have any man on the planet. You're sure he's not gay?"

Vanessa smirked. "There's not a gay bone in his body. My theory of being able to have any man on this planet is perhaps a bit exaggerated."

"Why don't you just tell him how you feel?"

"And ruin the best relationship I've ever had with a guy? No way!"

"Maybe what you guys have will last a lifetime. Or maybe you need to quit going out with so many other guys."

"Can we change the subject? Or better yet, I gotta go. I'm meeting some friends at the library. We're studying for an art history exam together."

"Okay. I'll let you know about Christmas in L.A. It sounds like it could be a lot of fun."

"Oh," Vanessa spoke casually. "I almost forgot to tell you. Mitch's grandfather, the one we'd be staying with, is the one and only 'Runaway Senator.'"

Allison's mouth dropped open. "What? You've got to be kidding? Why didn't you tell me sooner? Of course I'll find a way to go."

"Geez, Allison, I kind of thought that the beach, sun and snorkeling with your sisters would be the selling point. I didn't know Mitch's grandpa would be that much of a draw for you."

"He's in the history books, Vanessa. This is too cool—the 'Runaway Senator'. Maybe he'll tell us why he did it."

"We know why—his heart was no longer in politics. And as Mitch reminded me, the nickname 'Runaway Senator' is a misnomer, because he didn't run from anything. He finished his second term. The only thing he did was drop out of the presidential race."

"Yeah, but he dropped out of politics altogether—at the peak of his career."

"It's a free country, or so I thought."

"Okay, whatever, I just hope he'll talk about it."

"It'd be rude to ask. Am I going to regret inviting you, Allison? Are you going to embarrass me?"

Allison laughed. "I guess I've gotten used to being the embarrassment of the family.

"Great." Vanessa said sarcastically. "I gotta go. Give Jason a big ol' kiss for me."

28

Three days before Christmas, James Rothman drove his year old Chevy Blazer up the long drive to the stunning, two-story home that had been in his family for over sixty years. Just a hop, skip and a jump from downtown L.A., Glendale was home to many wealthy families, including some of the Hollywood elite.

At one time the Rothman family was Glendale's most respected family among the many wealthy and famous inhabitants, but today they blended in with several aging Hollywood stars that appeared to have outlived their time in the spotlight.

Not that James minded. As a psychiatrist, his life was far removed from the fast paced hustle and bustle of the crowd that sought fame. As he pulled into the three-car garage, his wife Lacey was opening the door to her silver Mercedes when she turned, smiled, and waved her fingers at him. James grinned. He had told her years before that her wave was ultra-feminine, and it ignited a desire in him to take her to bed each time she did it. Much to his satisfaction, she seemed to know just when it would have the greatest effect on him.

We'll be lighting candles tonight.

He grabbed his briefcase and stepped out of the Blazer. "Where are you headed?"

Lacey opened the car door and dropped her purse into the passenger seat. She turned around just as James reached her side. "I'm meeting Mindy at the mall. She needs a new dress for the New Year's dance." She wrapped her arms around James and lifted her chin in anticipation of his kiss. "You're home early."

"I had a cancellation." James nestled into her neck, loving her soft, flowery scent. "I stopped by to see Mitch. Did you know he and Jeannine broke up?"

Lacey's hand made a beeline for her mouth. "That was over a week ago. Didn't I tell you?"

"No," James drawled in a deep, husky voice.

"I'm sorry. We've both been so busy lately." She stepped closer, and caressed his arm. "How's he doing?"

"He seems to be handling it well—says a girl friend of his has been helping him through it."

"Must be Vanessa."

"Have you met her?"

"Yes, I met her when Mitch sprained his ankle way back when. They've been buddies for a long time." Lacey quickly reached up and kissed James cheek. "I've got to go. Mindy will think I forgot about her."

After watching Lacey pull out of the drive, James entered the house and headed straight for his office. Something was bothering him, but he couldn't put his finger on it. He walked over to the desk, tucked his keys and wallet in the top drawer, and sank into a brown leather chair. Scattered thoughts raced through his mind: his current caseload, his visit with Mitch, his father's upcoming visit.

His thoughts turned to work as he mentally scanned his caseload, but nothing seemed out of the ordinary. Most of his patients were dealing with typical stresses and life-defining situations.

Maybe it's Dad?

James wondered if they'd spend more than a few token hours together while his dad was here. But James realized it wasn't likely, since Lacey, Mindy, and he were going back east to spend the holidays with Lacey's family.

What is it?

Frustrated, he stood up as he decided to go for a run.

Maybe I just need to burn some energy.

Just before heading upstairs to change into a pair of jogging shorts, he passed by the long, antique table where all their family photos sat in various frames.

A quick glance brought him up short. *That picture.*

While he was at Mitch's house, sitting on the sofa, there were a couple of pictures strewn casually on the coffee table. James had leaned forward to get a closer look when Mitch walked in carrying a couple of cokes.

"Those were taken a few months ago but Hank just gave me copies. We were playing beach volleyball." Mitch sat down beside James and looked over his shoulder. "You've met my friend Hank haven't you?"

"Yes. I recognize him and his girlfriend JoJo. Who's the other girl?" James studied the striking girl with the dark auburn hair. She was wearing a red bikini top and a short pair of cut-offs and looked as if she was about to hit an incoming ball.

There's something familiar about her.

"That's Vanessa. She's been a good friend of mine for a couple of years now. Haven't I told you about her?"

"Is she the one studying dance?"

"Yeah, that's her. I'd like you to meet her. Mom met her a long time ago."

"Yeah—I'd like that."

But that was it. The subject had turned to school, and Mitch's plans to apply to med school.

But so what? What is bothering me about the picture?

He thought about the young woman with the deep tan and the dark, auburn hair. *Madeline.* The resemblance between Madeline and this young woman was enough to bring a smile to his face.

That's it! She looks like Madeline.

There were differences to be sure, but the similarities were striking. He sighed knowingly.

Puzzle solved—just a coincidence.

Still feeling like a run was a good idea, he bounded up the steps and into his bedroom to change. He stopped at the dresser and pulled open the second drawer.

Wait a minute—Madeline has a daughter named Vanessa.

Knots in his stomach seemed to get tighter. Resignedly he sat down on the bed, trying to figure out why he was so keyed up. Something was wrong.

Memories of Madeline came flooding back to him, like the first time he saw her, at school, in first grade. She had been crying and when he asked her if she was okay, she looked up at him with the biggest, saddest eyes he had ever seen. He didn't know it then, but that first look bonded the two of them forever.

James rubbed his forehead, thankful that Lacey and Mindy were out tonight. He needed time to think this through. His mind switched gears, something Mitch had said started replaying in his mind. Mitch had invited Vanessa and her family to spend time with James' dad at the beach house. It was Mitch's chance to provide them with some enjoyment, since Christmas brought up painful memories. Their mother had abandoned them more than four years ago.

Abandoned them?

James sprang from the bed and nervously resumed pacing.

But it's just a picture, a coincidence. Shaking his head no, he admitted to himself that it could be Madeline's daughter. *But abandoned?*

James went to his desk, retrieved an old address book and opened it up to the A's. Averson, Madeline. He picked up the phone, dialed the number, then spoke with some man who told him he had the wrong number.

James quickly dialed information and was promptly told there were no

Averson's currently living in Bismarck, ND.

Okay, so the Aversons moved. People do it all the time.

But the words, "their mother abandoned them," circled around in his head.

James could have called Mitch but, acting on instinct, he walked briskly to his office, grabbed his keys and wallet out of the drawer, and less than half an hour later was knocking on Mitch's door.

"Door's unlocked. Come on in, Vanessa."

Feeling like an unwanted visitor, James yelled through the door. "Mitch, it's me—Dad."

A moment later, the door swung open and Mitch was asking James if he had forgotten something when a car drove up. As James mumbled "no—just wanted to talk to you," they both turned and watched Vanessa get out of her old yellow bug.

Noticing the surprised expression on Vanessa's' face when she saw he had company, Mitch quickly glanced at James. "Looks like you get to meet Vanessa right away." When she got a little closer, Mitch began the introductions. "Vanessa, this is my dad, James Rothman."

Vanessa extended her hand and smiled brightly. "Hi, I'm Vanessa Averson."

"Averson?" James took her hand, but the slight hesitation intensified the moment. "That's not a name I hear frequently." He was about to say more, but an uneasy feeling settled into his stomach.

"Does that mean you've heard of the name? There are not too many of us."

"An old friend of mine married a guy named Averson." James had come over here for answers, and he knew that getting to the point would expedite matters. "Are you Madeline's daughter?"

No way. As the blood rushed to her heart, Vanessa's skin turned a pasty white. Trying to speak calmly, she asked, "You know her?"

"Yes." Mr. Rothman said cautiously. "We went through grade school and junior high together."

"Um, have you seen her lately?"

"No. Not for years." James glanced at Mitch. Vanessa knew something had passed between them.

Mitch grabbed her hand. "Come in and sit down." With his hand on her arm for support, he gently guided her inside and over to the sofa. He glanced over at his father with a concerned frown. Turning around, he knelt down, and at eye level whispered to Vanessa, "Can I tell my dad?"

She nodded her head before grimacing with embarrassment. "Of course.

I don't know why it's getting to me."

Mitch squeezed her hand and sat beside her on the couch. "Have a seat, Dad."

James awkwardly sat down in the chair opposite the sofa.

"Vanessa hasn't seen her mom in more than four years. Her mom took off while the rest of the family was at a family reunion." Mitch absently rubbed Vanessa's back. "They don't know where she is or who she's with. They haven't seen or heard from her since."

The shock hit James, knocking the breath right out of him as he did a mental calculation. *Four years ago: family vacation.* As he spoke, he tried to make sure the sincerity in his voice was stronger than the anxiety. "I'm sorry to hear that."

Vanessa's shrug didn't match her strained facial expression. "I'm used to it."

James rested his elbows on his knees as he rubbed the palms of his hands together. There were so many things he wanted to ask, but a sense of caution overrode his other thoughts. Thankfully, Mitch broke the ice.

"I can't believe you know Vanessa's mother."

Mitch's tone perked Vanessa up. "What was she like?" she asked timidly.

Forcing himself to relax, James leaned back and thought back on years gone by. He grinned slightly as he glanced at Mitch then made eye contact with Vanessa. "She was special."

"Really?" Vanessa smiled encouragingly. "In what way?"

Under the circumstances, James felt it would be disloyal to Madeline to share personal stories. But he could paint an overall picture for Vanessa. "Everybody loved your mom. She was smart and had a great sense of humor." James was a bit taken aback by the surprised expression on Vanessa's face. "We were in the same classes first through fourth grade. After that, because we had different teachers, we drifted apart. We became good friends again in eighth grade."

"How come?"

James smiled, reliving the memory. "In eighth grade I ran for Student Body President against your mom's boyfriend." James smile turned into a boyish grin. "She chose to help me in the election instead of him. I asked her why she wanted to help me." James hesitated a moment, remembering her exact words.

Buck for president? What a joke. He's a good kisser and fun to hang out with, but he'd make a lousy president. You, on the other hand, will make this a year our class won't ever forget.

James decided to tweak that version. "She said Buck was a great linebacker but I'd make a better class president."

"Did you win?"

"Yes." He thought about how it played out. I won the election. *Madeline lost her kissing partner.* "We were good friends after that and up until she was gone."

"When her grandmother died."

James nodded, wondering if Vanessa knew anything about Madeline's grandmother's death. He was curious—Madeline had left town even before the funeral. In the few times he'd spoken with Madeline over the years, he'd never felt it was his place to ask about it, and Madeline never brought it up.

The young woman glanced nervously at her watch. "I've got to go, Mitch. I, uh, I just stopped by to tell you that everyone's coming—they'll arrive Christmas evening—but they can only stay a couple of days."

"Great!" Mitch's enthusiasm lightened the discomfort in the room. "We'll have a blast."

James and Mitch could see Vanessa was uncomfortable. They both stood at the same time she did.

"It was nice to meet you, Mr. Rothman," Vanessa said, holding out her hand.

James grabbed her hand with both of his. His eyes were warm and his voice sincere when he said, "Nice meeting you, Vanessa. I look forward to seeing you again soon."

As Mitch walked Vanessa out to the car, James stood alone in the small living room. The turmoil within him seemed a booming thunder amid the silence in the room.

What happened to you Madeline? Where are you? Are you okay?

Anxious to leave, but giving Mitch and Vanessa privacy, he paced the floor a few times. He thought about that night, four and a half years ago in Bismarck.

You were distraught, hiding something. But you told me you were okay!

James remembered how weeks later he had tried to contact her one more time, despite her adamant statement that she was fine, he could tell she wasn't. When one of her daughters answered the phone, James hung up. He felt like an intruder in Madeline's personal life.

Ah hell, there's nothing I can do about it now. He ran his hands through his thinning, gray-streaked hair.

James heard Vanessa's VW start at the same time Mitch opened the front door of the apartment. Making a beeline for the door, James mumbled a hasty goodbye and headed toward his car. Mitch, leaned out the door, watching his dad leave in as big of a hurry as Vanessa had.

Vanessa's nerves were jumping by the time she arrived home. She parked in her designated parking space by the side of the garage, opened the door, grabbed her backpack and purse, then stepped awkwardly out of the car. Her legs, wobbly since the shock of meeting James, barely seemed able to carry her weight. Out of habit, and per Sharlene and Dan's house rules, she put her things in her bedroom.

Not wasting a minute, she glanced at the clock before reaching for the phone. She dialed Allison's number at work. The receptionist at the bank answered the call and after Vanessa explained that it was a family emergency, she was put on hold and waited anxiously until she heard Allison answer.

"It's okay, Allison. It's me."

"What's the matter?"

"Look, it's not an emergency, but something happened today that I just had to tell you about."

Allison glanced nervously at the line of people needing assistance in the teller line. "I'm real busy. Make it quick before I get into trouble."

"I met Mitch's dad today."

"So?" Allison asked impatiently.

"Just listen for two seconds." Vanessa let out her breath. "He knows Mom—or knew her."

"What?" Allison squealed in a high-pitched voice.

"They went to the same school, first grade through tenth."

"No way."

"Unbelievable, isn't it?" She didn't wait for the answer. "He says they were good friends. His name is James."

"James? That sounds familiar."

"It didn't to me."

"Yeah. I'm pretty sure Mom mentioned him before."

"It was so weird, hearing more stories about Mom that we'd never heard before: first from Carlotta and now from Mitch's dad."

"It is weird. Have you told Dad?"

"No. And I'm not sure we should. It took him a long time to deal with Carlotta."

"True." Allison could see the concerned expression on her supervisor's face. "I've gotta get back to work. Let's talk about it later."

"Okay. Call me tonight."

29

Randall parked his truck in the closest spot he could find and practically ran into the airport, knowing, since he was ten minutes late, he would not be there to greet Stacie as she got off the plane. He should have taken Carlotta up on her offer to pick Stacie up, but he missed his daughter so much he could not wait to see her. How could he know that one of the large kilns at the cement factory was going to break down? Each minute it was down cost the company a lot of money. He had to get a repair team going before he could leave.

He paused for the traffic to pass, then ran across the street. He was about to run through the opened sliding glass doors when, off to the side, he heard a soft-spoken "Dad." The smile was already plastered across his face as he turned toward the familiar voice.

"Stacie!" Stacie's smile melted the stress right off him as he reached for her.

"Hi, Dad." she whispered.

"You cut your hair." He rocked her back and forth a few times, then stepped back away. "It looks good on you." Stacie's wispy blonde hair was cut in layers that ended at the nape of her neck. He also noticed her clothing had become a bit more sophisticated. "You've only been gone five months, but you look like you've grown up a whole lot during that time."

"New York can do that to a person. You gotta go with the flow or it will swallow you whole."

With a chuckle, Randall asked, "Is that the city's motto or did you make that up?"

"Debuted right here for the first time."

Randall grabbed her carry-on and a large tote bag filled with wrapped gifts. "Let's go get the rest of your luggage."

"That's it."

"Isn't this just your carry-on?"

"No, that's everything."

"You're traveling light."

"I managed to stuff everything in there. Bikinis don't take up much room."

"But it's winter." They headed towards the truck.

"Yes, but winter in L.A. is a whole lot different than winter in New York."

"True."

"And I've learned how to pack. My roommate, Sarah, travels a lot. You won't believe how much stuff I've got in this thing."

Randall unlocked the door to the truck. "That's a handy thing to learn. You'll have to show me." A minute later they were heading home. "Tell me about New York."

Stacie laughed. "I tell you about New York every week when we talk."

"Isn't there more you want to tell me in person?"

"No, but I'll repeat everything. It's big—a *big* city. It's cold." She mocked a shiver. "It's beautiful." Her eyes took on a light glaze as she thought about it. "The energy is amazing. Life always keeps moving. Nothing stays the same. I haven't stayed the same. It's like I was a turtle in Bismarck, changed into a desert tortoise in Avra Valley, and now I'm on my way to becoming a cheetah."

"So that explains the sleek haircut and sophisticated clothes."

Stacie grinned at his insight. "Hmm—I never thought of that, but I guess I would rather look like a cheetah than a turtle."

"I don't know, in that city you might need a protective shell."

"If I did, I wouldn't be able to run as fast."

"True. It would be cumbersome." Randall steered the truck into the left-hand turn lane to get onto Valencia Road. "Do you still find time for your artwork?"

"Between working two jobs and taking one class, about the only time I have to draw is when I'm in a taxi. I started drawing sketches of cab drivers, then giving them the drawing as sort of a tip. One guy liked his so well he covered my cab fare."

"Well that's the least he should do. They all should do that. Don't they know you're going to be famous someday?"

She giggled. "Stacie Averson, world famous taxicab driver sketch artist. You'd be so proud." She met his gaze and smiled when she saw his thoughtful expression. "You don't have to say it."

He said it anyway. "I am proud of you."

Stacie smiled in return and looked back out the window. "I can't wait to see what you've done so far on the house."

"It doesn't look like much yet. I'm behind schedule. The perk tests were a hassle. It took three tests before we found the right area for the septic. But now the footings are dug and the walls are going up. It'll be awhile before we're ready to move in."

"Are you still building it per Grandma Helen's specifications?"

"Mostly, but I changed a few things: extending the ceilings, stuccoing the exterior and adding a bedroom."

"How come, with only you living there?"

"The design only had three bedrooms. I want this house to be a family home. Each of you girls will have your own bedroom when you come and visit."

"Neat."

"No fighting over where to sleep."

"What are you going to do with the trailer and Spartan Manor?"

"As soon as the house is built, I'll get rid of the trailer. But of course we'll keep Spartan Manor."

"I'm glad you're keeping it. Spartan Manor is special. Are Spencer and Lizzie still living in it?"

"No. Spencer was able to stop the foreclosure on his mother's house. He and Lizzie moved back last week." Noticing a change in her expression out of the corner of his eye, Randall glanced over at her. "What?"

"Nothing." Her smile was a mixture of shyness and contentment. "You're a good guy, Dad, helping them out."

He shrugged. "Well, maybe, but Spencer has more than made up for it. He has helped out a lot with the house and still plans on helping every weekend." Randall chuckled. "He's been worth every ounce of aggravation that Lizzy has given me."

As Stacie's face flushed, she hurried to get the conversation to a safer topic. "She's still giving you problems?"

Randall laughed. "That little girl is a handful times ten. She can cause more damage in five minutes then all three of you girls put together." He turned thoughtful. "I give Spencer a lot of credit. Between him working full-time and taking care of Lizzy, he still finds time to help me out. He talked me into putting the cooling system for the house underground."

"Why's that?"

"More energy efficient. The vents are at the base of the floors."

Stacie smiled gently. "He's like the son you never had."

Randall looked over at her with a surprised expression. "I was always happy with my girls."

"I know, Dad. But I think it's pretty neat that you have helped each other. You're probably the only father figure Spencer's ever had."

"Hmm. You're probably right. In that case, he's long overdue for a little help. And as much as I hate to admit it, it was lonelier without you than I thought it would be. I guess there's something to that empty nest syndrome stuff. It helped having Spencer—and even Lizzy— around."

Wondering if she would get to see Spencer during her brief visit and not really sure if she wanted to, she opted for changing the subject. "So when are we leaving for L.A.?"

"Christmas day. Allison didn't want to miss out on Jason's Christmas, so we're leaving right after Jason opens his presents."

"Is Jason coming with us?"

"No. Todd's parents are coming into town. They haven't seen Jason since last Christmas, so they get priority."

Stacie sighed. "I can't wait to see my little nephew."

The butterflies Stacie had been feeling in her stomach ever since the Avra Valley road exit seemed to triple as they crossed the canal bridge of the Central Arizona Project.

"Home?" He asked. "Or new house construction zone?"

"New house."

She sat up straight, looking for signs of the new house. They passed the short driveway to the bigger trailer, then the one for Spartan Manor, then made a left hand turn down a curved road Randall had put in parallel to the state land road.

"There it is!" Stacie pointed up ahead, seeing the outline of a two-foot, rustic adobe brick wall. The truck was barely stopped when Stacie hopped out and ran toward the construction area. Randall laughed when she suddenly stopped, dropped to the ground and pretended to kiss the dirt. While still on all fours, she turned around, giggling. "I didn't realize how much I missed this place—this land." She got back up and stepped over the wall. "Where am I standing right now?"

"You're in one of the spare bedrooms. You could be standing in your room."

"Cool. Show me the rest."

Randall stepped over the wall and walked Stacie through the floor plan. "I'm so glad you're doing this, Dad," she said, looking at him fondly.

"Yeah, me too." He sat down on the partially-built wall. "This is one place that will be for us." His tone of voice deepened. "It's the one thing your mother can still give us."

Stacie walked over and sat next to him, laying her head on his shoulder as his arm came around and squeezed her tight, shoulder to shoulder.

They sat in silence for a few minutes, both in their own visions of what the house was going to look like, until Stacie spoke. "Hey, Dad?"

"Yes?"

"Can I ask you a personal question?"

"You can always ask."

"Where are you getting the money to build this house? It looks like it will cost a fortune."

With only a slight hesitation, he answered. "Your mother's trust fund."

"There was enough money in it?"

"Yes. I never intended to use any of it other than to continue paying the property taxes, but Carlotta can be very persuasive."

"Yeah, thank God for Carlotta." With a contented smile, Stacie realized she didn't just say 'thank God' from habit—she meant it. For good measure, she silently thanked God again and liked the feeling of peace she got along with it.

"By the way, Stacie, I forgot to tell you. Carlotta wants to see you before we go to L.A., so I told her we'd drop by "Props" for a piece of pie this afternoon."

"Good, I can't wait to see her. And I've got presents for her from Lena."

They drove back to the trailer. Stacie had mixed feelings when she walked in the door. "I think you can fit all this furniture into the living room of that house."

"Probably could." Randall closed the door behind them. "I'm sure we'll need to buy some new furniture after it's built."

"That'll be fun." Stacie grabbed her things and started walking to the back of the trailer. "I'm going to put this in my room and call Allison." Her bedroom was just as she had left it, bed made, dresser and closet empty, a few photos on the wall. She dialed the number and heard Allison's 'hello' after the second ring.

After a few minutes of catching up, and deciding to have Mexican food for Christmas Eve dinner, including green corn tamales and mini chimichangas from "Lerua's," Allison asked Stacie if she was alone.

"Yes, Dad's in the kitchen," Stacie whispered.

"Did Vanessa tell you about Mitch's dad?"

"No. What about him?"

"He knows Mom. He went to school with her in L.A. up until tenth grade. They were good friends."

"No way! What did he say about her?"

"Just a few stories. I'll tell you about it later. I'm getting ready to take Jason to see Santa Claus. Do you want to come with us?"

"I'd love to, but I can't. Dad and I are going to see Carlotta soon." Stacie wanted to hear as much as she could before Allison got off the phone. "Are we going to get to meet him when we stay with Mitch's grandfather?"

"No. He's going to be out of town with Mitch's mom and sister. They're going back East somewhere to spend the holidays with family over there—but Stacie, don't mention it to Dad, okay? Vanessa and I think he might take it hard, and we don't want to ruin the holidays for him. We think he's heard of this guy before."

The tiniest pause in the conversation seemed a much longer moment as nervous energy gathered in Stacie's throat. "What's his name?"

"James Rothman."

As Stacie felt the beginnings of a panic attack coming on, she was grateful that Allison was in a hurry to get off the phone. After hastily said 'goodbyes' and 'we'll talk more later,' Stacie hung up the phone with a shaky hand. She crouched down on the floor by the bed and took several slow, deep breaths. Although her gut was telling her otherwise, she silently tried to comfort herself.

It doesn't mean anything. It's just a coincidence, that's all.

She willed herself not to dwell on things she had no control over. Isn't that how she had finally learned to survive these past few years? With determination, she stood up and left her room as one last thought surfaced.

Is the Runaway Senator my grandfather?

30

It was after dark on Christmas day when Randall, Allison, and Stacie arrived in Malibu at the beach house, lit by the half moon and festive Christmas lights. Vanessa and Mitch ran outside to greet them as Greg Rothman stood in the doorway.

"Merry Christmas!" Vanessa yelled as she flew first into Randall's arms, and then hugged her sisters. Echoes of "Merry Christmas" resounded in the air. Mitch and Randall shook hands. Mitch hugged Stacie, then Allison. "Merry Christmas and nice to meet you" greetings were volleyed back and forth. The Arizona travelers gathered their luggage, with Mitch and Vanessa's help, and headed toward the house.

Greg Rothman purposely stayed behind—a habit born of necessity in his previous political life to 'size up' the people he was about to encounter. It was perhaps no longer necessary, but forever ingrained. Any apprehensions he may have had, due to Mitch's warnings of what the Averson family had been through, dissipated when he saw what appeared to be a healthy, loving family, despite the absence of a mother. Greg walked down the steps to join the others in greetings and introductions, and to help with the luggage and gifts.

Although he loomed over Randall by several inches, Greg felt the strength and integrity of Randall's handshake and liked him instantly. As he greeted Allison, he saw the enthusiastic, wide-eyed look he'd seen thousands of times over the years—of a person enthralled with meeting a 'so-called' celebrity.

There was one more introduction to be made, but before he even turned around, Greg could almost sense her hesitation. He heard her say, "Hello, Mr. Rothman, I'm Stacie," in a voice that sounded lacking in confidence. When their eyes met, Greg felt his own hesitation. He was momentarily suspended in time. For a brief second he was twenty-two again, standing at a rickety shed door, in the middle of the desert, during the hottest part of summer, and he was looking into Helen's eyes for the first time. He fought an overwhelming urge to take this girl in his arms and tell her how much he loved her still. But she wasn't Helen. Gathering up all his previous life experience at making good first impressions, he greeted Stacie warmly. As he followed the Aversons and his grandson into the beach house, where dinner was ready to be served, Greg Rothman did what he had learned years earlier; he let go of the past.

———

The stores of Malibu sat like sparkling jewels against the backdrop of the ocean. Vendors lined up in front of the stores, selling their wares street fair style. It was two days after Christmas and Vanessa was keeping her promise to her sisters by taking them to the store where she first purchased the "Bailey's Hearts" necklaces.

"Here they are." Vanessa pointed at the display of inexpensive necklaces in the middle of the store.

Allison and Stacie followed Vanessa to the display. "Healing Heart," Allison said. She picked up the crystal heart painted with a red line near the bottom and green strands representing grass protruding up from it. She read the card. *The Healing Heart—Is your heart broken? The healing heart gives us the courage to feel our pain but reminds us to seek the healing energy of our natural surroundings.*

They read each of the messages attached to the hearts. *Inspirational Heart—Is your heart longing for something more? Is your life urging you to wake-up? Trust that you will find the inspiration within to guide you on your true path once you discover your heart's desire.*

Truthful Heart—Are you seeing the reality of what you have created with your life? Or are you only seeing what you wish to see? Truthful heart gives us the courage to remove the haze through which we view our life's situations and to see with clarity. Only then do we have the strength to embark on our true path.

There was also "Grieving Heart," "Loving Heart," "Playful Heart," and "Heart of Courage." Allison chose "Heart of Courage," which was painted with a ray of light at the top of a mountain peak. To her it was symbolic of the changes she needed to make in her life.

Vanessa chose "Inspirational Heart," since she wanted to create an exciting dance career for herself. Stacie chose "Truthful Heart." She told her sisters it was because something touched her about the simple design, which was clear and spoke of clarity. In truth, she felt it was symbolic of her life. She wanted the courage to learn the truth of her identity.

Vanessa was the last to pay. As she tucked her wallet back in her purse, she frowned. "Well, I'm done shopping. I don't have any money left."

"You and me both," Allison agreed. "Why don't we stop for something to drink? I'm thirsty and I'd like to sit down." A few minutes later they found a corner table in a coffee shop.

Vanessa hadn't wanted to come right out and ask Allison and Stacie what they thought of Mitch and his grandpa, but they hadn't volunteered any information since Christmas night when, after the men called it a night, the girls had stayed up talking. Allison had said that Mitch was cute and seemed like a great guy and that Mr. Rothman was super cool and in such great shape for a man his age. Now Vanessa was itching to talk about them. She took a sip of her blackberry iced-tea. "It was a great day out on the boat yesterday."

Allison answered sarcastically, "Yeah, it was a great day. We didn't catch anything worth keeping, the water was rocky, I got seasick, and we froze our buns off after getting drenched. It couldn't have been any better!"

"Dad seemed to have a good time," Stacie said. She sensed Vanessa wanted to talk about Mitch and Mr. Rothman.

But how can I? If Mitch's dad is the 'James' that is my father, then Mitch is my half-brother and Mr. Rothman my Grandfather. This is insane!

There was a part of her that didn't believe it. It was too outrageous to be true, and it left her feeling like she was making it all up. *But Dad said it— he said my father's name is James, a childhood friend of Mom's. How many childhood-friends named 'James' did Mom have?*

"Yeah, he did." Allison answered. "For a man who has never set foot on a boat—other than a catamaran in the Icelandic State Park lake—Dad looked like he could hold his own as a sailor."

"He and Mr. Rothman seemed to hit it off," Vanessa said.

Allison smiled. "Are you having trouble calling him 'Greg' too? Even though he asked us to, it just doesn't feel right. I mean—he's so nice and down to earth—and he has a way of making you feel so comfortable with him—but he's a former senator! It seems disrespectful to call him Greg."

"I agree." Vanessa grinned. "So I haven't been calling him anything! And that wasn't easy to do when the three of us were cooking Christmas dinner together. When I was baking pies, instead of asking him where the roller was, I started looking through the cupboards. I mean—what kind of logic is that? All I did was avoiding what felt rude for something that was obviously rude—going through his cupboards!"

Allison laughed. "Did he say anything?"

"Yes. He looked over and nonchalantly said, 'the rolling pin is in the bottom drawer next to the stove.' I guess my three balls of dough sitting on the counter were a dead giveaway."

Allison and Vanessa chuckled, and Stacie, only half listening, managed a smile.

"Well, Allison, I give you credit," Vanessa said. "As far as I know you haven't asked him—Greg—one question about his past life in politics."

"That's because it's been so much fun talking to him about Mexico. The dolphins that love to swim in the wake of the boat, and the diving. I can't believe sea lions play with the divers while they're diving! That's so cool! Maybe we should try it sometime."

Stacie didn't answer Allison.

Only if I have the guts to tell Dad I know the truth. I don't think I could do a repeat of this trip: staying with 'Grandpa Rothman' and spending a day with him on the boat.

Allison looked at her two non-responding sisters who were gazing off in different directions. "Or—maybe not," she said flippantly.

Stacie glanced back at Allison while reaching for her cup of coffee. "I'm sorry, Al, it's just hard to think of learning to scuba dive when I'm living in New York and its winter."

"Speaking of New York, I feel a need to bring up something that's been bothering me." Vanessa leaned forward, closer to Stacie. "Stacie—what are you doing in that city? New York, of all places? That place is too rough for you. Geez—you weigh all of a hundred pounds. You couldn't defend a flea from a grasshopper." Vanessa took a breath and tried to soften her voice, but it came out in a whine. "You're an angel living in the armpit of the nation."

Stacie's eyes widened as if in disbelief. "I thought L.A. was considered the armpit of the nation."

Allison laughed at Stacie's comeback. "And like you should talk Vanessa. You're a dancer with a weight problem living in a city where a woman owns more bikinis than shoes."

"I don't have a weight problem!"

"Maybe not on the outside—but on the inside you sure do."

"What is that supposed to mean?"

"It means that whether or not you're overweight, your weight is your occupation. Every little morsel you eat registers on your brain—every calorie added up."

"I don't have an eating disorder."

"You're paranoid about food. I wouldn't exactly call that normal."

"You know what I don't consider normal? It's you, Miss High and Mighty Valedictorian, who had the world in the palm of her hand, yet hasn't dared set foot in a college door."

"Don't you two ever give it a rest?"

Two heads, Allison's and Vanessa's, turned toward Stacie in surprise. But

Vanessa had struck a nerve in Allison, and Allison spoke without thinking. "I can't believe Vanessa the slut thinks she has a better handle on life than I do."

Stacie's eyes widened in disbelief as she saw Vanessa's expression. Allison, who was waiting for Vanessa's typical retort, caught Stacie's expression and turned toward Vanessa. The tension in Vanessa was obvious. She looked like she was about to explode.

"Vanessa, what is it?" Stacie said in a whisper. "What's wrong?"

Allison wasn't as comforting. "I don't believe it. Are you about to cry?"

It was like the dam broke. "Mitch thinks I'm a slut, too." And before she got the "what do you expect?" lecture from Allison, she continued. "Mitch and I took a walk along the beach a couple days before you guys got here and he asked me, 'You sleep around a lot, don't you?' He said it like it was no big deal."

"What'd you say?" Allison asked.

Vanessa gave an exasperated sigh. "I told him, 'I happen to like sex. So what's the big deal?' And he said, 'You aren't very choosy.' I said, 'Sure I'm choosy. If they aren't any good, I choose not to sleep with them again. If they are good, I do.'"

Allison rolled her eyes. "And you wonder why you have that reputation?"

Stacie could see by Vanessa's expression that something deeper was going on. "Let her finish, Allison."

Allison stopped short. "I'm sorry, Vanessa, it's just a bad habit of mine to say that. What did Mitch say?"

"He said that my 'air of confidence' seemed a little too much for show—that there was nothing to back it up. Then—" Vanessa hesitated, "He said, 'I don't think you like sex at all. I think you're lonely and insecure and looking for attention wherever you can find it.'"

Allison and Stacie looked at each other in surprise. That thought had never occurred to them, but before they could respond, Vanessa continued. "I was so angry—I said, 'Why don't you try me and find out?'" Vanessa almost started crying again. "And he said, 'Too risky.'"

Surprisingly, Allison kept the sarcasm out of her voice. "But, Vanessa, that's how you act."

"I—" Fresh tears welled up in Vanessa's eyes. "I know. But—I'm really confused when it comes to sex." As much as she didn't want to tell the truth, she knew she needed help. "I've only had sex with one guy."

Two audible gasps were a pitch higher than most of the chatter in the coffeehouse. Allison lowered her voice and spoke quietly. "What about high school—Ian—Steve? You slept with them, didn't you?"

"Only with Ian. You know that I had had a crush on him for a long time, but he just used me. I thought he was going to be my boyfriend. I was so stupid. And even worse is that it wasn't very pleasant. It happened so fast—in a car. It was, I don't know, not at all like I imagined. It didn't feel very good—and it was—messy." Vanessa sort of chuckled, something between laughing and crying, before continuing. "Then Steve asked me out. I was feeling so insecure I went out with him. He started kissing me. When I pushed him away, he said that Ian told him how easy I was. After that, Steve told everyone I was easy. It was his convenient way to make it sound as if he had scored with me that night."

"Those jerks." Anger sprung forth in Allison. "Why didn't you tell the truth?" Allison's compassionate tone didn't disguise the anger completely.

"Who would've believed me?" Vanessa shook her head. "You know—when I slimmed down, it was like I became the new girl in school, and it seemed like all the guys wanted me. It confused me. I liked the attention, but I also hated it. I was still the same person inside, but nobody cared about that. The truth is—I'm scared to get too close to a guy. I'm not sure if I can trust them, and I don't trust myself either. I feel so screwed up."

Allison reached over and grabbed Vanessa's hand. "Vanessa, you need to tell Mitch the truth. That poor guy is probably so confused. You guys have been good friends for several years now. It's obvious there's something more between you. I think you should trust him—at least give him a chance."

"I agree." Stacie leaned forward. "He seems like a special guy. I think he really cares for you."

Vanessa wiped her tears with her napkin. "Thanks guys." She giggled slightly. "When I think about it now, I wonder—why in the world have I wasted so much time and energy cultivating a reputation that had nothing to do with who I am inside? I mean—Sharlene even called me on it when we lived in Bismarck. She figured out it was just an act, but I went ahead and continued it here anyway, without her knowing. I've led people to believe I'm having the time of my life—that I'm sexually promiscuous and loving every minute of it. Instead, I'm scared to death to get close to a guy. I figure he'll just—" Vanessa bowed her head in embarrassment as tears started flowing again. "He'll just use me then dump me."

Allison and Stacie glanced at each other with compassion in their eyes. But it was Stacie that spoke. "Vanessa, there are a lot of great guys out there. We have the best example of that." There were things that Stacie could not admit to her sisters, like the fact their dad had loved their mom so much that he raised her daughter by another man. But some topics were safer. "I asked Dad, the day before we came here, if he had started dating yet."

Allison and Vanessa looked at Stacie in surprise. "What did he say?" Allison asked.

"He said that he's dated a few nice women—," Stacie got choked up and tears formed in her eyes as she put her fist up to her heart. "But in his heart, he still feels married to Mom." Her voice got shaky and she couldn't continue without a few tears falling. "And he said that no matter how he tries to forget her, to be angry with her, and even to hate her, the truth is that he still loves her. And that no matter where he is, or who he is with, nothing changes that truth. So he's learned to live with it. He figures someday that will change—and he'll be able to open his heart to someone new."

By now, all three of them had tears in their eyes. "Wow," Vanessa whispered. "Why didn't I see that kind of love exists? It was right under my nose."

"Amma and Afi are still crazy about each other too, and some of our aunts and uncles," Allison said, "but I sure haven't found it."

Vanessa looked at Stacie as if she had just gotten a lens into focus. "Do you know that I know nothing about your love life? Come to think of it, I don't even know who your first kiss was—or if you've ever had a boyfriend."

Stacie sat silent for a moment, filtering a barrage of scattered thoughts.

The truth. Wasn't what Vanessa had done meaningful? Isn't the truth a bridge to bring us closer to the ones we love and to help each other through the tough times? Can anybody ever really love us, for who we are, if they don't know who the real 'us' is? Oh, God—the truth. I've wanted the truth about my parents for so long, but aren't I being a hypocrite to want it from others when I can't speak it myself?

"Stacie?" Allison whispered after she and Vanessa had exchanged puzzled looks.

As Stacie avoided eye contact with both her sisters, she thought of everything Allison had been through.

She wasn't able to hide her struggles from the world: they were there for all of us to see. Nobody knows about my struggles, and I don't have to talk about them either. But as these thoughts sprang forth, truth expanded inside of her and wanted to come out. *Does the truth set you free?* In an impulsive moment, she decided to give it a try. "Well—," Her voice was unsteady. "Do you want to know about the guys in my life when I was sober or not sober?"

"What do you mean?" Allison asked hesitantly.

Stacie sat forward in her seat to be closer to her sisters and out of earshot of nearby people. "It means that I've done some things that I wish I hadn't. And—and one of those is having sex with guys when I was using drugs."

Stacie watched Allison's face form a perfect circle as she said "No," and

Vanessa's eyes widen in disbelief as she said, "You're joking."

"I wish I was." It wasn't that Stacie felt the need to apologize. The only person she had hurt was herself, but she did yearn for some sisterly support. "Look guys, it was a tough time for me—a time when I didn't really care what happened to me. It was the car accident, and meeting Carlotta that snapped me out of it."

"I had no idea." Allison looked stricken with guilt.

Stacie didn't want to dwell on that difficult time. "On a lighter note, I had my first sober kiss before I left for New York."

Stacie's giddier tone didn't allow Vanessa and Allison to linger in their shock and guilt for long. "With who?" Vanessa asked.

"You guys promise not to tell?"

"Promise," was answered by both.

"Spencer." Stacie smiled innocently. "It was pretty sweet, and kind of a funny story. I'll tell you about it, I mean—if you want to hear it."

"Yes!" Vanessa said excitedly.

"Tell us." Allison leaned closer.

"It was when Spencer and his little sister Lizzie were staying in Spartan Manor shortly before I left for New York. I was outside sketching and I saw Lizzie, off in the distance, just standing really still. I knew something was wrong—she seemed almost paralyzed. I rushed over to her, but slowed down as I got closer because I could see a coiled rattlesnake. I told her to be still and, well, to make what seemed like a tremendously long story short, I grabbed a big stick, walked slowly over to her, and helped her back away." Stacie smiled as she told how Spencer had come running over. "He started teasing me. He asked, 'how did a little thing like you tackle that rattlesnake?' And I giggled and said, 'I'm stronger than I look, thank you very much.' He told me, 'I'm forever in your debt. You ever need anything, you just tell me.' And well, I can't believe I said this, but I said, 'How about a kiss?' I was immediately embarrassed—mortified really. But he didn't respond, so I thought maybe he didn't hear me."

"What did he do?" Vanessa asked, perched on the edge of her seat.

"He just sort of looked at me sideways and got a funny expression on his face. Then he started talking about his mother who was in rehab and that the only good thing coming out of it was that he was getting to know his little sister. I was so relieved he didn't hear me."

"Then what?" Allison prodded.

"Well—he kind of sneaked it in. Right after talking about his mom and Lizzie, he said, 'Do you really want me to kiss you?'"

"Oh, how embarrassing!" Vanessa squealed.

"No kidding," Stacie said. "Heat rushed to my face—but, for some reason, I felt like I could say anything to him. So I told him, 'I've only been kissed when I've been wasted. It would be nice to go to New York City with at least my first real kiss over with.'"

"Dang girl—you're gutsy," Allison said. "Did he kiss you?"

"Not yet. First I got a little lecture. He said 'Okay, but there are two things I'm a little worried about. First, you said 'at least,' which implies you may be willing for more, and we hardly know each other. And secondly, I'm not sure how I feel about you saying 'first kiss over with,' but here goes."

"He kissed you then?"

"Yes, but I wouldn't call it a kiss. He caught me off guard and gave me a swift peck on the lips. My mouth wasn't even closed at the time!" Vanessa and Allison laughed along with Stacie. "I told him it didn't count—that I wanted to think of this as my first kiss."

"Wow, that's sweet." Allison said. "What did he say?"

"He grinned and said, 'Oh, you mean a real kiss, one with feeling and tongue action.' I wanted to clobber him. Instead, I took off in a hurry. But before I got very far, I heard him whisper my name. When I turned around, I swear he had this mischievous twinkle in his eyes. He said, 'I'm going to kiss you before you leave for New York. It's going to be great and we'll both want more, but we aren't going to take it any further because we are completely wrong for each other.'"

"He said that?" Allison asked.

"Yes." Stacie said dejectedly. "And then he said, 'Stacie, you have to go out in the world and slay those dragons that are on your back and I have to focus my energies on my sister, my job, and taking care of my mom's problems.' His voice was so soft, but husky at the same time. I don't quite know how to describe it."

Allison and Vanessa smiled at one another, then Allison commented, "Oh, I think you did a pretty good job, Stacie. We got the picture."

"So, is he a man of his word?" Vanessa asked.

"Yes." Stacie grinned.

"Well?" Allison inquired.

"He was right on all accounts. The kiss was amazing. I wanted more, and we're definitely wrong for each other."

"Wow." Vanessa said. "That's a perfect love story—just as it is. You have a hero—you—saving his sister from a deadly rattlesnake, and you have a passionate yet responsible knight, but you can't be together. You're not going to ruin it by trying to make something of it are you?"

Allison and Stacie laughed at Vanessa's theatrics, and Stacie didn't bother to answer the question with anything other than a shrug.

Stacie grabbed a small bag out of her purse. "Let's put on our necklaces." They took their necklaces out of the bag and helped each other put them on.

"It looks like we have everything we need to embark on our futures." Vanessa said as she rubbed her crystal heart absently. "We have each other and our 'Bailey's Heart' necklaces for the words of wisdom that we aren't getting from Mom."

Allison took a drink of her ginger-peach tea, glanced at Vanessa, then at Stacie in surprise. "Do you guys remember when mentioning Mom started an argument?"

Vanessa and Stacie looked at each other then back at Allison, shrugging their shoulders. Vanessa asked Stacie, "Do you want to argue?"

"I don't." Stacie turned to Allison. "Do you?"

Allison set down her glass. "I don't want to argue about her, but there's something that's been bugging me lately." As the attention turned to her, Allison sighed. "It's something I realized recently." She hesitated a moment. "You guys know the way I've talked about Mom—like I didn't really respect her. I mean I loved her—love her still—and I thought she was the greatest Mom, but I didn't really respect her as her own woman. Do you know what I mean?" By her sister's expressions, Allison realized they didn't have the same issue with their mom. "Anyway, now that I'm a mom myself, I realize there are lots of opportunities every day to either help someone else become a better person, or spend that time on your own needs, wants, education, or whatever it is." Allison looked. "Mom gave so much of herself to us and Dad, and I guess I'm just saying that now that I'm a mom—I respect who she was so much, as a mom and as a woman." Tears came to her eyes. "And I wish I could tell her that."

Vanessa leaned back in her chair and gazed out the window for a moment. "I know what you mean." She looked back at her sisters and leaned forward again in her chair. "There's been something stirring up in me. Ever since I met James, Mitch's dad, and he told me about Mom, I just, well, it's like the anger I felt toward her is dissipating." When Stacie and Allison didn't respond, Vanessa continued. "Now when I think of the ugly things I said about Mom after she left, it sends a sickening chill down my spine—and I'm disgusted with myself. I mean, I'm still sad—I still can't believe she's gone—but I guess I'm not as mad at her anymore." Vanessa took a deep breath. "I don't know. It's confusing. I don't really know how I feel about her anymore."

Words from a conversation more than four years ago resounded in Stacie's thoughts. She felt a comforting sense of peace flow through her heart like slow, warm molasses. Her voice was smooth velvet when she spoke. "Pastor Ron said something to me once—something like 'our greatest lessons and strengths come through in the bad times, and that someday we may look back on those times as our greatest blessing.' He also said that 'in order for us to heal, we would need to forgive Mom.'" Stacie looked at both her sisters and thought she saw a sense of peace within them also. "Maybe we're getting there. Maybe we're forgiving her for leaving us."

There was nothing more to say. After a few minutes, as if by mutual consent, the three sisters left the coffee shop with linked arms. On the way home, Vanessa took a detour to show her sisters the house their mom lived in with Great-Grandma June.

Later that afternoon, Allison borrowed Vanessa's car and drove to Pepperdine University, where she sat alone on the lawn, silently making peace with the life she would never have.

31

After having been in the air for only ten minutes, the hum of the plane at ten thousand feet had already lulled his daughter Mindy to sleep. His wife, Lacey, was currently engrossed in the book "Endurance," by Alfred Lansing, about the 1912 Antarctic Expedition. Mindy had insisted her parents read, what was according to her, the "greatest real life adventure story ever!" So, for the first time in about ten days, James Rothman had time to think about something other than holiday festivities and relatives. With three idle hours before they'd land in L.A., thoughts he had kept under wraps during the holiday now filled his mind.

What happened to you, Madeline? He tried to replay the conversation with Vanessa and Mitch, but as he tried to focus on it, various snapshot memories of him and Madeline would interrupt. It was obvious after a few minutes of warring between his conscious and subconscious mind that trying to control his thoughts would not work.

He sat back and relaxed as images started coming faster: he was eight years old. His mother—what was she saying to him? Before he could grasp it, his mind darted to an image of when he visited his dad at the senator's office. Just as quickly his thoughts were back on Mom; he was a little boy talking to his mother. An image of Madeline interrupted. *Madeline!*

Suddenly, words his mother spoke years ago sprang forth as if from an empty well. *"Don't ever mention this girl, Madeline, to your father. It will only make him upset."* The memory was followed by the question he asked his mother. *Why would his father get upset?* The memory was so vivid James recalled his mother's tone and the determined look in her eyes. *"Now, James. Don't talk back to your mother. It is very important to your father's career that you don't talk about your friend to anybody else. In fact, you really shouldn't be friends with her at all. Their family is just not friends with our family. But you must be discreet, James, and not let anyone know this. Can you do that? Can you do that for your father?"*

James had shaken his head yes. Pleasing his father was the most important thing he could do. Sometimes his father would go beyond kindness and they'd have a lot of fun together, but James always understood that he wasn't his father's first priority. Sometimes James felt his father looked right through him, as if his mind was on more important matters.

The scattered images began flowing together, and James knew—just as he had counseled many people up until now—that his time had come to resolve issues he hadn't faced. Counseling others had been his life work, and he was proud of the accomplishments he had made—the lives he had touched in a positive way, but he hadn't faced some truths in his own life. Realizations had come years earlier during the time of grad school: feelings of abandonment by his father, whose career as a politician seemed to come before his duties to his family. That was easy to uncover. What was harder to recognize was a sense that James had been manipulated by his adoring mother. Her actions frequently opposed the things she said, leaving James with an uneasy feeling that he could not trust his mother.

James forced himself to continue with these long buried thoughts. His own voice echoed in his ear, as he had told so many patients when it came time for them to face their problems.

Find the truth. Go where the discomfort is. Let the pain and confusion lead you to where you need to dig deeper. That's where you'll discover who you are and begin to heal.

He knew it was his moment to face some hard truths in his own life.

I need some answers. He took a deep breath and focused on trying to relax. It was past ten p.m. when they exited the plane. As they waited for their luggage, James called his father and arranged to meet the following morning.

Unable to sleep, James arose early the next morning and slipped quietly out of bed—careful not to awaken Lacey. He put on a pot of coffee, showered, and dressed casually. Although it was on the warm side for a winter's day, he grabbed a sweatshirt and a windbreaker, then headed toward his dad's beach house in Malibu.

Arriving early, James drove up slowly and parked next to his dad's Jeep. Hoping not to awaken him, James closed the Blazer door gently and walked toward the beach. The ocean's edge barely touched the rising sun. Soothed by the sounds of the softly breaking waves rolling up the sand, he let his mind go wherever it led.

The images came back. He was a boy, trying to please both of his parents, feeling the immense weight of his father's politics on his shoulders, and that of his grandfather's before him. Everyone in his family had their sights on Gregory Rothman becoming President of the United States, and everyone expected James to keep up the family legacy, but—as much as he tried to love the political arena—he couldn't see that in his future. Even as a teenager, he had disappointed his grandfather immensely. The necessary drive and insincerity of politics didn't seem to be in him. Curiously, his father didn't seem to mind. He would just say, "Son—you can choose a different path." James felt closer to his father at that time than any other.

It wasn't long after James' own rebellion from politics, shortly after he enrolled in Stanford, that his father became known as the "Runaway Senator." James' mother, Sandra, was devastated. Her dreams of being the future First Lady fell in a heap all around her. The truth of their 'fictional lives' undid the ambitious couple, and they soon separated. Determined to maintain her status in the community, despite humiliation and anger, she held her head high and continued with charitable work and social functions.

Sitting down in the sand, just out of reach of the teasing water, James thought about the satisfaction he normally felt due to creating a life of his own. By becoming a counselor, he was able to help others. It was a different form of service to people, without the power or the fame. But, with the realization that he had not helped his own family face truths or heal from the past, his previous contentment in helping others seemed hypocritical.

Look at the distant relationship I've accepted with Dad for years. When did we ever really connect?

Images from the past continued rolling like an old 8mm film: Madeline crying on the steps outside school; a field trip in fourth grade when he sat beside her on the bus and they shared each other's lunches. In fifth grade they were square dance partners in a school production. His memories were vague, but he could see her pretty hair flopping around as she twirled and the two of them giggling when she stepped on his toes.

That was around the time he first mentioned Madeline to his mother. *"Madeline Kiser? Are you sure? And you say she's living with her grandmother?"* His mother's behavior puzzled him now as it had then. As questions began forming in his mind, he stood up and walked back to the beach house.

—————

Greg was dressed and about ready to go when he heard the knock on the door. "Come in, door's unlocked." He grabbed a few sodas and bottled water out of the fridge and packed them in the ice chest along with sandwiches and fruit. He turned toward the front door. Father and son gazed awkwardly at each other for a moment before greetings were issued.

Because of the moderate weather, they opted for sailing and drove the Jeep to the boat docks, parked the car, grabbed the ice chest and hats, then headed to Sam's sailboat that Greg had borrowed for the day.

Greg started the engine and headed the boat out to sea. He sensed James' mood, but Greg wasn't yet ready to talk and was grateful that James seemed to be lost in his own thoughts as well. When they neared a cove, Greg released the anchor.

With the slowing and anchoring of the boat, James thought he should help, but he couldn't escape his thoughts. Something was wrong. He glanced up at his dad, then out across the water again. Nothing was making sense, and yet the images were merging again: Madeline as a young girl—crying on the school steps, helping him make posters for his eighth grade election, leaving L.A. without saying goodbye, and then the visit a few years ago in Bismarck.

I should've done something—made her talk to me. I should've helped. What happened to her?

James glanced back at his dad. "Before I left for the holidays, I stopped by to see Mitch." The tension in his voice was apparent. He willed himself to relax. "It was nice of you to invite his friend, Vanessa, and her family, to stay at the beach house."

"It was fun. We had a great time." With the boat gently rocking, Greg sat down next to his son. "What is it, James?"

As James met his father's gaze, he felt the weight of a thousand words left unsaid. "I'm not sure, really. I got the chance to meet Vanessa shortly before the holidays. I had been at Mitch's one day and saw a few pictures of him with his friends. Vanessa was in several of them, and she looked quite a bit like a girl I've known since grade school. When I went home, I couldn't quit thinking about it, so I drove back to Mitch's place right before Vanessa pulled up."

The seriousness of James' tone made Greg uneasy. "Is Vanessa the daughter of the girl you knew?"

"Yes—she's Madeline's daughter. But there's something else." The tension inside of James built. His pulse increased with each passing second, throbbing louder and louder inside his head.

He tried to calm himself. *Don't make it such a big deal.*

"I've remembered some things I now find a little odd. She was a good friend of mine, but Mom made me keep my friendship with her a secret from you."

Greg's eyes narrowed. "Why would she do that?"

"She said it would upset you if I remained friends with her because our families were enemies. She said to never mention it to you because it would make you very angry."

A puzzled look passed between them. "I can't imagine ever getting upset with you for being friends with a young girl." Apprehension built within him as he asked, "What is, or was, Madeline's last name?"

James hesitated; a secret kept for so many years was about to be revealed. *But what harm can come of revealing a name?*

He said it nonchalantly. "Kiser."

Greg froze, stunned.

Coincidence? But why in God's name would Sandra keep a little girl a secret from me?

As possibilities came to mind, his world started spinning. *Helen's mother still lived in Glendale at that time.* "James, how long have you known this girl?" The question was filled with disbelief.

James looked taken aback at his dad's strong response. "Since first grade."

Oh, God. Could she be Helen's child? Could she be mine? Is Stacie's resemblance to Helen more than just coincidence?

Greg jumped up, feeling as if he would explode.

Startled, James leaped up and grabbed his father by the shoulders. "Dad." No response. "Dad!" When he saw the wide-eyed look of shock in his dad's eyes, James went and grabbed a bottle of scotch Sam kept on board. He brought it back, took off the cap and handed his father the bottle.

Greg accepted it gratefully, took a swig and willed his nerves to calm. "This can't be."

"What is it?"

"Oh, God." Realizations were coming one after the other, Greg's mind moving rapidly as random pieces of information revealed themselves, yet the punch line seemed evasive. "I talked to Randall about the house he's building north of Tucson."

"What does that have to do with anything?"

"It's got to be Helen's house—the one she designed. And this girl, Madeline, could be my daughter!"

James backed up a step. "Who's Helen? And how—is it—that my friend Madeline—can be my sister?" His words were sharply enunciated.

Greg heaved a loud sigh. "I don't know where to start." Inadvertently speaking his thoughts out loud, he said, "I felt a connection with those girls, especially Stacie." He realized his thoughts were scattered. "Give me a minute." He paused, looking out over the water until he was ready to speak.

"Oh, boy, it's taken me years and hundreds of miles out on the open water to sort out the debris I left in the wake of my decisions. Here I was—raised to reach the highest office in the country. My education was the best. I graduated from Stanford University with honors. My parents were proud. But then I deviated from the path they had laid out for me. I took a summer school entry-level law course at the University of Arizona. In hindsight, it's among the best decisions of my life."

Greg paused, looked at James, and then down at his folded hands. "My parents weren't happy about it. I had to convince them it was a good decision. The only point in my favor was that Earl Kiser, an old friend of my father's, lived just outside of Tucson. My father asked me to stop by and see him while I was there. Your mother and I were engaged, and she wasn't happy about my decision either. I don't know why I was so determined to go to the UofA. Maybe because it was reasonably close, but far enough away to get the chance to breathe. Or maybe I just needed a change after four years at Stanford. But while I was in summer school, the thought occurred to me—I didn't want to marry Sandra. I cared for her, and she'd been in my life for as long as I could remember, but there was no real love between us. Her visit to Tucson confirmed my feelings. It was an awkward time for us."

But I slept with her anyway, he thought.

"The morning I went to see Earl Kiser, I told Sandra over the phone that the wedding was off. She seemed to take it well and said that we'd talk about it when I got back. I assumed she felt the same way I did. Then I drove out to Earl Kiser's place." Greg smiled at the memory. "On this long, miserable, dirt road that ended up at this small trailer in the middle of nowhere, I met Helen—Earl's daughter. I fell in love with her the moment our eyes met."

The affectionate tone in his father's voice touched James. "Tell me about her."

Greg warmed at the memories. "She was in a shed working on a small bowl on a pottery wheel. She was completely lost in what she was doing—didn't even know I was standing there. She looked adorable. Her hair in a ponytail with bits of clay in it, and wearing an oversized men's shirt I later learned was her father's. She made a perfect little bowl, and I could feel her excitement. She removed the bowl from the wheel, lifted it up closer so she could examine it, and looked right into my eyes. To this day I've never experienced another moment like that one. It was unforgettable. I fell so hard, so fast, that my life slipped right away from me. I knew right then I would never be the same. Nothing about my current goals or my family's dreams mattered at that moment." Greg smiled at the memory.

James recalled another memory. "Do you remember when my 8th grade history class came to the government buildings on a field trip? Madeline and I took a detour and went to your office. You weren't there but your secretary, Mrs. Heiserman, said we could see your office if we made it quick. Madeline looked around and was immediately drawn to a shelf behind your desk. She picked up a small bowl, looked at the bottom, then had a puzzled look on her face. When I asked her about it, she said, "I don't know—it reminds me of something."

"It was Helen's very first bowl." Greg smiled at the memory. "I watched her initial it right after we met." Greg leaned back against the boat. "We had three days together—the best time in my life—and I was about to change all of my plans, move to Arizona, and spend the rest of my life with Helen."

Comprehension stirred deep inside James, as part of the puzzle became clear. "But Mom was pregnant with me." It was a statement of understanding. Times were different then, and there was only one honorable choice for his father at that time.

Greg looked into his son's eyes, at once seeing the strong, successful man he was but also the young boy he hadn't given enough love to. "God knows I haven't been the best father to you."

James shook his head in acknowledgment. Instead of feeling angry, he felt immense relief at finally understanding some of his father's choices and behavior.

Eyebrows raised, Greg continued, "I'm sorry. I raised you the way generations of Rothman's were raised, at arm's length, and with the wrong expectations."

"Its okay, Dad, it really is." James grinned. "I'm just overwhelmed at the possibilities." He had loved Madeline all these years, feeling a connection with her that he had chalked up to feeling protective toward her from the first moment he saw her. "Dad, is she your daughter?"

"She must be." Greg's eyes widened as another memory surfaced. "That must be why Helen tried to reach me before she died." He turned to James. "Something triggered my secretary's memory about a month after Helen called. Mrs. Heiserman asked me if my wife gave me the message. When I asked her 'what message,' she said 'Helen, the woman who called, sounded urgent,' but that my wife had walked in while I was still talking to her. Sandra took the message and said she'd give it to me."

Greg tried to understand his ex-wife, tried to see her motives behind her actions, but all he could see was a selfish woman who had made vital decisions for him, all because she had her sights set on living in the White House. "Sandra knew about Madeline." The words sounded defeated as he thought of all the years lost without his daughter. "I called Helen as soon as I found out. It was her attorney who returned my call and told me the news, Helen was gone—a brain aneurysm. He didn't tell me about a little girl. But James, if she's your age, she's my daughter."

"And my sister." James sat down beside his father, grabbed the offered bottle of scotch and took a swig himself. He smiled at the thought that Madeline Kiser was his sister. "This is one for the books, Dad. It really is."

"I don't believe it." Greg said. "Do you realize I have three more grand-daughters and a great-grandson?"

James laughed. "You sound pretty sure of yourself."

"The pieces fit." Greg smiled contentedly as he shook his head in disbelief. "Are you okay with this?"

James smiled. "You're going to love Madeline as much as I do."

"Did you know that Madeline left her family while her daughters were still in high school?"

"Yes. Mitch and Vanessa told me."

"They think she left with another man. Mitch told me that a next door neighbor had seen Madeline with a man the night before she left."

Since James had already heard about the mysterious man and knew it was him, there was no hesitation in his response. "That man was me. Madeline and I had stayed in contact occasionally over the years—sent a Christmas card a time or two, and I had even visited her once when in route to a business conference. And, for some reason, I would think of her when Lacey and I went to Minneapolis to see Lacey's grandparents. So a few years ago, actually over four years ago now, Lacey and I were heading to Minneapolis for her nephew's wedding. On a whim, I tried Madeline's old phone number. The moment she answered I could tell something was wrong. So once in Minneapolis, Lacey and I booked a charter flight to Bismarck. Unfortunately there was a delay and the flight didn't get in until after 9 pm. By the time we arrived, Lacey had the beginnings of a migraine, so she stayed at the hotel. I went over to the Averson's house and Madeline and I talked for over an hour—maybe two. She seemed a bit scattered, but assured me she was fine, that she was just having everyday stress, fighting off a flu bug, and missing her family. Lacey and I were supposed to meet Madeline for an early breakfast before we caught our flight out, but Madeline didn't show up or answer the phone when I tried to call. Lacey and I were worried, but we assumed Madeline was resting. She was probably already gone."

"So she may not have left with another man." Greg felt an urgency to get going, needing to find the answers. But first, he had to hear everything his son could tell him. "Tell me about her. Maybe you'll be giving us some clues as to where to start to sort this out."

James began with the story of the first time he laid eyes on her, crying at the side of the building. When he saw her, her big eyes peering up at him with those wet lashes, he knew he wanted to take care of her, and he had. They became good friends throughout the years, always able to count on one another through good times and bad. He told his father about the election and how Madeline had helped him. "Come to think of it, she frequently seemed sad. It's funny—I think that's what drew me to her. I wanted to take care of her. I thought it was just who she was, and I felt glad I was able to help. But then there were times when she'd laugh or stick up for the underdog. Her strength was there, just under a veil of vulnerability."

Greg felt an urgency to begin looking for his daughter, but first, he felt, there were other things that needed to be said. "You know, I didn't sleep much last night. When you called, I thought by the tone of your voice that you were looking for answers. I figured you wanted to ask me why I did what I did all those years ago—when I withdrew from the presidential race, and drastically changed my life. I thought you may have wanted a better answer than the one I gave you at the time."

James smiled. "You said your heart wasn't in it. But I always figured you must've had a major mid-life crisis."

Greg chuckled at James' reasoning. "Maybe that's as good an answer as any."

"What is your answer? I mean—if you don't mind me asking. Why did you throw it all away, the way you did—the family, and your career?"

Greg didn't know where to start. That time in his life was so far away from him now it was hard to go back. He looked out at the open water, as Helen's image, her warm smile, seemed to envelop him. After meeting Stacie Averson, Helen had been on his mind frequently the past few days. He could almost hear her saying, *"This is what matters. No matter how hard it is, take the step. Tell him who his father really is."* He closed his eyes and let her image melt into him, a woman he had never forgotten, the one woman he would always love—even if death kept them apart.

"I have a lot of regrets in my life, but leaving that life isn't one of them. Hurting you and our relationship though, is at the top of the list." There were some things Greg couldn't tell his son.

The man I wanted to be died on the day I found out Sandra was pregnant. Through the years, I both loved and resented you, my son. It was because of that pregnancy I didn't ever drive that long dirt road to Helen again. I always believed there'd come a day when I could go back to her. The day I found out she had died, I wanted to die, too. I felt I had nothing else to look forward to, but then I would look at you and know how truly selfish I was being.

Greg drew strength from James' calm manner until he found the courage to unburden himself. "Protecting the family name was no longer my priority. I didn't leave because of Helen. I had long since learned she had died. The truth is, when I couldn't be with Helen, it broke my heart. Later, the war broke my spirit. I received the Medal of Honor for saving a squadron during an ambush by the North Koreans, but my 'bravery' was more of a death wish than any heroics. I felt so trapped by my life. But when I almost died, you were all I could think about. It took a near death experience for me to appreciate that I had a son, a son that was counting on me to be there for him. All of a sudden I had hopes of raising you and being there for you, but after I came back, real life began to chip away at me, bit by bit, and my high hopes were buried under the broken man that I had become. I had seen too many of my buddies get blown away, and I couldn't come to terms with any of it. On my return, everyone took care of me—your mother and my parents. The worst part is that I let them. Everyone doted on the returned war hero. I hate to think how they loved that. It was going to be so much better for my political career to have that Medal of Honor under my belt. They couldn't give up the dream of seeing me in the White House, but it was all a façade, and it didn't even occur to me to change it. I lived out my days being a dutiful son, husband, and politician, but everything about my life rang false. The way my family interacted—the formal dinners—left me hollow. I found myself longing for the life I would've had with Helen, and when it hit me that I needed a change, it came on me suddenly."

"What triggered it?"

Greg looked out at the water. "There was so much pressure around the upcoming presidential nomination. The party wanted me to run, my family expected me to run. It was my good old buddy Sam that saw it was getting to me. He convinced me to take a diving trip to San Carlos. He said, 'Come on—two days, tops. We'll take a quick flight into Guaymas, hook up with a dive shop, and get four, maybe five, dives in. Nobody will even miss you!'"

"What happened?"

"Just like he said. We got some dives in—had a few beers. At dusk the night before we left, I took a long walk along "Catch 22" beach. There was a rock outcropping about fifty yards off shore that had a large cardon cactus. It reminded me of my time spent in Tucson with Helen. In all honesty, during my busy life as a politician, I had done my best not to dwell on losing her, but in that moment I felt her love so strongly. In that moment I realized how far I was from the life I would've shared with her. That's all it took to fully realize a career in politics was not what I wanted. I knew I wasn't going to waste one more minute of my life doing something that was becoming more and more repulsive to me." Greg looked at James. "Even though Helen was gone, I felt she was leading the way. She changed me, James. The life I am living today—a simpler life—close to nature, is how I would have lived had she been in my life. It's a freedom she gave me."

"I wish I could've known her," James said.

A mixture of relief and exhaustion from their candor left them oddly quiet for a few minutes. In silent agreement, they pulled up anchor, started the engine, and headed back.

After they arrived at the dock and secured the boat, they hurried to the Jeep and drove the short distance to the house, feeling a mutual urgency to find answers. The question as to what had happened to Madeline weighed on both of their minds.

Back at the house, they showered, put some steaks on the grill, made a quick salad, and heated up a can of barbecue beans. They ate at the dining room table where Greg, Mitch, and the Aversons had gathered for Christmas dinner just five days before. They told each other everything they could think of: the smallest details about Madeline's life and that of her family, the Aversons.

They called it a night with thoughts of Helen, Madeline, and the amazing connection they had with them foremost in their minds. As James lay in bed, he smiled—acknowledging it was Madeline who had closed the gap, bringing father and son together at last.

As Greg lay awake, he thought about the empty pit of loneliness he had carried with him most of his life. He had always felt something was missing and had mostly attributed it to losing Helen, but now he knew it was more than that.

All these years I've had a daughter—my daughter with Helen.

As he drifted off to sleep, first his memory, and then his dreams, took him back to another time.

Do you know why I chose that particular story for you?" Greg asked as she playfully touched his nose with the tip of her finger, then kissed him at the nape of his neck.

"Because this is a perfect night, just like the night you stayed by the lake with your grandfather."

He interwove his fingers with hers. Before he replied, he looked deeply into her eyes. "For the first time in my life, I know what he means. You're my angel. You've changed me forever."

Overcome with love and gratitude, she kissed the tips of his fingers. "Thank you."

He brushed his lips at the corner of her eye where a teardrop hovered, then dropped onto his back. "Okay, your turn."

Helen leaned toward him and propped herself up on her elbow. "I can't top that one!"

Gregory winked at her. "Probably not—but give it your best shot."

"All right, but my story is more recent. Every summer, as soon as school got out, the school bus driver would drive me to the municipal airport. Dad would be waiting for me, sometimes in the pilot's lounge, sometimes looking over the plane or refueling. There was always this anticipation inside of me as to when our eyes would meet. Sometimes I'd see him first, but sometimes he'd be waiting for me to spot him. The moment our eyes met, he would throw out his arms and I'd run toward him as fast as I could. It became a tradition in grade school, but I quit doing it when I was in junior high. When Dad came for my graduation from high school, I spotted him as he was wiping down the plane. I stood on the tarmac, waiting for him to spot me. Several minutes passed before he looked my way. As soon as our eyes met, I broke out in a run. I could tell from a distance Dad was taken off guard, but he recovered and threw his arms out to meet me. We were both in tears when I finally reached him."

Helen's eyes glistened in telling the story.

Gregory wrapped his arms around her as she rested her head on his chest. "You lost so much when your father died."

"Yes, but I was so blessed to have him for my dad. I have no complaints that he's gone other than I miss him so much."

———

Three weeks later, Greg and James called it a night after another long day of fruitless searching for Madeline. Greg was relying on his staff in Mexico to keep the dive shop running smoothly, and James worked around his patients schedules as well as he could. They had spent hours, every day, calling public record agencies. They searched under vehicle registrations, utility companies, and hospitals. They used Greg's old connections to gain access to some private databases. As many calls as they had made, they had a whole lot more ahead of them. Checking obituary records would be a last resort, one they hoped never to use.

"How about a beer?" Greg stacked the papers on the desk and headed for the fridge.

"Sure." James' voice was heavy with disappointment until he suddenly remembered a story he had neglected to tell Greg. "Oh, man, I remembered something last night I wanted to tell you. It's probably the only sneaky thing I ever did to Mom." His voice took on a mischievous, lighter note. "In junior high, Madeline made beaded necklaces and bracelets. She did a great job. They looked nice. Well, remembering what Mom said about Madeline in grade school—that I shouldn't be her friend—I asked Madeline if I could buy a necklace for my mom for Christmas." James grinned. "Mom wore that necklace all the time, at least around the house. I took some satisfaction in seeing the trouble she went through, having to change necklaces all the time when she went to one of her functions. She would've died had she known where I got it."

Greg smiled the genuine smile of a parent who is proud of his child but, in this case, it wasn't just his son's clever way of seeking harmless revenge, it was also pride in his daughter's talent. "I remember that necklace. I can't believe it was my daughter who made it."

As Greg set his fork down, he was struck by an earlier conversation his granddaughters had when they returned from shopping. "Wait a minute, that could be it!"

"What?"

"Bailey's Hearts! The girls—they bought the necklaces. They considered the sayings as 'words of wisdom' from Mom."

"What does that have to do with Madeline?"

"Maybe nothing, but I've got a hunch about this. Allison explained to me they had learned their mom's nickname was Bailey." Greg was so touched by the name that tears came to his eyes. "My last night with Helen, we were outside—it was a beautiful night. She wanted to exchange special stories, she wanted a story I hadn't shared with anyone before. I told her a story that my grandpa had told me—how a special man, a drifter named Tom Bailey, had brought love into his and my great-grandparents hardened household one winter, and how my grandpa considered him an angel. Helen was touched by the story. She told me if we had a daughter, we would name her Bailey."

"You think these 'Bailey's Hearts' could be Madeline's creation?"

Greg knew it was a long shot. But right now it was all he had. "It's worth checking out."

32

With luggage jammed into the trunk and Allison behind the wheel of her red Mazda 323, Stacie in the front passenger seat, and Vanessa and Mitch in the back seat, the car was filled to capacity as they left the airport.

"Can you believe this weather? I haven't seen sky this blue in months." Stacie tried to distract herself from thinking about Vanessa and Mitch.

My half-sister is dating my half-brother! She tried to find humor in the situation. I guess its okay. Since I share a mom with Vanessa and a dad with Mitch, they're not related to each other.

"What about when you were in L.A?" Vanessa said defensively. "It wasn't raining when you guys were there. At least not all the time."

"L.A. doesn't have blue sky—ever, only a persistent cloud of pollution," Allison piped in while braking for the stop light at Tucson Boulevard and Valencia.

Vanessa ignored the comment and leaned forward with her hand on the headrest of Stacie's front seat. "I'm glad you flew in first, Stacie. Did you take my advice on how to kill time at the Tucson International Airport?"

"Didn't need to," Stacie said flippantly. "Allison picked me up as soon as I arrived. We went and got something to eat while we were waiting for your flight to arrive."

"No fair," Vanessa said teasingly. "How come nobody did that for me? I was stuck there for two hours."

Allison giggled while replying, "Knowing we would be spending the next week together, maybe we didn't *want* to spend an additional two hours with you."

"Hey—I'm beginning to feel picked on." Vanessa gave an exaggerated huff and turned to Mitch. "That was when my grandparents had their fiftieth wedding anniversary in Mountain that I told you about."

"Are you guys going this year?" Mitch asked innocently. "If you are, I'd really like to go. I mean—if you'll have me. I realize I don't have an ounce of Icelandic blood in my veins, but we can keep that our little secret, can't we?" He shrugged his shoulders apologetically. "I think I can blend." He raised his fist in the air, and with as much conviction as he could muster, he said, *"Islanskur Mater!"* He was rewarded with giggles and smiles from

Allison and Stacie.

"What?" He asked innocently when he saw Vanessa's bewildered expression. "It must be a blast to spend a week with dozens of relatives, where you eat, toss a ball around for awhile, play cards, listen to your cousins play the guitar, get bit by mosquitoes, sit in front of the fan to escape the suffocating humidity, eat some more, walk around, see the sights—you know—the bars and the graveyards."

Allison laughed. "You nailed that description. But we love Mountain just the same."

While giggling, Vanessa smacked him in the arm. "I don't believe it. It was more than a year ago when I told you about my last North Dakota trip, and I didn't even think you were listening. You're good, Rothman. You hung on my every word while beating the pants off me in miniature golf."

"A big family reunion is being planned for this year." Stacie said. "Uncle Barney told Dad that cousins and second cousins who normally don't make it are going to try to attend. We should think about going."

They made a pact to return to Mountain, with a brief visit to their hometown, Bismarck, in the summer. Allison stretched her head up to peer at Mitch in the rearview mirror. "How about you, Mitch, are you in?"

He backed down. "I don't know—that may be too soon. One has to prepare for a trip like that."

"What would you possibly need to do to prepare for a trip to Mountain?" Vanessa asked.

"Eat prunes." He said seriously.

Vanessa smacked him teasingly across the leg. "What are you talking about?"

"You know—that 'tarta' stuff."

"You mean vinarterta?"

"Yeah, that Icelandic prune cake stuff. You've got to work up to eating that kind of thing." He grinned mischievously. "You can't just jump into it. I mean, who would ever think of making a cake using prunes?"

"It's good!" Vanessa squealed. "Especially Aunt Marge's. She adds a secret ingredient."

"Speaking of Aunt Marge," Allison said, "she and Uncle Barney are coming down to see the house next month."

Stacie turned toward Allison. "Have you seen the house since it's been finished?"

"No, Dad wanted me to wait so we could all see it together." Allison's heart skipped a beat as she decided to voice something she had meant to keep to herself. "I don't think this trip is just about the house."

"What do you mean?" Vanessa asked.

"I think this is about Mom." Allison glanced over at Stacie and knew they had both been thinking the same thing.

Vanessa leaned forward in her seat. "Why do you think this is about Mom? Dad just finished the house and he's excited for us to see it."

"Then why did he fly you guys out here on such short notice? And why did he suggest that it would be better if Jason didn't come?"

"Jason won't be there? I just assumed he was with Dad already."

"No, I dropped him off at Todd's." Allison cast a puzzled glance toward Mitch.

Vanessa saw Allison's confused expression. "Mitch's dad called and told him to come with me, said that he would pay the airfare."

"Really? That was nice of him, but why would he do that?"

Mitch shrugged his shoulders. "I thought it was a little strange, but he said he had to get going and that we'd talk later."

Stacie's stomach flipped.

Oh, God. It's all going to come out.

A deep panic ballooned quickly. *I don't want anyone to know.*

She slumped a little in her seat. As she felt the truth was about to be revealed, she realized why she had never questioned Randall.

As long as nobody says otherwise, I'm still his daughter.

"What's the matter, Stacie? You look like you're about to pass out."

"Just tired—probably jet lag or something."

As they exited onto Avra Valley road, Vanessa pointed out Arizona Portland Cement to Mitch and the long conveyer belt that connected the plant to the mine. "That's where Dad works—an eyesore if there ever was one."

Stacie looked out at the landscape and sat up abruptly. "We finally got 'em!" A partial smile brightened her face at the sight of the Mexican Poppies, in full bloom, scattered brightly over the desert floor in a colorful golden carpet.

"Wow," Vanessa responded. "Dad told us about them before we moved here."

"I won't ever complain about winter rains again." Allison explained to Mitch that the amount of winter rains determine if there will be a wildflower season in the spring. "In the four years we've been here, this is the best season yet."

A few minutes later they turned down Sanders road and saw the tall cement structures on either side. "It doesn't look like it," Vanessa explained to Mitch, "but we're about to cross over a bridge—it's the Central Arizona Project." She pointed out the chain link fence that ran along the canal.

"They cut through three acres of our property to build it."

A moment later they were on the other side of the structures. Oohs and aahs filled the small space in the car as the large, sand-colored stucco house, with midnight blue and burnt orange trim, came into view.

"It's beautiful." Vanessa exclaimed. She hadn't seen any of it since the footings were dug during the summer. "And look at the…." At first, the massive flagstone patio and its large pots of flowers caught her attention, but she was the first to spot her dad and—"Your dad's here!" She said to Mitch as she pointed to the two men who were sitting on a bench wall seat.

"What?" Three voices said in unison as Mitch leaned forward. "Why is he here?" Mitch asked.

Panting, Stacie wanted to get out of the car immediately and run far away. Remembering the panic attack she had the day she was with Carlotta, she tried to calm herself down. She took a few deep breaths.

Please not again. But she couldn't contain the overwhelming emotions. "Stop here." she said in a low, desperate tone.

"What?" Allison asked as she kept on driving. The atmosphere in the car was suddenly intense as all eyes gravitated toward Stacie.

"Let me out of the car." It came out in a whine.

"What's the matter?" Allison drove the remaining distance, then pulled in the circular driveway. By the time she put the car into park, Stacie had opened the door and bolted out.

"Stacie!"

Just a few steps were all Stacie's wobbly legs could handle. Her face went completely white as Randall ran up and grabbed her before she collapsed. She didn't want to cry, but tears came out with the words. "How could you do this to me?"

Randall had never seen such intense pain expressed by Stacie before, and just by supporting her weight he could feel the enormity of her emotions. "What do you mean? What am I doing?"

"Bringing him here like this!" Stacie cried.

Randall did not understand. "There's something I want to tell you." He turned to the girls, then back to Stacie. "Something you need to hear about your mother."

"Not this way." Stacie's face became awash with fresh unbridled tears. "Please don't say it." The sobs became harder. "Please, Dad, don't say it," she repeated in a whisper.

He held her while she cried. "It's okay, sweetie, its good news."

She pushed away from him. "I already know what it is! How can you say its good news?"

He stopped short. "What is it? What's bothering you?"

Stacie stared at him in disbelief. "How could you do this to me—and, and to you?"

Randall looked at her questioningly, and then looked at everyone else— who clearly seemed as perplexed as he was. He looked back at Stacie and spoke tenderly. "Do what?"

She looked at James and back to her dad, wondering how both of them could act like this was no big deal. "I know he's my real father." Another glance toward James conveyed whom she was talking about.

"No!" Randall yelled. Mouths opened and eyes widened as everyone looked around from one to another in shock.

James stepped closer to Stacie. "I'm not your father." His voice was tender, but he was clearly shaken.

Stacie looked at James, then at Randall. "You said it, Dad."

Randall shook his head as if he didn't know what she was talking about. "That night in Bismarck—Paul was over," she explained. "I was supposed to spend the night at Claire's. But I didn't. I came home. I heard you tell Paul you overheard Mom talking to a man named James, some childhood friend of hers, on the phone. I heard you, Dad," she said in a soft cry. "I heard you say you weren't my real dad—you said he was."

Allison and Vanessa stood close, speechless, with tears in their eyes. Mitch stood close to Vanessa with his hand protectively on the small of her back.

Randall rubbed the back of his neck. "Oh God, Stacie. That one time is the only time I ever mentioned those words out loud. I'm so sorry you heard that, but it isn't true."

Stacie's voice was a little steadier as she asked, "Why would you say something *so awful* if it isn't true?"

There were so many things to talk about, but this was the last thing Randall had expected to be brought up. He let out a deep sigh. "It's true I sometimes doubted you were my biological daughter." Randall began telling the story of what he had overheard Madeline saying on the phone to James. "She was about seven months pregnant and rubbing her belly. She said, 'James, do you want to raise this child as your own?' I left the room before she saw me."

"What did she say when you asked her about it?" Allison asked.

"At the time, I didn't ask her. I wish I had. It would have saved Stacie and me a lot of grief. I thought if I confronted Madeline about it, I'd be making it easier for her to leave me."

Randall turned again towards Stacie. "Let's face it. I was crazy about your mom. I didn't want to live without her. When you were born, it didn't matter to me if you were mine or not. I loved you from the first moment I held you in my arms. Deep down, in my gut, I believed you were my daughter. We were so close, and I'd forget what I had overheard, but my defenses were down after your mom left. That is the only time I ever said those words out loud. I'm so sorry. From the day you were born, you've been my daughter—just like Allison and Vanessa."

Stacie started crying again, but this time all the years of feeling isolated came out in tears of relief. "I know, Dad. That's the only thing that kept me going when I found out. I knew you loved me anyway."

"And it's a good thing, because you *are* my biological daughter." Randall reached out and firmly held her shoulders. With tears in his own eyes, he looked deeply into hers, making sure they were connected as he said, "I know it to be true. Can you trust me on that for now—and later you and I will talk more?"

Stacie nodded yes before she fell into her dad's arms, crying even more. She began feeling a sensation in her body she hadn't felt in a very long time—peaceful—safe. It felt so good. She squeezed her dad so tight; she never wanted to let him go.

Allison and Vanessa joined Randall and Stacie and hugged them both while Mitch, with a stunned expression on his face, walked over and stood next to his dad.

"How awful, Stacie," Vanessa said. "I can't imagine how hard it was to think you weren't related to Dad, especially after Mom leaving."

"I'm so sorry, Stacie." Allison said. "I wish you'd talked to us about it."

It was a poignant scene, until Stacie stepped away from the group and turned to James. "No offense, Mr. Rothman, but I'm so happy you're not my dad!"

James smiled, clearly touched by the exchange. He was thrown off track by Stacie's revelation, and wondered about the pain the misunderstanding must have caused. "No, Stacie, I'm not your father." James glanced at Randall and got an encouraging nod to continue. He looked at Allison, Vanessa, and back to Stacie, clearly getting everyone's attention. He smiled awkwardly before saying, "I'm your Uncle."

As mouths dropped open and eyes widened in shock again, the only thing that broke the silence this time was Vanessa's hand slapping against her mouth. All eyes turned to her as she screamed a muffled "No!" against her hand. "Oh, my God. Mitch?" Her eyes were wide with shock. "Mitch?"

Mitch looked at her quizzically. "What's the matter?"

"We're cousins!"

Allison and Stacie gasped at this realization.

Vanessa felt a searing pain, knowing she was going to lose him now after they had finally discovered their love for one another—and had gotten together in ways no cousins should.

Oh no.

Memories of their intimate times together bombarded her with hot, sexy, steamy images: kisses so wet and deep, the weight of his strong body on hers.

Ew! He's my cousin!

Mitch could tell where her thought process was going and mischievously would have loved to drag out her feelings for as long as he could, but there were other people involved. "Vanessa," he whispered to her. "I told you I was adopted."

A smile brightened her face. "You weren't joking?"

"No."

"Thank God." Vanessa flew into Mitch's arms for a brief, but reassuring hug.

"I remember that phone call with Madeline when she was pregnant with Stacie." James said. "She and I had just barely renewed our friendship. Lacey and I were going through a very difficult time because our best friends, Ryan and Kathy Larsen, Mitch's parents, died in a car accident. Mitch was only four years old. In their will, Ryan and Kathy had requested if anything happened to them, they wanted Lacey and I to adopt him and raise him as our own." James put his arm around Mitch. "Mitch was the child Madeline was talking about."

Vanessa whispered softly to Mitch. "I'm so sorry about your parents."

"Thanks." He leaned over and kissed the side of her cheek. "It was a long time ago. I was really young."

Allison seized the momentary silence. "Are there any other misunderstandings or can we get to the part about Mom?" Under the circumstances, that comment brought about a few light chuckles. Taking that as a yes, Allison turned toward her dad. "You did say you have some news about Mom. Are we ever going to see her again?"

He couldn't speak. The tears in his eyes and the slight upward tilt of his lips said it all as he nodded 'yes.'

Allison's eyes opened as big as full moons. "When?"

Randall looked at his daughters one-by-one as memories of the past four and a half years without Madeline ran through his mind. So much heartache, so many wrong turns and challenging choices, but they had pulled through. He swallowed the lump in his throat. "The day after tomorrow."

"Is she okay? Have you seen her?" Stacie asked in a faint voice.

"Yes, I've seen her." Randall smiled. "She looks good."

A bit weathered perhaps, and much thinner, but good.

"Where is she?"

"She's in Phoenix."

Anxious to get to the details about their mom, Allison was the first to jump in and get the conversation moving forward. "Who is she with?"

Randall took a deep breathe before answering. "She was never with another man."

"What?" Allison and Vanessa asked at the same time. "Then who was the man Mrs. Deiko saw her with?" Allison asked.

"It was me." James leaned forward, as if admitting guilt. "As I mentioned, Madeline and I periodically kept in contact over the years. And, ironically, it was a trip to Minneapolis—for my wife's grandparent's 50th wedding anniversary, that brought Lacey and I on a junket over to Bismarck all those many years ago. The second trip, at the time of your family reunion, Lacey and I were booked to fly to Minneapolis for her nephew's wedding. Since it had been so easy to visit Madeline the first time, I thought of her again and, on a whim, called. She tried her best to sound upbeat, but it was obvious something was very wrong. I asked her about it, but she attributed it to not feeling well and missing her family. But by the following morning, I couldn't shake the feeling that something wasn't right with Madeline. I re-booked our flights so we'd have time to see her. Lacey and I arrived in Bismarck at around nine o'clock that night. Lacey would have gone with me to see Madeline, but she had a slight migraine and chose to stay at the hotel."

Vanessa was looking at James, "If Mom didn't go with you—," she turned to her dad, "then why did she leave?"

Allison jumped in. "And I don't understand. Mom didn't take the truck or the car. And you checked—and we double checked—every available mode of transportation."

"Your Mom left on foot." His words were heavy with guilt.

"That doesn't make any sense." Vanessa said. "She walked to Phoenix?"

Randall knew the telling would be difficult. It had been horrifying hearing the story from Madeline and from her caseworker. He took a moment to gather his thoughts. *Just say it straight—they can handle it—they've handled a lot worse.* "Your mother had a severe nervous breakdown caused by post traumatic stress disorder."

A symphony of "No," "It can't be," and "Oh, my God" resounded in the air.

Vanessa practically pleaded. "All this time we thought she was off having a good time, and that she just up and left us to be with another man. I can't believe it."

"Listen to me, girls. Mrs. Deiko's seeing James threw us, but it was your mom's own handwritten note that got us off-track. We did the best we could at the time." He hoped he sounded convincing. He felt enough guilt for all of them.

He gauged his daughter's reactions and knew this was going to be a very long day. "Listen, I suggest we take a break before we continue. Does anybody want to see the house?"

"No!" It came out in stereo between Allison and Stacie.

Stacie looked at her dad with subtle desperation. "The house looks amazing. It's truly more magnificent than I imagined, but there's so much to talk about."

"I know, Sweetie, but I need to get something to drink. And I think we should go inside and sit down. Can you wait a few minutes?"

"Sure, Dad." Stacie took pleasure in letting the name 'Dad' roll off her tongue.

"Okay," Vanessa added. "I'm thirsty and I have to go to the bathroom. Let's see the house, get some drinks, and use the toilet." Vanessa's face flushed with embarrassment, as she suddenly became more aware of her relationship with James. As they all headed for the front door, she asked him. "What do I call you? Uncle James or, since you're Mitch's dad, Mr. Rothman?"

James grinned along with everyone else. "Mr. Rothman is definitely out. If you're comfortable calling me Uncle James, I'd like that."

"Okay, Uncle James," Vanessa continued, "Is it okay if I date your son?"

Everyone snickered, grateful for a momentary respite from the emotional conversation. "Yes," James responded while still laughing. "That's fine by me."

33

Under the circumstances the tour of the house was anticlimactic, but the beauty of the house, with its arched entry, warm sandy yellow walls, rustic red accents, and large diagonally-scored concrete floors, was felt and expressed by all. It was a home built for family interaction. The living room, dining room, and kitchen shared in one large, great space. Each bedroom had inviting French doors leading out to patios, and the bathrooms were spacious, with an old world charm. Although the furnishings from the trailer made the house homier, they were inadequate in such a large house.

Randall quickly explained to his daughters that they would have to figure out which bedroom they wanted. "Draw straws if you have to. They're pretty much the same size. And I'd like you guys to go shopping and get some new bedding."

"That's great, Dad." Allison said. "But why don't you come shopping with us? You can pick out some things for the house."

"No way. I've been shopping with the three of you before. That's not my idea of a good time." He did not acknowledge the real reason he did not want to furnish it.

Maybe Madeline will want to decorate the house.

To end further questioning, he turned and headed toward the kitchen.

Allison followed him. She put her arm around him and leaned her head against his shoulder as they walked into the kitchen. "I'll help with the drinks."

"Carlotta made a gallon of lemonade and enough food for us so we won't have to worry about cooking unless we want to."

"Carlotta knows?"

"Yes, I told her. She knows your mom has a lot to handle right now, so Carlotta's going to wait until your mom calls, but she won't have to wait long. I told your mom about Carlotta, and she was very moved to have the opportunity to see Carlotta again."

Although James appreciated Randall's invitation to be with the family at this time, he knew Randall and his daughters needed time alone to discuss Madeline. James and Mitch talked briefly before James said, "If you'll excuse us, we're going for a walk. We'll be back in a bit."

Randall nodded as the girls waved. Vanessa ran over and gave Mitch a quick kiss close to his lips. "Watch out for snakes. It's a little early yet in the year, but if those baby rattlers are out there, they are the ones to really watch for. They haven't learned to control their venom."

"We'll be careful." Mitch suppressed a grin as he and his dad walked out the door.

Randall brought in a tray of lemonade while Allison grabbed a bag of tortilla chips and a bowl of Carlotta's jalapeno cheese dip. It was a nice gesture, but nobody was hungry.

Stacie resumed the conversation before Randall and Allison had a chance to sit down. "Can you start at the beginning, Dad? Tell us everything?"

"I guess that's a good place to start—the beginning." Randall set the tray of drinks on the large mesquite coffee table and sat in his recliner while Allison joined her sisters on the sofa. He grabbed a glass of lemonade and took a long drink. More than half of it was gone when he set it on the table.

"You girls were right about knowing more about your mom's childhood than she did. Until recently, she didn't remember. And after just speaking with Carlotta, I learned that, out of respect for your mom, Carlotta didn't tell us everything either."

"What are you talking about?" Allison asked.

"As you know, your grandmother, Helen, died of a brain aneurism before her scheduled surgery. What we didn't know is that your mom was alone with Helen when she died." Randall looked away, trying to blink away tears. The thought of Madeline's tiny six year old arms holding her dead mother for hours made him feel sick. He swallowed. "It was well over an hour when Carlotta got back from the grocery store, and it was over an hour after that when the fire department came and literally pulled your mom off Helen's body. Your mom temporarily stayed with Carlotta until the courts gave custody to your mom's grandmother, June—a woman she had never met. Your mom was screaming as two court officials pulled her out of Carlotta's arms."

As Allison, Vanessa, and Stacie absorbed their father's words and each formed questions, looks between themselves and Randall conveyed an agreement that for now they would try to just listen.

"We have learned that June was paranoid schizophrenic, but had a way of fooling most people. The time that your mother lived with her was emotionally and sometimes physically abusive. June convinced Madeline that her deceased mother, Helen, had been a wicked woman. In other words, when your mother needed love and support the most, she was sent to live with a monster."

Having learned a few things on their own, and through Grandma Helen's diary, this news was not a total surprise to his daughters.

"Over the years, your mother learned to survive by replacing the mother she remembered and loved with the woman June said she was. Madeline also learned to please her grandmother to reduce conflict. Every day of every year with that woman was a battle for survival."

"Another traumatic event happened when your mom was sixteen. She was almost raped by a boy in the neighborhood. The neighbor across the street, Mr. Smith, a black man, helped your mom."

"We met him! Mitch and I met him when we went looking for the house Mom grew up in. I knew there was something he wasn't telling us."

Allison turned to Vanessa. "You didn't mention he was African-American."

Vanessa shrugged. "I didn't know that was important."

Randall resumed his story. "Mr. Smith had heard a ruckus from his kitchen window. He saw Madeline in a dark corner of the yard trying to fight somebody off. He quickly and quietly ran across the street and came up behind the attacker. The attacker ran off. June, who was very prejudiced and had previously told Madeline to stay away from Mr. and Mrs. Smith, heard the commotion and came outside to find Mr. Smith helping Madeline. June was livid and yelled at Mr. Smith to let go of Madeline or she would call the police. Your mom gestured to Mr. Smith that she was all right, so he left. Madeline, still in a state of shock, ran into the house and up the stairs. June ran after her, yelling all the way and getting more and more hateful. When Madeline reached the entrance to the bathroom, close to the head of the stairs, June went after her, calling her a dirty whore for letting Mr. Smith touch her. Madeline swung around, finally yelling back. It frightened June." Randall paused. "And—her grandmother backed away, fell down the stairs, and broke her neck. It killed her."

"Oh, my gosh—that article." Vanessa exclaimed.

"What article?" Randall asked.

"We did some of our own digging, Dad, and we found the article that said June Kiser died from falling down a staircase. It said they were investigating the possibility of foul play."

"And it was Mom." Allison shook her head in disbelief.

"It was an accident." Randall said. "And one more memory your mother buried. She had already lost the memories of a loving mother, and her mother's tragic death, and had forgotten about Carlotta, or, more accurately, these memories were practically beaten out of a little girl. Over the years, Madeline felt her whole family was bad, so she erased any memory of them as best as she could."

"But then her memories started coming back." Stacie said.

"In the past, your mom had learned to shut down memories as they surfaced, or pretend it was her imagination. All that changed when she received the letter from the attorneys, regarding the Central Arizona Project. It was in her hands—a document, proof of land in her name, and with her deceased mother's name on it. Your mom had tried for so long to keep the memories buried, but all of a sudden reminders seemed to be everywhere: Stacie growing up and looking more and more like Helen, Allison looking at colleges in California, so close to where she had once lived, the Native American woman in the grocery store reminding her of Carlotta."

"The memories confused your mom. Some wonderful memories surfaced, but she didn't trust them. She said her grandmother's voice grew louder and louder in her head, criticizing everything Madeline did. But worst of all was June's voice criticizing your mom for being a terrible mother. Your mom somehow transferred the words June had said about Helen being a bad mother to words meant for her. By the time your mom left, she believed all of us would be better off without her."

"I don't believe it," Stacie said. "She was the best mom. How could she not know that?"

Randall shook his head. He was doing his best in conveying the facts, but it would likely take time before they gained understanding.

Vanessa leaned forward in her chair. "What happened the night Mom left?"

Randall held back tears as the memory of Madeline waving good-bye surfaced again. "By the time we left for Mountain, her nerves were shot. She had already convinced herself she would be protecting us by leaving. She said she was a complete mess, but was used to holding herself together in front of others. She had learned that well with her grandmother and had continued living her life trying to please others. She kept herself together, barely, during her visit with James, but, as soon as he left, any resolve to appear normal was gone. She remembers playing over and over in her mind whether to take the truck, or to pack a few things, or grab a credit card out of the drawer, but she couldn't concentrate long enough to do any of that. After several hours of pacing, lost in nothing but incoherent thoughts, she just left. She ran away—trying to get her mind to stop—the voices to stop. She has no idea how she ended up on the highway, but vaguely remembers a trucker stopped and asked her where she was headed. She answered, 'desert.'"

"Your mom's memories are fuzzy regarding that time, but she associated the desert with feeling 'safe.' She describes those first few weeks as being in a trance-like state, just wandering around. She walked, she got rides, she slept in alleys, or parks. She didn't know where she was headed except for the desert. She accepted food from strangers. Records at the sanitarium show she was found in the desert between Phoenix and Tucson, dehydrated and filthy, and couldn't remember who she was."

"What do you mean—sanitarium?" Allison asked.

Randall clasped his hands and looked away. At first Allison thought he was irritated with her for the interruption, but she soon realized he was fighting back tears. "I'm sorry, Dad."

Randall started crying. His words came out in muffled sobs, "I didn't see it. I should've seen it—I should've known she needed help. My wife was in trouble and I didn't help her."

As tears filled all of his daughter's eyes, Vanessa stood up, walked over, and knelt beside him. "We didn't see it either, Dad."

Randall half-smiled in gratitude as Vanessa hugged him. He vowed to pull himself together, knowing that getting caught in a cycle of blame wouldn't help anybody move forward. He wiped his tears with the back of his hand and looked lovingly at his daughters. "I love you girls so much."

Allison hesitated, trying to convey what was in her heart. When the tears began falling from her chin, she wiped her face and said, "You really did take care of us, Dad. You did great."

Randall's eyes misted over again.

"And you did look for Mom," Stacie said. "You looked for a long, long time. I heard you on the phone. I saw you looking through papers. You did all that, even when you thought she was with another man."

Randall pulled himself together, again. "Thank you, girls. It's been—" He hesitated, unsure of how to continue. "It's been difficult, as I'm sure you now know, learning the truth. And, unfortunately, there's more to tell." He took a slow, deep breath. "For most of this time, she has been in a mental hospital in Phoenix. Not too long ago, she was transferred to a partially assisted group home."

"Why weren't we contacted?" Stacie cried out while Vanessa simultaneously asked, "Is she crazy?"

"No, but she's had a difficult road—very difficult. We weren't contacted because Madeline wouldn't speak for a very long time. By the time she did, she said her name was Bailey Kiser." Randall was exhausted but, as difficult as this was on all of them, they weren't finished yet. The caseworker suggested it would be better for the girls to hear the truth from him. He steadied himself as he delivered the worst and final blow of the day. "Your mom attempted suicide several times at the mental hospital."

"No," the girls cried.

Randall nodded sadly. "It's hard to sum up the reasons a person would make that choice, but your mom really did believe we would be better off without her. Since she also believed she had been born of sin, as June had always told her, she felt even God didn't love her or care about her. After her suicide attempts, and since they were short staffed, your mom was medicated pretty heavily—so there was less concern about additional attempts. While the medication worked in keeping her from harming herself, it also greatly impeded her recovery."

"But what about the love we gave her, her life with us, her marriage? How was all of that trumped by her childhood memories?" Allison asked.

"The caseworker said post traumatic stress disorder can work that way. When the memories surfaced, Madeline felt she had been living a lie, only pretending to be a wonderful wife and mother."

"Your mom went through three therapists before she finally started coming around. But it was a—," Randall nodded his head in gratitude. "It was a nurse's aide—a young, large, black man with kind eyes and a big heart that brought your mom back from her darkness. He believed in her—he believed she was not mentally ill, and he was relentless until she believed that herself. She said he reminded her of Mr. Smith, and slowly she opened up to him. It wasn't long after that her therapist was able to gain your mom's trust. When she finally believed the therapists really wanted to help her, she began the long road to recovery." Randall took a deep breathe. "Eventually your mom faced the difficulty of her childhood head-on."

"Why didn't she call us?"

"It's taken a lot of work for her to sort out her past. Just in the last few months she's become a stronger, more independent woman. A few weeks ago, she finally called our old number. When a stranger answered and told her she had the wrong number, she was devastated and unsure of herself again. She was afraid we would never forgive her for what she did. Her therapist was working with her—they set a few goals for Madeline to work towards to help her deal with our reactions before contacting us."

"I wonder if she'd ever think to look here." Vanessa said. "Did you tell her about the house?"

"I did."

"What did she think?"

Randall smiled as he recalled Madeline's reaction. "She was speechless—in a good way."

"How did she find us?" Stacie asked.

Randall gave a huge sigh of relief as he looked at Stacie, then Allison and

Vanessa. "She didn't. And you know what? I'm exhausted—and I've told you everything I needed to tell you."

"What does that mean?" Allison asked.

"It means your Uncle James can fill in the rest."

"What?" Vanessa glanced at her sisters, who seemed as puzzled as she.

"The worst is over girls. We have the answers we've been wanting for more than four years now. The truth is unimaginable, but your mother is alive, she's put her demons behind her, and she loves us."

"She does?" Stacie asked with tears in her eyes.

"Yes, very much. And she knows we love her too."

"What does this mean for you and Mom?" Allison asked.

He thought back to the moment he saw her at the group home. He had hesitated, but the moment their eyes met they flew into each other's arms like the long lost lovers they were in their hearts. At the memory, his body ached with longing, wanting to hold her again, but he also recalled his conversation with the caseworker, who cautioned that a great challenge lay ahead of them: Madeline had carried her need to please into her marriage with Randall and into her role as a mother, without acknowledging her own needs and desires. Madeline was only now learning who she was, Randall was warned, and her discovery might or might not fit into a life with him.

"You know, there's never been anyone for me except your mother, but a lot has changed. We'll just have to see what happens."

Randall leaned back in his recliner. "I'm done talking. Your Uncle James can tell the rest." One by one, his daughters gave him a hug and a kiss before they headed outside. They saw Mitch and James off in the distance and waved at them. Satisfied the guys were heading back, the sisters walked around a bit, loosening up as if they'd just run a marathon—and avoiding, at least for now, any conversation.

34

Twenty minutes later everyone joined Randall back in the living room. Allison, sitting on the other side of Vanessa, leaned forward and looked at James. "Mr. Rothman—Uncle James, I'm confused about something. You said that during the time of that phone call—the one Dad overheard—you had just renewed your friendship with Mom. But, you weren't friends—you were brother and sister."

"I didn't know that at the time."

"You didn't?"

"I just found out a few months ago, after meeting Vanessa."

The realization hit Allison and Vanessa at about the same time. "Greg Rothman is our Grandpa," Allison said, eyes wide.

"I already thought he was my grandpa," Stacie grinned. "Since I thought James was my dad. So I'm already used to the idea."

"Yes," James confirmed with a big smile on his face. "And he's very excited about it. He's been bragging about his granddaughters for the past three months."

"He didn't know either?" Allison asked.

"No. He had no idea Madeline was his daughter. We put the pieces together shortly after you stayed with him in Malibu. After the holidays, I remembered things from my childhood that didn't make sense. I realized I needed to clarify a few things that had never been brought up."

"But why did Grandma Helen keep her pregnancy from your dad?"

"My mom was pregnant with me at the time." James hesitated briefly before giving a thorough, but edited, overview of what he and Greg had talked about that day on the boat. They had already decided they wouldn't tell the Aversons about James' mother's manipulations. Overall, Sandra was a good woman, and a good grandmother to Mindy and Mitch, but that didn't stop James from having an emotional discussion with his mother, who—at first—tried to defend her actions. Later, she broke down in tears of shame and admitted what she had done.

"One thing is for sure," James added, "your Grandmother Helen was the one woman my dad has never forgotten."

"So he really loved her?" Stacie asked.

"I'll let you ask him that question."

"Are we going to see him?"

"Yes. He's with Madeline now. He'll be bringing her home."

Before they had much of a chance to think about the homecoming, Stacie asked, "How did you find her?"

James smiled. "If we would've taken a cue from you girls earlier, it would've been easy. But at first, we did the usual search through public records, missing persons, utilities, all under the name of Madeline Averson. Then finally Dad remembered you girls talking about 'Bailey's Hearts.' Then it was a piece of cake."

"What do you mean?" Vanessa glanced at her sisters, then back at James.

"After more than a month of looking for her, we became frustrated with the search. We went over everything we could think of again. I remembered she had made some beaded necklaces in junior high, and when I mentioned that, Dad's eyes instantly lit up. He remembered you girls talking about your 'Bailey's Heart' necklaces. He told me how pleased he was that Helen nicknamed their daughter Bailey because of a special story he told her— one he hadn't shared with anyone else. It was how a drifter named 'Tom Bailey' had brought joy into the lives of his great-grandparents household."

"We know that story!" Stacie said excitedly. "It's in Grandma Helen's journal!"

"Yes—but she didn't mention any names—so we didn't know who our grandfather was," Vanessa added.

"Madeline never went by the name 'Bailey' in school, so the name meant nothing to me," James said. "But when I mentioned the jewelry, Dad put the two together. We knew it was a long shot, but by that time we were feeling desperate. I called Vanessa, asked her where she got the necklaces, went to the store, and then tracked down the manufacturer. He said the designer's name was Bailey Kiser."

"I don't believe it!" Allison jumped up and her sisters joined her. "Bailey's Hearts is Mom!" They all said at once.

"Bailey's Hearts—how did that happen?" Vanessa asked.

Randall laughed. "If we tell you everything, there won't be anything left for your Mom to tell you."

"I think there will be plenty," Allison responded.

With a grin, Randall looked at James. "You go ahead. I'm done for the day."

"All right," James replied, "I'll take it on." He faced the girls. "Your dad may have told you that Madeline didn't talk to anyone at the hospital for a very long time." As the girls nodded, he continued. "During that time, she drew the designs and wrote the sayings. She said they were things she wished somebody would say to her, but mostly—she wished she could be that example for you girls—to live life lovingly, truthfully, courageously. She never intended they'd be real jewelry someday. But Madeline's roommate at the mental hospital had a brother who owned several jewelry stores in California that marketed to the younger crowd. He happened to see your mother's drawings of heart designs and sayings. He liked what he saw and asked if he could contact a jewelry maker on her behalf. She didn't respond much, but she did give her permission. He set it up, and less than a year later the necklaces were in his stores, then soon spread to others. He encouraged her to keep designing, and he put the funds—less a reasonable handling fee—in an account for her."

By mutual agreement, everyone decided this was a good time to take a break. The rest of the afternoon was spent with everyone joining in group conversations, either outside on the patio or in the living room, some seeking alone time to work though their thoughts. In the evening they barbecued chicken on the grill, made a pasta salad, and steamed fresh green beans for dinner.

After dinner, Allison made plans to meet her sisters at the mall the next day. "I'm going home tonight. I've got some things I need to take care of, but, if it's okay with you, Dad, I'll have Jason stay with Todd over the next few days. It may get pretty emotional around here. I think it'd be better for Jason to wait a bit before he meets his grandma."

35

Excitement ran through the group with an underlying theme—'let's make the house look great for Mom's arrival,' and they did. With the house sparkling clean, new comforters on beds and new towels in bathrooms, additional flowers planted in the courtyard, and a large bouquet of fresh cut flowers on the coffee table, the house looked beautiful. The final touch was a huge welcome home sign, artfully painted by Vanessa and Stacie, hung in the spacious entry.

"Where've you been?" Vanessa asked Allison as she walked in the door.

"Cleaning up some of my messes."

Vanessa figured she knew what Allison was talking about. "Which ones?"

Allison was about to say, 'shut up.' Instead she looked at Vanessa seriously. "It's time for me to start with a clean slate. I talked to Judy and admitted that I didn't think about her feelings when I slept with Todd. And that, yes, of course, I knew how she felt about him, but I didn't think about what I was doing at the time."

"Whoa, how'd she take it?"

"She forgave me. But time will tell if we can be friends again."

"What about Todd?"

"Todd and I have pretty much been okay. We've both made mistakes and already worked through them for Jason's sake. I apologized, though, for keeping him and Judy from being together for so long."

"Wow. That must have been a difficult conversation." Vanessa walked over and wrapped her arms around her older sister. "I'm proud of you."

"Thanks," she whispered. "I'm proud of you, too, but I haven't known what to call you since I haven't been able to call you my 'slutty' sister."

Vanessa giggled. "Oh, don't give up on me yet. I'm making up for lost time. I'm keeping Mitch very busy."

They laughed together as Vanessa, with a hand on Allison's back, turned them toward the hall. "Let's go find our little sister." They walked down the hall until they came to Stacie's room. They quietly stood at the door and watched Stacie sketch, then looked at each other questioningly.

The ghost? Allison mouthed quietly to Vanessa.

Vanessa shrugged her shoulders. They watched as Stacie sat silently, peering at the gray form.

Stacie knew her sisters were there, but a sudden urge to look at the unfinished drawing had come over her, and now she felt a strong desire to complete the shapeless form before seeing her mother again. She took a charcoal pencil and drew the shape of a head, then shoulders, over the original formless figure. Stacie worked quickly, purposefully. She filled in the eyes, a turned up nose, and a contented smile. She drew her short, sassy haircut.

"What are you doing?" Vanessa asked innocently.

"Oh, not much," she answered noncommittally. "Just—finishing this."

"Can you finish it later?" Vanessa asked as she turned to look at Allison, who had nudged her arm.

What? Vanessa silently mouthed.

Allison smiled knowingly. *This is important,* she mouthed back to Vanessa.

Stacie held the sketch away from her and studied it for a moment. Born from an inner peace, she had captured a look of contentment in her penciled eyes. Feeling the sudden quietness of her sisters behind her, she had a moment of awareness that left her spellbound.

But it's not just about me. It never was. We all lost our way. Knowing she was running out of time, she quickly resumed her sketching. She penciled in a likeness of Allison, and then Vanessa. She smiled.

We're like a trilogy: body, mind, and soul, now defined. The gray forms on the paper suddenly reminded her of what Vanessa had said years before: *"There is NO gray area here. It's as clear as black and white—Mom ran off with another man."*

Suddenly Stacie was overcome with another realization and started giggling.

"What is it Stacie? We've got to hurry." Allison said—her patience now gone.

But Stacie couldn't talk, instead she started drawing again. She had sat down just fifteen minutes earlier feeling a strong desire to draw her own form, a symbolic drawing showing she now knew who she was. And that would've been enough, but, she realized, it wasn't the full story; her sisters had gone through a similar experience. Then, when she thought she had captured it all, another realization had hit: *this started with Mom not knowing who she was and was followed by Dad falling apart.*

Stacie continued her drawing—fast and furious. She knew she was moving too quickly for it to meet her usual standard of work, but when she had finally captured everyone in her family's likeness, she held the drawing in front of her and knew she would never touch it again. It was perfect—just as it was.

Allison and Vanessa peered over Stacie's shoulders as tears filled their eyes. They had witnessed the stages the drawing had gone through, seeming to understand Stacie's intentions.

"Oh, look." Vanessa leaned over the sketch. "The paper has a tear in it."

"That's too bad." Allison said, finally understanding the importance this sketch held for Stacie. "Oh well—as Dad would say, 'it's an imperfect world.'"

Stacie stood up and leaned the portrait against the desk. "I don't know," she smiled self assuredly. "As Grandma Helen would say—perhaps 'life is perfect—despite its seeming imperfections.'"

Vanessa and Allison exchanged a smile at Stacie's self-confident glow. "Well said, Stacie."

"Is it time?"

Allison glanced at the clock. "Yes. Mom should be here any minute."

Vanessa reached up and touched the necklace that hung below her neck. "We're all wearing our 'Bailey's Hearts' necklace."

"That's right," Allison said. "We have our words of wisdom from Mom."

"And we have each other," Vanessa said.

"And we have Dad, too," Stacie added.

Allison smiled. "Now let's go get Mom."

The three sisters walked arm in arm out of the bedroom, down the hall, and out the double entrance doors. They joined their dad on the large flagstone patio. It wasn't long before they glimpsed a forest green Jeep Cherokee cross the bridge over the Central Arizona Project canal. As it got closer, they could see the reflection of the yellow and orange Mexican Poppies in the bottom side panel of the Jeep. With tears in their eyes, and hands clasped together, Randall, Allison, Vanessa, and Stacie quickly glanced at one another, clearly needing to experience this pivotal moment together. With the sun in their eyes, they could barely see the outlines of the two people in the vehicle as it came to a stop. They sensed, rather than saw, a comforting gesture between their mom and their Grandpa Greg.

The song of the 'Curve Billed' thrasher filled the silence as a ground squirrel scurried past. The passenger door opened slowly—and Madeline 'Bailey' Kiser Averson stepped out of the car and stood before them.

If you would like more information regarding "Defining Gray" or the upcoming sequel, please visit **www.defininggray.com**

DEFINING GRAY — A novel by Denise Bjornson

ORDER FORM

EMAIL ORDERS: orders@soaringturtlepress.com

TELEPHONE ORDERS: +1-520-419-0567

POSTAL ORDERS: PO Box 35403, Tucson, AZ 85740 USA

WEBSITE ORDERS: Paypal available through website at soaringturtlepress.com

Name: _____

Address: _____

City, State/Province, Postal Code:

_____

Telephone: _____

Email: _____

Payment:　　☐ Check　　☐ Credit Card

　　　　　☐ Visa　　☐ MasterCard　　☐ Discover

Card No.: _____ Exp: (mm/yy) _____

Name on Card: _____

Signature: _____